PUFFIN BOOKS

GREAT NORTHERN

'Wake up, Ship's Naturalist!' said Nancy.

'Hey, DICK!' said Roger.

Dick looked up from his book with a start.

'What's the matter, Professor?, said Captain Flint.

'I can't make out about those birds,' said Dick.

'What birds?'

'The ones I saw today,' said Dick. 'The book says they don't nest here, only abroad, and the ones I saw were nesting.'

'Different sort of birds,' said Captain Flint.

Dorothea looked up from her exercise book. 'Didn't you say they were Divers?' she asked. 'The ones you'd been wanting to see?'

'They were Divers,' said Dick. 'One of them was a Black-throated Diver. It's the other two I can't make out. I thought they were Great Northerns, but they can't be.'

'I don't see that it matters,' said Nancy. 'They're all Divers, and it's Divers you wanted to see. The whole of the first ten days you talked about nothing else.'

'But it matters most awfully,' said Dick. 'Those birds were nesting and the book says they don't.'

But it was difficult for Dick to stir up the others to much interest. It was the end of their holiday and they were just about to return their borrowed boat *Sea Bear* to her owner. There was no point in getting excited now, they thought – until they discovered that the horrible brute of an egg-collector on the *Pterodactyl* intended to shoot Dick's wonderful birds and steal their precious eggs.

Arthur Ransome was born in Leeds in 1884 and educated at Rugby. He wrote books of literary criticism and on storytelling before he went to Russia in 1913 to learn the language and study the folklore. In the First World War he was a war correspondent from the Russian Front, and travelled widely in Russia, China and Egypt. He gave up journalism in 1929 and between 1930 and 1945 wrote his famous *Swallows and Amazons* series of children's books. He died in 1967.

SCRUBBING THE *SEA BEAR*

Great Northern?

ARTHUR RANSOME

The Great Northern Diver
'nests abroad . . . usually seen solitary'
SANDARS

'nests in eastern North America,
Greenland and Iceland'
'may nest in the Shetlands, as it is
often round these islands all summer,
but this has never been proved.'
COWARD

ILLUSTRATED BY THE AUTHOR

PUFFIN BOOKS
IN ASSOCIATION WITH
JONATHAN CAPE

Puffin Books, Penguin Books Ltd, Harmondsworth, Middlesex, England
Viking Penguin Inc., 40 West 23rd Street, New York, New York 10010, U.S.A.
Penguin Books Australia Ltd, Ringwood, Victoria, Australia
Penguin Books Canada Ltd, 2801 John Street, Markham, Ontario, Canada L3R 1B4
Penguin Books (N.Z.) Ltd, 182–190 Wairau Road, Auckland 10, New Zealand

—

First published by Jonathan Cape 1947
Published in Puffin Books 1971
Reprinted 1973, 1974, 1975, 1977, 1980, 1982, 1984, 1987

—

—

Made and printed in Great Britain
by Richard Clay Ltd, Bungay, Suffolk
Set in Monotype Caslon

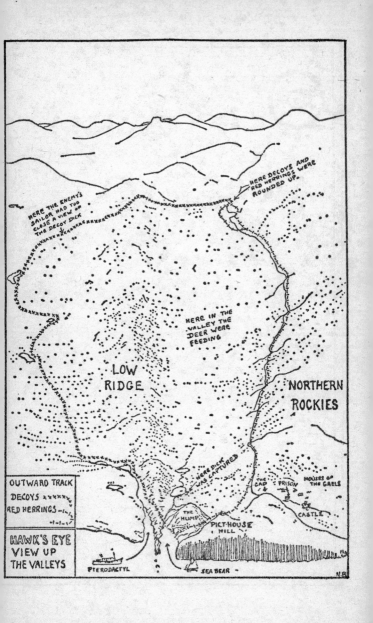

HERE THE ENEMY'S
SAILOR HAD TOO
CLOSE A VIEW OF
THE DECOY DICK

HERE DECOYS AND
RED HERRINGS WERE
ROUNDED UP.

HERE IN THE
VALLEY THE
DEER WERE
FEEDING

LOW
RIDGE

NORTHERN
ROCKIES

HERE DICK
WAS CAPTURED

THE
CAP

PRISON

HOUSES OF
THE GAELS

THE
HUMP

PICT-HOUSE
HILL

CASTLE

OUTWARD TRACK
DECOYS ×××××
RED HERRINGS —·—·—·

HAWK'S EYE
VIEW UP
THE VALLEYS

PTERODACTYL

SEA BEAR

N.B.

CONTENTS

ILLUSTRATIONS

NOTE

Every effort has been made (short of falsifying the course of events) to prevent the inquisitive reader from learning the exact place where the *Sea Bear* was scrubbed and the Ship's Naturalist made his discovery. Persons who pester the author for more information (whether or not they enclose stamped envelopes with their letters) will not be answered. Further, should anyone with particular knowledge of the Hebrides identify the loch where the Divers are nesting and be the means of disturbing them, they will make enemies of John, Susan, Titty, Roger, Nancy, Peggy, Dorothea and Dick, as well of the author, who will in that case be sorry he has written this account of what happened.

CHAPTER I

THE *SEA BEAR*

ON a hill above the cliff a boy in Highland dress turned from watching the deer in the valley to look out over the sea. He saw a sail far away. It was no more than a white speck in the distance, and presently he turned his back on it and settled down again to watch the deer.

The *Sea Bear*, with Nancy at the tiller, was lolloping comfortably along in bright sunshine, heading towards the rocky coast of one of the islands of the Hebrides. She was an old Norwegian pilot cutter and had been borrowed by Captain Flint (Nancy's and Peggy's Uncle Jim) for himself and his crew of Blacketts, Walkers and Callums. The Minch can be a stormy sea, but they had been lucky in their weather and now after a happy fortnight of good sailing with almost every night spent in a different harbour they were going to put her aground in a sheltered cove, scrape off the barnacles and weed, put a fresh coat of paint on her below the waterline and take her back to the port on the mainland from which they had started, to hand her over to her owner all spick and span and ready for him to take to sea again at once.

'Nobody much likes lending boats,' Captain Flint had said. 'The least we can do is to let Mac have her back better than before we had her.'

'Then, perhaps, he'll lend her to us again,' Roger had agreed.

Nancy was at the tiller. Peggy, her mate and sister, was in the cockpit beside her, ready to give a hand with a rope if need be. Captain Flint was smoking a pipe, sitting on the cabin skylight, watching for the square-topped hill that would show them the way to the cove they had to find. Roger was sitting on the forehatch, keeping a look out and wondering how soon the others would agree that the wind, which had been dropping since the early morning, had weakened so far that it would be worth while to start the engine. The rest of the crew were down below, in the cabin, except for Susan, who had been keeping an eye on the clock and had just gone forward into the fo'c'sle, to light a Primus stove and to put a kettle on it for the ship's company's tea.

The cabin had been little changed since the days when the *Sea Bear* had been a working pilot cutter. There were still the six berths of the pilots, built as it were in the walls of the ship, above the long settees. Going to bed, as Titty had said, was like getting into a rabbit hutch. But, once you were in, you could shut yourself off from everybody else by pulling a curtain across. Many a tired pilot must have slept in one of those bunks while the other pilots, only a yard or two away, were playing cards with each other under the cabin lamp. Farther aft were two more bunks, one on each side, close to the companion ladder and handy for going on deck. They had been used in old days by the men whose business it was to take the cutter to sea to meet the big ships coming in, put pilots aboard them and pick up other pilots from the big ships outward bound. John and Captain Flint slept in these bunks. Nancy, Peggy, Susan, Titty, Dorothea and Dick had each one of the cupboard bunks in the main cabin while Roger, being the smallest, had a bunk in the fo'c'sle which once upon a time, no doubt, had belonged to a Norwegian ship's boy.

John, feet wide apart to steady himself, was leaning over the chart table by the companion ladder, looking now at the big chart that showed the coasts on both sides of the Minch, the Scottish mainland and the Outer Hebrides, and now at a much smaller chart that showed in detail the tiny cove for which the ship was making. Mac, the owner of the *Sea Bear*, had left a lot of these little charts aboard her. John and Nancy had spent happy hours looking through them and, when Captain Flint had said that he meant to give the ship a scrub before handing her over they had brandished this particular chart before him. 'Look at this,' Nancy had said. 'Mac didn't bother about taking her to a harbour for scrubbing. Look at that anchor and look at that cross and what he's scribbled in pencil in the margin ... "Scrubbed *Sea Bear*" ... Let's do the same. She's got her own legs. There's no need to take her into a harbour and lean her up against a pier.' Rather unwillingly, Captain Flint had agreed.

Titty was lying on her stomach in her cupboard bunk, sucking a pencil and bringing up to date her private log of the voyage, a rather different log from the business-like one kept by John and Nancy, which was all courses and distances run and remarks on changes of wind and weather. It was a good deal easier to write lying on your stomach in a bunk than sitting at the cabin table while the *Sea Bear* was crashing her way to windward. (Not that she was crashing very hard at the moment, with only a failing wind to drive her, but there had been times when she had crashed very hard indeed and Titty had got into the way of writing her log in her bunk.) Dorothea was also writing, but her writing had nothing to do with what happened aboard ship. She had wedged herself into a corner by the mast, leaning back against the bulkhead that divided cabin from fo'c'sle, and was making up her mind whether the villain in her new story should have a black beard and ear-rings or be clean-shaven with a scar across his cheek.

Dick, who had been appointed Ship's Naturalist, was sitting on the starboard settee with a pencil in one hand, while with the other he was keeping the *Pocket Book of Birds* and his notebook from sliding off the cabin table. He was making a list of the birds seen during the cruise and telling himself that the voyage had been a success in spite of his disappointment at not seeing the particular birds for which he had been keeping a look-out. 'I say,' he had said when he had first heard of the northern port from which they were sailing and the islands they were to visit, 'we'll be seeing Divers.' 'With brass helmets,' Dorothea had said, 'going down under the sea and coming up with bars of gold from sunken wrecks.' 'Not that kind of Diver,' he had explained. 'Birds. Redthroated and Black-throated. We might even have a chance of seeing a Great Northern though they'll most of them be in Iceland by now.' All through the cruise he had been watching for them, and now, with the cruise all but over, he was consoling himself by remembering how many others he had been able to add to the list of birds he had seen with his own eyes ... Gannets, guillemots, terns, petrels, fulmars, puffins, razorbills, mergansers, and so tame some of them. He was almost sure that some of his photographs of gulls would come out all right, and perhaps, though it had been taken from a long way off, that one of a shag in the act of swallowing a fish. But he had seen no Divers, and if, tomorrow, they were all going to be hard at work scrubbing the ship, there would be no other chance.

'I say, John,' he asked, 'you know the lakes shown on that chart? How far are they from the place where we'll be anchored? Can I have a look?'

John dropped on the settee beside Dick and held the little chart so that they could look at it together. It showed an inlet in the coast-line, divided into two by a promontory and a line of rocks. There was flattish country to the south, a cliff and hills to the north, and inland were a number of small lochs, two of them drained by a stream that came out at the head of the cove that was marked with an anchor and a cross on the shore. On those lochs, Dick thought, there might be

Divers to be seen. John was interested not in the lochs but in a neat sketch at the head of the chart showing the outline of the hills behind the coast, with a dotted line ruled straight down from one corner of a square-topped hill, and a note written beside it, 'N. end of Sq. Top bearing W. $\frac{1}{2}$ N. leads to cliff on N. side of Entrance.'

There was a sudden stamp of feet on the foredeck. Roger's voice shrilled out, 'Sail HO! ... At least, not sail. Motor boat ... Starboard quarter ...'

It was the first vessel to be sighted that day. John, the little chart still in his hand, was up the companion ladder in a flash. Dorothea wriggled round the table to follow him. Titty rolled out of her bunk and made a dead heat of it with Dorothea. Even Susan, after a careful glance at the stove to see that the flame was neither too high nor too low, banged at the underneath of the forehatch, in case Roger was on the top of it, pushed it up and climbed out. Dick, who had glanced back to his bird-book, where it said that Black-throated Divers were to be found on mountain lochs near the coast, looked up to find that he had the cabin to himself. Everybody else was on deck.

There was a lot of chatter up there. People were taking turns with glasses and telescope. 'Look here, it's my turn now. I spotted her first.' That was Roger. 'Only a motor boat, anyway.' That was John. 'She's going to pass us pretty close.' That was Nancy. 'You carry on, Nancy. We've the right of way. You've nothing to worry about. She'll pass under our stern.' That was Captain Flint. 'She's coming up a terrific lick.' That was Roger. 'Probably carrying dispatches.' That was Titty. 'Or taking a doctor to one of the lighthouses.' That was Dorothea.

Dick hardly heard the chatter. He was looking at the coloured pictures in his bird-book, showing the Divers he had never seen. Tomorrow would be the very last chance.

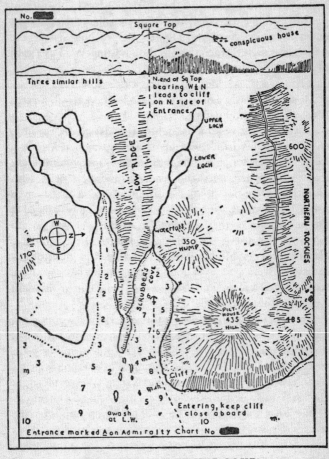

MAC'S CHART OF THE COVE

We put in some of the names. (Not very well. Sorry.) N. B.

The chatter on deck meant nothing to him until, suddenly, he heard his own name.

'It's Dick's boat.' That was Peggy's voice. 'Dick! Take a look. Where is he? Hey! Dick!'

Dorothea called down the companion ladder. 'Dick! Dick! Hurry up. It's your bird-man and he's going to pass us quite close.'

Dick was already working his way along the slanting cabin floor and reaching for the ladder. Dorothea pushed the glasses into his hand as he came on deck. He had no need of them to recognize the bird-man's boat. He knew her the moment he saw her, but, balancing as best he could and trying to hold the glasses steady, he used them to read at least some of the many letters of her name. 'P.T.E.R. . . .' The *Sea Bear* lurched and the glasses were pointing at sky instead of boat . . . He swung them down and read the last lot of letters . . . 'A.C.T.Y.L.' Yes, she was the *Pterodactyl* all right, on her way back. Earlier in their cruise they had seen her in that harbour on the other side of the cape and Dick had told the others what her name meant, PTERODACTYL, a sort of half-bird half-lizard, prehistoric, of course, and extinct. And then, while they were ashore, coming along the quay, all laden with provisions, they had seen her moving out, and had stopped to watch her. 'Off again after his birds,' a longshoreman had said. 'Shetlands, he's bound for. Looking for birds. His fourth trip this year.' 'What did you say he was?' Dick had asked. 'One of those bird chaps,' the man had said. 'Tell him of a rare bird and he'll go five hundred miles, they say. Pays good money, too, to anybody who tells him where to find one.' Dick had watched the big motor yacht slip away beyond the pierheads and, after they were back aboard their ship, he had climbed the rigging to the cross-trees and caught just a glimpse of her outside, already no more than a white speck of flying spray, on her way to the far northern nesting

places of the sea birds. Some day, perhaps, he too would have a
boat like that. He would have a whole library of bird-books
in her, and a dark room for photography, and a camera with
a telephoto lens to take photographs of birds without having
to come near enough to disturb them. He would have given
anything to have been able to go aboard the *Pterodactyl* and
talk with a real bird-man who was doing all the things that he,
Dick, would like to do. The others had laughed at him (all
except Roger, who liked engines) and had said that she was
only a motor boat anyway, and that you could go to look for
birds in a sailing vessel and have all the fun of sailing as well.
Every time they had seen a motor boat after that, someone
had said, 'There's a ship for Dick,' but he had not minded
their teasing. The *Pterodactyl*, even if she was moved by a
motor, belonged to a bird-man who was using her just as
Dick would like to use a vessel of his own, big enough to live
in, as a travelling observation post. With a boat like that, you
could migrate with the birds.

The *Pterodactyl* crossed the bows of the *Sea Bear* with
twenty or thirty yards to spare.

'Beastly rude,' said Nancy.

'Quite within his rights,' said Captain Flint. 'Going at
that lick, he'll be thinking of us as practically standing still.
All the same it would have been better manners not to rub it
in.'

Dick, with the glasses, was trying to catch a glimpse of the
bird-man himself. But the *Pterodactyl* was steered from inside
a deckhouse and he could not see who was at the wheel. There
was no one on deck as the big motor yacht drove on her way,
foam flying from her bows.

'He's probably seen lots of them,' said Dick to himself.

'Seen what?' said Peggy.

'Dick's thinking about birds,' said Dorothea.

'Divers,' said Dick.

20

'An hour's time and that boat'll be in port,' said Captain Flint, glancing into the companion at the clock that was screwed to a beam so as to be easily seen from on deck. 'That is, if she's going back to . . .' (For a very good reason the name of the harbour where they had first seen the *Pterodactyl* will not be mentioned in this book.)

'If we're going in there to get petrol before starting across you'll be able to see her again,' said Dorothea to her brother.

'Of course she may be going somewhere else,' said Dick.

'Let's start our engine,' said Roger, who had come aft and had very much disliked seeing the *Pterodactyl* moving so much faster than the *Sea Bear*.

'Shiver my timbers,' said Nancy. 'What are you doing here? You're on the look out. Get away forrard and shut up about engines.'

'You'll be calling for engines yourself pretty soon,' said Roger, and scrambled forward again. 'The wind's getting weaker and weaker.'

Captain Flint looked about him. 'Roger's about right,' he said. 'Looks like a change coming. It's a paltry wind. But there's no petrol to spare, except just for getting in. With that calm yesterday we ran the tanks pretty nearly dry. Never mind. We haven't got far to go. We ought to be getting a sight of that hill any time now.'

Roger was back on the foredeck. Susan was once more in the fo'c'sle watching a kettle that had begun to steam. Dick was trying not to lose the vanishing speck of the bird-man's boat. Nancy was glancing now at the compass, now at the sails, keeping them full but not too full, intent on getting the very best out of the old cutter. All the others, Captain Flint, Peggy, Titty, Dorothea and John, were looking at the blue hills ahead of them.

'Square Top,' Roger suddenly shouted, pointing along the bowsprit.

'I can't see it,' said Titty.

'Where?' asked Dorothea.

'Might be it,' said John. 'Just coming up now.'

The skyline ahead of them was changing. Hills near the coast were lifting to hide the bigger hills beyond them. John gave the little chart to Peggy and went up the port shrouds to the cross-trees to get a view from higher up.

'Square Top all right,' he shouted.

Captain Flint took the chart from Peggy.

'Fine on the starboard bow,' called John, and came quickly down to have another look at the chart.

'Looks like it,' Captain Flint was saying. 'That little sketch must have been made from just about where we are now. How's she heading, Nancy?'

'West and a half north,' said Nancy.

'And we're coming in on the right bearing. Couldn't have struck it luckier.'

'Good for the *Sea Bear*,' said Titty.

'Carry on just as we're going,' said Captain Flint, 'and this tack will bring us close off the entrance.'

A hand, Susan's, showed in the companion way and took hold of the rose knot worked in the end of the bit of rope that dangled from the clapper of a small ship's bell.

'Ting . . . Ting . . .'

'Two bells! Five o'clock. Tea!' called Nancy, almost as if she wanted to hurry the others off the deck.

'We'll get it over,' said Captain Flint. 'We'll be in in no time if only the wind lasts out.'

Roger, at the first 'ting' of the bell, had opened the fore-hatch and was already disappearing below. Susan's hand came up again through the companion, this time carrying a mug for the steersman. Peggy took the mug and put it on the lee-ward side in a corner of the cockpit where it could not slide about. Susan passed up a huge rock bun. Peggy handed it on.

'Shall I have mine on deck too?' she asked.

'No need,' said Nancy.

Titty and Dorothea went down and Peggy after them.

'Go on, John,' said Nancy. 'You'll get a better view when we're a bit nearer . . . Get along down, Dick. Your *Pppppppp-terodactyl*'s out of sight.'

Dick took a last look towards that long lump sticking out from the coast-line away to the south. It looked almost like an island, but he knew it was really a cape, the Head, that hid the harbour where they had first seen the bird-man's boat. He could not see the motor yacht any longer. He followed John down the companion.

Nancy, at the tiller, was alone on deck. The clink of mugs and plates sounded from below. She took a gulp of tea and then a mighty bite of the rock bun. This was better than going into any harbour with buoys and lighthouses and shops and quays. Sailing towards an unknown coast, watching for a tiny break in the coast-line, she had the ship to herself and wished that tea in the cabin would last for ever.

Sitting at the cabin table, Dick saw two tea-leaves floating in his mug. He dipped them out.

'Strangers,' said Titty.

'Perhaps your Divers,' said Dorothea. 'Perhaps you're going to see them after all.'

Dick, as a scientist, did not believe in tea-leaf prophecies. 'There's not much hope left,' he said.

'You never know,' said Dorothea.

Nobody wants to stay below when the ship has made a good landfall and is coming in towards an unknown anchorage chosen by the crew and not by the skipper. Nancy did not have the ship to herself for very long. Nobody dawdled over tea and presently they were all on deck once more, watching the coast coming nearer and nearer, watching the square-topped hill, glancing at the compass, comparing the cliff, now clear to see, with the little drawing of it on Mac's chart, and eager for the first glimpse into the little cove where the *Sea Bear* had once been scrubbed and was going to be scrubbed again.

'Got it!' called John who had taken his telescope up to the cross-trees. 'Just to the left of the cliff . . . Low ground to the south of it. Plumb on the bowsprit end.'

Presently they were all able to see it from the deck, the narrow inlet close under the cliff, the ridge above the cliff stretching up to the hills, and, north of the ridge, some cottages and a grey house.

'Conspicuous house,' said Peggy, looking at the chart.

'Anyhow,' said Titty, 'it doesn't show any houses where we're going.'

'Those houses don't matter,' said Dorothea. 'They're in a different valley, over the top of that range. They won't even be in sight.'

'I can't see them very well even now,' said Roger.

There is no certainty at sea. At the very last minute, with the cove opening before them, things were changing fast. Away to the south the Head was showing less and less clearly. The wind was slackening. The *Sea Bear* was moving slower and slower. The sunlight had weakened. Something odd was happening to the coast. The tops of the hills inland showed sharp and still clear but it was as if a white veil hung over their lower slopes.

'I told you we ought to start the engine,' said Roger.

Captain Flint took a worried look round.

'We may have to change our plans,' he said suddenly. He went down the companion ladder, and, looking down, they could see him busy with parallel rulers on the Admiralty chart.

'Oh look here,' said Nancy, 'he can't be thinking of giving up now.'

'Why, we're nearly there,' said Titty.

Suddenly the sails flapped. Nancy had to change course to fill them again. The air was suddenly cooler. It was as if somebody had turned down the light of the sun.

'I can't see the Head,' called John.

There was a yell from below. 'Hey, Nancy! What are you changing course for?' Captain Flint had glanced up from the chart table at the tell-tale compass under the cabin roof.

'Wind's changed,' said Nancy. 'Mist or fog coming. And we can't see the Head.'

Captain Flint came storming up the companion ladder. He took one glance at the cliff ahead and jumped for the starboard jib-sheets.

'Ready about!' he called. 'Helm down!'

The *Sea Bear* swung very slowly round. A gentle breath was coming from the north-west.

'Fair wind for the Head,' said Captain Flint. 'What about using it and doing our scrub in harbour tomorrow?'

'And not go into the cove at all?' said Nancy. 'But you promised we should.'

'Well, look at it,' said Captain Flint.

Already there had been another change. The square-topped hill was standing in a mist that hid its lower slopes. It was like an island in a white sea. The white sea was rolling towards them. It had covered the low-lying ground and was eddying round the foot of the cliff.

'Fair wind for the Head,' said Captain Flint again. 'And Dick'll be able to have another look at his boat . . . Eh, Dick?'

'But it's the very last chance of seeing Divers,' said Dick.

'Look here,' said Nancy. 'This wind'll be dead against us

once we're round the Head and we'll be beating all the way up to the harbour with rocks on both sides of us. . . .'

'That's true enough,' said Captain Flint. He looked south towards the invisible Head and then up at the cliff. Mist was already pouring over the top of it.

'We're nearly in already,' said Nancy.

'It's pretty late,' said Susan.

Captain Flint stooped and glanced at the clock. 'Slack tide,' he said. 'I wouldn't try it otherwise. But the fog'll be on us in a minute.' Once more he pulled out his pocket compass and took a bearing of the square-topped hill, now no more than a grey ghost above the mist. 'All right, Nancy,' he said. 'You win. Lower all sail! We'll start the engine, Roger. And I hope to goodness the petrol lasts long enough to take us in.'

'Oh, good!' said Titty.

'Aye, aye, Sir,' said Roger and, as he followed the skipper below, 'I told you we'd be wanting it.'

There was a whirr from below as the engine started and a steady throbbing as it was warming up. Captain Flint was on deck again in a moment. The staysail was already down. Peggy and Susan, working together, were bringing in the jib. Captain Flint gave John a hand with the topsail and took the weight of the boom on the topping lift. 'You and Susan take the peak halyard,' he said. 'I've got the throat. Lower away.' This was all old drill to the crew of the *Sea Bear* and in a very few minutes all sails had been lowered and the old cutter was wallowing uncertainly in the swell.

'Nancy's the best hand with the lead. John takes the tiller. Slow ahead, Roger!'

'Aye, aye, Sir.'

The *Sea Bear* began to move again as the engine changed its tune.

'West and a half north, John, and as steady as you can.'

'West and a half north it is.'

'But what are we going to do?' said Dorothea.

'We're going in,' said Nancy, taking the lead and its line out of a locker in the cockpit.

'If we can,' said Captain Flint.

The coast had disappeared altogether. The square-topped hill had been swallowed up. The chug . . . chug . . . chug of the engine was driving the *Sea Bear* slowly forward into a wall of white wool.

The boy high above the cliff had seen the mist coming. It had filled the valley and hidden the deer he had been watching. He felt a cold breath on his forehead. The wind was changing. He had written up his diary for the day and eaten all he meant to eat of the cake he had brought with him. A faint sound of bagpipes was calling him home. He put his diary and what was left of his cake in the biscuit box he used as a safe, pushed it well out of sight at the back of his private hiding-place and, as the mist reached him, set out carefully to pick his way among the rocks and heather. No one on land saw the *Sea Bear* lower her sails. No one heard the quiet throb of her engine as she crept slowly on towards the cliff.

CHAPTER 2

FEELING HER WAY IN

THE whole feeling of the day had changed. This was no longer careless summer sailing. The wall of mist was moving to meet them. John, steering, was watching the compass as if his life depended on keeping the needle steady. Everybody was on the alert, waiting for orders, knowing that there must be no mistakes and that if anything needed doing it would need doing at once. The hatch over the engine room was open. Roger, his eyes sparkling, was standing by, his hands hovering over the controls. The mist rolled over the *Sea Bear*, and from the cockpit it was hard to see the little flag at the masthead. A clanking of iron told that Nancy and Captain Flint, grey ghosts on the foredeck, were making ready the anchor.

Captain Flint came aft and glanced at the compass.

'Keep her going as she is, John,' he said.

'West and a half north,' said John.

'We want someone at the cross-trees ... Dick ... No ... I forgot your glasses.' (Dick was cleaning his dimmed spectacles.) 'Peggy. I may want Susan to lend a hand with the anchor. Nancy'll be busy from now on. Everybody else, keep your eyes skinned and sing out the moment you see anything. *Anything*. Don't wait till you are sure what it is. Sing out if you see anything at all. Roger, stand by to stop her at once and go astern if I shout.'

'Aye, aye, Sir,' said Roger.

'Titty. Nip below and bring up that tin of tallow for the lead. Fo'c'sle. Starboard side, top shelf.'

'Aye, aye, Sir.' Titty was gone.

'Chug . . . chug . . . chug . . . chug . . .'

The *Sea Bear* moved on in a white world of her own.

'It's like being a caterpillar inside a cocoon,' thought Dick, hurriedly wiping his spectacles, putting them on and trying to see, not quite sure whether or not the mist was on his spectacles as well as all about him.

Nancy, at the starboard shrouds, a lifeline round her made fast to the rigging, so that she could use both hands without fear of falling overboard, was getting ready to swing the lead. Now, now . . . The lead dangled three feet or more below her right hand, the big coil of the lead-line, with its marks at

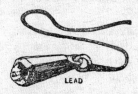

LEAD

every fathom, in her left. She was swinging the lead, fore and aft, in wider and wider swings. She was whirling it over and over, round and again and away . . . She had let go of it and the lead was flying out ahead of the ship. Nobody aboard could do that as well as she. Dick could see her feeling for it as the ship caught it up, dipping, as if she were fishing with a handline.

'No bottom at twelve fathoms,' she called out.

'Carry on,' called Captain Flint.

Titty came up through the companion instead of through the forehatch because that was closed to give more room for the chain that lay ranged ready to pour out through the fairlead as soon as the anchor was let go. She had a tin in her hand. She crouched by the mast, to be ready with the grease the moment it was wanted. Dick, as so often before, felt that, in this ship-load of experienced sailors, he and Dorothea were no more than passengers. They knew how to sail their little *Scarab*, but this was the first time they had been to sea. There was nothing for them to do except to keep out of other people's way and to be ready to obey orders in case anybody should think it worth while to give them any.

Splash. Again the lead fell after Nancy had sent it flying forward. Again she was dipping, dipping. Again she was hauling it in hand over hand.

'No bottom at twelve.'

There was a sudden shrieking of gulls. Captain Flint, who had been glancing at the little chart, looked up from it to watch Nancy, as if he were waiting for the answer to an urgent question.

Splash.

'No bottom at twelve.'

'We must be pretty near in,' said Captain Flint to John. 'We ought to be getting the bottom by now.'

Splash.

Nancy, hauling in the line and dipping, turned suddenly to shout, 'Twelve fathoms.'

'Arm the lead,' said Captain Flint.

Dick saw Titty scoop something out of the tin with her fingers and poke it into the hole he had often noticed at the bottom of the lead.

'Hurry up,' Captain Flint was saying, low, to himself, not for Nancy or Titty to hear. Anybody could see that they were being as quick as they could.

Splash.

Nancy was hauling in. She was dipping. 'Eleven,' she shouted, and went on hauling, coiling as she hauled, grabbed the lead as soon as she could reach it and looked at the bottom of it. 'Eleven and soft mud,' she called out.

So that was how it was done, thought Dick. The grease on the bottom of the lead brought up a sample of the bottom to

INTO THE MIST

help the skipper who was feeling his way in. He knew now what was the use of those little notes dotted about on the charts . . . 's' for sand, 'm' for mud, 'sh' for shell, and so on. This was the first time he had seen them bother about arming the lead. They had often sounded to make sure of the depth when they were making ready to anchor. This time they wanted to know more. They wanted every little bit of knowledge that might help them with this white mist blindfolding their eyes.

Splash.

'Nine and a half . . . Mud and shell . . .'

'Do we . . .?'

'Shut up,' said Captain Flint. 'Listen!'

Gulls were squawking somewhere to starboard, high above them.

'Cliff?' muttered Captain Flint.

The chugging of the engine sounded suddenly different, as steps do when they go over a wooden bridge after walking on solid road.

'West,' said Captain Flint to John.

'West it is, Sir,' said John quietly.

'If that's the north side of the place,' said Captain Flint, 'we must be clear now of any tide there is across the entrance.'

'He's very pleased,' Dorothea whispered to Dick.

'Nine fathom . . . Mud and shell.'

A bird flew close by the stern of the ship.

'Guillemot,' said Dick. 'At least, I think so.'

'Eh! What's that?'

'Sorry,' said Dick. 'It was only that I saw a bird.'

'Something to starboard,' yelled Peggy, high in the mist. 'No . . . It's gone. I can't see anything now, but there was something.'

'She may have caught a glimpse of the cliff,' said Captain

Flint to John. 'We must be pretty near. Sorry. Don't listen to me.' He grinned at Dick. 'You watch your steering.'

'West,' said John.

They were startled next by a noise that had nothing to do with the sea. 'Go back. Go back. Go back!' It was the cry of a grouse alighting.

'We jolly well won't,' said Roger, and earned a grim look from Susan.

Captain Flint gave the chart to Dick. 'Hang on to this,' he said, and went forward to join the misty figures on the foredeck.

'Eight fathom,' called Nancy. 'Eight fathom . . . Mud.'

'Seven fathom,' said Nancy, looking round to find Captain Flint close beside her.

'Stop her,' called Captain Flint, and the throbbing of the engine quickened for a moment as Roger instantly put it out of gear.

'Hard a starboard!'

'Starboard,' repeated John, putting the tiller over.

'Let go!' called Captain Flint and himself obeyed his own order. There was a heavy splash and then the rattle and roar of the chain pouring out through the fairlead on the stem.

'Finished with engine.'

The throbbing of the engine turned to a cough and ended.

The *Sea Bear* was at anchor. Looking over the side Dick could see small flecks of foam moving slowly past her as she swung. Looking away from her he could see nothing at all but white mist.

'Have we got in?' Nancy was asking.

'We're in,' said Captain Flint. 'But I wouldn't like to swear to the exact spot. Lend a hand to get that dinghy over.'

There was a rush to set up the davits and in a few minutes the dinghy was swung out and lowered into the water.

'John in charge of the ship,' said Captain Flint. 'Come on,

Nancy. Bring the lead. Somebody keep on ringing the bell
. . . all the time. We're not going far, but it may help us not
to lose you.'

He rowed away, with Nancy in the stern coiling the lead-
line at her feet. In a few moments the dinghy, with Nancy
and the skipper in it, was no longer even a dark blob in the
mist. It had gone. Listening for the gentle splash of the
oars, the rest of the crew were looking at each other as if to
ask what was going to happen next.

'We're close in shore anyhow,' said John. 'Hear that
grouse again?'

'And anchored,' said Susan. 'Well, it's much better than
being at sea in a fog.'

'We may have to shift again,' said John. 'We may be too
near in.'

'Is that what they've gone to find out?' said Dorothea.

'What about Peggy?' said Susan. 'He forgot about her.
She isn't wanted up there now.'

'Come along down, Peggy,' called John.

'BELL!' A shout came at them out of the mist.

'Ting . . . Ting . . . Ting . . . Ting . . . Ting . . .' came
the answer. The shout had met Roger just as he came happily
up from the engine room after shutting off the petrol and
giving the engine a wipe over with an oily rag.

'He said we were to keep on ringing,' said Titty, and took
the rag with which Roger was wiping his fingers and used it
to wipe the grease off her own.

'All right,' said Roger, 'I will,' and he kept the bell
ringing, 'Ting . . . Ting . . . Ting . . . Ting . . .'

'Quiet a minute,' said John, coming aft from the foredeck
where he had been making a neat stow of the staysail so that it
could be hoisted again at a moment's notice. 'Listen!'

'Seven fathom,' they heard Nancy's voice away in the mist.

'Ting . . . Ting . . . Ting . . .'

'And again.' That was Captain Flint.

'Eight fathom.'

Aboard the *Sea Bear* they listened for the oars, trying to make out where the dinghy was.

'Seven fathom.'

'Where now?' said Titty. 'That sounded as if Nancy was close by.'

'Somewhere astern,' said Peggy. 'They've been moving round that way. Pheeu! It was clammy up there.'

'Could you see anything?' asked Dorothea.

'Not a thing,' said Peggy. 'But I've got ears.'

'Good long ones,' said Roger.

'Let me get at that boy,' said Peggy.

'Bearing about west,' said John.

'BELL!'

'Ting ... Ting ...' 'Shut up Peggy, I've got to keep ringing.' 'Ting ... Ting ... Ting ...'

'Eight fathom.'

'That sounded off the port bow,' said John.

'Ting ... Ting ... Ting ...'

'Seven fathom.'

'Amidships now,' said John. 'Funny how hard it is to tell.'

'There they are,' cried Titty. Dimly, a shadow dinghy had shown for a moment.

'That's a bit too near,' they heard Captain Flint's voice. 'Half a minute ... Now, try again.'

'Seven and a half.'

'Ting ... Ting ... Ting ...'

'John!'

'Sir!' John shouted back into the whiteness.

'Have the kedge ready.'

'Aye, aye, Sir ... Come on, Susan,' said John, and ran forward.

'That means we're all right,' said Titty.

'Does it?' said Dorothea.

'Of course it does,' said Peggy. 'He's going to put the other anchor down. We're going to stop where we are for the night.'

The shadow dinghy showed again, clearer now, and was presently alongside.

'Hop out, Nancy, and give them a hand when they're paying out the kedge rope.'

'All ready with the kedge,' called John.

Nancy was aboard, very wet with working the lead. Captain Flint brought the dinghy under the bows. John lowered the smaller anchor.

'Not in the boat. Half a minute. Hold it so, while I get it slung from the stern. Good lad. That's the way. Now, pay out rope and give a shout when you're nearing the end. It's made fast, isn't it?'

'Just going to be,' said John.

'Wouldn't help us much to lose the lot,' said Captain Flint. 'I did that once, so I know.'

He pushed off from the *Sea Bear*'s side, and rowed away into the mist, passing along her side, and then disappearing astern, the grass kedge rope towing after him as John, Nancy and Susan paid it out and made sure that it should run free. Dick and Dorothea from the cockpit watched the rope sliding away like a snake on the top of the water until it vanished like every thing else a few yards from the ship.

'Three fathoms to go,' John shouted.

There was a splash far astern, and presently Captain Flint came rowing back, climbed aboard and went forward to make the kedge rope fast to the chain of the main anchor before paying out another two fathoms of that.

'Well and truly moored,' he said as he came aft. 'She won't hurt now.'

'What's the shore like?' asked Dick. 'It must be quite close because of those grouse.'

'Never got a sight of it,' said Captain Flint. 'We've been all round the ship and saw nothing. But we've got a good depth and a good bottom and plenty of room to swing.'

'Where are we?' asked Dorothea.

'We'll know that when the mist goes,' said Captain Flint. 'It won't last. The wind's coming off the land. It'll be clear enough in the morning.'

'We're stopping here?' said Susan.

'We jolly well are,' said Nancy. 'Shiver my timbers but that mist's clammy.'

'You ought to say, "Chatter my teeth!"' said Roger.

'Well, they do it without my saying it,' said Nancy.

'Mine too,' said Peggy. 'Let's have a fire in the cabin.'

'Good idea,' said Captain Flint.

There was a stampede down the companion ladder. Half an hour later, the cabin stove was burning brightly and the whole ship's company were sitting in the warmth. It was hard to believe that only a few hours before they had been sailing in bright sunshine. The cabin lamp had been lit. Dorothea was thinking that a misty chapter would go well in her *Romance of the Hebrides*. John was writing up the log . . . 'Closed with the coast. Thick mist. Anchored in seven fathoms. Mud bottom. Laid out kedge. Land to north.' Captain Flint was poring over a book of sailing directions. Nancy was looking yet again at the small chart on which the *Sea Bear*'s owner had marked the place where he had put her ashore for a scrub. Dick was looking at the big Admiralty chart that showed a lot of small sheets of water not far inland from the coast, just the place for Divers if only he were able to go ashore and look for them. Peggy and Susan were debating supper and agreeing on macaroni and tomato with poached eggs. Titty was back at her own private log . . . 'Anchored in white mist. We may be anywhere.' Roger was fingering his penny whistle trying to think of a suitable tune to play. He grinned to himself and startled everybody by shrilling out at a good pace, 'We won't go home till morning.'

'Oh, shut up,' said John. 'If you want to play that thing, we'll put you in the dinghy at the end of a long rope and you can go and play it in the fog.'

Roger played a bar or two of 'God save the King!' to show that he was bringing his private concert to an end, and said, 'Well, if you don't like real music, get Captain Flint to lug out his accordion.'

'All right, Roger,' said Captain Flint. 'We'll cheer them up by playing duets.'

'We don't need cheering up,' said Nancy. 'This is the best thing that's happened on the whole cruise. But we don't mind helping you to make a noise.'

'It'll be like being in the Arctic,' said Titty. 'Nansen could make all the noise he liked, drifting in the ice, with nobody to hear except Polar bears.'

'We're Sea Bears ourselves,' said Roger, 'and we can make all the noise *we* like, and there isn't even Nansen to listen.'

Captain Flint laughed, and took the accordion that Peggy pushed into his hands, and presently there was a din in the cabin enough to lift the roof. They sang all their old favourites that they used to sing in the houseboat on the lake, stamping with their feet, and banging on the table. Peggy and Susan, the cooks, busy in the galley, were singing while busy with their eggs and macaroni. But Nancy, now and again, looked doubtfully at Captain Flint. She knew very well that he was not really happy.

'It's all right, Uncle Jim,' she said. 'It couldn't be righter. Mac'll be delighted. We're in his bay, just where we wanted to be.'

'Are we?' said Captain Flint. 'I wish I knew. If only this infernal mist would clear and we could see. She's safe enough as things are, but we shall have to keep an anchor watch.'

'What's that?' asked Dorothea.

'Somebody on deck while we're asleep,' said Titty, 'to rouse out the rest of us if anything goes wrong.'

There was more singing after supper. Then, before turning in, everybody went on deck for a last look round. The mist was as thick as ever. Water dripped from the furled mainsail. The decks were wet. The light coming up through the skylight shone into whiteness overhead. It was very quiet, but for the distant sigh of waves. The *Sea Bear* lay in smooth water. They knew that those waves must be somewhere outside.

'Even in real harbours she hasn't lain as quiet as this,' said Nancy. 'I don't see why you shouldn't go to bed too.'

'Look here,' said Captain Flint, 'she isn't mine. I wouldn't care twopence if I drowned the lot of you, but I'm not going to get Mac's ship into trouble if I can help it.'

'You can't stay up all night.'

'Not going to. You can set the alarm for three, and then, if it's still thick, you and John can take a watch. But it should have cleared by then.'

The crew stowed themselves in their bunks. The lamp burned on in what might have seemed an empty cabin, except that a pair of large feet showed near the top of the companion ladder where the worried skipper of the *Sea Bear* was sitting and smoking and, every now and then, looking uselessly round into the misty night.

CHAPTER 3

PUTTING HER ON LEGS

IT was a restless night in the *Sea Bear*. Steps on deck woke sleepers in their bunks. They turned over and went to sleep again only to be waked once more by the whirr of an alarm clock, instantly suppressed. Dick lay thinking of the small lochs that were shown on the chart and wondering how long the scrubbing of the ship would take and whether he would be able to go ashore for his last chance of seeing Divers before going home. People were moving in the cabin. There was the noise of somebody slipping on the way up the companion ladder. 'Jibbooms and bob-stays! I wish shins were made of iron!' It must have been Nancy who slipped. There were snatches of quick eager talk up on deck. 'Look! Look! That's the place.' 'Don't shout.' 'All right. But they're sleeping like logs.' Then there was the gentle bump of the dinghy being brought alongside, the squeak of rowlocks. Silence . . . Then, 'What's he doing? Stamping to keep warm?' 'Finding the best place to beach her.' 'Why's he shifting that stone?' 'Making marks, so that we can see where to bring her in when the tide's up.' 'He's coming off again.' Silence for a long time. Bump. Captain Flint's voice outside: 'Nice bit of hard. Mac knew what he was doing. Ten foot rise and fall . . . Low water about one . . . If we put our backs into it we'll have the barnacles off and the anti-fouling on with time to spare.' There were more noises in the cabin. Dick rolled out of his bunk, to find that almost everybody else had had the same idea. Titty, Dorothea, Peggy and Susan were all going up to see what was happening. Dick hurried after them, but hardly had time to get half-way up the companion ladder before there was a roar of 'Go to bed, you idiots! You've only a few more hours for sleep and a hard day ahead.' The fog had gone, high clouds were driving across, and the sky was full of light.

'We couldn't have done better even if we'd been able to see,' said Titty.

'Anchored right in the middle,' said Dorothea.

'We really had better go to sleep again,' said Susan.

'He's been ashore and looked at the place where she's going to be put on legs,' said Peggy.

'Put on legs . . .' Dick wanted to see how that was done, and perhaps all the crew would be needed for it, but they might not be needed all day and if the Ship's Naturalist could be spared . . . Dick scrambled back into his bunk and was asleep again. He did not hear John, Nancy and Captain Flint come down into the cabin. There was quiet for an hour or two. Then more noises. Heavy bumps in the fo'c'sle. Bumps on deck. Someone was reaching into his bunk to get at something high up under the deck. The winch was clanking. There was the sudden roar of a newly started Primus stove. Dick, half asleep, heard Roger say, 'Shut up!' and somebody else say, 'Engine!' and Roger bounce out of his bunk with 'Coming. Coming! Don't let him start it till I get there.' Dick dozed again. It seemed only a moment later when he awoke and knew that he was the only one below decks. Bright sunshine was sweeping round the cabin. The engine was throbbing. Dick rubbed his eyes, grabbed his spectacles, scrambled out of his bunk and up the ladder to find all the rest of the crew on deck and the *Sea Bear* moving very slowly across the smooth water of a sunlit cove where yesterday she had lain blindfold in the mist.

The north side of the cove, towards which they were moving was steep and rocky. A lump of rising ground, covered with heather, hid the valley that was shown on the chart. At the mouth of the cove, Dick saw the seagulls circling about the cliff that had thrown back the sound of the engine when they passed close under it in the fog. The top of the cliff sloped up to a little hill, behind which a high ridge hid the buildings they had seen from the offing. Looking astern, he saw a line of rocks, rising into a promontory that divided the cove from another to the south of it. At the head of the cove a stream was coming down over a waterfall. The *Sea Bear* was moving towards a little bay with rocks on either side. She was in perfect shelter, though small white clouds, high overhead, were racing seaward, and outside, beyond the cliff, were white-topped hurrying waves.

'Just ticking over,' Captain Flint was saying. 'No need to ram her ashore.'

'Aye, aye, Sir,' said Roger.

'Chug ... chug ... chug ...'

A lot of work had been done since, in the early morning, the mist had blown away. A great coil of rope was on the after deck, close by the cockpit, with the kedge anchor aboard again and ready for letting go from aft instead of from the bows. More coils of rope were on the foredeck, and the end of one of them went down into the dinghy which, with an anchor in it, was made fast to the starboard shrouds instead of towing astern. Susan was at the tiller. That must mean that John and Nancy and Captain Flint were going to be needed for something else, and needed at once.

'Doing fine, Susan,' said Captain Flint. 'We're on the marks now. One white stone above another ... Keep them so.'

'Dick,' said Dorothea, 'it's too cold to be on deck in pyjamas.'

'I'm warm enough,' said Dick. 'I'll change afterwards.'

'It's a lovely bit of beach,' said Nancy. 'We saw it as soon as the fog went, and Captain Flint went ashore and put the marks.'

'But where are her legs?' said Dick.

'Look over the side,' said Nancy. 'Didn't you hear us putting the bolts through.'

Dick looked over, and saw that heavy posts had been slung alongside, one to starboard and one to port, their forward ends pivoting on huge bolts close to the shrouds.

'Isn't it a gorgeous place?' said Titty. 'Better than any harbour.'

'It's just the place for a story,' said Dorothea, looking at the blue hills far inland, and the steep cliff that sheltered the cove from the north winds.

'Better than any harbour,' said Titty again. 'It's the sort of place where something's simply bound to happen.'

'I hope to goodness not,' said Captain Flint, hurrying past after making sure that all was ready on the foredeck. 'She's a big ship and we can't afford to let anything happen at all.'

'Not that kind of thing,' said Titty, but he did not hear her. Already he was at the stern, looking to and fro as if to judge his distance.

'Let go the kedge,' he said.

There was a splash and, as the *Sea Bear* moved slowly on, he paid out rope.

'John,' he called, and John was there in a moment. 'Watch the kedge rope. See it runs out clear but be ready to check it and haul in fast if we have to go astern. We don't want it fouling the propeller.'

'Aye, aye, Sir,' said John.

'I'll take the tiller to put her aground,' said Captain Flint. 'You're doing all right, Susan. Stand by to take charge again. Nancy,' he called. 'Ready with that bow warp?'

'All clear to go,' sang out Nancy.

'Chug . . . chug . . . chug . . .'

Slowly, slowly the *Sea Bear* was moving on towards the shore.

'Stop!'

'Stopped,' said Roger, pulling the gear lever half-way back. The chug, chug of the engine suddenly quickened, now that it was no longer turning the propeller.

Slowly and more slowly the *Sea Bear* moved into the little bay. There were rocks close ahead to port and starboard. On the starboard side they were already beginning to hide the mouth of the creek and the open sea beyond it. Another twenty yards and she would be ramming her bowsprit into more rocks above a narrow strip of curving beach.

'Any minute now,' said Captain Flint quietly.

Nobody breathed.

'Scrrrunch.'

The next second Captain Flint had left the tiller, was in the dinghy and rowing for the shore, Nancy paying out the warp as he rowed.

'Scrunch.'

'He's got there,' exclaimed Titty.

They saw him step out of the dinghy, jerk it a foot or two up the beach, take out the anchor, stagger up the shore with it and bed it among the rocks.

'Haul it on the bow warp and make fast,' he shouted, and Nancy had it taut in a moment.

'Stern warp, John! Haul in and belay!'

'Aye, aye, Sir.'

'Port warp, Nancy.'

He was coming off again in the dinghy. Nancy passed down the end of a rope, and he took it ashore and made it fast round a rock.

'Starboard warp!'

In a very few minutes the *Sea Bear* was moored stem and stern, with ropes ashore on either side.

"LEGS. Stout posts so fastened in an upright position on each side of a vessel as to support her when left high and dry by the receding tide"

SEA DICTIONARY.

Ship ashore

without legs   with legs   Leg ready for lowering

Easing leg into position

The bolt acts as a pivot

Leg in position

HOW LEGS WORK

'Scrunch. Scrunch.'

'She's afloat again,' called Roger. 'Shall I give her another push with the engine?'

'Finished with engines.'

Roger disappeared below. The throbbing of the engine came to an end and Roger bobbed up again on deck, wiping his hands on a greasy rag and looking extremely pleased.

Captain Flint, very hot and out of breath, came aboard.

'Scrunch' ... A very gentle scrunch this time.

'She's tickling the ground,' said Titty.

'That's all right,' he panted. 'Tide's got another inch or two to rise. And now we'll put our feet down. Starboard side first. We've plenty of time to get them both down before she settles.'

Nothing could have been simpler. The after end of the long timber that had been slung along the starboard side was lowered. Nancy pulled on a rope in the bows while John paid out a rope from the stern until the timber was standing straight up and down. Captain Flint had a good look, and both ropes were made fast. The upper end of the post was lashed to the shroud. The same thing was done to the leg on the other side, and there was the *Sea Bear* ready to take the ground with her keel and with a leg on each side of her to hold her up as soon as the tide should leave her.

'You'd better get dressed,' said Dorothea to Dick, and he bolted below. Any minute now he would know whether he would be free to go ashore.

'That's all we can do for now,' said Captain Flint presently. 'Well done, everybody. What about breakfast?'

'Porridge'll be cold,' said Susan.

'Who cares?' said Nancy.

'There'll be hot coffee anyway,' said Peggy. 'I got the Primus going again while you were fixing the legs.'

They had hardly begun their porridge when they felt the

ship meet the bottom once more and they knew that the tide which had lifted them after they first touched had begun to drop. There was a general stampede up the companion and up the fo'c'sle ladders.

'She's sitting very pretty,' said Captain Flint.

'What about her legs?' said John.

'They'll be doing their share in a minute.'

'This one's on the bottom anyhow,' said Roger. 'I can see a fish nosing round it.'

'Her waterline's showing,' said Nancy a minute or two later.

'Another couple of hours and we'll be at work.'

'Do let's get breakfast finished,' said Susan.

They went down again and Dick, still thinking of those lochs marked on the chart not so very far away, put his question.

'Will you want all of us for the scrubbing?' he said.

'All hands,' said Nancy.

'Don't you think it,' said Captain Flint. 'Not enough brushes and scrapers for one thing. No. The four toughest are the ones I want. John and Nancy with Susan and Peggy to lend a hand. And we'll ask the others to keep out of the way. Better let them have a run ashore.'

'We'll explore,' said Titty joyfully.

'Of course if you really don't want us,' said Dorothea, who also was thinking of adventure on land.

'Good,' said Roger.

Dick, thinking of Divers, was too pleased to say anything at all.

'Stow your grub away,' said Peggy, 'and then Susan and I'll make sandwiches so that the land party can clear out.'

'The land party!' Titty and Dorothea and Roger looked at each other with eyes full of plans. Dick was running over in his mind the things that, as Ship's Naturalist, he must not forget to take.

'May we take the little chart?' asked Titty.

'It doesn't give names to anything,' said John.

'All the better,' said Titty. 'We'll put in names ourselves . . . Scrubbers' Bay for a start.'

'And Gull Cliff,' said Dorothea.

'I don't suppose Mac'll mind,' said Captain Flint.

The *Sea Bear* was settling firmly on her keel and legs. People talked a little less loudly than usual. Throughout the cruise they had known her alive under their feet, swaying along with a reaching wind, punching into head seas, alive always, even when moored in harbour for the night. Now, suddenly, she was dead. Nobody said anything about it, but each one of them kept glancing at the faces of the others to see if they felt it too.

'I wonder what she's like underneath,' said Nancy suddenly.

'We'll soon know,' said John.

'Most of these old pilot cutters are the same,' said Captain Flint. 'Deepest at the heel.'

'Won't she settle on a slant with her nose down?' said John, who had been thinking it out.

'She would on flat ground,' said Captain Flint. 'But this beach has a slope to it. She's very nearly level, and she must be pretty well solid on her legs by now.'

'I've had enough to eat,' said Nancy. 'I'm going up to have a look.'

Captain Flint followed her, stuffing tobacco into his pipe. John made a large mouthful of the last of a slice of bread and marmalade, gulped the last of his coffee and was gone. Titty and Dorothea hurried after John. Dick had already finished his breakfast and was getting out the things he needed and putting them in a row on the settee below his bunk.

Camera. Telescope. Pencil. Notebook. Nothing was to be forgotten. Roger stood up, glanced at the companion ladder and then back at the table. He sat down again and passed his empty mug to Susan. He was the engineer and his job for the moment was done. He helped himself to another slice of bread. Susan laughed.

'Still hungry?' she said.

'Why not?' said Roger. 'I am, if you want to know.'

'Better eat now,' said Susan, 'and then you won't have to carry so much grub when you go ashore.'

Roger looked at her with some suspicion. Was Susan laughing or not? 'We'll all be hungry again if we go a long way,' he said.

'We won't starve you,' said Peggy.

Dick was sure he had forgotten nothing. He put the small things in his pocket, put the camera in his knapsack, to make sure of keeping it dry, and, with his knapsack ready on his back, went up on deck.

'Look over the side,' said Dorothea. 'The tide's gone down a lot already.'

Dick looked over. A broad strip of the dark green under-water body of the *Sea Bear* was showing along her sides.

'The sooner we all get ashore the better,' said Nancy. 'Come on, John. Cargo of paint, brushes, scrapers. Much easier now than when she's high and dry.'

'Scrapers?' said Dorothea.

'For the barnacles,' said Nancy. 'She's fairly covered with them. And slimy with weed.'

'What about putting the folding boat over?' said John.

'We shan't need it,' said Captain Flint. 'We'll only have it to stow again.'

'Let's have it all the same,' said Nancy, looking at the queer shape of the folding boat, stowed almost flat, and lashed alongside the skylight. 'We've never used it once. And to-day's the last chance.'

'Get the scrubbing done and you shall play about in the folder this evening, once the *Sea Bear*'s afloat again.'

'Right,' said Nancy. 'That's a promise.'

Everything had gone well and everybody knew it. They had only to look at Captain Flint, sitting on the cabin skylight smoking his pipe, to know that he was no longer the worried skipper of the night and the early morning. He was not even bothering to give advice as John and Nancy brought up mops and long-handled scrapers, and two great tins of Mariner Brand, Best Quality, Gold Medal Anti-fouling Paint out of the stores in the fo'c'sle, and lowered them down to Titty and Dorothea, who were already in the dinghy, hoping to be the first ashore.

Peggy put her head out of the fore hatch. 'Susan wants to know if we'd better get grub ready now for the scrubbers as well as for the others.'

'Much better. Horrible job climbing aboard again for it.'

Ferrying began, and long before it was finished the tide had dropped far enough to make it difficult to reach the dinghy even with the rope ladder.

'Isn't Captain Flint coming?' asked Titty.

'The captain's always last to leave the ship,' said Dorothea.

'But the *Sea Bear* isn't a wreck,' said Titty.

'He wants to be last anyway,' said Dorothea.

Nancy went back once more to fetch him, and there was a cheerful moment when Roger said, 'He's going to fall in,' as Captain Flint climbed heavily down to the dinghy by way of the bobstay. He did not come straight ashore but sat in the stern of the dinghy while Nancy rowed him round the ship.

'He's got his long boots on,' said Roger.

'He'll want them,' said John. 'He'll be able to get going long before we can.'

It was quite like a camp on the beach, what with all the stuff that had been brought ashore, and the whole crew of the *Sea Bear* waiting by it, watching the tide fall lower and lower round their ship. The sun poured down into the little bay. There was a blue sky overhead. Little clouds flying across it were like scattered flecks of cotton wool, 'A grand drying day,' said Captain Flint.

'Her starboard side'll be dry first,' said John, glancing towards the sun.

'That's the one we'll begin on,' said Nancy. 'Gosh! what waste of time it is going into harbours. This is ten times better.'

'Hadn't the explorers better get going?' said Dorothea.

'Let's just wait to see her really standing out of the water,' said Titty.

'You needn't go at all if you don't want to,' said Nancy.

'But we do,' said Titty, and Dick looked at her gratefully.

'You won't find anything inland half so exciting as this,' said Nancy.

'I bet we do,' said Roger.

'Unknown country,' said Titty.

'It'll be real exploring,' said Dorothea.

'Instead of just paddling and scrubbing,' said Roger.

'Well, get along with you,' said Nancy.

But the explorers lingered, as the legs of their ship stood higher and higher out of the water, and Captain Flint in his long sea boots waded out with a stiff scrubbing brush and began work on the *Sea Bear*'s stem. They waited, with Dick growing more and more anxious, till John and Nancy waded out to join the skipper, able at last to stand in the shallow water under the *Sea Bear*'s bows.

'Do let's start,' said Dick.

'What time have we got to be back?' asked Dorothea, and

Susan repeated the question. 'What time had they better be back?'

'Oh, sevenish,' called Captain Flint. 'We'll give them a hoot with the fog horn as soon as she floats.'

'Come on,' said Dorothea.

'Don't get into trouble with natives,' said Susan.

'There aren't any,' said Titty. 'It's beautifully uninhabited.'

'There are houses the other side of that ridge,' said Nancy.

'But not this side,' said Titty. 'Anyhow not on the chart.'

'So long, you scrubbers,' called Roger, and the land party turned their backs on the *Sea Bear* and climbed up from the shore, explorers in a strange land.

CHAPTER 4

THE FIRST DISCOVERY

FROM above the little bay the land party looked down just for a moment on the *Sea Bear* and the scrubbers working at her in water up to their knees. Then they plunged forward over springy peat among rocks and short heather.

'Now!' said Titty.

'Now what?' said Dorothea.

'They're out of sight,' said Titty.

'Yes,' said Dorothea. 'Anything may happen any minute.'

'What's the time?' asked Roger.

'Dick,' said Dorothea. 'What's the time?'

Dick was looking westward over wild, broken moorland, hoping to see the lochs marked on the chart, but they were still hidden by a lump of rising ground.

'Dick,' said Dorothea again. 'Time?'

He started, pulled himself together and looked at his watch.

'Seven . . . seven and a half minutes to twelve. We've wasted a lot of time already.'

'We've got six hours at least,' said Roger. 'That's six times sixty minutes for things to happen in. Three hundred and sixty different things.'

'One'll be enough,' said Titty. 'If it's the right sort of thing, and it's bound to be in a place like this.'

'Those tarns must be about due west,' said Dick.

'We'll see them when we get higher up,' said Dorothea.

'Let's get to the top of this one,' said Titty, pointing up the hill to the north of them. 'Up there we'll be able to see all ways at once.'

'If we work north-west,' said Dick.

'No,' said Roger. 'Much better go straight up, and be able to look all round.'

'This is the best day of the whole cruise,' said Titty, and climbed on.

'I know why,' said Dorothea. 'It's because it wasn't planned.'

That was it. For the four able seamen, as well as for Nancy and John, the cruise had been too successful. The *Sea Bear*, sailing from port to port, from one famous anchorage to another, had been as regular as a liner. Everything had gone according to programme, and that programme had not allowed for such days as this, with four able seamen exploring by themselves and their elders thoroughly busy and out of the way.

'Indian trail,' exclaimed Dorothea a minute or two later, and stopped short, looking at a trodden path between clumps of heather. The others joined her.

'No footprints,' said Titty.

'Sheep-track,' said Roger.

'Deer,' said Dick. 'Look at that mark. The hoof's much bigger than a sheep's.'

'John said he thought he saw a stag early this morning when the fog cleared.'

'We'll see them drinking their fill at eve,' said Titty.

'At those tarns perhaps,' said Dick, 'unless the chart was wrong and there aren't any.'

'If they're marked on the chart they'll be there,' said Titty. 'We'll see them as soon as we get a bit higher.'

They climbed on, with the world about them growing wider as they climbed. Looking southward they could see how the coast curved out towards the distant Head. White crests of foam flecked the blue sea.

'You'd never think it was blowing like this when you're

down in our creek,' said Titty, leaning against a gust of wind that blew her hair past her cheeks. 'Dot's jolly lucky to have pigtails.'

'I'm luckier,' said Roger, 'and so's Dick, except for his goggles.' In the harder gusts, Dick was putting a hand to his spectacles which shook in the wind so that he found it hard to see through them. 'Come on, Dick. Don't let's stop before we get to the top.'

'Coming,' said Dick who, besides having trouble with his spectacles, was finding it hard to steady his telescope while he searched as much of the valley as he could see for a sign of the two lochs. 'I can see deer,' he said suddenly.

'Where?' said Dorothea.

'A whole lot of them, grazing like cows.'

'We'll see them better from higher up,' said Roger. 'Race you to the top.'

He raced alone. The others plodded after him. Dorothea had picked a small purple flower, and was showing it to Dick.

'It's a butterwort, I think,' said Dick. 'But I don't know for certain.'

'Sticky leaves,' said Dorothea.

'Fly-catcher,' said Dick, stooping over a small patch of the flowers.

'Roger,' called Titty. 'Wait a minute. We ought to keep together,' she said to the others. 'We're in unknown country and anything may happen.'

'Something has,' said Dorothea. 'Look at him.'

Roger had reached the top of the hill. He was urgently beckoning to them, pointing at something close beside him and beckoning again. He was not shouting. That in itself was enough to tell them that he was not simply trying to hurry them.

'He may have seen enemies,' said Titty.

'What is he doing?' said Dorothea.

Roger, after one more bout of beckoning, had dropped to the ground. A moment later he had disappeared. It was not as if he had crawled on over the top of the hill. He had not seemed to be moving. One moment they had seen him crouching on the ground with his back towards them. The next moment he had gone. He simply was not there.

'Come on,' said Titty, and raced up the steep slope of the hill. 'He must have found a cave. Come on.'

'The top of the hill's a queer shape,' said Dick.

'It's like . . . Dick . . . I know what it is,' panted Dorothea.

They could all see it now, a green, turf-covered mound on the very top of the hill, and, as Titty came breathlessly up to it, Roger came scrambling out.

'What about this?' he said.

'It's a Pict-house,' said Dorothea. 'A real one. Prehistoric, like that one they showed us on Skye.'

'Well, nobody showed us this one,' said Roger. 'I found it myself.' That day on Skye had been a wasted one. Well-meaning natives had shown them things and they had felt more like trippers than explorers.

'What's it like inside?' said Titty, stooping to look into the hole out of which Roger had crawled.

'The hole doesn't go very far,' said Roger. 'It's a square sort of tunnel. Stone walls. Beastly dark.'

'I say,' said Dorothea. 'How would it be if I made my robber chief prehistoric? He'd wear skins and live up here and see the Danish longships coming into our bay.'

Dick had just glanced at the tunnel, and then climbed the steep side of the mound.

'I thought so,' he said. 'The roof's fallen in. It's just like that one in Skye. A room in the middle and a tunnel for getting in and out . . .' He stopped suddenly. 'There are the lochs!' he said, and, thinking of his Divers, was for setting off straight across country.

'Father'll want to know about it,' said Dorothea.

Dick, after one more glance at the lochs in the valley, pulled out his pocket-book.

Dorothea, Titty and Roger had all climbed up beside him. The middle of the mound was like a shallow saucer where it had fallen in, perhaps centuries before. Standing in the dip they looked round over the edge.

'It's like being on the top of the whole world,' said Titty.

On one side they looked out over the sea to Scotland, southward to the Head, northward to another great cape jutting out. Far out to sea were the black specks of two fishing boats, each with a long wisp of black smoke blowing from it. Looking down to the cove where they had left the *Sea Bear*, they could see the top of her mast. The rest of her was hidden close under the steep shore. They could see both inlets with the rocky spit between them, and then rolling moorland stretching towards big grey hills. Here and there were lochs. They could see part of one of the lochs, that had raised hopes in Dick, and the whole of the other. Looking up the valley they could see that there was a ridge to the south of it and another to the north rising slowly towards the mountains. Along the slopes of the northern ridge they caught glimpses of a cart track that seemed to come from the head of the valley and, not far away, turned sharply into a gap on the skyline.

'Crouch down,' said Titty. 'When you're on the bottom you can't see anything but sky. Not even the hills. If we were hiding in it, nobody could see us, unless they came here and climbed up to look in over the edge.'

The others crouched beside her. It was true. There was nothing to be seen but the great circle of blue sky overhead, from which the last white scraps of cloud had blown away.

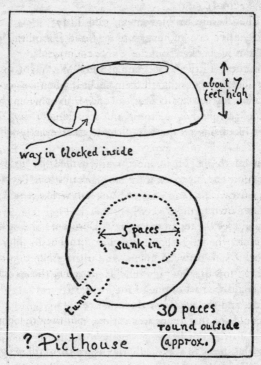

about 7 feet high

way in blocked inside

5 paces sunk in

tunnel

30 paces round outside (approx.)

? Picthouse

**A PAGE FROM DICK'S NOTEBOOK
SHOWING THE SHAPE OF THE 'PICT-HOUSE'**

'Buzzard,' said Dick, as a black speck swung across high over their heads.

'It's like being in a bird's nest,' said Titty.

'The hero could lie here laughing,' said Dorothea, 'while the villains were searching the whole countryside.'

'It's a bit like the igloo,' said Roger. 'We ought to fetch Nancy and Peggy. We'll tell them about it when we get back. They wouldn't come anyhow,' he added. 'Not when they're in the middle of their scraping and scrubbing. I say, it's an awful pity we haven't got that chart to mark exactly where it is.'

'But I have got it,' said Titty. She pulled the little chart out of her knapsack, unrolled it and spread it out flat.

'Pict-house Hill,' said Roger. 'Put it in with a pencil. You can ink it afterwards.'

'It's a good name anyhow,' said Dorothea. She stood up and looked round. 'That long ridge can be the Northern Rockies. Then there's Low Ridge on the other side of the valley. It gets lower and lower till it turns into those rocks we didn't want to hit in the fog.'

'What about Dick's tarns?' said Titty.

'Upper and Lower,' said Dorothea, 'but they're lochs, not tarns.'

'And the lump that wouldn't let us see them till we got up here and still doesn't let us see the stream . . .'

'Burn,' said Dorothea, 'not stream.'

'It would be a beck if we were at Holly Howe,' said Roger.

'That lump's not big enough for a hill,' said Titty.

'Let's call it the Hump,' said Roger. 'It's very camelious.'

Just putting in those few names on the chart made the valley seem almost their own.

'I wish we weren't sailing tomorrow,' said Dorothea.

'I'm going in again,' said Roger, 'to see how far I can get.'

'Look out,' said Titty. 'Remember the tunnel in Kanchenjunga. More of it may cave in on the top of you.'

'All right,' said Roger, and slid down the steep side of the mound. Dick was down there, too, making a sketch of the entrance to show his father. Eager as he was to get away to the lochs, he was Professor Callum's son and, for the moment, had to turn from birds to ancient monuments.

Titty and Dorothea were alone in the shallow saucer where the ancient roof had fallen in, and long, long ago been grown over with green turf.

'It is a most gorgeous place,' said Titty. 'And wasted. Think of no one knowing about it but us.'

'Perhaps no one's ever been here since the last of the ancient Picts died fighting to defend it as the strangers from the sea came roaring up from their boats.'

Roger, a good deal dirtier than before, came climbing over the edge. 'Someone's using it,' he said, looking round over the wild moorland as if he expected to see that someone close at hand. He held out a tin biscuit box. 'I've been as far as I can, and I found this when I was feeling round where the tunnel comes to an end. It's somebody's provisions.'

He shook the box and they could hear something sliding about inside it. There was, alas, no doubt that the box had not been left by any ancient Pict. Much of its paper covering was still sticking to it and they could see the trademark and the name of a famous firm of Glasgow biscuit-makers.

'Oh well,' said Titty, 'it can't be helped . . . and it doesn't really matter. It isn't as if we were ever going to be here again.'

'I'm going to open it and see what's inside,' said Roger.

'But it isn't ours.'

'It's treasure trove,' said Dorothea. 'Roger found it. He can't do any harm by looking at it.'

She wanted to know what was in it, and so, in spite of her scruples, did Titty.

'Of course there may be a message in it, like the one we left in the cairn.'

'Urgent, perhaps,' said Dorothea. 'Think if people didn't open bottles cast up on the shore just because the bottles weren't theirs.'

'I'm going to open it anyhow,' said Roger.

He put the box on the ground and took the lid off. They saw at once that the thing that had been sliding about was a paper parcel.

'Provisions,' said Roger. 'I thought so. Bread ... No ... Cake of a sort ...' He had opened the paper and found a heavy hunk of cake, very dark, like Christmas pudding.

'It's not old,' said Dorothea, poking it with a careful finger. 'Soft and still sticky. What's that underneath it? I say, perhaps it's someone writing a story.' From the bottom of the box she pulled out an ordinary school exercise book.

'French verbs more likely,' said Titty. 'I had to fill a whole book of them the summer we found Swallowdale.'

'Do you think I'd better taste the cake?' asked Roger.

'Of course not,' said Titty. 'Wrap it up again and put it away.'

'All right,' said Roger. 'You never know. There may be poison in it.'

Dorothea had opened the exercise book. 'It's all in a foreign language,' she said.

'Let me look,' said Titty. 'If it's French ... But it isn't. And it isn't Latin either. Perhaps it's a secret code.'

'It looks like a diary,' said Dorothea. 'Those numbers must be dates.' She and Titty pored over the book together. Yes. It looked as if the figures at one side of the page might be dates, but they could make nothing of the words: 'Da fiadh

dheug ... damh a fireach ...' On and on it went, short
entries and each with its figure at the side, 'Damh is eildean.'
Here and there was a short word like 'is' and a shorter like
'a' but all the other words belonged to no language that they
knew, and if it was written in code, perhaps even 'is' and 'a'
did not mean what they usually meant.

'I know what it is,' said Titty suddenly. 'It's Gaelic. It
belongs to one of the natives. A savage Gael. Look here,
Roger. You put it back where you found it.'

All three of them looked at the ridge before them, and
up the long wild valley and down again at the cove far away
below them where the mast of the *Sea Bear* spoke to them of
friends and allies. There were no Gaels to be seen. Up here,
on that hill above the sea, on the top of the old dwelling place
of Picts who had been dead a thousand years, they might have
been the only people in the world. But there was the biscuit
box and its contents to show that someone counted the old
Pict-house so much his own that he could safely leave his
things in it.

'Dick,' said Dorothea, 'do look, before Roger puts it
back.'

But Dick took no more than a polite interest in biscuit box,
exercise book and hunk of cake. He was bursting to be gone
and had almost done what he had to do. He had made a sketch
of the mound from one side, giving a rough idea of its shape.
Now he was making a drawing of it to show as well as he
could the way in which it was built. There was a circle with
a smaller circle for the dip made by the fallen roof and dotted
lines to show how the tunnel lay.

'Bother whoever he is,' said Roger, slipping over the edge
with the box to put it back in the tunnel.

'Father'll want to know how big it is round,' Dorothea
was saying, looking over Dick's shoulder, as Roger came
climbing back, wiping the earth from his hands. 'It's for

Father,' she explained. 'He always wants to know shapes and sizes when anybody finds antiquities.'

'Boats are what Daddy always measures,' said Roger.

Dick was pacing earnestly across the dip. 'Five steps,' he said, 'and it's about thirty round. Very thick walls. And the dip isn't quite in the middle. That means that the wall is thickest where the tunnel goes in.' He wrote the figures beside his diagrams.

'And now,' he said, 'I'm off.'

'Much better come with us,' said Titty.

'I've got to go down to those lochs,' said Dick. 'It's the very last chance of seeing Divers.'

'Oh, let him go,' said Dorothea.

'We'll explore along the slopes of the Northern Rockies,' said Titty, glancing up the valley and then at the chart. 'We'll come back past Upper and Lower Lochs. They'll show us the way to the beck ... burn. And we'll follow the burn past the other side of the Hump until it comes to the waterfall and our cove.'

'Dick,' said Dorothea, 'are you going to stay at those lochs all the time?'

'I expect so,' said Dick. 'There's sure to be some birds, even if there aren't any Divers.'

'Good,' said Titty. 'We'll pick you up on our way back to the ship.'

'But don't wait for us if they sound the foghorn. Go straight back to the *Sea Bear*,' said Dorothea. 'Only do listen for it ... If he's watching birds, you know ...' She looked at the others. They laughed. They both knew that if Dick was looking at anything, even if it was only a caterpillar, you could shout at him from close by without his hearing.

'I'll hear all right,' said Dick, putting his notebook in his pocket. 'Good-bye.'

'Look here,' said Roger. 'Even if somebody else is using this place, we'll never find a better one for eating our grub.'

'Eat yours with us, Dick, and get it over,' said Dorothea.

'I can eat it going along.'

'Susan'll be very fierce if you forget it,' said Titty.

'Bother birds,' said Roger. 'Adventures are much better.'

But Dick was already over the edge of the mound, and hurrying on his way to the lochs, thinking of the time that he had already had to waste.

Dorothea watched him. Now and again, as he dropped into a dip in the uneven ground, she lost sight of him, and then saw him again as he came up on the other side of it, moving quickly slantwise down the slopes of the long ridge that sheltered the valley from the north.

She turned to find that the other two explorers had emptied their knapsacks and were opening their packets of sandwiches.

'Roger's quite right,' said Titty. 'Going a long way, it's easier to carry your grub inside.'

Dorothea wriggled out of the straps of her own knapsack and sat down beside them. In that hollow on the top of the old Pict-house, she thought, an escaping prisoner could hide from his pursuers. One moment, before sitting down, she could see for miles, out over the sea or up the valley to the mountains. The next, sitting on the ground, she could see nothing but sky and the short blades of grass stirring against the blue just above the level of her head. 'Invisible to all but the eagle, the fugitive rested and was safe,' she murmured to herself.

'What?' said Roger, taking a bite from a sandwich.

Dorothea started. 'Nothing,' she said. 'I was only thinking how secret this place is.'

'Listen!' said Titty. 'Listen!'

'Bagpipes!' said Roger.

DICK GOES OFF TO THE LOCHS

Faintly, from far away, the skirl of bagpipes drifted down the wind.

They jumped up.

'People . . . quite near . . .' said Titty.

'I can't see anyone,' said Dorothea.

'You can't tell,' said Titty. 'Somebody may be seeing you.'

'Come down,' said Roger. 'Come down, and then you can't be seen even if there's somebody watching.'

They dropped and for a moment waited silently, listening for the pipes. They could still hear them.

'It's the other side of the Northern Rockies,' said Titty. 'A road goes over where that gap is.'

'There's a robber castle just over the top of the range,' said Dorothea.

'Conspicuous house,' said Titty, looking at the sketch on the little chart.

'Far enough away, anyhow,' said Roger, and took another bite.

CHAPTER 5

'WE ARE BEING STALKED!'

THAT far away skirl of bagpipes had come to an end.

With little in their knapsacks but their empty lemonade bottles and all solid rations except chocolate stowed inside them for easy carrying, the three explorers looked out from the top of the old Pict-house and searched the skyline of the ridge before them. The gap in its rocky outline, and glimpses of a cart track winding up to it through the heather, told them where the house was that had been seen from far away when the *Sea Bear* had been sailing towards the coast the day before.

'I'd like to see what sort of a house it is,' said Dorothea. 'I'm sure it ought to be a castle.'

'I bet it's where that biscuit box comes from,' said Roger.

'We ought to know the worst,' said Titty. 'And if we go carefully up to that gap, we ought to be able to see without being seen.'

Watching the skyline, they dropped down from the hill-top and then began to climb again.

'It doesn't look much used,' said Roger when they came to the cart track.

'We could pretend it isn't there,' said Titty.

'But why?' said Dorothea. 'At dead of night, with the hoofs of their horses muffled to make no noise, the smugglers come this way over the hills. A light blinks out at sea. Boats land and are gone again before the morning and when the sun comes up the smugglers are far away and everything is like it is now.'

'Anyway,' said Roger, 'it's a lot easier walking on it. Come on.'

'We oughtn't to turn back without knowing what's there,' said Titty, as much to herself as to the others.

They knew almost at once. As soon as they were in the gap, with heather slopes to right and left, they could see down into the country on the further side of the ridge.

'Native settlement,' said Titty at once.

'I told you it must be a castle,' said Dorothea.

'Don't let them see you,' said Roger.

They were looking at a group of low thatched buildings, cottages, barns and sheds. Just beyond these, was the 'conspicuous house' of the chart and, though it was hardly big enough to be a castle, Roger and Titty were not inclined to quarrel with Dorothea about it. It was built into the steep side of the hill and looked down on a bay of the sea. In front of it was a stone terrace, level with the ground at one side but with a ten or twelve foot drop below it to the rocky face of the hill. It was a two-story house, but was turned into something as good as any castle by a turret with a battlemented tip that rose high above its steeply sloping roofs.

'Get down,' said Roger, and dropped to the ground.

But Titty and Dorothea were still standing, looking through the gap at a world very different from the desolate valley they had left. It was different because it was inhabited. Far away on the slopes of the hills that fell away towards the sea there were more of the queer low cottages, like those only a hundred yards or so in front of them, with their rough thatched roofs, the thatching held down by ropes weighted with big stones. Here and there on the dark slopes were little groups of men and women cutting peat.

'Let me have your telescope,' said Dorothea. 'There's a watcher in the tower.'

'Sister Anne,' said Titty. 'It's just the place for a Bluebeard.'

'It's a girl,' said Roger, lying at their feet, elbows on the ground and telescope to his eye. 'Flop, or she'll see you. She's looking straight at us.'

They flopped, but not quite quick enough. They heard the sudden, threatening barking of a dog somewhere among the cottages.

'Now you've done it,' said Roger, working hurriedly backwards along the ground. 'Even if that girl didn't see us,

that beastly dog'll stir everybody up. They'll come pouring out to see what it's barking at and our valley won't be un-inhabited any more. It'll be a mass of people asking questions, and we'll have to go back to the ship.'

'It wasn't a girl,' said Dorothea, as soon as she had wriggled back far enough to be able to lift her head without being seen from the top of the tower. 'It was a boy in a kilt. The young chief of his clan looking far and wide from the battlements.'

'Not far and wide,' said Roger. 'He was looking straight at us.'

'But what a place for a story,' said Dorothea. 'Smugglers or Jacobites . . . or just villains with a prisoner in the tower. They might easily have a dungeon cut in the solid rock.'

'Natives anyway,' said Titty. 'We must get away from here as quick as we can.'

'That dog's stopped barking,' said Roger.

As quickly as they could they were retreating out of the gap and down the cart track by which they had come. Already they could see down the steep slopes past the hill with the Pict-house to the creek, where the mast of the *Sea Bear* showed where all the older members of the crew were at work.

'Let's go back to my Pict-house,' said Roger. 'And then, if we see natives pouring out of the gap, we can just slip down the hill, and get away.'

'But we're going to explore up the valley,' said Titty.

'We'll never find anything as good as the Pict-house,' said Roger.

'Stop a minute and listen,' said Dorothea.

There were no sounds of pursuit.

'Well, if you won't come back to my Pict-house,' said Roger, 'what about creeping up to the gap again to have another look. I don't believe that was a boy on the tower. It looked much more like a girl.'

For a moment the others hesitated. Perhaps, if they had not known that they would be sailing next day, they would have waited and then crept up again to have another look at the native settlement beyond the ridge. But they knew that they had to be back at the ship before evening and that they would never see the place again.

'Oh look here,' said Titty. 'We can't just give up exploring. We shan't have another chance, not here anyway.'

'And there's Dick,' said Dorothea. 'We said we'd pick him up on the way home.'

So, though Roger looked regretfully up at the gap and back at that green mound on the top of the little hill, they presently turned west along the cart track leading towards the head of the valley. To the left, below them, they could see the two lochs, but no sign of Dick.

'He's made himself as invisible as he could,' said Dorothea. 'He always does when he's looking at birds.'

Far ahead of them blue hills rose like a jagged wall, and above them to the right was the skyline of the Northern Rockies. Not one other human being was in sight.

They walked on, following the cart track at first, but presently leaving it, because it kept on reminding them that they were not the first to discover the valley, and later coming back to the track again because they found it much slower work walking through heather and rocks and squashy patches of moss and peat. And anyhow, as Roger pointed out, the people who had built his Pict-house had discovered the valley pretty near the beginning of the world. Also, later inhabitants, cutting peats for winter fuel, had left deep trenches, some of them too wide to be jumped across. Good places to hide in, they agreed, but wasting a lot of time when you had to walk round them instead of going straight ahead.

They had been walking for a long time. Deer, moving on the flats below them, had made them forget the native settlement on the other side of the ridge. Roger was leading the way. Dorothea was close behind him. Roger had said something about exploration being wasted on Dick, and Dorothea was explaining that there were more kinds of exploration than one and that birds, for Dick, were a part of exploration that really mattered, and that anyway Dick was as good an explorer as Roger. 'Who got first to the North Pole?' Titty heard her say, and then, though Dorothea went on talking, and Roger too, Titty did not hear a word. She had suddenly got the queerest feeling that they were not alone.

Down in the bottom, well behind them now, she knew that Dick was somewhere by the lochs. Further away still, she knew that Captain Flint and the four scrubbers were hard at work scraping and painting the *Sea Bear* before the tide could come up once more and float her off. So far as she could see there was no one else in the valley and the three explorers had the hillside to themselves. Yet, suddenly, she had the feeling that they were being watched, and watched from close at hand. She looked all round her, but could see nothing but rocky slopes and patches of heather and moss. There were no trees, no bushes. She shook herself, hurried on and tried to hear the end of Dot's argument about different kinds of explorers. Of course there was nobody there, nobody but the three of them, walking the hillside in sunshine under a wide blue sky.

A little later she had that feeling again. It was as if she were reading a book and someone had come up unseen and were reading it over her shoulder.

'Dot!' she said.

'Hullo,' said Dorothea. 'Want a rest?'

'Oh, not just yet,' said Roger.

'What is it?' said Dorothea.

'Nothing. Sorry,' said Titty. It was clear that neither of the others had felt what she had felt. And now, with the two of them stopping and looking back at her, she did not feel it herself.

'More deer,' said Roger. 'Dot, you've got my telescope.'

Down below them on the wide flats in the bottom of the valley a herd of hinds were grazing like cattle.

'They look as tame as anything,' said Roger.

'They wouldn't let us get near them,' said Dorothea.

'Let's try,' said Roger, '. . . Stalking . . .'

'No, no,' said Titty. 'We haven't got half as far as we meant to do. If we go down now we won't see anything. Let's keep on and not go down till it's time to start home.'

'I've never seen them before except at the Zoo,' said Dorothea.

'I expect they belong to those natives,' said Titty.

'In winter,' said Dorothea, 'the natives harness them like reindeer and fly in sledges over the snow.'

'Bet they don't,' said Roger. 'Hullo!'

From a patch of heather only a hundred yards ahead of them, a huge stag rose to his feet and was gone, in great leaps, down the slopes towards the head of the valley. All the deer grazing below stopped feeding and began to move.

'Keep still,' said Titty.

'I'm glad he didn't charge this way,' said Roger. 'But I didn't think much of his horns. Did you?'

'Perhaps they'll grow,' said Dorothea.

Presently the deer below stopped moving and began to graze once more.

'Come on,' said Roger, and the explorers set out again.

'They've seen us,' said Dorothea. 'They'll be off again in a minute.'

'We can't help it,' said Titty. 'Let's just keep going and then they'll see we're not trying to stalk them.'

'Pretty hard to stalk,' said Roger. 'I expect they're accustomed to it and know just what to do.'

It was clear that the deer in the valley knew very well that there were explorers moving along the hillside above them. They kept lifting their heads, and shifting a few hundred yards, stopping and then once more walking on.

'They won't let us get anywhere near them,' said Dorothea. 'They probably don't approve of being stalked. I wouldn't like it myself.'

Again Titty had that queer feeling. She turned suddenly towards the top of the ridge. Just for a second she thought she saw something move beside a rock close under the skyline, but she stared at the place and could see nothing but the rock itself.

'Dot,' she said, 'look up there, where there's a big rock sticking right up out of the heather.'

'What is it? Another stag?'

'No,' said Titty. 'I believe we're being stalked ourselves.'

'Not really?' said Dorothea.

'Yes, really,' said Titty. 'I'm sure we are.'

'Keep still,' said Roger, 'and listen. And throw up your heads. We ought to sniff the wind like the deer. And the wind's just right. It's coming from up there.'

For a minute or two the three explorers stood still as rabbits that have scented danger but do not yet know where it is. Their eyes searched this way and that along the ridge. Not a thing was moving.

'There's no harm in pretending,' said Dorothea. 'We could be prisoners escaped from the castle, with the villain hunting us for our lives.'

'I wasn't pretending,' said Titty.

Roger looked at her, and so did Dorothea. No. She was not pretending. Titty really did believe that on that wild hillside above them somebody was watching them and keeping hid.

'I thought so before,' said Titty, 'but I wasn't sure.'

'If we *are* being stalked,' said Dorothea, 'the thing to do is to pretend we don't know. We must just go on, pretending we don't know we're being stalked, and all the time getting further and further away.'

'And then the stalker will get a bit careless and let himself be seen,' said Roger. 'And then, when we know who it is and where he is, we'll know what to do next.'

'It's a pity we stopped,' said Dorothea.

'We could be picking flowers,' said Titty, looking about her and, as it happened, not finding any.

'Fossils,' said Dorothea. 'Plenty of stones. It's just the sort of place Dick finds them in.'

The three explorers grovelled, picked up stones and earnestly showed them to each other.

'Come on,' said Roger loudly, to be heard by any stalker

within a hundred yards. 'There'll be lots more fossils further on . . . Ammonites.' He finished in a shout.

'Belemnites,' shouted Dorothea, and explained in her ordinary quiet voice, 'They're the straight ones with pointed ends. That's it. We're geologists. We ought to be tapping the stones with a hammer.'

'We can make the noise all right,' said Roger, picking up a stone. 'Bang one stone on another and the stalker'll never know the difference.'

Roger and Dorothea moved on. Titty followed. She knew that though they were ready to pretend to be looking at stones both Roger and Dorothea believed she was mistaken. She could not be sure herself. But whether they were right or wrong, whether there was a stalker or not, Dorothea's plan was a good one. If there were no stalkers, it would do no harm, and if there were, it was the best thing they could do. All the same, they had come a long way up the valley. She glanced back. Dick's lochs were far behind them. The *Sea Bear*, out of sight behind the Hump, was further still, and she wished they had turned and were going the other way.

The three explorers, now geologists for anyone who might be watching them, walked on with bent heads, staring at the ground. They stooped, picked up stones and threw them away again. Roger, who had found a very good stone for a hammer, beat it loudly on every rock he passed. Down below them, the deer, now really worried, were restlessly on the move, but the geologists hardly noticed them. Whenever they stooped, they took the chance of looking up sideways towards the skyline, hoping to catch the stalker (if there was a stalker) unawares.

'What about eating our chocolate?' said Roger at last.

'All right,' said Titty. 'We can sit on these rocks and watch. If there's anybody there, we're bound to see him move.'

'I wonder if Dick'll remember to eat his?' said Dorothea.

'We ought to be turning back and looking for him soon,' said Titty.

They rested pleasantly, sitting on rocks, eating their chocolate, and looking at a hillside on which nothing was moving whatever. Even Titty lost faith in her stalker, and she could see that Roger and Dorothea were no longer much interested in something they could not believe.

Dorothea was the first of the other two to change her mind. She and Roger both knew that Titty had not been pretending but had really believed they were being watched from a distance by someone hiding in the heather. But they both thought she was wrong, though they were quite ready to get as much fun out of the idea as they could. They had eaten their chocolate and had just started again on their way up the valley. Suddenly Dorothea sniffed the air. She stopped. Titty, close behind, almost walked into her. 'What is it?' she said.

'Tobacco smoke,' said Dorothea. 'I smelt it. There it is again.'

'I knew there was someone,' said Titty. 'But I can't smell anything.'

'Sniff again,' said Dorothea. 'Sniff harder. It's rather faint. But there can't be anything growing here to smell like a railway carriage.'

'I can smell it too,' said Roger. 'Try blowing your nose.'

'I can't smell it,' said Titty. 'But if you can, it must be coming down wind. And the wind's blowing straight down on us. If there's someone smoking, he must be pretty nearly straight up the hill from here. But I can't see any smoke.'

'I'm going to charge straight up,' said Roger, and was off.

'Much better not,' said Titty. 'If there is somebody, we can't frighten him off. Hey, Roger! Come back.'

'There's no one,' shouted Roger. 'Come on and see.'

'We'd better make sure,' said Dorothea.

They left the track and scrambled up the steep slope after Roger. It was very hard work, climbing through heather and over rock and loose stones. Roger, struggling uphill, shifted a biggish stone that rolled down past Titty and Dorothea. It rolled, jumped, gathered speed and went bounding down into the valley.

He stopped to watch it taking longer and longer leaps until at last below them it disappeared with a splash into what must have been boggy ground.

'It might have hit a deer,' said Titty, climbing up beside him.

'I didn't send it down on purpose,' panted Roger. 'Anyway, there's nobody here.'

'There isn't,' said Dorothea. 'Funny. I'm sure I smelt that smell.'

'What about going down and starting home?' said Titty.

'Why should we?' said Roger.

'Time's getting on,' said Titty. 'Look where the sun's got to.'

'Let's go a little bit further,' said Roger, 'just so that if there *is* a stalker anywhere, he'll see we don't care.'

They went on, working sideways down the slope, no longer bothering about being geologists. That false alarm of the tobacco smoke, and that rush up the hillside, that had seemed as empty as any hillside could be, had made the geology seem less worth while.

A startled grouse, high up on the hillside, made them think of geology again.

'There must be somebody,' said Titty. 'That grouse wasn't startled by us.'

Roger picked up a stone and began tapping with it on a rock. He grinned at Dorothea, and Titty knew that his geology was for her more than for stalkers who were not there.

A moment later a shrill whistle sounded above and behind them. The smile left Roger's face.

'There's no doubt about that anyhow,' said Titty. 'We all heard it.'

'But where *is* it?' said Roger.

A whistle sounded again. They stared up towards the top of the ridge.

'That wasn't in the same place,' said Dorothea. 'The first one was over there.'

'Different whistle, too,' said Roger.

Titty looked back down the valley. They had come a long way from the cove where the *Sea Bear* was being scrubbed by the rest of her crew, who could do nothing to help the explorers, supposing help were needed. 'We're going back now,' she said.

'We must just make them show themselves,' said Roger. 'I'm going on.' He beat a tattoo on a rock and took a few steps forward.

Titty and Dorothea followed him. After all, those whistles had not sounded very near. They might have been over the skyline, on the other side of the ridge.

Dorothea squeaked. Something was moving on the hillside at last. Two dogs were leaping through the heather. Clear of it, they came racing down the rocky slope.

Roger looked back rather doubtfully. Titty plunged forward past Dorothea to join Roger. The dogs were coming at a terrific pelt.

'What do we do?' gasped Dorothea.

'We'd better stand quite still,' said Titty. 'It's the only way.'

'You have to look them straight in the eye,' said Roger.

'But there are two of them,' said Dorothea.

Again there was a shrill whistle on the hillside. The explorers heard it gratefully. At that moment they would have welcomed any stalkers. The dogs stopped as if unwillingly. They crouched on the ground, but kept edging forward a foot or two at a time. One of them stood up and growled.

'That one's coming on,' said Roger, and looked at the stone he had picked up for use as a geological hammer.

'Put that stone down,' said Titty. 'He may think you are going to throw it.'

Roger dropped the stone. The dog that had stood up looked back over its shoulder. It dashed forward once more. The other jumped up and came racing after it.

The whistle shrilled again, twice. Both dogs stopped dead, turned as if unwillingly, and went, slowly at first, and then faster, up the hillside towards the heather they had left.

'Gosh!' said Roger. 'We couldn't have done much anyway. It was like Christians waiting for the lions.'

'But who called them back?' said Dorothea. 'I can't see anybody.'

Then, for the first time, they saw someone on the ridge above them.

'It's a boy,' said Titty, 'in a kilt. It's that boy we saw on the tower.'

'A savage Gael,' said Dorothea.

'What a beast,' said Roger, 'sending those dogs after us.'

'He called them back,' said Titty.

Without more talk, the three of them turned off the track straight down into the valley. There was no point in getting into rows with natives.

Worse was to come. They dropped over a steep brow to the flats and disturbed yet another lot of hinds that had been quietly feeding out of sight from above. The hinds set off up the valley at full gallop.

There was a furious yell from the ridge behind the explorers. Somebody was shouting at them or at somebody else in a language they did not know. Somebody else was shouting back.

'Gaels,' said Dorothea, 'talking Gaelic at each other.'

'They're shouting at us,' said Titty.

There was another burst of angry shouting. They could not see the boy but, looking back, they saw a man coming down from the ridge further up the valley. He shouted again, shook his fist, turned as if he meant to get ahead of the moving deer, changed his mind and came leaping towards the explorers.

That was enough. The explorers turned and ran, and at that moment, far away, they heard the long drawn hoot of the *Sea Bear*'s foghorn.

'She's afloat,' said Titty. 'We ought to have turned back long ago.'

'We're done,' said Dorothea. 'We'll never get there before that Gael catches us. I do hope Dick's gone back already.'

'He'll have heard the foghorn,' said Titty.

'Not if he's looking at birds,' panted Dorothea.

'That man's stopped running,' said Roger.

They paused and looked back. The man had indeed stopped running, but he was shouting his Gaelic and someone they could not see was answering him.

'He's shaking his fist at us,' said Roger.

'Don't stop,' said Titty, 'he'll only come after us again.'

'And we've got to find Dick,' said Dorothea.

The three explorers hurried on down the valley to the lochs and were presently looking for Dick along the rocky shores.

'What would have happened if they'd caught us?' said Roger.

'Native trouble,' said Titty. 'Just what we've got to keep out of. But anyhow we've been beautifully stalked.'

CHAPTER 6

FIRST SIGHT OF THE BIRDS

DICK, notebook in one hand, pencil in the other, telescope lying handy and triumph in his heart, crouched among some rocks on the shore of the upper of the two lochs. For the first time in his life he had seen a Diver. After leaving the others at the Pict-house, he had gone straight to that upper loch, so that, if the signal for return came too soon, he would at least be able to pass the other loch on the way back to the ship. Almost at once he had seen one of the birds the thought of which had leapt into his mind the moment he had known that he and Dorothea were to join the others in a cruise among the Western Isles. He had heard it, even before he had seen the long line of splashes far out that showed where a largish bird had taken to the water.

'Cuck . . . cuck . . . cuckcuckcuck . . .'

He had never heard a cry quite like it before. The splashes had shown him where to look, but in the rippled water he found it very hard to see the bird. Something was moving on the water out there. But what? The wind made things very difficult. Every time he had caught sight of the black moving spot he had lost it again before he had been able to bring his telescope to bear. The wind was blowing from behind him over the loch, so that the roughest water was on the far side, where that bird had come down. At first, he had hardly let himself hope it was a Diver. It might have been a duck, or any other largish bird. Whatever it was, he would wait until he knew for certain.

There had come a lull in the wind. Smooth water spread

81

out over the loch from the shore, and far out on the loch he had seen the bird swimming out of the rippled water into the smooth. As he watched, it disappeared. It had come up again, nearer. He had known then that it was a diving bird of some kind. It was swimming low in the water. Very like a grebe. It must have gone under and come up again without a splash. No. It did not always go under like that. He had seen it hump itself above the water, half rise and go down as if it had taken a header. It had come up again, a minute later, and he thought it had brought something with it. There had been splashing for a minute or two after it had bobbed up. It had probably got a fish. The bird was a bit big for a grebe. Dick had crouched, hardly daring to move while he took off and cleaned his spectacles and, finding that made no difference, unscrewed and cleaned the eye-piece of his telescope, misted over with his breath.

When he had screwed it back on the telescope and looked again the bird had gone. Then it had come up much nearer than it had been. It was swimming straight towards him and now, in smooth water, he had a chance of seeing what it was like. In spite of all that he could do to keep them steady, his hands had begun to shake. The bird had dived again. There was no splashing when it came to the surface. Either it had caught only a small fish and swallowed it without a struggle, or else it had failed to catch a fish at all. Dick was almost certain that he knew now what it was. Nearer the bird had come and nearer yet.

'It is,' Dick said in a whisper. 'It must be.'

Resting the telescope on a rock, he had at last got a steady view. He had seen a black and white dappled back, a greyish head and nape, a neck striped black and white at the sides and a broad stripe of black down the throat.

There could be no doubt about it. 'Black-throated Diver,' he had whispered reverently, put down the telescope, pulled out his pocket-book and added that name to his list of birds seen on the cruise.

For hour after hour he had stayed there watching that bird diving, coming up again, dipping its head under water as if to peer into the depths and then diving again. He had made a drawing of it and then another, showing the markings just so that he could compare them with the pictures in his book, but he knew for certain what it was. Then, at last, a long line of splashes had shown that the bird was getting up off the water. Again he had heard that strange 'Cuck ... cuck ... cuck-cuckcuck.' He had seen the bird in flight, like a cigar with busy wings. It had circled overhead and flown away as if towards the lower loch, but he had seen it swerve southwards and then had lost sight of it altogether.

Dick put his notebook back in his pocket. What matter now that the cruise was ending? He had seen a Diver with his own eyes. He wanted to tell Dorothea. The others would hardly guess how pleased he was.

He stood up, rather stiffly, took his glasses off, cleaned them, put them on again and looked up to the little hill where he had left the three explorers on the top of that prehistoric dwelling-house. There was nobody there now. He looked along the ridge with a gap in it where that cart track climbed over into the next valley. Nobody there either. He looked up the valley towards the hills and saw specks moving against the heather. He thought he heard a shout ... probably Roger. Well, if they had gone so far, they would soon be turning back and coming to look for him, and he knew there would be small chance of watching birds with Roger larking round. That bird had done its fishing and flown away. He could do no more here, but there was the other loch to see. He had better go and have a look at it while there was still time, though there was not likely to be anything there so well worth looking at as that Black-throated Diver. That sort of good fortune was not to be expected twice in an afternoon. Dick did not care. Already his day was the most successful of the whole cruise.

Rejoicing in what he had already seen, he walked along the shore, sometimes having to climb up into the heather, sometimes dodging marshy bits, sometimes finding it hard to keep his footing on loose stones. It was slow going along the shore, but he came at last to where the loch narrowed into a stream flowing through the flats that divided one loch from the other. Once upon a time, thought Dick, looking at those flats, the two lochs must have been one. Perhaps, he thought, when the ancient Picts had built that place on the hill, the whole valley had been one great lake, or even an arm of the sea.

He saw a dipper, bobbing its white shirt front, on a stone in the stream, but did not bother to put it in his notebook. He had seen dippers before. A family of baby water-hens scuttered across and a mother water-hen flapped along close to the bank on which he was walking, pretending to have broken her wing and trying to draw him after her, to give her young ones time to get away. But that, too, he was not seeing for the first time. On a day when he had seen a Black-throated Diver, dippers and water-hens did not mean as much as usual. Presently he was skirting wide reed-beds. The lower loch lay before him, and as he looked at it and at a little island far out towards the middle of it, he became alert once more. After all, seeing one Black-throated Diver need not mean that he would never see another.

Three Mergansers came flying together from the foot of the loch, lifting suddenly at the sight of him, but flying straight on over his head. Dick watched the quick black and white flashes of the three birds until he could see them no more and knew that they must have dropped to the water in the loch that he had just left. He wrote 'Three Mergansers' in his notebook and thought of going back there to have another look at them. He looked at his watch. The afternoon was gone and it seemed to him that he had only just begun his day. But now, at any moment, he might hear the *Sea Bear*'s foghorn telling him that the day was over. It would be silly to go back now.

Beyond the reed-beds, the banks of the loch rose higher and Dick kept close along the water's edge, knowing that a bank behind him was as good as rocks in front by way of cover. The one thing you must not do is to let birds see you against a background of sky. He went very slowly along the edge of the loch, looking this way and that over the water but mostly towards the little island. No matter what birds might be about, he knew that islands were magnets, alike for birds and for human beings. And this particular island was a very good one. Reeds at one end of it, boulders in the middle and, as he now saw, a flat bit of grassy shore at the end furthest from the reeds. What was that, swimming not far from it? Dick's heart leapt again. Whatever it was, it looked most awfully like that Diver. Perhaps he had been wrong in thinking it had flown south and out of the valley.

There was water at his feet and small stones, but a few yards further on he saw there was a rock big enough to give him cover and a place behind it that might have been designed for the comfort of a bird-watcher. He crept on, dropped beside the rock, pulled out his telescope, focused it on the island and searched the water where he had seen that swimming bird.

Thank goodness the wind had gone and the waves with it. The water was still and the sun, well away to the right over the western hills, was not in his eyes. But there was no bird . . . and then, in the circle of smooth water he could see through the telescope, there were ripples on one side. He followed them to their centre and found the bird. It had just come up and he saw it dip its beak and lift its head as if swallowing a drink. There it was, swimming, its body low in the water, its neck lifted, its head turning now one way, now another. It was a Diver all right. Lucky he had not gone back after the Mergansers. He made up his mind to stay exactly where he was. He could hardly be in a better position from which to watch it.

The Diver was swimming towards the island, and Dick was following it with the telescope, when he saw something blackish move on the flat grassy point of the island, a few feet from the water. Yes. It moved again. For a moment he thought it was some sort of animal. Then he saw that it was a bird, moving in an odd way, as if it could not get properly up on its legs. It shuffled along the ground until it almost fell into the water, when, at once, it swam off, another Diver, like the first. He was sure now that it was the bird he had seen on the upper loch together with its mate. 'Exactly like grebes,' he thought, watching the two swimming together. 'Like grebes, only enormous.'

'Hoo . . . hooo . . . hoo . . . hoo!'

He was startled by a long wavering cry. It was like wild laughter, as if the two great birds were sharing some fantastic joke.

'Hoo . . . hoo . . . hoo!'

He heard it once again but no more. Both birds dived together. They came up wide apart.

One of them was swimming towards the island. He could not be sure if it was the same one that he had seen launch itself into the water, but it landed at that same place. Whether it was the same bird or not, it had that same weakness in the legs. It seemed to slide itself along the ground, helping itself with its wings. It stopped, close to the water, just where he had first seen a bird move.

Through the telescope he could see the long mottled body of the bird, resting low on the ground. The other Diver was swimming about, moving further and further from the island, diving now and again, staying under water a long time and coming up sometimes where Dick was expecting to see it, and sometimes in quite a different place. The bird on the island scarcely moved.

'If it's nesting,' thought Dick, 'its eggs can't have hatched yet. Or only just. But it's too far off to see them.'

He kept perfectly still and watched, keeping the telescope trained on the sitting bird, thinking that if it moved again he would be able to see what sort of nest they made. There might be no nest at all. He remembered puffins and shelduck and their use of rabbit holes, and the many birds that laid their eggs on the bare ground, lapwings nesting in open fields, gulls with their eggs hard to see among the pebbles. He wondered whether these Divers took turns to sit on their eggs. If so, he wished the swimming bird would not take quite so long a turn in the water. At any minute now, Titty and Dorothea and the noisy Roger might be coming to hurry the Ship's Naturalist back to the ship, not thinking for a moment that his adventure, of lying still and watching two dark blobs through a telescope, was more exciting than any they could have. Carefully he turned his head, but the bank above him made it impossible for him to see if they were coming down the valley. He turned back to his birds.

He wished he had had Captain Flint's big binoculars instead of the little telescope which, useful as it was, did not show things large enough to let him see much at this distance. If only he had had a boat, so that he could row out nearer to the island and see what sort of nest the Divers made . . . He thought of the folding boat carried on the *Sea Bear*'s deck. But it was no good thinking he could persuade the scrubbers and painters to leave their job and bring it ashore and carry it to the loch. And anyhow, it was too late. There was a nest there all right. He was sure of that. Dick pulled out his notebook and scribbled in it, 'Pair of Black-throated Divers on the lower loch. Nesting.'

Five minutes later, he pulled out the notebook again and put a question mark against what he had written. It may have been that the trout in the loch had begun their evening movement towards the shore and the Diver was moving after them to better fishing grounds. The swimming bird, with one dive after another, had come nearly half way from the island towards the place where Dick lay hid. He was getting a better view of it each time it came to the top of the water. Its head seemed very dark on the top, and the whole bird seemed even larger than he had thought it at first sight. It dived, and came up a minute later with a fish, struggled with it on the surface, swallowed it, sipped water and swam nearer still. Dick was puzzled, but he knew very well that nothing is more difficult to judge than the size of things seen at a distance through a telescope. The bird dived again. Dick watched the spot where it had gone under, but it must have been swimming straight towards him. When it came up it was no more than thirty yards off, and Dick was so startled that he nearly shouted aloud.

'It's a Great Northern,' he said to himself, and had added it to his list before he remembered that Great Northern Divers did not nest in Great Britain.

'It can't be,' he said to himself. 'But it isn't a Black-throated.'

He made rather a mess of the page in his notebook where he had written of those birds. He had drawn a line through 'Black-throated' and had written 'Great Northern' before, remembering that there could be no nest, he put a line through that. He jammed down some question marks.

Again he had a good view of the bird and saw clearly that it had two patches of black and white stripes on its dark neck.

'It *is* a Great Northern,' he said, made another entry in his book, and then, looking out once more at that dark blob of the bird on the island, still where it was, he crossed it out again and turned over a fresh page.

If only he had had the bird-book in his pocket. There was not time to go and fetch it. The only thing he could do would be to make a sketch of the bird's head and neck and compare it with the picture in the book when he was back in the cabin of the *Sea Bear*. He made a drawing, not as good a drawing as Titty would have made, but showing clearly just how those two striped patches were placed on its neck. There could be no doubt that, whatever the bird was, it was different from the Black-throated Diver he had seen. He sketched in a small picture on the same page to show what its head had looked like. There could be no mistaking them. And this new bird was certainly a Diver. And it was not a Red-throated Diver. There was not a touch of red about it. What other Divers were there that it could be?

He was just finishing the drawing, had written 'Great Northern Diver', crossed it out, written it again, set a question mark beside it, and crossed out the question mark after yet another look at the bird, and put down a few more notes to help his memory, when he heard Roger call.

'Ahoy! Dick! Dick! Ahoy!'

Then Dorothea's 'Cooee!'

The bird must have heard those shouts and seen the explorers. It was swimming fast towards the island, looking more than ever like a big grebe, swimming with its whole body under water and only its head showing.

Botheration! There was nothing to be done. Dick stood up, saw the explorers coming along at a jog trot and waved to them.

'Buck up!' shouted Roger.

Hurriedly stowing pocket-book and telescope, Dick climbed up from the shore.

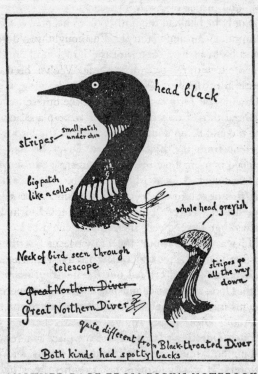

The following labels appear within the illustration:

head black

stripes — small patch under chin

big patch like a collar

Neck of bird seen through telescope

~~Great Northern Diver~~

Great Northern Diver

whole head greyish

stripes go all the way down

quite different from Black-throated Diver backs

Both kinds had spotty

ANOTHER PAGE FROM DICK'S NOTEBOOK SHOWING THE KINDS OF DIVERS

'Back to the ship!' called Titty. 'Quick.'

'Didn't you hear the foghorn?' said Dorothea, without stopping.

'No,' said Dick.

'Ages ago,' panted Titty. 'We thought you'd gone only Dot said we'd better shout in case.'

'Hurry, hurry!' said Dorothea. 'We've been pursued. Hostile islanders.'

Dick found himself running with the others.

'Divers,' he said to Dorothea. 'I've seen a Black-throated . . . And two I can't make out.'

'We've been stalked,' said Titty.

'That man isn't in sight,' said Roger.

'Booooooom!'

That was the *Sea Bear*'s foghorn again and, as he heard it, Dick half remembered hearing it before, when he had been too busy watching those birds.

'That's the second time,' said Dorothea.

'Two sorts of Divers,' said Dick. 'At least I think so.'

But Dorothea had no breath to spare for answering.

They kept up a steady trot along the side of the loch, and then along the bank of the little stream that ran from the loch to the sea, and came at last to the place where with little foaming eddies it flowed out into the salt water. The *Sea Bear* was no longer in the little bay where they had left her standing on her legs as the tide fell. Already the tide had risen again and floated her off. There she lay at anchor. They could see Captain Flint, sitting on the cabin skylight, smoking. They could see blue puffs of smoke drifting slowly away. Nobody else was in sight, until from behind the *Sea Bear* John and Nancy appeared sculling round in the folding dinghy.

'If I'd only known,' said Dick, thinking that once they

had put the folding boat in the water he could have persuaded
them to bring it to the loch.

'Ahoy!' shouted Roger.

'Half a minute,' Nancy shouted back, 'we'll bring the
dinghy. No room for anybody else in this.'

'They've given up the chase,' said Dorothea to Titty,
looking back up the stream.

'We did them beautifully,' said Roger. 'All that stalking
for nothing.'

Nancy had climbed from the folding boat into the dinghy
and came rowing ashore while John and Captain Flint were
hoisting the folding boat on deck.

'Where are Peggy and Susan?' asked Roger.

'Cooking. We sounded the foghorn for you ages ago.'

'We're nearly starving,' said Roger. 'We've been a
thousand miles since we had our grub.'

Everybody was talking at once as the shore party climbed
in and the dinghy pushed off for the ship. 'Savage Gaels!' 'A
castle!' 'A young chieftain . . .' 'Bagpipes . . .' 'We've been
stalked . . .' 'Hunted for our very lives.'

'Dick,' said Dorothea, 'what's the matter?'

'Three Divers,' said Dick, 'and two of them look exactly
like Great Northerns, but they can't be . . .'

'Dick,' said Dorothea, 'when did you eat your sandwiches?'

'Oh, I say . . . I forgot about them. The thing is, those
birds were nesting and I know my book says they don't.'

'Doesn't she look a beauty?' said Nancy, resting on her
oars a moment to look at the *Sea Bear*. 'We made a proper
job of it. We worked like slaves. We only just had time to do
it before the tide came up.'

CHAPTER 7

IS IT OR ISN'T IT?

NOTHING could have fallen flatter than the explorers' tale of their adventures. Captain Flint and the four scrubbers were thinking only of their ship. They had done a solid job of work. They had scrubbed and scraped the whole of the *Sea Bear* below the waterline. They had slapped on two coats of anti-fouling paint and done it with a minute or two to spare. They had floated their ship off and moored her with anchor and kedge in the old place. And now, very pleased with themselves, and hungry for a well-earned supper, they were not in the least interested in stories of savage Gaels, ferocious dogs, mysterious whistles and what not, which they thought were no more than what might be expected when Dorothea and Titty and Roger had been off by themselves and ready to make romance out of anything.

'Oh yes,' said Peggy, almost as if she had not been listening to Titty's story of how first she came to feel that the empty valley held a secret watcher.

'Oh yes,' said John, when Roger had told of the charging dogs, pulled up, only just in time, by a whistle from their invisible master.

'Not bad,' said Nancy between mouthfuls, when Titty had told of a huge and savage Gael roaring strange words and striding after them as they fled.

'But it's all true,' said Dorothea. 'We were stalked like deer, and at the end there were whistles going all over the place and furious natives yelling their war cries.'

'Every bit of it's true,' said Roger, 'and before that I found a prehistoric house. You can see it from our deck.'

93

'Oh yes,' said Susan. 'Pass the salt to Captain Flint.'

'Dick's got some sense,' said John. 'How many savage Gaels did you see, Dick, scientifically speaking?'

'I didn't see any,' said Dick.

'I thought so,' said John.

'Dick was looking at birds,' said Dorothea, 'and you know he doesn't see anything else when he's doing that. He didn't even hear the *Sea Bear*'s foghorn the first time.'

'What birds did you see?' asked Captain Flint.

'Divers.'

'What sort of Divers?'

'That's just what I don't know,' said Dick. 'I was just looking them up in my book, only supper got in the way.'

'Ungrateful young hound,' said Captain Flint.

'I don't mean that,' said Dick, 'only Dot made me put away the book till afterwards.'

'Well,' said Dorothea, 'you know you forgot to eat your sandwiches.'

Dick looked rather sheepishly at Susan. 'I'd have remembered them if I'd been hungry,' he said.

'Come on,' said Nancy. 'What really did happen? You were prowling about and some of the natives told you you were trespassing.'

'Much more than that,' said Roger. 'They were creeping and lying low so that we couldn't see them until they were ready to charge.'

'They stalked us,' said Titty.

'There's a young chieftain,' said Dorothea. 'We all saw him, except Dick.'

'Complete with claymore?' said Captain Flint.

'Well, we didn't see that,' said Roger. 'He was a long way off.'

'There really were natives?' said Captain Flint.

'Lots of them,' said Roger.

'I bet they weren't interested in you at all,' said John. 'Just rounding up sheep or something.'

'I don't care what you say. We were stalked,' said Titty.

After supper it was 'All hands to wash up!' so as to get the table clear. Nancy lit the stove in the cabin, more for pleasure than for warmth. Peggy lit the cabin lamp although it was still light outside. The big chart was spread on one end of the cabin table where everybody who wanted could have a look at it. John and Captain Flint were working out tides. At the other end of the table, Dick settled down with his bird-book. Titty lay on her stomach in her bunk, writing up a log of the day's adventures that was a good deal more lurid than it would have been if anybody besides herself had been going to read it. Dorothea, sitting as usual in her corner by the mast, was busy with an exercise book, sometimes looking far away through the walls of the cabin, sometimes writing down a sentence or two, sometimes scratching one out and writing it again.

Dick had the bird-book open at the page with pictures of the Divers. His notebook was open beside it at the page with the drawing he had made that afternoon. He was more and more puzzled to know what he had seen. The book was clear enough: 'Nests abroad. Usually seen solitary.' But his birds were not solitary. There were two of them. And they were not nesting abroad, but nesting here. Therefore, they could not be Great Northerns. Then he looked at the picture in the book and compared it with his sketch. The sketch was very rough, but there could be no mistaking it for the head and neck of any other bird than the one shown in the book and labelled 'Great Northern Diver'. On the same page was the account of the Black-throated Diver: '*Colymbus arcticus.* Length 28 inches' and the account of the Great Northern Diver: '*Colymbus immer.* Length 31 inches.' Yes, he had noticed himself that the Great Northerns, if they were Great

Northerns, were bigger than the Black-throated. His sketch of the Black-throated was just as unmistakable. He was sure he had seen both kinds that day. And yet . . . He looked from his sketch to the picture in the book and was sure they showed the same bird. Then, looking not at the pictures but at what was written, he read those two words, 'nests abroad', and was full of doubt once more. He did not hear a word of the talk that was going on close beside him among the mariners looking at their chart.

'Aren't you jolly glad we came in here?' Nancy was saying.

'We were well enough in here during that fog,' Captain Flint admitted. 'Better luck getting in than we deserved.'

'And we've scrubbed her,' said Nancy. 'And I bet she liked being scrubbed here where Mac used to scrub her instead of being taken into a beastly harbour.'

'All very well,' said Captain Flint. 'But it's costing us a lot of time.'

'Why? We can sail straight across from here in the morning.'

'Just what we can't,' said Captain Flint, with his finger on the chart. 'I'm not going to take the risk of being held up in those narrows with a head wind or a calm. We might lose two days instead of one. We've got to go into port first to get a can or two of juice for Roger and his engine. We used very nearly the last we had getting in here. If we'd gone to the harbour we could have filled up last night.'

'How soon shall we be starting in the morning?' asked Roger.

'Good and early,' said Captain Flint. 'Two or three in the morning, if we can. I'd start now if there was any wind, but there isn't, and we want the tide with us round the Head and up the other side into harbour. And I don't think we've juice in the tank for more than a mile.'

'Well,' said Nancy, 'that's all right. It won't take ten

minutes filling up. We dash into the harbour, get the cans filled and sail for the mainland right away. We won't have lost any time at all.'

'And what if there's no wind? This morning's draught has blown itself out. There hasn't been a breath since tea-time.'

'There's always some,' said John. 'We haven't been stuck for a calm on the whole cruise.'

'We would have been, but for the engine,' said Roger. 'Twice. That day getting out of Tarbert and the other day getting into Portree. We'd have been stuck each time if it hadn't been for the engine.'

'Oh well,' said Nancy, 'we found a good wind outside, and that day at Portree we were close to before the wind dropped. We could have towed in with the dinghy.'

'Roger's right,' said Captain Flint, 'and you're wrong. You never know when you may want the engine and want it badly. If our tanks were full now, we could start straight away, wind or no wind. Hullo! What's the matter with Dick? Worried about something?'

'Wake up, Ship's Naturalist!' said Nancy.

'Hey, DICK!' said Roger.

Dick looked up from his book with a start.

'What's the matter, Professor?' said Captain Flint.

'I can't make out about those birds,' said Dick.

'What birds?'

'The ones I saw today,' said Dick. 'The book says they don't nest here, only abroad, and the ones I saw were nesting.'

'Different sort of birds,' said Captain Flint.

Dorothea looked up from her exercise book. 'Didn't you say they were Divers?' she asked. 'The ones you'd been wanting to see?'

'They were Divers,' said Dick. 'One of them was a Black-throated Diver. It's the other two I can't make out. I thought they were Great Northerns, and they can't be.'

'Let's have a look at the pictures,' said Captain Flint.

Dick handed over the bird-book, and, when Captain Flint had looked at the pictures of Red-throated, Black-throated and Great Northern Divers, he pushed his own notebook across the table, open at the page on which he had made his sketches.

'They're not very well drawn,' he said, 'but I'm sure I got the markings about right.'

'Your bigger one's certainly like the Great Northern Diver in the book,' said Captain Flint, 'and the other's obviously a Black-throated.'

'That's what I thought,' said Dick.

'Had you got the book with you when you made the drawings?'

'No. That's why I made them,' said Dick.

'You seem to have changed your mind several times,' said Captain Flint. The page of the notebook had turned over, and he was looking at that other page where Dick had written 'A pair of Black-throated Divers on the lower loch. Nesting,' had crossed out 'Black-throated' and written 'Great Northern', had crossed out that and written it in again, besides dotting question marks all over the place.

'They all look very much alike to me,' said Nancy.

'Divers Divers,' said Roger. 'Or Diverse Divers. Several different Divers. Divers because they're diverse or Divers because they Dive.'

'Don't be an idiot, Roger,' said John.

'I'm trying to help.'

'Are you?'

'I don't see that it matters,' said Nancy. 'They're all Divers, and it's Divers you wanted to see. The whole of the first ten days you talked about nothing else.'

'But it matters most awfully,' said Dick. 'Those birds were nesting and the book says they don't.'

98

'Of course it matters,' said Dorothea, who had been listening and now came to the support of her brother. 'It's just the sort of thing that does matter.' She knew very well what a question like that meant to Dick. She knew that he would not be happy until he had settled it one way or the other. She had not minded the pooh-poohing of the story of the explorers' adventures, and by now had begun to doubt whether those Gaels had not really been busy with something of their own and not concerned with explorers at all. The adventures had been good fun while they lasted. But this was different. She was not going to have anybody, even Nancy, pooh-poohing the work of the Ship's Naturalist. 'Of course, Dick's got to make sure. It's like Father's diggings,' she said. 'Once, in Egypt, when he couldn't be sure whether a tomb was third or fourth dynasty, or something like that, he couldn't think of anything else at all until he'd found out.'

'How soon are we going to be home?' asked Dick.

There was a horrified silence in the cabin. It was almost blasphemy. They all knew the cruise was over, except for taking *Sea Bear* across to the mainland to hand her back to her owner, but they could hardly believe their ears when they heard one of the crew talking as if he were in a hurry to leave the ship.

'There's a man at the Natural History Museum,' explained Dick. 'He'd know in a moment. You see, there may be all kinds of changes between moults that this book says nothing about. They may look quite different at different times of year.'

'It's an awful pity Dick didn't see the Divers at the beginning of the cruise,' said Dorothea. 'He could have asked that man in the bird-boat.'

'It may not be too late yet,' said Captain Flint. 'We may see him again tomorrow. He was going straight for the Head when he barged across our bows yesterday. We may find him in harbour tomorrow if he hasn't gone off again somewhere else. What was the name of his boat?'

'*Pterodactyl*,' said everybody at once.

'Do you think I could go and ask him?' said Dick.

'Of course you could,' said Nancy. 'Good excuse, too, for you to have a look at your boat.'

'Look here,' said Captain Flint, 'we shan't be in port for a minute longer than we can help, but if your *Pterodactyl*'s still there, we'll put you aboard while John and I go ashore to fill up the cans. How's that?'

'Thank you very much,' said Dick, thinking that the bird-man would settle his doubts one way or other, and thinking too of seeing the inside of a boat fitted out for the very purpose for which, some day, he hoped to have a boat of his own.

'Of course she may have sailed,' said Captain Flint.

'Pushed off with her beastly motor, you mean,' said Nancy.

'It's a jolly good motor,' said Roger.

'How soon do we start?' said Dick, half getting up.

Captain Flint laughed. 'Not now,' he said. 'But as soon as tide and wind'll let us.'

Dick had one more look at the picture in the book and at his own sketch, and then put bird-book and pocket-book resolutely away. Tomorrow, if things went well, he would know for certain.

Presently Susan, backed by the skipper, began to urge people to go to bed. As usual, when this happened, the whole crew wanted to go on deck for a last look round and a smell of the night air before turning in. Late though it was, they could still see the dark shore and the way out between the cliffs and rocks into the open sea. There was no breath of wind and the *Sea Bear* lay hardly stirring in the still water, sparkling with reflections of the stars. John and Nancy hoisted the riding light up the forestay, according to custom, though even if another boat did come into the cove, which was unlikely, there was no fear of her not seeing the *Sea Bear* in that northern night that was never wholly dark. John went below through the forehatch. Nancy came aft along the deck to find Dorothea, Titty and Roger still lingering in the cockpit.

'Lights out in five minutes.' Susan's voice came from below.

'Coming, coming,' said Roger, and explained to the others. 'It's not that I'm sleepy but I've got to be up early in case he wants the engine.'

'Look here, Dot,' said Nancy, after he had gone. 'Was it all a story of yours and Titty's about being hunted through the valley?'

'Of course it wasn't,' said Titty.

'No,' said Dorothea, and suddenly grabbed Nancy's arm. 'There's one of the Gaels watching us N O W.' Not fifty yards away, in the shadow of the shore under the cliff, all three of them saw the flicker of a match. Someone was lighting a pipe. The tiny spark quavered and died. They could see nothing where it had been but the dark mass of the cliff against the sky.

'What's he there for?' said Dot.

'Why shouldn't he be?' said Nancy.

'Hostile natives,' said Titty. 'We told you and you wouldn't believe us.'

'Um,' said Nancy regretfully. 'Well, anyway, we're sailing in the morning. It's too late to do anything with them now. But if they're really hostile it's an awful pity we'll never be seeing them again.'

'All hands below,' Captain Flint roared from under their feet. 'We're off early. I'm asleep already.'

CHAPTER 8

'HE'S STILL THERE!'

DICK was the first of the crew to come on deck. He found Captain Flint there before him, standing by the mast, licking the back of his hand and holding it up, this way and that, feeling for a breath of wind.

'Hullo, Dick, you're in a hurry.'

'I am, rather,' said Dick. 'It would be an awful pity if he's gone before we get there.'

'Who? Oh, your bird-man. It doesn't look as if we're going to get there very soon. Just bad luck. There isn't wind to stir a candle flame.'

'Shall I go and wake up Roger?'

'There isn't enough in the tank to do it under power,' said Captain Flint.

Dick looked round. In the early morning light the little cove was like a mill pond and out at sea there were no waves but only a gentle swell to shake the long glittering path laid there by the sun.

'Pretty hopeless,' said Captain Flint.

Dick had a new idea.

'If we can't start, would it be all right for me to go and have another look at those Divers?'

'No,' said Captain Flint, 'it would not. No shore-leave on the day a ship sails. The wind might come and we'd have to send more of the crew to collect you, and likely enough the rest of the crew to collect them . . . Hullo!' Again he licked the back of his hand and held it up. 'No. No going ashore. There's just a suspicion of a wind. It's coming all right. And we'll have the tide with us at the start. Yes. Down you go and dig up the engineer. We'll maybe find a breath to help us when we get outside.'

Dick shot down the ladder, shouting, 'Roger! Engine!'

Captain Flint looked at his watch, and came aft. 'They can have their sleep out later,' he said to himself, and reached into the companion.

'Ting . . . Ting . . . Ting . . . Ting . . .'

The ship's bell clanged.

'Coming!' yelled Roger.

'Four bells,' said John, rubbing his eyes. 'I thought we were starting earlier.'

Everywhere people were rolling out of their bunks.

'All hands!' came a cheerful shout from on deck, and there was a general rush for the ladder.

'But there's no wind,' said Nancy as she reached the deck.

'Going out to look for it,' said Captain Flint. 'I felt a breath just now.'

A much worried Roger came up from the engine room.

'Tank's nearly empty, Sir,' he said. 'You haven't forgotten?'

'Worse luck,' said Captain Flint. 'But we'll shut off as soon as we have her outside. Start her up and have her ticking over in neutral.'

'Aye, aye, Sir,' said Roger, and was gone.

The next few minutes were full of the regular drill of getting under way. Tyers were cast off the sails. Everything was made ready for hoisting. John and Nancy were working the winch. Clink, clank, clink, clank . . . The chain was coming in. Peggy hauled the flag to the masthead, where it dangled without a flap against the bamboo flagstaff.

'Straight up and down, Sir,' said John, looking over the bows.

The first 'Chug, chug' came from the engine.

'Dick,' shouted Roger, 'see if the water's coming out of the exhaust.'

Dick leaned over and saw puffs of blue smoke and little jets of water spurting as they should.

'Yes,' he called.

'Engines ready, Sir,' said Roger, coming on deck.

'Anchor off the ground,' called John.

'Slow ahead,' said Captain Flint. 'Here you are, Nancy. Keep her in the middle. I'll get the anchor aboard.'

The tune of the engine changed. The *Sea Bear* was moving. There was a thump as the anchor was settled in its chocks. The mainsail swayed aloft and hung idly in the windless air. The staysail climbed to its place and hung there, like the mainsail, waiting for a wind.

'That'll do,' said Captain Flint.

'Well, good-bye to Scrubbers' Bay,' said Nancy. 'I'm jolly glad we came here.'

'I'm not,' said Captain Flint. 'If we'd scrubbed in port we could have filled up with petrol at the same time.'

'The Scrubbers missed the best of it,' said Roger, who was waiting in the cockpit, with the engine-hatch open.

'You and your Gaels,' laughed Nancy.

'Well, you saw one yourself,' said Titty. Her voice changed. 'There's one of them now,' she added. 'I wonder if he's been watching us all night.'

They were not the only people to be early astir. As the *Sea Bear* moved slowly out towards the open sea, they saw a tall, grey-bearded figure standing on the cliff.

'That's the one who came charging after us,' said Dorothea. Roger turned to look at him.

'He can't catch us now,' he said. 'Let's give him a wave.'

The crew of the *Sea Bear* waved cheerfully. The man did not wave back, but stood there watching them, leaning on a long stick.

'What a dogmudgeonly brute,' said Roger.

'Dogmudgeon's a good word,' said Nancy.

'Isn't it?' said Roger. 'I'll lend it you if you like.'

Clearing the point, the *Sea Bear* lifted gently to the swell, and the explorers, putting Scrubbers' Bay behind them for the moment, thought of their Gaels no more.

The little flag at the masthead lifted half-heartedly. The mainsail filled. The *Sea Bear* was sailing, though there was so little wind that the mainsheet never properly hardened but hung, dipped in the water, rose dripping and jerked taut as the *Sea Bear* rolled, and then slacked and dipped again. The jib had been broken out, the topsail set, but it was still the engine that was doing the work.

'The wind's trying to be north-west,' said Nancy. 'That'll take us to the Head.'

'How soon?' asked Dick.

'This time next year if it doesn't come a little harder,' said Captain Flint. 'Who wants to steer? Titty? Dorothea?'

Everybody laughed except Dick. Titty had more than once complained during the cruise that neither she nor indeed any of the four younger ones was ever asked to steer except in a calm.

'No thank you,' said Titty.

'I'll steer,' said Dorothea, with just a glance at Dick.

'South-East by East,' said Captain Flint. 'But don't you worry about the compass. You can see the Head. Keep it clear on the starboard bow and you can't go wrong. I'm afraid we've got to stop that engine.' He took the dipstick that hung just inside the engine-room hatch, unscrewed the filler cap of the tank that was hidden under the after deck, and dipped.

'How much?' asked Roger over his shoulder.

Captain Flint looked at the dipstick. Only the very tip of it was wet.

'Put her in neutral, Roger. Stop her. There's hardly a drop left, and we must keep that for later.'

'Gosh!' said Roger. 'We'll never get there at all.'

He slipped below. The engine was silent. The *Sea Bear* lost speed. She was hardly moving. Dorothea very gently moved the tiller, to reassure herself that the ship still had steerage way.

'It doesn't matter,' said Nancy. 'We're at sea, and we're not in a hurry.'

'But we are,' said Dick.

'I forgot you and your *Pterodactyl*,' said Nancy. 'But your bird-man may not have been going back there when we saw him. He may be anywhere by now.'

Captain Flint lit his pipe and dropped the dead match overboard, where it slowly, very slowly, drifted astern. 'Going in there to scrub is losing us two days instead of one,' he said. 'If only we had full tanks we'd be half way across by now.'

'If we hadn't gone in I wouldn't have seen the Great Northerns,' said Dick, '. . . if they *were* Great Northerns.' But he, like Captain Flint, looked at the dead match in the water and then at the far away lump of the Head, sticking up out of the sea. Going at this pace it would take them a very long time to get there. And even then they would be a long way from the harbour.

'We may as well have breakfast anyhow,' said Peggy. 'Where's Susan?'

She was answered by the sudden roar of a Primus down below.

They had breakfast in the cabin, porridge, sardines and tea, with condensed milk out of a tin which gave its usual queer taste to the tea and the porridge, and made Susan scribble on a bit of paper.

'Hullo,' said Captain Flint, 'you taking to writing too?' He glanced up through the companion, thinking of Dorothea, who, on deck, was earnestly steering the hardly moving ship.

Susan showed him the paper, on which were only two words, 'Bread. Milk.' 'We ought to be able to get some fresh milk in the town while you're getting the petrol. It'll make all the difference to tomorrow's breakfast. And we've run right out of bread.'

'Susan,' said Captain Flint. 'I've said it before and I say it again. Gold. You're worth your weight in it.'

'It's three days since they had honest milk,' said Susan.

Dick hurried through his breakfast and took Dorothea's place at the tiller while she went below to have hers. He did not trust any of the others to take steering seriously while there was not enough wind to make it seem worth while. He was afraid that even a minute, more or less, might make all the difference between finding the bird-man in port or meeting the *Pterodactyl* at sea, already on her way to some other place where there were birds to watch.

They were still sitting round the cabin table when they heard the first faint ripple of water round her bows.

'She's sailing,' said Titty.

Captain Flint put down the coffee cup from which he was just going to drink. Nancy was already running up the ladder. He went after her. Steering, for the moment, was really steering, and Dick, full of hope, with both hands on the tiller, was looking earnestly at the compass, at the distant Head and at the compass again.

Captain Flint glanced at the compass.

'Carry on,' he said. 'You're doing all right.'

'Please get out of the way, Nancy,' said Dick. 'I can't see right ahead.'

'Come along down,' said Captain Flint. 'We'll leave the Professor in charge. He's found a better wind for her than we had.'

But the wind was no more than a promise. It kept dying down and then raising false hopes by new catspaws off the land that rippled the water astern, filled the sails and for a moment or two sent the *Sea Bear* on her way.

Worse was to come. The tide turned. When they first came out it had been flowing south, taking them in the right direction no matter how slowly they sailed. For some time Dick did not notice what was happening, looking only at the compass and the far away Head. Suddenly, glancing astern, he saw the near-by cliffs moving the wrong way against the inland hill.

'I say,' he called, 'please come on deck. I think she's going backwards.'

It was true, and even before they had come pouring up from below, Dick had understood the reason for it.

'She isn't really going backwards,' he said. 'It's the tide. It must have turned and begun going the other way.'

'Not enough wind,' said Captain Flint, 'that's all.'

'She's moving all right,' said Titty, looking down at the steady ripple running from her bows.

'Yes,' said Captain Flint, 'but not so fast as the tide is taking her back.'

It was a strange feeling, to be sailing and yet to see by the land that though she was going ahead she was losing ground with every minute.

'Hadn't we better go near the shore and anchor?' said Nancy.

Captain Flint hesitated, but only for a moment. 'No,' he said. 'Anywhere else, we would,' he said. 'But not in these waters. Deep until close under the cliffs. Remember your soundings the day we came in? No. We've made a fair offing, and we'll keep it. Stick to your course . . . South-East by East . . . She won't make it, because of the tide, but she'll be working out across it all the time.'

'South-East by East,' said Dick.

'Six whole hours of ebb,' said Titty.

'Not quite as bad as that,' said Captain Flint. 'And the wind may harden ... or it may not,' he added, looking grimly round.

'We're going back quite fast,' said Roger.

'Get out and push,' said Nancy, 'if you're in a hurry.'

'Dick wishes he could,' said Dorothea, 'and so do I.'

Foot by foot the *Sea Bear* was losing ground, though slowly working across the tide. Those inland hills seemed to be moving northwards. Presently the crew of the *Sea Bear* were able once more to look into Scrubbers' Bay, though from a long way off. Then the entrance to the Bay was closed again, though they knew where it was from the cloud of gulls about the cliff. They were looking up at the little hill from which, at the door of his lair, prehistoric man a thousand years ago and more had looked out over the sea.

'There's someone on the top of my Pict-house,' said Roger, but, if it were so, the somebody had vanished before anyone could bring a telescope to bear.

And still the tide was carrying them slowly northwards. Before the wind strengthened again they were looking up at Dorothea's 'castle' and its cottages on the northern side of the long ridge that shut in the valley of the explorers.

'Funny,' said Nancy. 'All those houses on one side of that ridge, and you said that the valley on our side was empty.'

'It was,' said Titty, 'until we were stalked. There are no houses at all.'

'Deer forest, probably,' said Captain Flint.

'We saw lots of deer,' said Titty.

'But no trees,' said Roger.

'They call it a forest just the same,' said Captain Flint.

The wind strengthened and they began to creep south

once more. It slackened, and they hung motionless between wind and tide. It strengthened again and slackened.

'Just can't be helped,' said Captain Flint.

'Who wants to help it? said Nancy. 'It's a grand day.'

'I know one who wants to help it,' said Captain Flint, looking at Dick.

'Two,' said Dorothea.

'Three,' said Nancy with a grin, looking at Captain Flint.

But, with no petrol to spare, even Dick knew there was nothing to be done, even if it meant that he was going to miss his chance of going aboard the *Pterodactyl*, and getting his question answered by the bird-man.

Most of them did not mind at all. If they were going to be another day late in getting across to the mainland, it meant that the cruise would last another day longer. They were at sea and that was enough for them. If there was not enough wind, even Columbus suffered from calms. They might for a moment envy half-a-dozen fishing boats shooting northwards with the tide, but they were perfectly content to sit in the cockpit and on the foredeck, in bright sunshine on blue water. And as for being sorry they had spent those two nights in the wild anchorage of Scrubbers' Bay, they were all agreed that yesterday had been the best day of the whole cruise. Even Roger thought that, though it was a pity that today of all days the tank should be running dry, just when the lack of wind would have given the engine and the engineer a noble chance of being useful.

The morning passed. Roger sounded eight bells for noon.

'Corned beef,' said Susan. 'Pemmican, I mean. Cold. It's too hot for any cooking.'

'There's still lots of tinned fruit,' said Peggy.

They ate their dinner on deck . . . The wind strengthened while they were washing up.

'Too late now,' said Captain Flint.

But, about two o'clock, they began to feel that they were really moving, and presently the tide was with them instead of against them, and everybody wanted to be steering, while the far away blue lump of the Head grew bigger, turned from being an island into being a promontory of grey rock with patches of green fields.

'Too late,' said Captain Flint. 'Once we're round it we'll have the wind against us all the way into port. I daren't let Roger do his stuff till the very last minute. We'll have to beat in. Tide'll help, but we'll be lucky if we don't find the shops closed. All right, Susan. No sailing for the mainland tonight. Good night's rest for everybody and off in the morning.'

'Good,' said Nancy.

'Good be blowed,' said Captain Flint.

'Anyway, he hasn't come out today,' said Dick. 'At least not since we've been near enough to see.'

'We'll have a grand beat in,' said John.

They had tea as they were coming near the Head. They passed it with half a mile to spare, to clear the outlying rocks, jibbed, hauled in on the sheets and brought the *Sea Bear* to the wind. Instantly it felt as if there was twice as much. The *Sea Bear* had been on an even keel all day, as if she had been sailing on a mill pond. Now, she heeled over, not much but suddenly and enough to send Roger's mug sliding across the floor of the cockpit and spilling the last drop that he had been carefully saving to wash down his last mouthful of cake. The little flag at the masthead rippled gaily. The *Sea Bear*'s stem no longer cut silently through the water, but drove it with a curl of foam. It was as if, at the very last minute, she were showing what she could do. To and fro she beat in the narrowing channel. The lighthouse on the Head was left astern. That other lighthouse on the rocks outside the harbour came nearer. To and fro. To and fro. Already they could see the houses and the masts of fishing boats at the quays.

'It's the only harbour we've been into twice,' said Titty.

'If he's anchored where he was last time,' said Dick, 'we shan't know if he's there till we get right in.'

They were coming very near the harbour mouth. A fishing boat was coming out, high-bowed, with a short stumpy mast and a wheel-house. The fishing boat changed course for them slightly and passed astern of them. Everybody waved, by way of saying Thank you, and a large hand came out of the wheel-house door and waved back.

'Better manners than your *Pterodactyl*,' said Nancy.

'I don't expect the bird-man was steering himself,' said Dick.

Then, almost in the harbour mouth, after letting the *Sea Bear* show what she could do when newly scraped and scrubbed, the wind dropped again.

'Get your engine going, Roger,' said Captain Flint. 'There may be a pack of boats inside. And even less wind. Stand by to lower sails. We've enough in the tank to take us in now.'

The sails were lowered and, with the engine chugging, the *Sea Bear* moved in between the piers. John, after bringing in the jib, ran up the ratlines to the cross-trees. Dick watched anxiously. John looked down at the cockpit, nodded and pointed at something they could not see from the decks.

'He's there,' cried Dick. 'Oh, good.' And his hand flew to the pocket where he kept his notebook with his sketches of the Divers.

'Steamer coming up astern,' shouted John.

They looked aft. Far out at sea, a line of smoke and a dark blob showed on the horizon.

'Bit of luck,' said Captain Flint. 'That'll be the mail-boat. Just time to get the letters done. She'll have them across long before we can do it. Save a few posts anyway. Now then. Nancy and John on the foredeck. Stand by for letting go.'

The *Sea Bear* had passed the pierheads and was in harbour.

'There he is,' cried Dorothea. 'We're in time after all.'

'We'll bring up near him,' said Captain Flint. 'It's not too far from the quay. Ready with that anchor, forrard?'

'Aye, aye, Sir.'

The engine faltered, went on again, and faltered once more.

'Not one drop too much,' murmured Captain Flint, looking into the engineer's startled eyes. 'Tank's empty. Lucky we didn't turn it on a minute sooner. She'll do now. Finished with engines.'

The engine coughed and stopped. The *Sea Bear* slipped on in silence towards the big white motor yacht that everybody called 'Dick's ship'.

She rounded up perhaps forty yards away.

'Let go!'

There was a splash and a rattle of chain. Captain Flint lashed the tiller and went forward. 'Now then, all hands! Stow sails. Let's show these fishermen we know our jobs. All right, Dick. We'll have the dinghy over for you the moment we've got the decks clear and all ship-shape.'

With everybody working together and everybody knowing what to do, in a very few minutes the *Sea Bear*, with her headsails neatly furled, tyers on her mainsail, ropes coiled, was a model of what a ship in harbour ought to be. John, Nancy and Captain Flint were lowering the dinghy into the water. Dick, his notebook in his hand, was waiting, looking across at the motor yacht and suddenly fearing that the bird-man might not be aboard.

'Now then, Dick,' said Captain Flint. 'Better let John take you across. Don't be too long. I'll be writing a word to all the parents warning them to bear up under the news that I haven't drowned you and that they'll have to put up with seeing you again. And then John and I will take the cans ashore for petrol, put the letters aboard the mail-boat and send a wire to Mac to tell him his ship's still afloat and that we'll be bringing her across tomorrow.'

'Don't tell him we've scrubbed her,' said Peggy.

'I won't,' said Captain Flint. 'He'll be pleased as Punch about that. She was sailing like a witch today, whenever the wind gave her half a chance.'

'What's going to happen now?' asked Roger, coming up on deck and wiping his hands on a bit of cotton waste after putting his engine to sleep.

'Dick's going across to the *Pterodactyl* to ask his bird-man about the Great Auk.'

'Great Northern Diver,' said Dick gravely, and was surprised at Nancy's chuckle.

CHAPTER 9

CROSS PURPOSES

'*PTERODACTYL*, Ahoy!'

John held the dinghy steady a few yards from the accommodation ladder that hung between fenders on the shining white side of the motor yacht.

A sailor with '*Pterodactyl*' in red letters on his blue jersey came to the side and looked down on them.

'Tell him what you want,' said John.

'Can I speak to the owner?' asked Dick. 'It's about birds.'

'Have you got news for him?' asked the man. 'What is it? Buzzards? Another eagle? I'll tell him.'

'It's just a bird I'm not sure about,' said Dick.

'He's busy,' said the man. 'But I'll ask him.'

'What did he mean by news about buzzards and eagles?' said John, when the man had gone into the deckhouse.

'Perhaps he's been watching some,' said Dick, 'and is waiting to get a photograph when the young ones have hatched out.'

'You can come aboard.' The man was back again, looking down at them from the deck. 'But he can't give you more than a few minutes.'

John put the dinghy neatly alongside the handing fenders. Dick climbed the ladder.

'Aren't the both of you coming?' asked the man.

'I'll hang on here,' said John, who was not in the least interested in motor boats and thought that Dick would manage his bird business best by himself.

'This way,' said the sailor, and showed Dick into the deckhouse. There was no one in it. 'Down there,' he said, and

Dick, feeling his pocket to make sure he had his notebook handy (though he had taken it out and put it back only a moment before), went down a flight of steps into the saloon.

The saloon was full of light and seemed enormous after the cabin of the old pilot boat, and the first thing Dick saw was that there were pictures of birds the whole way round the walls. That, of course, was just the sort of thing he would have some day when he had a ship of his own in which to visit all the famous sanctuaries. The next thing he saw was that, in spite of the daylight that came through a row of portholes, there was a powerful electric lamp over a table at the far end of the saloon. The lamp lit up the thin reddish hair of a man, the bird-man himself, who was busy at something on the table. The lamp was close to his head. A reflected glitter of white skin showed through the thin hair. The man was writing in a large book. Dick waited silently for him to finish. The man looked up. Dick saw clever eyes behind spectacles rather like his own, a long, narrow nose and a straight, thin-lipped mouth.

'Who are you?' asked the man.

'I'm Dick Callum.'

'You're not one of my regulars, are you?' said the man. 'Never mind. Never too soon to begin. What is it you've found?'

Dick tried to pull out his notebook. It stuck in his pocket.

'Well?' said the man.

The notebook came out with a jerk and fell on the floor. Dick picked it up and went forward to show his drawing. The man, whom he had interrupted when he was busy, had not waited before taking up his work again. In one hand he held an egg, in the other a pair of micrometer callipers. He was measuring the egg.

'I wanted to ask you ... You'll know at once what it is ...' Dick stopped short. He had seen that beside the egg

IN THE CABIN OF THE *PTERODACTYL*

that the man was measuring, there were a lot of others in a long rack in front of him. All eggs of the same kind. 'I . . . I say . . . You're not an egg-collector?'

It was instantly clear that Dick could not have said anything to please his host better. He put the egg he had been measuring in the rack with the others, and, twiddling the micrometer between his fingers, smiled at Dick.

'You've heard of the Jemmerling Collection,' he said, almost as if he were speaking of St Paul's Cathedral. 'Well, I'm Jemmerling. I've the biggest private collection in England . . . probably in the world. British birds only, of course. It would take more than one man's lifetime to do as much for the foreigners . . .'

Dick's mouth fell open. It was the very last thing he could have expected. He thought of his friends of the Coot Club and their long struggle to protect the birds. He remembered their fight with George Owdon, who took eggs and sold them to collectors. Why, this man was a George Owdon, only grown-up and worse. This man of whom, without knowing him, Dick had begun to make a hero, was an enemy. A bird-man! He was as dangerous an enemy as birds could have.

Mr Jemmerling laughed. He mistook Dick's horror for admiration.

'Yes,' he went on. 'I have eggs of every bird known to nest in the British Isles and some, indeed, of those that used to nest but do so no longer.'

'Here?' stammered Dick, looking round at the row of cupboards that lined the walls of the saloon below the pictures.

Mr Jemmerling laughed again. 'No room here for a collection like mine,' he said. He got up from the table, came out from behind it, took Dick by the shoulder and marched him up to a bookcase.

'Look at that,' he said, and pointed to a large fat book bound in crimson leather. On the back of it in gold lettering were the words, 'Jemmerling Collection. Preliminary Catalogue.'

' "Preliminary", mind you,' said Mr Jemmerling.

'All those eggs . . .' stammered Dick, glancing back at the table.

'Just a bit of what I'm working on this trip. Measurements. Average and extreme. There's greater variety than you would think. I have eighteen Golden Eagle's eggs. No other collection has such a range. And no two of those eggs are exactly alike.'

Dick glanced away at the steps out of the saloon. Never again would he be able to think of the *Pterodactyl* as of the sort of ship he and Dot would one day have for themselves. He almost wished he had never come aboard. His eyes went back to the table, to that long rack of eggs, puffins' eggs, he thought they were, and he saw in his mind the puffins themselves, with their bright eyes and comic beaks. It was dreadful to think of them. And eighteen eggs of the Golden Eagle. Eighteen dead and empty shells with labels instead of those eighteen noble birds.

'Are you a collector, too?' asked Mr Jemmerling kindly.

'No,' said Dick.

'Then what was it you wanted to say to me?'

Dick hesitated only for a moment. He was a scientist first of all. He had to know. It was horrible to think that the owner of the *Pterodactyl* was an egg-collector, but the very pictures round the walls of the saloon told Dick that no one would be better able to settle his doubts about those birds. For twenty-four hours he had been waiting to ask his question. There could be no possible harm in asking it. The birds were far enough away and there was no need to say where he had seen them. He had only to show the picture in his notebook.

'It's this,' he said. 'It's a bird I saw. I wanted to be sure what it was. It's a Diver. I know that, but . . . That's what it looked like ... It's head, I mean ...' He opened his notebook and held it out for Mr Jemmerling to see. 'It was a long way off,' he added. 'I watched it through a telescope.'

Mr Jemmerling looked at Dick's drawing.

'Great Northern Diver,' he said at once.

'I thought it was,' said Dick, 'but the picture in my book is very small.'

'I can do better than a picture,' said Mr Jemmerling, and touched a bell-push at the side of his table. A bell rang somewhere in the ship and a moment later a sailor with '*Pterodactyl*' on his jersey, came through a door into the saloon.

'Great Northern Diver,' said Mr Jemmerling, and the sailor turned and went back into the forward part of the boat.

'Yes,' said Mr Jemmerling, 'I can do better than that. We've had three on this trip. One a very good specimen indeed.'

The sailor was in the saloon again, handing to Mr Jemmerling the dried skin of a large bird. It was like a feathered balloon from which the air had escaped. There could not have been anything deader. Dick did not like looking at it, remembering the live bird he had seen, swimming, diving and fishing in the loch. But Mr Jemmerling had laid it flat on the table and was turning the neck for him to see.

'There are your two sets of white markings. Yours is a good drawing. Nobody could mistake it. Far away? Pity you couldn't let me know about it earlier. I leave for Glasgow tomorrow. Yes. It's a Great Northern Diver all right. There are always a few stragglers hanging about. If you saw it well enough to make that drawing you must have had a pretty good view. What made you doubtful about it?'

'I thought they didn't nest further south than Iceland,' said Dick. 'It says that in the big book I've got at home.'

'No more they do,' said Mr Jemmerling. 'That's why we never see more than single birds. Migrants, staying late.'

'But I saw two,' said Dick. 'And they were nesting. I've only got a little book with me, and it says "Nests abroad". That's why I didn't think they could be Great Northerns.'

'WHAT?' exclaimed Mr Jemmerling.

His whole attitude changed. He had been a great man, showing off to a visiting boy. Now he was something different. He looked hard at Dick, sat down, half stood up and sat down again. One of his hands, lying on the table, kept opening and closing.

'Did I understand what you said?' he asked. 'You saw a pair of Great Northern Divers nesting? Let me see that drawing of yours again.'

Dick held out his notebook with the picture.

'That other is a Black-throated Diver,' said Mr Jemmerling. 'Did you make these drawings from the birds or did you copy them from a book?'

'I made the Great Northern while I was looking at him,' said Dick.

'What have you done with the eggs?' said Mr Jemmerling suddenly.

'I didn't actually see the eggs,' said Dick. 'They were too far off. But I'm sure I wasn't mistaken about the nesting. One of the Divers was sitting on the shore, close to the water . . .'

'Mainland or island?'

'Island.'

'On the sea?'

'No. In a loch.'

'It's impossible, but . . . Go on. What made you think they were nesting?'

'One was sitting on the shore of the island, and the other one was fishing. I saw the fishing one first. Then I saw the one that was sitting move . . .'

'How did it move?'

'I thought at first it had been hurt,' said Dick. 'It didn't walk very well. It seemed to help itself with its wings . . .'

'They do. They do,' said Mr Jemmerling. 'And then?'

'It flopped down into the water, and after a bit one of them went back and struggled up out of the water and sat in the exact same place. I'm not sure if it was the same one or the one that I saw swimming first.'

'How long were you watching them?'

'I didn't look at my watch,' said Dick.

'An hour?'

'Much more than that.'

'And the bird that was sitting kept still all that time?'

'All the time except that once when it came into the water.'

'Where are they? I'll come back with you at once . . .'

'But . . . but . . .' Dick suddenly wished he had never asked his question. He picked up his notebook. 'Thank you very much for telling me,' he said. 'I'd been wanting to see them and then when I saw them I thought it was impossible because of the nesting.'

'It *is* impossible . . . but it sounds to me as if it was true.' Mr Jemmerling's eyes were glittering. '*Credo quia impossibile.* I believe you because it's impossible. We won't waste a minute. We'll go there at once.'

'But . . .' Dick wished more than ever that he had never come aboard the *Pterodactyl*.

'Most important to prove it,' said Mr Jemmerling, 'and we can't do that without the eggs.'

'But you wouldn't take them?' Dick blurted out.

'Eggs of the Great Northern Diver, found here for the first time! Don't you see, man? Unique. Absolutely unique. It'll mean that every bird-book so far written is out of date . . . Witherby, Coward, Morris, Evans . . . all the lot of them, confuted by the Jemmerling Collection . . . I'll have the eggs, the actual nesting site, copied exactly . . . the birds themselves, shot in the presence of witnesses. You shall be a witness yourself and have your place in history. Proof. Proof. That is everything. The incredible thing must be proved beyond all manner of doubt . . .'

'But if you take the eggs and kill the birds they won't be nesting here any more.'

'What matters is to prove the new scientific fact that they have nested. There is an old saying, "What's hit's history: what's missed's mystery." We must have the proof, once and for all . . . in the Jemmerling Collection.'

'Wouldn't photographs prove it?' said Dick.

'Certainly,' said Mr Jemmerling. 'A photograph of the bird *on* the eggs would settle the point for ever . . . We'll have a photograph and an exact model of the nest, the actual eggs and the actual birds. We'll leave no loophole for any busybody in fifty years' time to question authenticity.'

Dick stood first on one foot and then on the other. He had got his answer and now he was only wanting to get away from the *Pterodactyl* as soon as he could.

'I must go back now,' he said. 'They told me to be as quick as possible because the dinghy's wanted.'

'Don't you live here?' asked Mr Jemmerling.

'No,' said Dick, glad to change the subject. 'We're on a cruise, and we're going across tomorrow to give up the boat.'

Mr Jemmerling went to a porthole and looked out across the harbour.

'That cutter your ship?' he said.

'Yes,' said Dick.

'I've seen her before. Passed you at sea the day before yesterday . . . And when did you see your birds?'

'Yesterday,' said Dick before he could stop himself, and went on hurriedly. 'Thank you very much for telling me what they were. I must go now.'

But he had already said too much. Mr Jemmerling was between him and the way up out of the saloon.

'They can't be far away,' said Mr Jemmerling. 'My boat

does fifteen knots. I can bring you back as soon as you've shown me the place. Or how would you like to stay aboard? I was going to Glasgow tomorrow but a discovery like this alters any plans. You can sleep in the *Pterodactyl* and I'll take you to Glasgow as soon as we've done our business. You'll be there as soon as you could be in any sailing yacht.'

'No thank you,' said Dick. 'And thank you very much for telling me what they were. I must go now.'

'Wait a minute. Wait a minute,' said Mr Jemmerling.

He was feeling for his pocket-book. Dick slipped past him towards the stairs. Mr Jemmerling grabbed at him.

'No. No,' he said. 'No hurry. I don't mean you to get nothing out of this. You're not one of my regulars, or you would know. I gave ten shillings to the boy who put me on to my last Golden Eagle. Here's a sovereign for you.'

'No thank you,' said Dick unhappily. 'I've simply got to go. They're waiting for me.' He bolted up the stairs to the deckhouse and out on deck.

'John!' he called.

Mr Jemmerling was close behind him. Looking down, he saw John in the dinghy.

'Your brother?' he said, and then, to John, in a welcoming voice, 'Tie up your dinghy and come aboard. I'd like a word with you, and perhaps you'd like to have a look over my ship.'

As John said afterwards, 'I couldn't tell him I wasn't interested in his beastly motor-biscuit-box.' He made the dinghy fast against the fenders and came up the ladder. Dick stood in his way and one glance at Dick's face told John that something had gone wrong.

'Glad to see you,' said Mr Jemmerling. 'Your young brother has come upon some very interesting birds. More interesting than he seems to understand. But he tells me you are leaving tomorrow so that he can't come with me to show me where they were. What was the name of the place where he found them?'

'I don't really know the name,' said John. 'It hasn't got a name on our chart.'

'Could you show it me?' said Mr Jemmerling. 'I'll fix you both up on board and we'll start at once. No time to lose. We don't how long those eggs have been laid. They may be hatching any day. I'll make it very well worth your while.' He still had the pound note in his hand. He took four others from his pocket-book and held the five out to John.

John looked from Mr Jemmerling's eager face to Dick's anxious one.

'I didn't find them,' he said. 'Dick found them. I didn't go ashore.'

'Share it between you,' said Mr Jemmerling. 'If you can't come with me, just come into the deckhouse and show me as near as you can. Our chart's on a very large scale.'

'John!' said Dick, and started desperately down the ladder.

'I don't think I could,' said John. He looked across to the watchers on the deck of the *Sea Bear*. 'And we can't stop now. They're waiting for us.'

For one moment John thought that Mr Jemmerling was going to hit him. Then, as Mr Jemmerling turned furiously on his heel and went into the deckhouse, he followed Dick quickly down into the dinghy.

'You didn't tell him?' said Dick.

'No,' said John. 'But what's the matter? What have you done to make him lose his hair?'

'Be quick,' said Dick. 'He's back again.'

Mr Jemmerling, red in the face, was glaring down at them from the *Pterodactyl*'s deck. Dick, hunched in the stern of the dinghy, did not look round again, while John, his eyes on the angry figure of the *Pterodactyl*'s owner, rowed silently across to the *Sea Bear*.

CHAPTER 10

MUTINY ABOARD

FROM the deck of the *Sea Bear*, the crew watched John and Dick row the dinghy over to the *Pterodactyl*. They could not hear what was said, but they saw the *Pterodactyl*'s sailor talk to them, go away and come back. They saw Dick climb aboard.

'Why hasn't John gone too?' said Roger.

'Why should he?' said Susan. 'It's Dick who wants to ask questions.'

Dorothea watched Dick follow the sailor into the deck-house.

'The bird-man must be at home,' she said.

After that, all but Dorothea lost interest in the motor boat. Titty sat on the cabin skylight, writing a very short letter home. Susan and Roger sat beside her and told her bits to put in. Nancy and Peggy had not thought it worth while to write a letter as Captain Flint was writing and anyhow they would be home themselves in another two days. They were keeping more or less of a look-out for the mail-steamer coming in. Captain Flint, down in the cabin, had told them to sing out as soon as they saw her funnel above the pierhead. They were all of them feeling a little sad. The two nights at Scrubbers' Bay had seemed to put off the end, but tonight, they knew, was their last night in the Hebrides. The next time the anchor went down, it would not be they but a different crew that would haul it up again. The cruise was all but over.

Dorothea was still looking at the *Pterodactyl*, and wishing she had been able to go with Dick instead of John. Dick had talked so much of the boat he would one day have, in which he and Dorothea were to voyage all over the world looking at

126

birds, that she would very much have liked to see what a bird-watcher's boat was like inside, if she was some day going to live in one. She sat on the coaming of the *Sea Bear's* cockpit, looking across at the big motor yacht and thinking of Dick somewhere inside that white shining hull talking with the bird-man, whom she saw as somebody rather like Dick him-self, only grown-up.

Dick seemed to be a long time talking to him, and when he did at last come bolting out on deck, followed by Mr Jemmer-ling, Dorothea knew at once that something was amiss. Dick had come shooting out of that deckhouse door as if he had been slung from a catapult.

Nancy happened to be looking that way. 'Hullo!' she said. 'If it was Roger instead of Dick, I'd know he'd been saying something cheeky.'

'Dick never would,' said Dorothea, scrambling to her feet and looking very worried.

'He couldn't,' said Roger. 'He would never think of the right thing to say.'

They were all watching now. The next thing they saw was that John was going aboard, then Dick missing his footing as he hurried down the ladder and dropping very clumsily into the dinghy. They saw John talking to Dick's bird-man. They saw the bird-man angrily turn his back on John and go back into the deckhouse. They saw John join Dick in the dinghy, push off and begin rowing back, just as the bird-man came out of the deckhouse again to stand looking down on the little boat that was already on its way across to the *Sea Bear*.

'He's mad with John too,' said Roger.

They watched in silence while John rowed towards them. As soon as the dinghy was near enough for them to see Dick's face, every one of them knew that something had gone seriously wrong.

'Whatever's happened?' asked Nancy, grabbing the painter that John threw up to her.

'I don't know,' said John. 'Ask Dick.'

'Wouldn't he tell you?' asked Dorothea. 'Or wasn't it a Great Northern after all?'

Dick climbed aboard.

'He's an egg-collector,' he said grimly.

Dorothea, who had shared the adventures of the Coot Club on the Norfolk Broads, was the only one of the others who could guess what Dick was feeling. She knew he had been thinking of the owner of the *Pterodactyl* as of the sort of man he would like to be. She knew Dick dreamed of having a boat like that in which he and she would cruise together from one haunt of birds to another. She knew how horrible a shock it must have been to him to find that the owner of that boat was not a watcher and protector of birds but one of their most dangerous enemies.

'He's here just to collect eggs and shoot birds,' said Dick. 'The rarer they are, the more he wants to take their eggs, and the more he wants to shoot them.'

'That's how the bitterns died out on the Broads,' Dorothea explained. 'They've only come back since people have been protecting them against the egg-collectors.'

'But what was the row about?' asked Nancy. 'Did you go and tell him what you thought of him?'

'No,' said Dick. 'It was because I wouldn't tell him where I saw those Divers.'

'Were they Great Northerns?' asked Dorothea.

'Yes,' said Dick. 'That's just it. They're the first ever known to nest in the British Isles. So he wants their eggs for his collection. And he wants the birds too. He said, "What's hit's history and what's missed's mystery." My seeing them isn't enough. It's got to be proved. He's right about that. I've got to prove it. We've got to go back there at once.'

'But you don't want to take the eggs,' said Titty.

'You've seen the birds,' said Susan.

'I've got to go back,' said Dick. 'Don't you see? It's something all the books are wrong about. It's something nobody knew before. Nobody will believe it unless it's proved and I've simply got to prove it.'

'But how can you?' said Susan.

'Photographs,' said Dick. 'He said himself that that would do it, but he wants the eggs as well, and the birds. We've got to go back. We can take the folding boat to the loch so that I can get to the island, and I've still got a film only half used in the camera.'

'Did you see the eggs?' asked John.

'No,' said Dick. 'That's another reason why I've got to go back. I'm sure they're there. But I've got to see them, and I've got to take a photograph. I've simply got to.' He looked at Nancy who, so far, had listened but had not said a word.

'Captain Flint'll never agree,' said Susan.

'He'll have to,' said Nancy suddenly, and Dick knew he had found an ally worth having. 'Don't you see? We've got to go back. Of course we've got to. Dick's absolutely right. Supposing Columbus had sailed to within sight of America and then come tamely home with nothing to show it was there! Of course he must get his photographs. Jibbooms and bobstays! We were just cruising. This makes it a voyage of discovery. Dick's made the discovery. The cruise of the *Sea Bear* will go down in history. It'll be remembered for ever and ever, just because she had the Professor aboard. Good for the Ship's Naturalist. It's like the *Voyage of the Beagle*. Dick's a sort of Darwin.'

'It's not that,' said Dick. 'But we can't go away without making sure.'

'But it can't matter all that much,' said Susan.

'That man was dotty with excitement,' said John.

'I'd better tell Captain Flint at once,' said Dick.

'He's writing letters home,' said Titty. 'He'll have to change them and say we're not going to be home quite so soon.'

'He won't want to,' said Susan.

'He'll have to,' said Nancy. 'Go on down, Dick, and explain.'

'You'd better tell him,' said Dorothea, 'he's your uncle.'

'Right,' said Nancy, 'I will,' and charged down the companion way into the cabin.

'Jolly good,' said Roger. 'It means the cruise isn't over after all.'

'Shut up,' said John.

'Get out!' They heard the roar of a disturbed letter-writer down below.

Nancy came up again, pink-faced and angry.

'Won't listen,' she said. 'Writing letters like mad. Not interested. All he wanted to know was whether the mail-boat was in. Come on. Nothing for it but a first-class mutiny. All hands! Off with those tyers! Get her ready for sailing at once. That'll show him we mean business.'

'Oh, but look here,' said Susan, 'we can't. He's just made us do a harbour stow.'

'We're going to,' said Nancy. 'Don't go native just when things really matter.'

Susan looked at John for support, but John had seen the egg-collector at close quarters. He was on Dick's side and Nancy's.

Two short hoots on a ship's siren made them all jump.

'Mail-boat,' said Roger. 'She's coming in.'

'Shiver my timbers!' said Nancy. 'Don't stand gaping. Off with those gaskets. Get the halliards ready to hoist the sails. Buck up. He'll have heard that steamer and be on deck in a minute . . .'

The whole crew of the *Sea Bear* flung themselves at the

job of undoing everything they had done on coming into port. Gaskets were flicked loose and tied into bundles. The mainsail flopped in heavy folds down on the skylight. The staysail halliard that had been doing its harbour work of lifting the clew of the rolled staysail clear of the foredeck was shackled once more to the head of the sail, which was laid all ready for hoisting at a moment's notice. John cast off the lashings from the tiller. Nancy was fitting the handle to the winch ready for getting the anchor when Captain Flint came up on deck with a bundle of letters in his hand.

'What on earth's all this?' he exclaimed.

'I told you,' said Nancy, 'but you wouldn't listen. We've got to go back to Scrubbers' Bay.'

'But you've just come from there, you silly idiots.'

Everybody began to talk at once. Captain Flint gathered from the general hubbub that it had something to do with Dick. He heard the name of the *Pterodactyl*. He turned to Dick.

'What's gone wrong?' he asked. 'Wouldn't the prehistoric bird answer your questions?'

'It isn't his fault that all birds aren't prehistoric,' said Dick bitterly. 'He grabs the eggs of any rare bird he can find. Common ones, too. Even puffins' eggs. Dozens and dozens of them.'

'Well, that's not our business,' said Captain Flint. 'But what abut the bird you weren't sure about? Wouldn't he tell you its name?'

'They're what I thought they were,' said Dick. 'Great Northerns. He showed me the skin of one he'd killed. And now he wants to go and take the eggs and kill them both.'

'He can't if you haven't told him where they are.'

'I haven't. But it isn't only that. He says we can't prove they were nesting if we haven't got the eggs. But photographs would be just as good.'

'But who wants to prove it?'

'We all do,' said Nancy. 'Anybody would.'

'No one's ever known them nesting in the British Isles before,' said Dick.

'Are you sure?'

Dick bolted down into the cabin. Nancy, John, Titty and Dorothea took up the argument. Dick came up again with the *Pocket Book of Birds*, to find Captain Flint with his hands over his ears. He opened it at the page, and showed Captain Flint the words that mattered.

'Nests abroad.'

'They were nesting *here*,' said Dick. 'I saw them. I'd have seen the eggs if I'd had the folding boat. It was too far to swim.'

'But *you* don't want to take the eggs.'

'Of course, he doesn't,' said Dorothea.

'No,' said Dick. 'But it's got to be proved. He's right about that. I've got to take a photograph. I say, *must* we start home tomorrow?'

'Of course we must,' said Captain Flint. 'Time's up. We'll be one day late as it is.'

'Then Dot and I'll have to stay behind. We've got to get back there somehow.'

'Can't leave you,' said Captain Flint. 'And anyway I don't see that it really matters.'

'Barbecued billygoats!' exclaimed Nancy. 'Look here, when you were prospecting, if you'd spotted a lot of silver where no one had ever seen it before, would you have gone away without making sure?'

'It wouldn't matter if they weren't nesting,' said Dick. 'But it's most awfully important to prove they were. That beast thought so anyway. He gives boys ten shillings for showing him where he can find the nest of a Golden Eagle. He wanted to give me a pound to show him my Divers.'

'He tried to give me five pounds,' said John.

'Mad,' said Captain Flint. 'Mad.'

'It shows he thinks it's worth while making sure,' put in Dorothea.

Dick, desperate, took off his spectacles, wiped them and put them on again.

'I've simply got to go back,' he said. 'Don't you see? It's something all the bird-books are wrong about. It's a scientific discovery. It's something nobody knew before . . .'

'Well, you know it now.'

'I've got to prove it,' said Dick. 'I've got to go there again.'

'We'll both stop,' said Dorothea.

'We're going back,' said Nancy.

'We are not,' said Captain Flint.

'We've got enough stores left for an extra day or two,' said Susan, 'if we buy bread here, and a few more eggs.' Dorothea looked at her gratefully.

'Let's start right away,' said Peggy.

'Tide'll be turning,' said John. 'We'll have it with us.'

'We've just got the petrol cans to fill,' said Roger, and bolted for the companion way.

'Come out of that, Roger,' said Captain Flint. 'Shut up, all the lot of you. Listen to me. No mutinies aboard this ship. I'm going ashore for petrol, and to post letters. While I'm ashore the half-wits who cast off the gaskets and made a general mess can jolly well stow the sails again. We leave for Mallaig tomorrow morning. Mac wants his ship back. Your parents want you back, I suppose. There's no accounting for tastes. You don't want me to tear up these letters in which I've told them what a good crew you've been. You don't want me to write new ones saying I shall be thankful to be rid of a lot of mutinous riff-raff and never want to see you again. Have some sense, you blooming donkeys. Dick wanted to see Divers. Well, he's seen them. You can't expect me to go back on our tracks just because some lunatic has been pulling his leg.'

'One day wouldn't matter,' said Nancy.

'We've lost one day already.'

'He wasn't pulling my leg,' said Dick. 'He wants to prove it himself. But he wants to do it by killing the birds and taking the eggs. And I can do it by taking photographs.'

'Father would want Dick to make sure,' said Dorothea. 'It's like the discovery of a Pharaoh's tomb. When Father found one, he spent two winters working at nothing else. If the books are all wrong and Dick's found it out, he can't just sail away without making sure.'

'It must be pretty important,' said John, 'or that man wouldn't have been pushing five pounds at us and getting into a rage because we wouldn't take it.'

'If the *Sea Bear*'s owner knew,' said Titty, 'he wouldn't want her to miss a thing like that.'

'We're going back,' said Nancy.

'Don't deafen me,' said Captain Flint. 'There's no argument about it. Either the man is mad or he was pulling your leg. There isn't a bird's egg in the world worth five pounds to anybody. If you'd just grabbed his money and skedaddled he'd be after you now to try to get it back. Don't let's hear any more about it. Come on, John, and buck up. Here's the mail packet. We'll take the letters across, fill up our cans and get a wire off to Mac . . .'

'Look! Look!' whispered Titty. 'The *Pterodactyl*'s putting a boat over.'

The little steamer from the mainland was coming into the harbour. Ordinarily everybody would have been watching to see her tie up alongside the quay. Today, nobody took the slightest notice of her.

A boat in davits was being swung over the side of the white motor yacht. Two men were at the falls, lowering the boat to the water. For a moment the mutineers were silent. A man slipped down into the boat, cast off the tackles and brought the boat to the ladder, where the owner of the *Pterodactyl* was waiting.

'If he's coming to ask, don't tell him where I saw the birds,' said Dick.

'I won't,' said Captain Flint. 'But you flatter yourselves. He isn't interested. He's had his little joke with you and now he's going ashore.'

But the sailor had pushed off and, with the owner of the *Pterodactyl* sitting in the stern, was rowing straight across the harbour towards the *Sea Bear*.

'He's coming here,' said Dick.

'Why shouldn't he?' said Captain Flint. 'Pure politeness. Returning your call. But I hope he'll be quick about it. I want to get those letters off.'

'Don't tell him anything,' said Dick urgently.

'Get away forrard, all of you,' said Captain Flint. 'Or down below. And keep your mouths shut. Whatever he wants, there's no need to let him think we're nothing but a howling mob.'

CHAPTER II

THE EGG-COLLECTOR COOKS
HIS OWN GOOSE

NOBODY went below. There was a seething quiet on the foredeck where the mutineers waited, watching the dinghy from the *Pterodactyl* bringing Dick's enemy across the harbour.

'Plus fours at sea!' whispered Peggy.

There was certainly a contrast between the smartly dressed egg-collector, sitting in the stern of his dinghy, rowed by one of his men, and the stout figure of Captain Flint, in a shirt and a baggy pair of old flannel trousers, leaning against the boom and busy with the lighting of his pipe.

The egg-collector thought so too, and made his first mistake.

'Will you please inform your owner that I wish to see him?' he said.

Peggy turned round to hide her face and nearly squeaked as Nancy gave her a ferocious pinch.

'He's going to put his foot in it,' whispered Nancy with sparkling eyes. 'Keep quiet. Listen!'

'Owner not aboard, Sir,' said Captain Flint politely.

'Are you in charge?'

'Skipper for the time being,' said Captain Flint.

'Hear that?' said Nancy. 'For the time being . . . We'll depose him if he doesn't agree to come back. Do be quiet. What's he saying now?'

'Everybody *is* quiet except you,' whispered Peggy.

'Don't be a thundering galoot. Listen!'

They had missed a few words, but they heard the next

plainly ... 'Proposition to make which may be much to your advantage ...'

The egg-collector had his hands on the *Sea Bear*'s ladder and was coming aboard.

'He never asked if he might,' said Titty.

Captain Flint was standing up. The egg-collector stepped on deck. His man was holding the dinghy steady against the ladder.

'That your owner's family?'

There was a general grin on the faces of the mutineers. It widened as Captain Flint replied:

'No.'

'That boy, in spectacles?'

'I am sorry if he was a nuisance to you coming aboard.'

'Uncle Jim's getting mad,' said Nancy.

Dick was wiping his spectacles.

'It's all right,' whispered Dorothea. 'He knows you weren't.'

'Not at all. Not at all. But he came to me with a very remarkable story. Right up my particular street, as it happens. My name is Jemmerling. May mean nothing to you, but your owner would know it at once ...'

'No doubt,' said Captain Flint.

The egg-collector glanced at the group on the foredeck, and lowered his voice. They heard only the last words of what he said: '... likely to be telling the truth?'

'Why should you think not?' Captain Flint asked.

Again they could not hear everything the egg-collector said. They heard only scraps that meant little except to Dick ... 'mistaken ... description certainly accurate ... inclined myself to think he saw what he described. If so, the matter is of some importance ... Useless, of course, unless confirmed by competent witnesses ... Prepared to confirm it myself ... The boy could not be expected to understand ... Unable to

MR JEMMERLING COMES ABOARD

tell me the exact spot . . . Now . . .' Again he lowered his voice so that they could hear nothing until Captain Flint replied.

'Never left the ship,' they heard him say. 'I did not see the birds.'

'Surely he would tell, if you advised him to.'

'His secret, not mine.'

'It is not a secret he should be allowed to keep. He came to the right place with it in bringing it to me. I told you my name. Jemmerling . . . of the Jemmerling Collection. Alters all previous ideas . . . Adds a new bird to the list of British residents.'

'I know nothing about it,' said Captain Flint.

'But, perhaps if you were to tell me where you were when he saw the birds.'

'Look! Look!' whispered Titty. 'He's tearing up the letters.'

Captain Flint, standing listening to the egg-collector, was slowly tearing into little bits the letters he had been so busily writing in the cabin.

'It's the letters home,' whispered Dorothea. 'He'll have to write them again.'

'He's changed his mind,' whispered Nancy. 'Good. Oh, good! The *Pterodactyl*'s cooking his own goose.'

The egg-collector had seen that his first view of Captain Flint had been mistaken. He spoke in a new manner.

'Nice little ship,' he said. 'Hired, I suppose. Now, I wonder what this holiday has cost you. It need have cost you nothing at all if you can persuade that boy . . . Prepared to write a cheque at once. Would fifty pounds cover it?'

'Shiver my timbers!' whispered Nancy. 'Now what? Look out for squalls.'

The egg-collector had pulled a long narrow cheque-book from his pocket. With the cheque-book in one hand and a fountain pen in the other, he was smiling at Captain Flint.

'Good day,' said Captain Flint, and moved a step towards him. The egg-collector moved a step back. He stopped smiling.

'You understand,' he said. 'The information would be worth nothing to the ordinary person. It may be worth nothing to me. I will take that risk ... Did I say fifty pounds? ... Let me write you a cheque for a hundred ...'

'Good day, Sir,' said Captain Flint.

The egg-collector could not take another step back without going overboard.

'You will forgive me,' said Captain Flint politely, though his face was very red. 'I am about to go ashore. Good day to you.'

The egg-collector went down into his dinghy. The sailor from the *Pterodactyl* rowed him away. Captain Flint stood above the ladder. He tore his letters into still smaller bits, dropped them overboard in pinches of half-a-dozen scraps at a time and watched the tide carry them away.

The mutineers on the foredeck came aft.

Captain Flint turned suddenly.

'Spit in the water,' said Nancy. 'You'll feel better.'

Captain Flint looked curiously at Dick, almost as if he were seeing him for the first time. 'Sorry, Dick, old chap,' he said. 'I ought to have known that the Ship's Naturalist knew more about birds than I do. Well, what do we do about it?'

'Go back there, of course,' said Nancy. 'And we're all jolly glad you've made up your mind. It would have been a pity to have to make you walk the plank in view of the whole harbour.'

'How do you know I have made up my mind?'

Nancy pointed to a tiny scrap of one of the torn-up letters which had missed going overboard and was lying at Captain Flint's feet.

'I was wrong,' he said. 'He's not mad but bad. Rotten bad.

It isn't only eggs he wants. He thinks Dick really has got hold of something and he wants to take the credit of it for himself. You're quite right. It's up to us, it's up to the ship, to see he doesn't. Mac'll understand. I'll leave it to you to explain to the parents.'

'They'll understand too,' said Dorothea.

'Did you say a photograph would settle it?' he asked Dick.

'Yes,' said Dick. 'But it may be all a mistake. They were a long way off. But I'm pretty sure.'

'How long will it take you to find out?'

Dick thought. 'I'd have to make a hide and let them get accustomed to it, and take the photograph the next day. But if it's a mistake, I'll know at once, as soon as I can get near the island in the folding boat.'

'What was all that yarn you were spinning last night about savage Gaels?' said Captain Flint, but himself brushed that idea aside before anybody had time to answer. 'I don't suppose the shepherds would mind if you photographed every bird in the Hebrides. It's that chap who's the difficulty. He isn't going to give up in a hurry. He'll be watching us like a hawk. If we go back, he'll follow. Come on, John. We've got to fill up with petrol anyhow, and I'll have to send telegrams instead of these letters.'

'Aye, aye, Sir,' said John, and hurried below for more cans. Roger had already brought two of them on deck.

'Mutiny over,' said Nancy. 'Lucky for you. For us too. If we'd had to depose you and make you walk the plank, we might have had a bit of a job to take the ship back by ourselves.'

'Mutiny? Eh? What's that?' Captain Flint's mind was busy on other things. 'Don't bother to put the gaskets back on those sails. Leave everything just as it is. Look as lazy as a crew can be. Hi! What are you doing with that bucket?'

Titty had just dipped a bucket over the side at the end of a rope. She hauled it up. 'I was going to give the decks a wash down . . . Where he stood, anyway.'

Captain Flint laughed. 'Oh well, you can do that,' he said. 'What a chap!'

John hauled the dinghy alongside and went down into it. Roger passed the petrol cans down one after another.

'I'll row,' said Captain Flint. 'I'd let you if you had a yachting cap and a blue jersey and the ship's name in big red letters on it, and if you knew how to look the part.'

They pushed off from the side, but they had gone only a few yards when Captain Flint backwatered.

'That chap may try to have another go at Dick when I'm out of the way. If he tries to come aboard again, don't let him.'

'We won't,' said Roger.

'Out marline spikes and repel boarders,' said Nancy. 'I'd like to see him put a finger on our rail.'

'We'll be back as soon as we can,' said Captain Flint. 'Don't keep staring at his ship. Be lazy and look lazy. Let him think nobody's interested.'

The dinghy was half way to the quay when Susan suddenly remembered. 'The bread and the milk,' she said. 'And I've never given them the milk-can.'

'You can't haul them back now,' said Nancy. 'We can manage with tinned milk for one more day.'

'Six loaves of bread,' called Susan, and they saw John turn and nod.

'Keep that bucket away from here,' said Roger quietly. The others looked round to see that he was lying full length on the deck. He yawned. 'I can't be properly lazy if the decks are swimming with water.'

Titty had waited till the petrol tins had been passed down into the dinghy before sloshing her bucket of water over the place where the owner of the *Pterodactyl* had stood talking. She did not dip another. The whole crew took up restful poses in the cockpit, on the deck or sitting on the skylight, being careful to look not at the *Pterodactyl* but at the distant quay ... the whole crew except Dick who, in a sort of panic, had slipped down into the cabin and was reading and re-reading the short paragraph in his bird-book about the Great Northern Diver, and looking now at the picture and now at his own drawing. He came on deck again with the book in his hand.

'There simply can't be a mistake,' he said. 'That man knew it was a Great Northern as soon as he looked at my diagram. He showed me a skin of one of the ones he's killed. It was exactly the same. And I know I saw two birds, and except for a minute or two there was always one on the island and it was always sitting in the same place.'

'Of course there isn't a mistake,' said Nancy. 'And you'll get a photograph and prove it ... Prove what, by the way?'

'That Great Northern Divers do nest in the British Isles,' said Dick. 'All the books are wrong, because no one's ever found them nesting before.'

'Even Captain Flint sees how much it matters now,' said Dorothea.

'The *Pterodactyl* taught him,' said Nancy. 'I say, what sort of birds are they anyhow? Big?'

'As big as geese,' said Dick.

'Golly,' said Nancy.

'They went into the Post Office,' said Titty about ten minutes later. She had been lying on the foredeck, watching the long quay through a telescope rested on the rail. 'They've been in a long time ... Four telegrams to write ... There they are, coming out ... Captain Flint's talking to the harbourmaster ... They must have got the petrol ... There's a man wheeling our cans on a handcart.'

'Don't look round too fast,' said Nancy. 'The old Dactyl's goggling at us through binoculars. I do wish he'd come and try to get aboard.'

'Shall I get a spanner from the engine room in case?' said Roger.

At last John and Captain Flint left the quay steps in the dinghy, but they did not row straight to the *Sea Bear*.

'What on earth have they gone to look at that buoy for?' said Nancy.

They very soon knew.

'Engine, Roger,' said Captain Flint the moment he stepped aboard. 'And let's have the funnel for filling up the tank. She won't start without a drop of petrol.'

'Aye, aye, Sir,' and the gleeful Roger disappeared.

Captain Flint opened the filling hole in the after deck, fitted the funnel and, with John to help, began pouring petrol into the tank.

'You can start on the winch, Nancy,' he said over his shoulder. 'Get the anchor a-trip.'

'Are we starting right away?' asked Nancy, hurrying to the foredeck.

'We are not,' said Captain Flint. 'We don't want to show him the way to Mac's Cove. We're shifting to that buoy. We'll run a warp to it and lie there. We can let go then without making a shindy. If we have to get our anchor when we leave he'll hear it and be off after us and stick to us like glue. We must get away without a sound when the time comes. We've got to give that fellow the slip.'

CHAPTER 12

WAITING FOR A CHANCE

THEY had not long to wait before they knew that Captain Flint was right and that they could not make a move unnoticed. Roger had hardly set the engine ticking over; there had not been more than a dozen throbs, a dozen pale blue puffs of smoke and water from the exhaust pipe at the *Sea Bear's* stern, before they saw that people were busy aboard the *Pterodactyl*. The egg-collector had come out of the deckhouse and was watching them through binoculars. There was the quiet hum of big engines starting up. A man hurried forward and stood by the *Pterodactyl's* windlass, looking aft for the egg-collector to give the word to weigh the anchor.

'They're starting too,' said Peggy.

'Ready to start if we do,' said John. 'It's his only hope . . . to see where we go and come after us.'

'Dinghy, John!'

'Aye, aye, Sir.'

'Take a hand with you and wait for us near the buoy . . . No . . . Not you, Nancy. We'll want you here to let him have the end of the warp.'

'Come on, Susan,' said John.

John pushed off with Susan in the dinghy, rowed across to the buoy and waited, paddling a stroke or two now and then, so as not to drift back on the tide. They saw Nancy and Captain Flint busy on the foredeck. They saw the anchor climb to the stemhead of the *Sea Bear* and hang there dripping. They saw Captain Flint go aft, to the tiller. They saw Nancy waiting with the end of a warp. They heard the throb of the little engine change, as the *Sea-Bear* began slowly to forge ahead.

She came nearer and nearer to the buoy.

'Slow,' they heard Captain Flint's voice, without a hint in it that anything unusual was happening.

John brought the dinghy alongside the *Sea Bear*'s bows. She was just stemming the tide, no more.

'Here you are,' said Nancy quietly, lowering the end of the warp to Susan. 'Pass it once through the ring and make a bowline knot . . . a long one, two fathoms at least, he says, so that we can let go from the deck when we're ready . . .'

Two minutes later, it was done. The warp had been made fast, the engine had stopped and Susan and John were climbing aboard again as Roger, hot and happy, came up through the companion and looked across the water to the *Pterodactyl*.

'He's stopped his engines too,' he said.

'Shut off the moment he saw our dinghy near the buoy,' said Nancy.

'Spotted what we were up to,' said Captain Flint. 'Can't help that. And much obliged to him for showing that if we leave he means to follow us.'

'And all for Dick's birds,' said Nancy. 'Whoever would have believed it? Jiminy, Professor! I don't care whether they're nesting or not. This is better than anything that's happened yet. Three cheers for natural history. Great Auks and Guillemots! I never thought birds could be half such fun.'

'I'm almost sure they're nesting,' said Dick.

'That fellow thinks so too,' said Captain Flint. 'He thinks you're really on to something, and he isn't going to let go in a hurry. We're going to have our work cut out to diddle him. Four times our speed. If he sees us go and catches us at sea, we haven't a chance of throwing him off.'

'We want ten miles start,' said John. 'Or a good thick fog.'

'Fog's no use to us,' said Nancy. 'We'd never have got into

Scrubbers' Bay if I hadn't taken us to right off the opening before it came on. And we couldn't do it now.'

'Trouble is, it's so light at night up here,' said Captain Flint.

'If he goes ashore,' said Dorothea, 'what about a Press Gang or something to keep him there till it's too late to follow us?'

'We'll find a way,' said Captain Flint.

'What do we do now?' asked Titty.

'Nothing,' said Captain Flint. 'Just nothing. Keep him wondering. Keep him watching us till he's sick of the sight.'

'Come on, Peggy,' said Susan, 'we'd better get the animals fed. Where did you put those loaves, John?'

'Gosh!' said John. 'We forgot all about them. At least I did. We were thinking about shifting her to the buoy.'

'Well, we're very hungry,' said Roger. 'Anybody would be.'

'I want some milk too, if we can get it. And we've run out of chocolate. And eggs.'

'Hen eggs,' said Roger. 'Not Great Northern's.'

'Nobody wants the dinghy,' said Susan. 'Peggy and I'll row across to the shops before they shut.'

The two cooks went down into the dinghy, rowed away and landed at some steps below the quay.

'Hullo,' said Roger. 'The old Dactyl's hungry too.'

Mr Jemmerling was standing at the rail of the *Pterodactyl*, talking to one of his men who was already in the *Pterodactyl*'s dinghy. They saw the man glance over his shoulder at the quay. He pushed off, rowed away as fast as he could and was presently tying up his boat at the steps where Peggy and Susan had left theirs. He went up the steps and looked up and down the quay. He sat down on a bollard, as if he were waiting for somebody. They saw him fill a pipe and light it.

'He isn't in a hurry,' said Roger.

'Everybody isn't as hungry as you,' cried Nancy. Suddenly

her voice changed. 'Jiminy,' she cried, jumping up. 'That beast's sent him to wait for our cooks. He'll find things out from Peggy . . . She's simply bound to blurt everything out if he asks her. It's too far to swim. Let's get the folding boat out quick . . .'

'Too late,' said Captain Flint.

Susan and Peggy had just come out of a shop on the quay and were looking into the window of another. The *Pterodactyl*'s man was crossing the road towards them.

'We can't do anything now,' said John.

'Susan'll never tell him,' said Titty.

'Jibbooms and Bobstays!' exclaimed Nancy. 'Peewits and Puffins, I mean . . . Peggy's letting him carry her basket. She's always ready to chatter to anyone.'

'The innocent child was easy prey for the smooth-tongued, smiling villain,' murmured Dorothea and, though really worried, fumbled in her pocket for a pencil.

'They're going into the shop together,' said Roger.

'Do you think she really will tell him?' said Roger.

'We'll drown her if she does,' said Nancy.

'But it'll be too late,' said Dick.

There was horrified silence aboard the *Sea Bear* as they saw Susan and Peggy come out of the shop with the *Pterodactyl*'s sailor, now loaded up with loaves of bread as well as the shopping basket. They could see that he was talking to his new-made friends, as the three of them crossed the quay and came down the steps. They watched the *Sea Bear*'s cooks step into their dinghy and take basket and loaves from the sailor. They saw the sailor pull his forelock and then, as Susan rowed towards the *Sea Bear*, they saw the sailor go sculling back to the *Pterodactyl*. Nobody said a word until Susan and Peggy had handed up the provisions and come aboard.

'That was a sailor from the *Pterodactyl*,' said Peggy cheerfully.

'What did you tell him?' asked Nancy, very grim.

Peggy grinned. 'We saw him rowing after us,' she said, 'and when he came and spoke to us we had everything ready.'

'What did you tell him?' asked Nancy again.

'He said, "Where might you be voyaging in that bonny wee ship of yours?" and I said we'd got to take her back to her owner.'

'Good for you,' said Captain Flint.

'Not bad,' said Nancy.

'It was Susan's idea,' said Peggy.

'Well, so we have,' said Susan. 'And when he asked where her owner was, it was quite all right to say he worked in Glasgow.'

'And then what?' said Nancy. 'You didn't let out about Scrubbers' Bay?'

'He said something about meeting us at sea, and Susan said she remembered a motor boat steering across our bows, and was that him? He was a bit sheepish, but he plucked up again and asked, "And where have you been since then?" and we both explained that we were the cooks and didn't exactly know. We told him how puzzling charts are, with figures all over the place.'

'Gosh!' said Roger. 'I wish I'd been there.'

'You wouldn't have done any better,' said John. 'Probably worse.'

'You've both done splendidly,' said Captain Flint. 'He's learnt nothing and we've learnt a lot. I thought he'd made up his mind to find Dick's birds. Now we know he has. His only hope is to follow us, and follow us he will if we give him a chance. We've got to get away without his knowing. None too easy. He'll be watching us. Down below everybody. Don't keep staring at him. We're a lazy ship with a bone-idle crew and we take no interest in anybody ... least of all in a chap like that.'

'There's just one thing I must do first,' said John. 'It's the staysail block. It squeaks like a canary.'

'More like a cockatoo,' said Roger.

'He'd hear it right across the harbour,' said John.

'All right. Up you go and give it a touch of grease.'

John went up to the cross-trees and greased that block till it made no noise at all. Then he came below to find everybody in the cabin and ready for a monster meal.

'Tea,' said Susan, 'and supper.'

'And likely enough breakfast too,' said Nancy. 'We don't know what's going to happen in the night.'

Every now and then during that tremendous meal, somebody slipped through into the fo'c'sle to look through a porthole at the *Pterodactyl*. For a long time the egg-collector himself was sitting in a deck-chair, watching the *Sea Bear*. Then he disappeared, but left a sailor on deck, who seemed to have nothing to do.

They were washing up after the meal when they heard the sudden patter of rain overhead.

'Oh I say,' said John. 'And the sails aren't stowed.'

'They'll take no harm,' said Captain Flint. 'Don't go on deck. First bit of luck for us. A cloudy night's the very best thing we could have hoped for.'

'The rain's driven that sailor in,' said Titty.

'Do you think they've stopped watching?' said Dick.

'Not they,' said Nancy. 'I bet there's somebody in the deckhouse all the time, and they're ready to start the moment they see us move.'

'When are we going to?' asked Roger.

Captain Flint was looking at the tide tables. 'We'll want the ebb to help us,' he said, as much to himself as to anybody else. 'High tide close on nine. Ebb'll run till getting on for three. We must be off before then if we're to do any good.

Look here. Everybody had better get to bed. Put in all the sleep you can.'

Nobody wanted to turn in so early, and for half an hour or so they waited, someone going up the companion ladder every few minutes to look out at the rain, and bringing back the cheerful news that there was a grey sky, and a steady drizzle that would be as useful as a fog. At last Susan put her foot down, and reminded them that they wouldn't be much good if they were to sail in the middle of the night and had had no sleep before starting.

'Dick's asleep now,' whispered Dorothea, and pointed to him.

Dick, tired right out by the shock of finding his bird-man an egg-collector instead of a friend, by worry over his birds, by the disappointment of finding that Captain Flint would neither change his plans nor even agree to leaving Dick and Dorothea behind, and then by joy at finding not only the rest of the crew ready to help him but Captain Flint himself throwing all plans overboard and agreeing to do exactly what he wanted, was asleep over his bird-book.

'Sensible chap,' said Captain Flint. 'No. Don't wake him. Let him sleep. Get into your bunks, you others. I'll wake you when the time comes.'

'Sleep in our clothes?' asked Nancy.

'As you like,' said Captain Flint. 'Susan, lend me your alarm clock.'

'It makes an awful noise,' said Susan.

'Muffle it in a towel,' said Nancy, 'and shove it under your pillow.'

It was darkish in the cabin when Dick woke but though the lantern was not lit other people were still awake. He had hardly moved before he felt Captain Flint's hand on his knee.

'You can get into your bunk without a light, old chap,' he

heard him say. 'We put out lights an hour ago, and we want him to think we're all snoring.'

'Has it stopped raining?'

'No, but I'm afraid it will.'

'Can't we start now?'

'Not yet,' said Captain Flint. 'He's still got his eye on us. Look at that . . .'

There was a sudden flash of brighter light through the portholes on one side. The open companion was lit up and the white sail hanging in folds from the boom above it.

'That's his searchlight again,' Dick heard Nancy say.

'Every half hour,' said Captain Flint. 'We've got to wait until he's sick of doing that.'

'We really are going back?' said Dick.

'We are. You roll into your bunk and go to sleep.'

CHAPTER 13

GIVING HIM THE SLIP

JOHN, lying in his bunk neither asleep nor awake, felt a hand on his knee. He opened his eyes. It was darkish in the cabin and for a moment he was puzzled by two spots of light, one red and one green, on the cabin floor at the foot of the companion steps.

'We've got to take our chance now,' he heard Captain Flint whisper.

'Has he stopped watching us?' asked John.

'An hour and a half since he last turned that searchlight on us. Daren't wait any longer or we'll be late for the tide. It's stopped raining, worse luck, but there's a north-west wind.'

'Shall I wake Nancy?'

'Blooming cheek,' he heard another whisper. 'If it hadn't been for me we'd have left you snoring.'

'Don't knock the navigation lights over. We won't bring them on deck till we have to.'

John slid quietly out of his bunk, put on his shoes, wriggled into a warm sweater, tip-toed between the red and green lanterns and went on deck.

It was not dark, though no stars were showing, but it was very cold. A lamp glimmered faintly on the quay. Rippled water broke its reflections. A riding light dimly lit the deck of the *Pterodactyl* where she lay asleep a hundred yards away.

'Wind north-west,' said Captain Flint again. 'Couldn't ask better for getting out of here. Ready? Good. Slip along forrard. You get the staysail up. I'll give her a sheer to starboard and Nancy will let slip from the buoy. We won't start playing with the mainsail till we're outside . . .'

John went forward. Away to the south he could see the revolving flash of a lighthouse . . . a long flash, repeated three times in every minute. Over the land, to the north-east, a double flash, seen only as a sudden pale loom in the dark sky, showed where the lighthouse on the Head was hidden by the higher ground of the long promontory.

'I've cast off the tyers already,' whispered Nancy. 'And we left it ready for hoisting. But look out for the flapping when it goes up.'

John found the staysail halliard. A good thing that he had belayed it himself after greasing the block, and could put his hand on it at once. He glanced up the dim height of the mast. Was that block going to squeak or was it not?'

'Are you ready?' he asked.

'Half a minute. I haven't got hold of the knot yet. Give me a hand. There's a pretty hard pull on the warp. Now . . .'

Suddenly Captain Flint was beside them, putting his weight on the warp as well as theirs. 'That's right. We can't use the winch.'

'She's coming,' said Nancy. 'I've got the knot . . . Now. One second. All ready to slip . . .'

'Don't want her drifting,' said Captain Flint. 'And we'd better have no shouting. Just say one word, "Now," quietly, the moment we've slipped. We'd have done better to take the warp to the stern, but I think she'll come round all right. Plenty of room.'

'Aye, aye, Sir,' whispered John.

'I've taken a turn with the end of the rope,' said Nancy. 'I can slip any minute you like.'

'Give him time to get back to the tiller . . . Now. Nancy, I'm hoisting.'

Hand over hand he hauled on the halliard and the big staysail went up. 'Not a squeak from that block,' said John to himself. There was a single flap of canvas, but only one. John

THE SEARCHLIGHT

grabbed at the port sheet and quietened the sail. 'Quick, quick,' he whispered.

There was the faintest splash as the warp dropped in the water.

'Now,' said John.

The lamp on the far away quay, the white *Pterodactyl*, the houses of the town, the darker hills against the sky were swinging round. The lamp on the quay showed wide on the beam . . . on the quarter . . . astern . . . The flash of the lighthouse that he had seen as he came out of the companion now showed ahead. The *Sea Bear*, no longer facing the ebb, was moving with it.

Nancy coiled down the wet end of the warp as she hauled it aboard.

'We'd better stay where we are,' she said. 'He'll want a look-out.'

The *Sea Bear* was gathering speed. With the ebb tide under her, and the north-west breeze filling her staysail she was moving towards the dim grey pierheads of the harbour mouth.

'He's got the lighthouse to steer for,' said John, as the point of light swelled to a white flash, swept round the sky and dwindled to a point of light once more.

'John!'

John scrambled aft.

'Take the tiller while I rig our navigation lights. We don't need them, but you never know. There may be a fisherman coming in or some busybody to shout from the shore to know what we are doing without them. It's not the lights that matter now, but a shout carries a long way over water . . . Here you are. Keep the lighthouse fine on the starboard bow.'

'Fine on the starboard bow, sir,' said John, and took the tiller, warm from the skipper's hand.

A moment later the two lanterns were on deck, and John saw that Captain Flint was taking no risks. He was being careful not to let them show a glimmer of red or green astern to anybody aboard a boat in the harbour who might happen to be looking through a porthole. One at a time, they were taken forward and fixed in their places on the shrouds.

'Have we done him?' John heard Nancy ask.

'He hasn't turned that searchlight on again,' said Captain Flint.

He came aft. 'Our lights are pretty dim,' he said. 'But nobody can say we haven't got them.'

John gave up the tiller and looked back across the harbour to the faint gold speck that showed where the riding light hung from the *Pterodactyl*'s forestay. It was still there. Nothing had changed. The egg-collector and his men were still asleep.

'Gosh! When they find we've gone!'

'We want all the start they'll give us,' said Captain Flint. 'And we've only just got away in time. Dawn'll be on us before we know where we are.'

'What about the mainsail?'

'As soon as we're clear outside.'

The *Sea Bear* had slipped away without a sound. Her tired crew, all but three on deck, slept in their bunks and did not, unless in dreams, know that she was moving. With the wind off the land, the ebb tide carrying her with it, and only the big staysail pulling, she slid out of harbour like a ghost.

Half an hour later, as she began to lose the shelter of the shore, a gentle murmur began under her forefoot. It grew louder. Dorothea was the first one to hear it down below. 'Wind,' she thought. 'There must be a lot of it to make that noise when we're in harbour.' She heard new noises, the rattle of blocks, the flap of heavy canvas, the creaking of the gaff as it swayed aloft, all the noises that go with the hoisting of the mainsail. Then she guessed. In a moment she was out of her bunk, tip-toeing into the fo'c'sle and looking through a porthole. The dim grey light before the dawn showed a rocky shore slipping quickly past.

'Dick,' she said, prodding urgently into his bunk, 'we've started.'

Dick reached for his spectacles, rolled out of his bunk and joined her at the porthole.

'Hullo,' said Roger, sitting up and then 'Hey! They've started without us. What beasts!' He wasted no time in looking through portholes, pushed past Dick and Dorothea and was before them in scrambling up the companion steps.

They came on deck to find John at the tiller, and the mainsail just going up, with Captain Flint and Nancy at the halliards. Looking aft they could see the pierheads of the harbour they had left, already far astern.

'Why didn't you wake me?' Roger was asking.

'Ask the skipper.'

The mainsail was set, and the jib was going up.

'Harden in that starboard jib sheet, now you're here,' said John.

'You'd have got away a lot better if I'd been there to help,' said Roger, as he hauled in on the jib sheet. 'I can manage,' he added as Captain Flint coming aft gave him a hand.

'Not too hard.'

Dick and Dorothea were watching the harbour. A lamp flickered like a dying match and went out. They were looking for the white blur of a fast motor cruiser coming after them. Nothing was moving.

'Sodden with sleep,' murmured Dorothea, 'the villain little knew that his prey had slipped his evil clutch . . .'

'But have we?' said Dick.

Titty's face showed white at the companion. She did not say a word. She looked astern, then forward, shivered with the sudden cold and then sat on the top step, pushing the *Sea Bear* on her way with all the will-power she had.

'Let me out,' said Peggy, and Titty made room for her to pass. 'And Susan's sent your woolly for you. You're to put it on. Susan's just coming. She stopped to start a Primus.'

'Good for Susan,' said Captain Flint. 'But why aren't all you idiots in your bunks?'

'I like that,' said Roger. 'You and Nancy and John sneaking all the fun for yourselves.'

'Your turn's coming,' said Captain Flint. 'Once we've rounded the Head we'll be close-hauled for that cove, and we'll give her the help of the engine.'

'You ought to have used the engine coming out of harbour,' said Roger. 'We've got plenty of petrol now.'

'And told the *Pterodactyl* just what we were doing,' said John.

'I forgot that,' said Roger. 'Sorry.'

'Have we done him?' asked Dick.

'Can't tell yet,' said Captain Flint. 'If he doesn't come out before we round the Head, we've a goodish chance. But even that's not a certainty, because that thing of his can go at such a lick. We can't say we've done him until we're tucked away out of sight.'

'What'll we do if he comes out and sees us?'

'Carry on out to sea. Go and have a look at Cape Wrath. Lead him a dance anyhow. Don't you worry. We won't show him the way to your birds.'

There was never a moment when someone was not looking back towards the harbour as the sky brightened in the east and the *Sea Bear*, with every sail drawing, rushed on her way towards the light. The lighthouses no longer flashed. Sunrise was coming nearer every minute. They could see sheep and cows moving on the southern slopes of the Head. 'If he comes out now, he'll be able to see us,' said Dick.

'There's no sign of him yet,' said Dorothea.

A smell of coffee drifted from the companion way.

'The egg-collector'll be pretty bad-tempered at breakfast,' said Roger, glancing down into the cabin.

'You hungry already?' said Captain Flint with a grin.

'Porridge,' Susan called from below.

'Get along down to it, all of you,' said Captain Flint. 'No work on deck till we clear the Head.'

Roger took particular care to be the last to go, lingering to look at the compass when everybody else but the skipper had gone below.

'Go on, Roger. Tuck in, and then get ready with your engine.'

'Aye, aye, Sir,' said Roger gratefully, and bolted down after the others.

Susan brought up a bowl of porridge for the steersman.

'They ought to be asleep, you know. Roger and Titty, anyhow.'

'There's always a time to break every rule that was ever made,' said Captain Flint.

'Oh well,' said Susan, 'they can sleep all the rest of the day.'

'We can't expect them to sleep now,' said Captain Flint, looking anxiously over his shoulder.

Down in the cabin of the *Sea Bear* there was a new feeling among the crew, a feeling that had not been there when they had been merely cruising from one good harbour or anchorage to another. There is a tremendous difference between just going somewhere and having an enemy to dodge.

'I don't care what anybody says,' said Nancy, finishing her porridge. 'I'm jolly grateful to that beastly egg-collector. All right, Dick, I know what you're thinking. But I am. Just look what he's done for us. But for him we'd be on our way home. And now anything may happen. Nothing any of us could have said would have made Uncle Jim change his mind. Three cheers for the *Pterodactyl*!'

'He may be starting after us already,' said Dick.

'We'll dodge him all right,' said Nancy.

'What does he want?' said Susan. 'I don't see why it matters so much to him.'

'He wants the eggs and the birds,' said Dick.

'It's more than that,' said Nancy. 'Much more. He wants to be able to make everybody think it's his discovery, not Dick's. That's what made Uncle Jim see red.'

'I thought it was his offering all that money,' said Susan.

'That only showed Uncle Jim how important it was.'

'It isn't that that matters,' said Dick. 'I mean, so long as somebody proves that they really do nest. Only he would prove it by killing them and a photograph would do just as well.'

'Who found them? You did. Not the bird-man of the *Pterodactyl*. The bird-man of the *Sea Bear*. And the *Sea Bear*'s going to be famous for ever, not that beastly motor boat.'

'We can't let the birds be killed,' said Titty.

'They aren't going to be,' said Dick. 'Only, whatever happens, we've got to get our photographs without his seeing where we go to get them . . . No thank you. I don't want any more. I'm going up on deck.'

'He's gulped his breakfast,' said Dorothea, as Dick disappeared up the companion. 'But it's no good saying anything. Father's just the same.'

'It's three cheers for Dick as well as for the *Pterodactyl*,' said Nancy. 'But for him none of this would be happening. We'll be having another look at your Gaels.'

'We'll keep out of their way,' said Titty. 'We don't want to be stalked again.'

'We'll be seeing my Pict-house,' said Roger.

'Buck up with your grub,' said Nancy. 'I heard Uncle Jim say we'd be using the engine.'

'I'm ready,' said Roger. 'At least I will be as soon as he is. But it's silly to starve if you don't have to. Please pass the marmalade, John.'

They came on deck again to find the harbour out of sight. They were rounding the Head. There were hints of sunshine on the tops of the hills inland. Dick was putting Captain Flint's big binoculars back in their case.

'So far, so good,' said Captain Flint. 'But the sun'll be up in a minute or two. Somebody's sure to wake up soon, and the first thing he'll do will be to look across at our buoy.'

'And see the buoy all by itself,' said Dorothea. 'And no *Sea Bear*.'

'Five minutes after that he'll be coming hell for leather.'

'Won't you go down now and have the rest of your breakfast?' said Susan. 'It's all ready.'

'In a minute,' said Captain Flint. 'Come on, Roger. Let's see what the engine can do to help. Keep her as she's going, John.'

Captain Flint and Roger disappeared below. Sunshine crept lower on the Head. A golden glitter spread over the sea from the east.

'Go it, old *Sea Bear*,' said Titty.

Throb ... throb ... throb. The engine was starting. Captain Flint and Roger came on deck once more. Roger looked over the side not so much to see how fast she was moving as to see how much faster she would be moving when Captain Flint gave him the word.

'Full ahead!'

It was as if somebody had given a sudden push behind.

Chug ... chug ... chug ... With sails drawing and the engine going full out, the old pilot boat fairly surged through the water.

'Seven knots at least,' said John. 'She's never gone faster.'

Dick wiped his spectacles and looked astern.

'Do go down and have the rest of your breakfast,' said Susan to the skipper.

'All right. All right. Must just see what course she'll lay

close-hauled with the engine running. Now then, Nancy. Let's have your weight on the mainsheet. Bring her to the wind, John.'

Everybody who could get hold of the rope hauled in on the mainsheet, bringing the boom inboard. Nancy, Susan, Peggy and Captain Flint hauled in on jib and staysail sheets.

'That's it, John. Close-hauled. Keep the sails just full.' He looked forward across the wide bay north of the Head towards the coast they had left the day before. 'She'll all but lay the course. Wouldn't do it without the engine. Nothing we can do now but keep her at it. All right, Susan. Leave her to you, John.'

He went below while, with John at the tiller, the *Sea Bear* rushed across the bay towards those distant cliffs and hills. This was a very different passage from the long struggle through the calms and paltry winds of yesterday. Instead of having the tide against them for six hopeless hours, they had the ebb with them part of the way, and the passage was over before the flood had gathered strength against them. Instead of calms and a wind that was no wind at all, they had a sturdy north-west breeze that, coming off the land, did not raise a sea to stop her. Instead of having all but empty petrol tanks, they could let the engine run at full throttle. They were doing in a couple of hours what had taken them ten going the other way. It was as if the *Sea Bear* knew that everything depended on their getting tucked away in the cove and hidden by cliffs and rocks before the *Pterodactyl* came round the Head and sighted their white sails.

On and on she rushed, crashing through the little waves, leaving a foaming white wake far astern. This was Roger's moment. He spoke to no one, but kept coming on deck, looking over the side, to see that all was well with the water spurting from the exhaust, and dropping down below again to use his oil can and feel the bearings with a greasy hand.

But for two smudges of smoke far to the north, they still had the sea and the morning to themselves when Captain Flint came up on deck again. The Head was far astern. The early sunshine was showing them the places they had left never thinking they would see them again.

'That's the hill with my Pict-house,' Roger was saying.

'The Gael's castle is behind the ridge beyond it,' said Dorothea.

'She won't point up for our inlet,' said John.

'Right,' said Captain Flint. 'We're near enough now. We'll have those sails down.'

'But she'll go slower,' groaned Titty.

'Gummock,' said Nancy. 'It's because he doesn't want to tack.'

'Not so much that,' said Captain Flint. 'But we're near enough now to give him a hint of where we're going. If he comes round the Head now he'll see our sails with the sun on them. He'll never spot us without them. All hands to lower sail. We'll want you, John. Peggy at the tiller. Take no notice of us. Head her straight for the opening as soon as we have the sails down.'

Down came the headsails, down came the mainsail. The crew flung themselves at the job of putting on the gaskets to keep the sails from blowing about. The *Sea Bear* was closing fast with the shore.

'I'll take over, Peggy,' said Captain Flint. 'It had better be me to put her on a rock if anybody does.'

The *Sea Bear* slid under the cliff. Everybody took a last anxious look astern.

'We've done him!' said Captain Flint. 'How's that, Dick? Now for your birds. You've a clear field.'

'Except for the Gaels,' said Titty.

'There's no dogmudgeon to watch us come back,' said Nancy, almost as if she were sorry for it, glancing at the rock from which the tall Gael, who had not answered their cheerful waving of hands, had watched them put to sea.

'What's the matter, Dot?'

Dorothea was putting away the big binoculars. 'I thought I saw something for a moment,' she said. 'But I can't have if nobody else saw it. It was probably a breaking wave. Anyway it was miles away.'

'Don't you worry,' said Captain Flint. 'We've done him. Go slow with the engine, Roger. We'll put her where she was before.'

'There's the place where we scrubbed her,' said Peggy.

The *Sea Bear* crept on. John and Nancy were busy with anchors on the foredeck. The engine coughed and was silent. The anchor went down. The dinghy was put over the side, and Captain Flint rowed away with the kedge at the end of its warp. Twenty-four hours after they had left it, as they thought for ever, the *Sea Bear* was moored again exactly in her old place.

The tide had turned and was coming in and the *Sea Bear* lay with her head towards the sea.

'There's only one thing,' said Nancy. 'Anybody looking in could see her, and if the old *Dactyl* comes nosing after us . . .'

'She'd have to come close in shore to see us here,' said John.

'We got clear away,' said Captain Flint. 'He's probably given it up as a bad job. Anyway we can't hide her any better, unless we put her under water, and Mac wouldn't thank us for that.'

Roger suddenly pointed out between the cliff and the rocky spit that divided Scrubbers' Bay from the narrower inlet to the south of it. Far out at sea, a long white splash, like the furrow of foam cut by a great bird coming down on the water, was moving fast. Captain Flint grabbed the binoculars.

'Spoke too soon,' he said. 'He hasn't lost much time.'

'He knew which way to go because of meeting us at sea that day,' said Dick in despair.

'We're done,' said Titty.

'Cornered with no escape,' said Dorothea.

'He hasn't seen us yet,' said Peggy.

'Can't miss us,' said Nancy. 'He'll turn in any moment.'

'Rubbish,' said Captain Flint. 'He's far enough out, and he's not stopping.'

'Gone,' said John, as the cliff hid that flashing furrow and they could see nothing beyond it but empty glittering sea.

'Lucky he's in such a tearing hurry,' said Captain Flint.

'Pretty narrow squeak,' said Nancy.

'Good enough,' said Captain Flint. 'He can go to the North Pole and welcome, if his petrol holds out.'

'All the better if it doesn't,' said Roger.

'He'll drift for ever in the Polar ice, a frozen ship with frozen men, until the albatrosses pick the corpses clean,' said Dorothea.

The moment of gloom had passed.

'I'm going up to my Pict-house,' said Roger. 'I'll be able to see from up there. It's a splendid coastguard station. And we wasted it the other day. I'll watch him out of sight, and keep a look-out so that we know if he comes back.'

'Let him rip,' said Captain Flint. 'If he thinks he'll find us at sea, he's got plenty of room to go hunting for us. But go and watch if you want to. Look here, Dick, I'm not an egg-collector, but I'd like to have a squint at your birds. I'd like to know what all the fuss is about.'

'We'll all come,' said Nancy.

'Not me,' said Roger. 'I'm going up to the Pict-house. Somebody's got to be sentinel.'

CHAPTER 14

'I'VE GOT TO HAVE A HIDE'

A MIRACLE had happened. For the first time not Nancy, nor John, nor even Captain Flint was the leader of the expedition. It was Dick who knew about birds; it was Dick's discovery that had brought them back to Scrubbers' Bay, it was Dick, the humble Ship's Naturalist, for whose directions everybody was waiting . . .

Everybody but Roger, who was in a desperate hurry to be off, to climb the hill and to be alone in his Pict-house, a coastguard station, looking out over the sea. 'The old *Dactyl* will be out of sight if you don't let me get ashore quick,' he was saying.

'Oh put him ashore, somebody,' said Captain Flint. 'And bring the dinghy back. Dick, you said you'd be wanting the folding boat, didn't you?'

'What about rations?' said Roger.

'You've had breakfast,' said John.

'You don't want me to stop watching and come down again for grub,' said Roger.

'Feed the young cormorant and be quit of him,' said Nancy. 'Dick. Are you going to take the photographs right away?'

'Peggy's making his sandwiches,' said Susan.

'Here they are,' said Peggy, coming up with a paper packet and a bottle of lemonade. 'Come on, Roger. I'll put you ashore.'

'Thank goodness,' said Nancy, as the dinghy moved off towards the little bay where the *Sea Bear* had been scrubbed. Roger, complete with telescope and stores, waved cheerfully from the stern.

'Keep an eye on my Pict-house,' he called. 'I'll signal as soon as I get there.'

Nobody answered. Aboard the *Sea Bear* everybody was lending a hand in making the folding boat ready to take to the water.

The folding boat was made of wood and canvas. When not in use, its canvas sides collapsed like Captain Flint's accordion. When opened, it made a sort of coracle with pointed bow and stern, and the thwarts that fitted across it kept it from folding up again.

OPENING THE FOLDER

'It's not much use for more than one,' said Nancy. 'Two at a pinch. John and I tried and when we took Peggy as well, we nearly put the gunwales under.'

'Dick'll be all right in it by himself,' said Captain Flint. 'You won't be wanting a passenger, will you? Or not more than one?'

'No,' said Dick. 'The fewer people go near those birds the better. I'm only going because I've got to.'

Peggy came rowing back in the dinghy just as the folding boat was being lowered into the water.

'Got rid of him?' said Nancy cheerfully.

'He's nearly at the top of the hill,' said Peggy.

'He's close to our Pict-house now,' said Titty. 'There he is, just climbing on the top.'

'Hullo! He's signalling,' said Nancy. 'Awfully slow,' she added. 'You ought to have given your ship's boy a bit more practice.'

On the little mound that topped the hill Roger was standing, clear, with blue grey sky behind him. He was signalling letters by semaphore, with an interval between each one, after a bit of waving at large to get the attention of the *Sea Bear*.

'H,' said Nancy. 'E ... A ... D ... Get on with it ... I ... Heading. Go on. N ... G ... end of word ... F ... O ... R ... end of word ... A ... R ... C ... T ... I ... C ...'

Working her arms like a windmill in a gusty breeze, Nancy signalled back, 'G ... O ... O ... D ...'

Roger disappeared.

'Well, that's all right,' said Captain Flint. 'I thought it was. But it's just as well to know for certain.'

'Well done, Roger,' said Titty.

'Useful for once,' said Nancy. 'Look here. Who's going in the folding boat now?'

Everybody looked at Dick. After all, it was he who was going to use her on the loch.

'I've never tried,' said Dick.

'The sooner Dick gets the hang of it the better,' said John. 'Don't try rowing in style. Take very short strokes. If you don't you'll find yourself spinning.'

'Round and round,' said Peggy.

'And if you catch a crab, she'll capsize,' said Nancy.

'Go on down into her, Dick, and see what you can do,' said Captain Flint. 'We'll have the other boat handy to pick you up if you turn her over.'

'All aboard the dinghy first,' said Nancy. 'Who's coming?'

'We all are,' said Titty.

'Pile in then and we'll get her out of the way, and stand by to pick up Dick before he's gone under the third time.'

'Do be careful,' said Dorothea to Dick.

'Just one minute,' said Dick, and dashed below for the bird-book and his telescope.

'Please bring your big binoculars,' he said as he came up again.

'Got 'em,' said Captain Flint. 'I want to see those birds.'

'With the binoculars we might even be able to see the eggs.'

The dinghy, loaded so that there was no more than an inch or two to spare, was lying a few yards from the ship, with Nancy at the oars. The folding boat floated empty, tied to the accommodation ladder.

'We've Susan and John and Peggy and Titty and Dot and myself and old Uncle Jim Turner and all,' chanted Nancy. 'Lucky we haven't Roger as well.'

'There he is, signalling again,' said Titty.

They looked up and saw the sentinel on the top of his Pict-house, now a coastguard station.

'You wave, Titty. I daren't stand up to signal back,' said Nancy. 'What's he got to say this time ... G ... O ... N ... E ... end of word. O ... U ... T ... end of word. O ... F ... end of word. Out of sight of course.' They had the message long before Roger had finished semaphoring the letters.

'Good luck to him,' said Captain Flint.

'Not too good,' said Titty. 'He doesn't deserve it.'

Dick went gingerly down the accommodation ladder and felt for the folder with a foot ... It was rather like stepping into a floating saucer. He sat down quickly with a hand on each gunwale.

'Well done,' said Nancy. 'Better row for the place where the stream comes out. See how straight you can keep her.'

Dick, thanks to Roger's last signal, had been able to put the egg-collector clean out of his mind. He was free of that worry at least. What he had to do now was to prove first to himself and then to Captain Flint and the others, and finally, by taking his pictures, to naturalists for all time, that he had been right about the birds. To reach the island he would have to use the folding boat. To use the folding boat, he must find out how. So, for the moment, he thought about nothing but that. He put out the little short oars, dipped the blades and pulled.

The folding boat, he found, was like a saucer in more ways than one. She simply would not go straight. The faster you tried to hurry her forward the more she seemed to want to turn round. He steadied her and tried again. Again she started turning. He gave a quick pull with one oar to straighten her, and at the next stroke all but missed the water with his other oar. There was a dreadful lurch and, from the dinghy, a squeak of 'Do take care!' Dick heard that squeak, knew it was Dorothea, and did his best to smile with proper calm.

'You're doing all right,' said Nancy. 'I nearly upset her first time.'

'Mac ought to be ashamed of her,' said Captain Flint. 'There are perfectly good folding boats to be bought, but he must go and make his own. Says she's quite good for fly-fishing. I'd like to see him get hold of a salmon in her.'

'Pull salmon, pull Mac,' said Nancy. 'I bet the salmon would win.'

'It's just finding out how,' said Dick who, if he had been on dry land, would have been taking off his spectacles and giving them a wipe while thinking about it. With an oar in each hand in this little boat, he could not do that. So he tried again, taking very short strokes indeed, just dipping the oars and never giving her time to get properly spinning.

'You've got it,' said John.

'We'll go on and find the best place to land,' said Nancy. 'As near the mouth of the stream as we can.'

The dinghy went on ahead, and, as soon as it was behind him, so that he could not see it and the waiting crew all anxious to pick him from the water, Dick and the folding boat began to get on better terms with each other. That was the way, short strokes, not hard, and never let her have a chance to play tricks. He made slow but more and more steady progress towards the top of the inlet, where the little stream from the lochs above came trickling out among the stones.

The others landed, pulled up the dinghy and laid an anchor out. They turned to watch Dick struggling after them.

'How are we going to bring her to the lake . . . loch?' asked Dorothea. 'Even above the waterfall there are rocks and not enough room for rowing.'

'Portage,' said Titty.

'She doesn't weigh anything if we all lift her at once,' said Peggy.

'Here's the place, Dick. Bring her in here.'

'Not too hard. Remember she's only canvas.'

Dick brought her in. It was still early morning, and the sun had hardly begun to warm things up, but his spectacles were blurred, and he felt a trickle of sweat between his shoulder-blades.

'Sorry I was so long,' he said.

'You'll be all right when you're not in a hurry,' said Captain Flint, giving him a hand out. 'Now then. What next? Your show, Ship's Naturalist. Do you think we'll frighten your birds if we all go up to your loch together?'

'What about the boat?' said Dick.

'Don't you worry about the boat,' said John. 'We'll do that. Hadn't you better go on and see if the birds are still there?'

'Let's see you under way with that boat,' said Captain Flint. 'Easy, there, Nancy. Don't rip her up on a stone in getting her out.'

Dick, putting a hand to camera and telescope and the bulge

in his pocket that was made by the bird-book, to be sure he had them all, watched the folding boat brought ashore. John and Nancy lifted her bows, Susan and Peggy her stern.

'All right,' said Nancy. 'We'll be there as soon as you or all but.'

'Now then, Ship's Naturalist,' said Captain Flint. 'Let's make sure you haven't brought us all back here for nothing.'

'They won't have gone if they're nesting,' said Dick, and set out, climbing up at the side of the stream.

'Do you want help with the portage?' asked Titty.

'No,' said John.

'Skip along,' said Nancy.

Dorothea, after one glance at the four who were already on the move with the folding boat, was already hurrying after Captain Flint and Dick.

'Listen!' Dick stopped suddenly, as he was climbing up past the waterfall.

'Hoo ... hoo ... hooo ...'

The loch was still out of sight, but there could be no mistaking that weird, laughing cry that he had heard the day before.

'They're still there. That's them.' Dick hurried on, dodging round rocks, and clumps of heather, eager for the first glimpse of the island on the loch. Dorothea and Titty hurried after him and Captain Flint, after a backward glance to see how the others were managing the portage of the folding boat, hurried, not quite so fast, after Dorothea and Titty.

Dick looked over his shoulder to see that they were coming. The water was in sight now. He could see up to the far end of the loch. He could see the island. Where the stream ran out of the loch there was a belt of reeds. John and Nancy would be able to launch the boat in the stream, just below those reeds. That would save them from carrying it further along the shore. For one second he thought of waiting for it, but he

PORTAGE

had not yet seen the birds and so, skirting along the shore, squelching in the damp ground, he hurried on. Then, at last, he saw them, saw one of them at least, the bird whose eerie laughter he had heard, probably, shooting low above the water, and flinging high a long line of white spray as it met the surface.

He stared towards the island, but could hardly see it. When Dorothea and Titty came panting past the reed bed, he was standing, wiping his glasses with fingers that shook. 'There's the island,' he said. 'And I've seen one of the birds.'

'What's the matter?' asked Dorothea.

'Nothing,' said Dick. 'But I'd been thinking how awful it would be if they'd gone and it was all a mistake.'

'I can't see the birds,' said Titty.

'They're a long way off,' said Dick. 'I was much nearer when I saw them before.'

'Have a look through these,' said the voice of Captain Flint. 'Better make sure.'

Dick took the big binoculars and trained them on the distant island. Yes. There was the sitting bird, close to the edge of the water, and there was the other swimming a little way off.

'It's them,' said Dick. 'The one in the water's gone under ... There it is. Just come up again.'

'Let me look,' said Titty.

'That black blob,' said Captain Flint.

'But it looks just like a duck,' said Titty.

'It's not a duck,' said Dick. 'Wait till we get nearer. It's a Great Northern Diver.'

He led the way along the shore, wondering how near he could come with somebody as large and visible as Captain Flint without disturbing the birds and at the same time very much wanting to make sure that the others should see what he had seen. Presently he stopped.

'Look at them now,' he said. 'But don't let's go any nearer till they come with the boat.'

'Very like grebes,' said Dorothea, when it came to her turn with the binoculars.

'They are a sort of grebe,' said Dick.

'Let's see that drawing of yours,' said Captain Flint.

'I've brought the book itself,' said Dick, and held out the bird-book, open at the page.

'You're right, so far,' said Captain Flint. 'They can't be anything else.'

'And it's the first time they've ever been known to nest so far south,' said Dick.

'If they are nesting,' said Captain Flint.

'Here comes the boat,' said Titty.

Peggy, Susan and Nancy were in sight, hurrying along the shore of the loch, and John, in the folding boat, was just coming out from behind the reeds.

'He must keep close to the shore,' said Dick urgently.

Titty climbed up the bank, and looked up at the long ridge with the nick in the skyline where the cart track went over to the next valley and the native settlement.

'Nobody in sight,' she said.

'You forget how early it is,' said Captain Flint. 'There'll be nobody about yet.'

'It's not the people that would matter,' said Dick. 'But if the birds see a whole crowd of us and the boat . . .'

But it looked as if John had had the same idea. He was paddling the folding boat along only a few yards from the shore where it was least likely either to frighten the birds or to be seen by any natives.

'Well?' said Nancy. 'Here it is,' as John brought it in and found a place where he could step ashore.

'There they are,' said Dorothea. 'Dick was right.'

'Of course he's right,' said Nancy. 'But are those

them? They look just like any other ducks. A bit big, perhaps.'

'But they aren't ducks at all,' said Dick. 'Great Northern Divers.'

'Off you go,' said Captain Flint. 'Get your photographs and we'll be away out of this in a couple of hours.'

'I don't think I can,' said Dick.

'You try,' said Captain Flint.

Dick stepped into the folding boat, and paddled away. This was all wrong, he knew before ever he had started. Nobody could row straight up to wild birds and photograph them as if they were trees. They wouldn't wait to be photographed. But he hoped he might come near enough to the island to be sure that they were indeed nesting. On the thwart in the stern he had his camera and Captain Flint's binoculars. He was finding the folding boat not quite so unruly as when he had first tried it, but not at all easy to manage, unless he was content to go slowly. Well, the slower the better. There was one dreadful moment when he thought the shore party were trying to walk along keeping pace with him. He stopped and urgently signalled to them to keep still. They sat down. That was better. He paddled on, looking over his shoulder every few strokes, to see how far he had yet to go. Then, gingerly, he turned the folder round, and backwatered instead of pulling, so that he could keep his eyes on the birds and the island all the time.

He was still a long way from the island, though much nearer to it than he had been when he had watched from the shore, when he knew that it was not safe to go nearer.

The bird that was swimming dived and vanished. That would not have mattered, if it was fishing. But the other bird, sitting on the island shore was suddenly floundering into the water. A moment later he saw it, swimming fast, flapping with its wings, beating the water again and again, until at last it rose clear and flew with quick wing-beats, and then brought his very heart into his mouth by a wild, mournful shriek . . . 'Heuch! Heuch! Heuch!'

He stopped paddling at once. It was not safe to go an inch nearer. He took up the binoculars and trained them on the place the bird had left. He very nearly upset the folding boat by a sudden jerk. There, on the shore, was an untidy circle of broken bits of reed, and in the middle of it was something that could only be eggs.

He began paddling back to the others, anxiously watching to see the bird come splashing down again along the water, and presently go back to the nest.

'Eggs,' he said, as he brought the boat in to the shore.

'What about your photographs?' asked Captain Flint. 'Got them?'

'No,' said Dick. 'It's no good that way. I was sure it wasn't. I've got to have a hide . . .'

'Well, how long will it take you to make it?'

'It can't be done like that,' said Dick. 'I'll have to make it and get it to the island tonight, to let them get accustomed to it before I take the photographs tomorrow.'

'Another whole day,' said Captain Flint. 'You take your chance now, with the egg-collecting fellow miles away and heading for the Pole, and nobody to bother you.'

'The birds won't stay to be photographed,' said Dick.

'Photograph the eggs and be done with it.'

'It wouldn't be any good without the birds.'

'You do it properly,' said Nancy. She turned firmly to her uncle. 'He's got to get the photographs, and the *Sea Bear* won't go till he's got them. It's no good mutinying now.'

'Don't spit at me,' said Captain Flint. 'Who's the mutineer? He's going to get them. But the sooner he does it the better.'

'He's got to do it the right way,' said Nancy.

GREAT NORTHERN DIVER

'There's nothing on the island to hide him,' said John who, now that Dick had come ashore, was looking at the island through the binoculars.

'Not even a bush,' said Dorothea.

'We could disguise him as a sort of tree,' said Peggy.

'Great Gannets and Guillemots!' said Nancy. 'What's the good of disguising him as a tree when there isn't a tree for twenty miles? If his birds saw a tree suddenly sprout on their island they'd be scared out of their lives.'

'I've thought of a way,' said Dick. He was looking about on the shore for stones, found what he wanted and scraped a rough circle to stand for the island. 'There are some big rocks on the island, like this. The nest's here, and the rocks are just behind the bit of smooth shore at the water's edge. If I could hang something over the rocks and creep in behind it . . .'

'What about a sail?' said Peggy.

'He'll have to cut a hole through it for the camera,' said John.

'No cutting holes in Mac's sails,' said Captain Flint.

'Netting would be best,' said Dick. 'So that I could see out and the Divers couldn't see in.'

'Like muslin curtains in windows,' said Titty.

'It's a pity Mac took his trammel nets ashore before we sailed,' said Nancy.

'If that's the only trouble, there's plenty of marline in the locker.'

'Marline's string,' Susan explained to Dorothea.

'But how do we make it into netting?' asked Titty.

'Peggy's a dab at it,' said Nancy. 'She'll show you. We made our own hammocks.'

'It needn't be a very small mesh,' said Dick hopefully. 'If I had a big bit of netting I could take it out to the island late to-night and hang it over the rocks in a moment. Then, to-morrow, I could get ashore on the island from the other end very early and the birds would have forgotten about it by the time I was ready to take the photographs.'

'Won't they think the net itself rather funny?' said Titty.

'It won't be just plain netting,' Dick explained. 'We can fasten bits of heather on it.'

'Oh good,' said Titty. 'So they'll just think the heather's sprouted a lot in the night.'

'It's a good idea,' said Peggy.

'For natives as well as for birds,' said Titty. 'Nobody'd notice an extra patch of heather anywhere about here.'

'Right,' said Captain Flint. 'Back to the ship. Quick. Don't let's waste time talking about it.'

'What about netting needles?' said Peggy.

'Have to make them for you. What are you going to do with the boat? Leave it here?'

'There may be some of those Gaels about later,' said Titty.

'Hide it in the reeds, just in case,' said Nancy.

Nancy rowed the folding boat along to the reed-patch, and when she had worked the boat into the reeds and stepped ashore, no one could have seen the boat was there if he had not known exactly where to look.

Dick, Captain Flint and Dorothea, hurrying together, were first to come to the beach at the head of the cove. They looked back for the others and saw Susan, Peggy and Titty dropping down past the waterfall.

'Hullo,' said Captain Flint. 'Where are John and Nancy?'

'Gone exploring,' said Titty, 'up the valley to look at the deer, and to see if there are any of those Gaels.'

'It didn't look to me as if there's anybody about at all,' said Captain Flint.

'It didn't the other day,' said Titty. 'But there was, and Nancy thought they'd better make sure.'

'They won't be long,' said Susan. 'They haven't any grub

with them, and they said they'd come back when they were
hungry.'

'Idiots,' said Captain Flint. 'But we've plenty of netters
without them.'

'You know, a hide's really the only way to take pictures of
birds,' said Dick, as Captain Flint rowed the dinghy out to
the *Sea Bear*.

'Well,' said Captain Flint, 'we'll do our best to make you a
good one.'

CHAPTER 15

INTERRUPTED NETTING PARTY

No time was wasted. Captain Flint pulled the lid off a cigarbox that he had meant to use for storing feathers for troutflies, split it into three lengths, roughly shaped each length into a netting needle and then filled the cabin with blue smoke that brought tears to the eyes, as he finished the needles by burning away the unwanted wood with the tip of a poker made red-hot by Susan in the flame of a Primus stove. Peggy dug out a couple of big balls of marline from the store in the fo'c'sle. Titty, Dick and Dorothea with knife and sandpaper smoothed the edges and rounded the corners of the sides of the cigar-box, to turn them into measures (usually called meshes). As soon as the first needle and the meshes were ready, Peggy showed the others how to use them and did quite a lot of Nancy-like shivering of timbers when people made slip knots by mistake instead of the proper herring knot, which is easy to make as soon as you get into the way of it. Presently Dorothea and Titty were at work, taking turns, on the first strip of netting, hung from the starboard shrouds. Peggy herself and Dick were at work on the second, hung from the port shrouds, and when Susan and Captain Flint came up with the last of the needles they started a third strip, hung from the boom, so that Captain Flint could work at it comfortably while sitting in the cockpit.

There were a few mistakes, slip knots and missed meshes, at first, but fewer and fewer as time went on and the netters grew more and more pleased with themselves as they saw the strips of netting growing longer and the knots coming right without having to be thought about.

'There isn't really much need to hurry,' said Peggy, opening and shutting her fingers after a long turn with the needle, 'now that the *Pterodactyl*'s gone off to the Arctic.'

'But there is,' said Dick. 'There really is. I've got to take the net to the island tonight, to give the Divers time to get accustomed to it. Every minute counts really.'

'Isn't it queer?' said Titty to Dorothea. 'It's the birds who matter most, and they know nothing about it. There's the

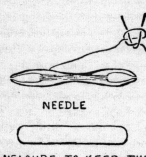

NEEDLE

MEASURE·TO·KEEP·THE
MESHES·ALL·THE·SAME
SIZE.

HERRING KNOT

NETTING

egg-collector dashing to the North Pole, and John and Nancy scouting up the valley, and you and me and Peggy and Susan and Captain Flint all working at nets, and Roger keeping a look-out, all because of the birds, and the birds themselves haven't any idea that if it had not been for them we'd be half way to the mainland by now, getting ready to give up the *Sea Bear* and go back to England in a train.'

'Why is it the birds aren't here always?' asked Peggy.

Dick's needle stopped in mid-air. 'I don't know why they come at all,' he said. 'The book says they're winter visitors.'

'But where do they go when they go away?'

'Arctic,' said Dick.

'That nasty fellow's gone in the right direction,' said Captain Flint.

'But luckily it's the wrong one,' said Dick.

'They probably want to get away from the winter round the Pole,' said Titty. 'When it gets too dark for anything up there, they come south to do a bit of fishing where the water isn't all solid ice.'

'But why didn't these ones go home again after the winter?' said Dorothea. 'Hi! Don't stop netting, Dick.'

'That's just what I don't know,' said Dick slowly, giving up his needle and mesh to Peggy who, with an eye on Susan's flashing fingers, set to work to make Dick's bit of netting catch up with the other two.

'Probably it was just an accident,' said Titty. 'The Great Northern Diver and his wife were getting ready to fly back to Iceland when something happened. He dived a bit too far and a crab or an eel grabbed his leg and hurt it. Or perhaps he hit a rock under water. Anyhow, something happened and he had to wait a bit before making the journey. And his wife wouldn't leave him. And then, when whatever it was that was wrong with him got better, the time was already pretty late, and they came slowly north to this bit of the Hebrides. Probably jolly like Iceland, too.'

'Go on,' said Dorothea. 'My turn at the netting. Go on. What happened next?'

'They saw that bit of a lake and thought they'd rest for a day or two. And then they found that island.'

'I know,' said Dorothea. 'And he said, "It's a home from home," and she said, "I don't see any Polar Bears," and he said, "Bears or no Bears there are plenty of fish," and he dived and came up with one in his beak, just to show her.'

'Yes,' said Titty, 'and they stayed on, day after day, until he began to think that it was a very long way to the Arctic and that probably all the best places there had been bagged already, and even she began to wonder if the Hebrides wasn't as good as Iceland or better.'

'He'd be like Dick,' said Dorothea, 'not wanting to think of moving if he was interested in something where he was, and she'd be like Susan at first.'

'How?' said Susan, looking up from her netting.

'Thinking of the clock,' said Dorothea, and was surprised when everybody but Susan laughed.

'Good thing somebody does think of the clock sometimes,' said Captain Flint.

'I know,' said Dorothea. 'What I mean is that at first the she-Diver would be saying, "Look here, we really ought to be getting on," but afterwards, when she saw that it really was a good place with no people, or not many, and plenty of fish, she'd begin to think that perhaps it was just as well for him not to have to make a tremendous journey before he'd fully recovered from whatever it was.'

'Anyhow,' said Titty, 'they made up their minds to stay and then she laid her eggs and they couldn't think of moving even if they'd wanted to.'

'The thing is,' said Dick, 'that if they bring up their young ones here, the young ones may come back to nest too, and their young ones after them. And that awful beast wanted to take the eggs.'

'Well, he won't get them now,' said Titty.

About the middle of the day, the netters knocked off for food. They had just had a signal from Roger up at his Picthouse.

'N ... O ... T ... H ... I ... N ... G ... end of word ... I ... N ... end of word ... S ... I ... G ... H ... T ... end of word ... C ... G ... S ...'

'C.G.S.,' said Peggy. 'That doesn't spell anything.'

'Coastguard Station,' said Titty.

'Tell him to come back,' said Susan, and Peggy stood up on deck and made the signals.

'N ... O ... end of word,' signalled Roger, and disappeared, making further orders useless.

'He's enjoying himself,' said Captain Flint.

'Well, he's got his food with him,' said Susan, looking up the creek in case John and Nancy should be in sight. 'The others haven't even a bit of chocolate. They'll just have to have something when they come back.'

'I do hope they get stalked,' said Titty. 'Nancy wouldn't believe that we were.'

'I hope they don't,' said Captain Flint. 'There's no point whatever in falling foul of the natives.'

After dinner (buttered eggs and tinned pears) netting went on again. Captain Flint, who had every excuse for it, as he had been awake all night, went suddenly to sleep in the cockpit, just after he had handed over his needle and strip of netting to Peggy. A gentle grunt and snore told the others what had happened, and his niece was going to wake him, but Dorothea stopped her in time. Everybody was feeling rather sleepy. Nobody else actually fell asleep, but there was a good deal of yawning and Captain Flint's snores, by making them laugh, probably helped to keep the others awake. He woke up when it came to his turn to net, but fell asleep instantly when his turn was over, woke again and slept again, and finally told Peggy to prod him whenever she wanted to take a rest from the netting.

Tea-time came, and there were still no signs of John and Nancy.

'You don't think they've got themselves lost?' said Susan.

'Oh no,' said Titty. 'John had his compass. I saw him looking at it when they started.'

'Old enough to take care of themselves,' grunted Captain Flint.

'They must be pretty hungry,' said Susan.

'They ought to have done their share of the netting,' said Peggy, stretching her fingers. 'If they're hungry, it serves them right.'

What was more surprising was that there were no signs of Roger, but after his mutinous 'No', even Susan did not feel inclined to climb the hill and fetch him down for tea. The six netters, by taking turns when they began to get cramp in their fingers and keeping three strips of netting going at once and all the time, had made a tremendous lot. Dick and Dorothea had been ashore in the dinghy by themselves and come back with scratched hands and a cargo of heather. All fear that they might not be able to get the netting done in time for Dick to take it to the island at dusk and set up his hide ready for next day's photographing was gone. After tea, which somehow put a stop to the yawning, they joined the three strips of netting into one, by running a length of string in and out through the meshes, and so lacing two edges together. Then they spread the whole net across the boom, so that it hung down on both sides.

Scraps of heather littered the decks and were being tied to the netting. Everybody was feeling that the work was as good as done. Everybody was in the highest spirits. They had given the slip to the egg-collector; they had brought the ship back; they knew that Dick had been right about his birds; the folding dinghy was already waiting for him, hidden in the reeds at the foot of the loch; the net was all but finished – and next day when the photographs had been taken the *Sea Bear* would be off to the mainland after a voyage that Dick's discovery would make memorable for ever.

And then the blow fell.

'We'll want another lot of heather,' said Peggy.

'I'll get some,' said Dick. 'But let's just try how it works.' He crawled under the heather-covered part of the netting.

'I can see out perfectly,' he said.

'But we can see you too,' said Dorothea.

'Of course you can see him with nothing behind him,' said Captain Flint.

Dick was already wriggling out. 'I'll get into the cockpit,' he said, 'and then you spread the netting over the top. That'll be the same as having solid rocks behind.'

It was done. The netting was hauled off the boom and laid over the cockpit. Crouched beneath it, looking up through net and scraps of heather, he could clearly see the rest of the crew standing round on the deck.

'Well,' he said. 'Can you see me now?'

There was no answer.

'Can you see me?' Dick asked again.

Again there was no answer.

He felt suddenly that something was wrong. He lifted a corner of the netting and put his head out. Standing round the cockpit, the netting party were not looking down at him but were staring out towards the sea. He heard Captain Flint say 'Damn!' under his breath. He saw the horror on Dorothea's face and Titty's, the anger on Peggy's. He scrambled out from under the netting and saw for himself what they were looking at.

Outside the headlands, off the mouth of the creek, a large motor cruiser was slowly circling round. There could be no mistaking her for anything but what she was. The *Pterodactyl*, the egg-collector's boat, had not gone to the Arctic after all. There she was, not three hundred yards away, and that figure standing by the deckhouse could be none other than Mr Jemmerling himself.

'He's seen us,' said Peggy.

'Oh, Dick!' said Dorothea.

'He's got brains, that chap,' said Captain Flint. 'He knew where he passed us at sea that day. He's gone north and then come into the coast and worked back, looking into every bay until he found us. Looks as if he's coming in.'

'If only the *Sea Bear* had guns!' said Titty.

But the *Pterodactyl*, after moving slowly across the mouth of the creek, turned again to the south.

'Perhaps he hasn't recognized us,' said Dorothea.

'He must have,' said Dick.

'Well, he's going away,' said Dorothea.

The *Pterodactyl* was hidden by the rocky spit south of the cove and, just for one moment, even Captain Flint let himself think that Dorothea was right. Then, much nearer, they heard the sound of her engines. She was close at hand although they could not see her.

'Coming into that other creek,' said Captain Flint. 'Probably knows the coast like the palm of his hand.'

Peggy was already hurrying up the shrouds to the cross-trees.

'He's coming right in,' she called down. 'I can see his beastly little mast moving. Just the other side of those rocks. I'll see the whole of him in a minute where the rocks aren't quite so high ... There he is ...' Watching her pointing finger and listening to the throb of engines, they knew, though they could not see, exactly where the *Pterodactyl* was.

'He's gone further in than we have ... He's anchoring. Going very slow.'

'Perhaps he'll hit a rock,' said Titty.

'If you'd only taken that photograph this morning,' said Captain Flint, 'we'd have been away out of this by now and he'd never have found the place.'

'Dick couldn't,' said Dorothea angrily. 'It isn't his fault.'

'He hasn't found the nest yet,' said Dick slowly. 'And there are hundreds of lochs marked on his chart. He won't know which it is unless we show him. We'd better give up and go away at once.'

'We can't without the others,' said Susan.

'I must say, I hate the idea of being done by him after all,' said Captain Flint.

'Done by him?' said Peggy from above their heads. 'We're not going to be. I wish Nancy was back, and John.'

'What surprises me,' said Captain Flint, 'is how he managed to come south along the coast without our coast-guard seeing him.'

'Why didn't Roger signal to us?' said Dorothea.

'We couldn't have done anything,' said Titty.

'He ought to have signalled anyway,' said Dorothea.

'What's that fellow doing now?' asked Captain Flint looking aloft.

'Anchoring,' said Peggy. 'Their anchor's just going down.'

'He can't do anything until he comes ashore,' said Dorothea.

'I don't know what we ought to do,' said Dick. He badly wanted to take the photographs and prove that the birds had nested. But he would rather not do that if it meant showing the egg-collector where they were. Perhaps, even if they gave up and sailed away, it was already too late. With the egg-collector so near, he would only have to hunt round one loch after another until he found them. And then he would take the eggs and kill the birds so that all chance of their coming back again year after year would be gone and there would be nothing but two stuffed birds and their blown eggs in the Jemmerling Collection to show that the Great Northern Divers had tried and failed.

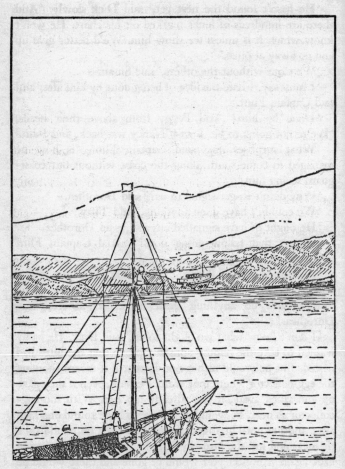

PEGGY AT THE CROSS-TREES

'It's awful having to give up,' said Dorothea. 'With the folding boat all ready and Dick's hide nearly done.'

'Could you see me through the netting?' asked Dick.

'Not a thing,' said Titty.

'The net's all right,' said Captain Flint.

'We may as well finish up the trimming of the net,' said Susan. 'But we haven't enough heather for all of it.'

'I'll get some more,' said Dick. 'But wouldn't it be safer for the birds if we just sailed away?'

'He might not come after us,' said Dorothea, 'and even if he did we couldn't stop him from coming back later on.'

'If he stays here he's only got to listen till he hears them,' said Dick

'We've only heard them make that noise once,' said Captain Flint.

'I do wish Nancy were here,' said Dorothea.

'Aloft there!' said Captain Flint. 'What are they doing now?'

'They haven't lowered their dinghy,' said Peggy from the cross-trees. 'Oh! They're putting it over now. No, they aren't. It's all ready for lowering, but they've changed their minds.'

'Dick,' said Captain Flint. 'I'm coming ashore with you . . . Just in case.'

'We can't do any harm by getting some more heather,' said Dick gloomily, 'even if we don't use it.'

'I'll tell you what,' said Dorothea. 'We could stay here on guard until he gives up and clears out.'

'Just what we can't,' said Captain Flint.

'Come on, you two,' said Susan to Titty and Dorothea. 'Let's get what's left of the heather tied on before Dick's back with a new lot.'

'Don't let's decide anything yet,' said Dorothea.

The cheerfulness of the day was gone. The *Pterodactyl* had

not, after all, been given the slip, and when Captain Flint
and Dick rowed ashore for a last lot of heather, no one could
have told whether there was deeper gloom in the dinghy or
aboard the *Sea Bear*.

CHAPTER 16

A GOOD LOOK-OUT

ROGER, as he went scrambling up the hill to the Pict-house, was very well pleased with himself, as he always was when the *Sea Bear* had been using her engine. He knew today that but for her engine (and, of course, her engineer) the *Sea Bear* would have had no chance of getting back into the cove without the *Pterodactyl* seeing where she was going. He was not in the least interested in Dick's birds but was grateful to Dick and to them for giving him such a chance of showing what the engine (and, of course, the engineer) could do. He, Roger, had beaten the *Pterodactyl* and, though the *Pterodactyl* would know nothing about it, he was looking forward to watching her steam away on a wild goose chase and to gloating as he watched. He chuckled. That was it. A Diver chase for the *Sea Bear* and she knew where to find them. The *Pterodactyl* was after Divers too, but her Divers had turned into wild geese and she was chasing them all for nothing.

He climbed as fast as he could, afraid that she would be out of sight before he came to the top. Just before he reached the Pict-house he saw her, a distant white splash moving fast across the blue sea. That was all right. He was not too late. Before climbing up the side of the mound that had been built who could tell how many thousand years ago, he looked warily beyond it to the ridge that hid Dorothea's 'castle'. There was no one moving on it. For a moment or two he watched carefully, remembering the invisible stalkers of two days ago, those dogs and the tall Gael who had sent the explorers flying down the valley. No. There was no one about. Roger scrambled up, dropped into the hollow where

195

the roof of the ancient dwelling had fallen in and became invisible unless to a hawk overhead. It was a perfect place for a coastguard station. There was even a dip in the wall on the side facing the sea so that Roger, himself hidden, could look out over the cliffs and watch the *Pterodactyl* hurrying on her fruitless journey. Roger chuckled to himself, thinking of the egg-collector and his men searching the horizon to the north of them for a sight of the *Sea Bear*'s white sails. Well, he had better let the others know. After another wary glance up at the ridge, he stood up and waved to get the attention of the *Sea Bear*'s crew.

Far below him in the nearer of the two inlets he could see his ship. They were just getting the folding boat over the side. He signalled, 'Heading for Arctic' and, through his telescope, saw Nancy's answering 'Good'.

He dropped down again into his hollow and watched the *Pterodactyl* keeping on her course to the north. Only just in time, he said to himself. In a very few minutes now she would be hidden by a headland that ran out from the coast. Gosh, what a pace she was going. Roger envied the engineer who had such engines to look after. He was almost sorry for the egg-collector. 'Cold . . . colder . . . Jolly well freezing,' he murmured, as he watched that racing white splash that was carrying the enemy in the wrong direction. 'And he's been quite warm. If he'd been half an hour sooner or we'd been half an hour later, he'd have been hot by now . . . Boiling . . . He'd have found us.' On and on went the white splash, far out at sea. 'If she doesn't turn quickly, we're safe. It doesn't matter where she goes then . . . Shetland or North Pole.' Even with the telescope it became hard to see her. More than once he lost sight of her. At last he could see her no more. She was gone.

'Good-bye,' said Roger, stood up and went to look down at the *Sea Bear*. He saw the dinghy lying beside her, full of the

crew, and somebody, Dick, climbing down into the folding
boat. He signalled 'Gone out of sight', got an answering wave
from somebody in the dinghy, and, for the moment, put the
Sea Bear out of his mind. Let them play with their birds.
He had the day before him and the Pict-house to himself.
He was not sure whether to be Primitive Man or Coast-
guard. He could be a bit of both, Coastguard, of course, if
the *Pterodactyl* had been in sight but, now that there was no
Pterodactyl to watch, he saw nothing against a morning as
Primitive Man.

In old days, as ship's boy, and even now, cruising in the
Sea Bear and rated as Engineer, he had had far too few
chances of planning his own day. There was always a captain
somewhere, or a mate, to tell him what to do next. Look at
the way the Pict-house had been wasted although it was his
own discovery. It was true that there had been some good
moments after they had left it, when they were being
followed up the valley and watched by savages they could not
see. But, if they had stayed at the Pict-house, something
even better might have happened. From the moment he had
found it, he had felt that it ought to be used. It was better,
far better, than the igloo of that winter holiday they had spent
in the lakes. In its way, it was as good as old *Speedy*, the
derelict barge in which they had found a boy living all by
himself in a creek on the East Coast. Today, Roger felt like
that boy. The Pict-house was his own.

But was it? He remembered the biscuit box he had found
hidden away in the blocked-up tunnel underneath it. He
slipped over the edge, went to the entrance, crawled in, found
the box and brought it out. Had the person who had left it
there come back and eaten that cake? He opened the box and
knew at once that somebody else had been at the Pict-house
since its discovery by the explorers two days before. The
packet of cake had gone. In its place was a slab of chocolate

in a red wrapper with gold lettering. At least the wrapper said it was chocolate. Roger slipped it out of the wrapper to make sure and unfolded the silver paper that covered it. Yes, it was chocolate all right and he did not think it could be poisoned. He broke off a small bit, but did not put it in his mouth. Two days ago, it had not been there. He could not persuade himself that he could rightly count it treasure trove and test for himself whether the chocolate was as good as the chocolate served out aboard the *Sea Bear*, of which, after all, he had a good supply in his knapsack. Bother it. Roger fitted the bit he had broken off to the rest of the chocolate, wrapped it up again, put it back in the box, took the box into the tunnel and left it where he had found it.

He crawled out once more, and almost guiltily, in spite of not having eaten the bit of chocolate, looked round. Up there, at the Pict-house, he was still alone in an empty world. There was nothing moving, even at sea. There was nothing moving on the ridge that walled out that other world of people and dogs that he had seen when they had gone up the gap to look down into the next valley. Down below him, in the cove, the *Sea Bear* lay deserted. Inland, he could see the blue hills, the slopes of rock and heather, but, though he could see some of the water of the loch, the little island and the further shore, he could see nothing of the near shore and the natural-history party. He was alone.

He climbed up once more into the hollow made by the falling in of the roof of the ancient dwelling, and settled down to be as prehistoric as he could. In a way, it was a pity Titty was not there. She would have known at once what Primitive Man would do. And Dorothea, of course, would have had a story about him ready made. Roger was not like that. Stories did not come easily to him. Being things did. Lying there in the hollow on the top of the Pict-house, he was the last of his race, or was it the first? He could have just finished building his house on the top of a hill so that he could see enemies long before they could arrive. The way in was too small for bears and easy to defend against wolves. But perhaps it would be better to be the last of his race. All, all had been eaten by wild beasts or wilder men and he, Roger, was alone, knowing that his turn would come and that any man he saw moving on the moorland or coming in a boat over the sea was an enemy. Properly, he thought, he ought to be naked. Primitive Man wore nothing but paint and perhaps a wolf-skin. But he had no skins and no paint and decided at once that too much realism would be chilly. So, though he had considered it for a moment, he did not take off his clothes. After all, his clothes were comfortable and loose and if Primitive Man had had the chance he would probably have swopped his skins for them, particularly if, instead of being snug inside his lair, he was up on the top of it keeping a sharp look-out.

A line of smoke far out at sea turned him from Primitive Man into Coastguard, and for a long time he followed with his telescope boat after boat of a fishing fleet steaming south. When the last of them had disappeared, he went to the side from which he could look down to the creek and saw that something was going on aboard the *Sea Bear*. With the telescope he could see half-a-dozen people busy on deck. They had come back from looking at those birds. He could not see what they were doing, but it looked very like work and Roger became at once an engineer on holiday. The harder the sailors were working the pleasanter it was to know that the engineer had nothing to do.

Once, late on in the morning, he saw that they were looking up towards him. He became Coastguard once more, and signalled to them to say that there was nothing in sight. He saw Peggy signalling back. What was that she was saying? Telling him to come back to the ship? Not he! He signalled an indignant 'No', and did not give them a chance of signalling again. Let them get on with their work and leave him to keep watch for all of them.

He settled himself comfortably in the hollow on the top of the Pict-house. He laid his telescope handy and unpacked his stores. It would be silly to take his grub down to the ship after carrying it up the hill. And anyhow somebody ought to be keeping watch in case the *Pterodactyl* came back. He opened his packet of sandwiches and divided it into two halves, one for dinner and one for a later meal. It was a pity he had not thought of bringing two bottles of lemonade. Looking out over the sea between mouthfuls, and being, at different moments, Prehistoric Man, Coastguard, Sentinel and Engineer taking a day off, he made a hearty meal, heartier in fact than he had intended, for, after eating the first half of his sandwiches, he ate the second, and then his chocolate, sucked an orange and, after drinking half his lemonade, decided that it was really not worth while to keep the rest.

Soon after that, he fell asleep.

There was every excuse for him. He had been up early the day before. He had slept but little during the night. He had been waked before dawn that morning. The sun was hot. He pulled a sunhat from his knapsack and put it on to shade his eyes. He had made himself very comfortable. In the hollow on the top of the Pict-house he was sheltered from the wind. He closed his eyes once or twice, opened them wide and let them close again. Without meaning to, he allowed them to stay shut, and was presently making up for all the hours he had missed from his bunk.

A sandy-haired boy in Highland dress stood in the gap where the cart track crossed the ridge and looked about him. The valley was empty. He smiled to himself, thinking of the invaders whom he and old Angus and the shepherd had kept in sight two days before and thinking of the way in which old Angus had sent them flying when he had seen them disturbing the deer. They had gone flying back to their boat and yesterday morning Angus had reported that they had cleared out, good riddance to them, and that he had watched them sail away.

Suddenly the smile left his lips. What was that, down in the near cove? A boat? He pulled a large pair of stalking glasses from a worn leather case that was slung from his shoulder. Angus was wrong. If that was not the same boat that had lain there two days ago, it was very like it. And if old Angus was wrong in thinking that they had sailed away it meant that he was right in thinking that they had been up to mischief. If those people had come back there would be work for the ghillies. This was no time of year for driving hinds. Once started, they might go far enough.

The day before yesterday when those invaders had stirred up the deer they had been chased off with no harm done, but Ian had been there when the old ghillie had told his father what had happened. Ian's father had been as angry as old Angus. He had been the more indignant on hearing that the deer-drivers had been children. 'More shame,' he had said, 'to them who set the bairns to such work.' Another time, he had ordered, there was to be no chasing off. The invaders were to be rounded up, and he had left it to young Ian and old Angus and the ghillies to make their plans and turn the hunters into the hunted. Old Angus had agreed with him. 'Lay hold of the bairns,' he had said, 'and we will soon ken who put them up to it. It is not the first time, but we will make sure it is the last.' It had been a dour and disappointed Angus who had come to the breakfast table next morning to report that the invaders had been frightened off for good and taken their boat out of the bay. It had been a disappointed Ian who had heard him.

For a moment he thought of turning back through the gap to bring the news that the boat was here again. But old Angus was away up to the head of the valley. And, of course, it might not be the same boat, though it looked very like it. He decided to go down from the ridge, climb the little hill to his private hiding-place, the grass-covered ruin that he called the broch, and from there get a nearer view of the boat. Besides, he had left a slab of chocolate in his biscuit box safe there, together with his diary, the diary that for the sake of practice he wrote in the Gaelic he talked with the ghillies, though he always talked English with his father.

Far away below, aboard the *Sea Bear*, the netting party was hard at work. Roger, the sentinel, was asleep on the top of the old Pict-house. No one looked up to catch a glimpse of the young Highlander coming nimbly down the heather-covered slope of the ridge. There were only a few moments when he could have been seen from the *Sea Bear*, for he slipped away towards the cliffs from the gap in the ridge, and came up again to the Pict-house from the seaward side of the hill. He moved silently and fast, as he and his ancestors, deer-stalkers all, had always moved, whether there was need or no. He came to the Pict-house and, close against its grass-covered wall, moved cautiously round it till he could look down the steep slope to the cove and the anchored boat.

He was sure it was the same boat. Lying on the ground beside the broch, he took his hunting-glasses from their case, and watched. There seemed to be a lot of people on deck, busy at something. Even with the hunting-glasses he could not see what they were doing, but he could see that two at least of them were those same interlopers whom he and old Angus had caught disturbing the deer. Yes, and this time there was one of the men who had put them up to it, a great fat brute lolling about on deck. Old Angus had been mistaken in thinking they had gone for good. Here they were again, and they would never have come back for nothing. They must have somebody working with them who knew the coast well, or they would never have dared to anchor where they were. Ian wondered who it could be. Somebody with land not far away. Angus had told him what they were up to. Deer are like salmon. They come back to the places where they began their lives, and by shifting the hinds in the breeding season a dishonest man could ruin his neighbour's deer-forest and improve his own without ever laying hand on a single beast. It was the very meanest of tricks. And to use children for the driving made it meaner. It would be too late for the scoundrels to do anything today and they were clearly busy with preparations of some kind. But they would not hang about longer than they needed. They would be up to their games tomorrow. Well, tomorrow, he and Angus and the ghillies would be ready for them.

The old Pict-house had been Ian's private hiding-place and look-out ever since he had been a very small boy. He worked round it now to the square entrance of the tunnel that had once led into the room where the ancient Picts had lived. He crawled in and brought out the tin box. He opened it and took out the packet of chocolate and his diary. There were several things to enter in that diary . . . the invasion of the valley by people who were using children to get the deer on the move . . . chasing them off . . . the departure of their boat . . . and now his own discovery that the boat, after sailing away, no doubt to lull suspicion, had come back and was even now lurking in the cove. The Gaelic words came easily to his pencil and he wrote them down, and put the diary back in the box, thinking of the next entry that should tell of the triumphant rounding up of the whole gang.

Then, sitting with his back against the wall of the Pict-house, he opened the packet of chocolate. Odd. It looked as if it had been opened before, but he did not remember opening it. Still odder. A bit had been broken off one corner and fitted back again, and he did, clearly, remember feeling the chocolate through its paper before he put it away and finding that he had not cracked it as he thought he had, when hurrying downhill he had slipped, and brought himself up hard against a rock. He must have been mistaken. Anyhow, the chocolate had come to no harm, and sitting there in the sunshine, where the ground below him hid all but the top of his head and his eyes from the boat he was watching, Ian ate it, thinking over how many ghillies would be needed to make sure that none of the invaders should get away if they came after the deer tomorrow.

He had finished the chocolate, folded up the paper and put it away in the deerskin sporran that served him for a pocket, when he was startled by a small noise close above him. It was not a sigh. It was not exactly a grunt. He listened. There it was again. Could it be a hare? Ian crept round the Pict-house till he could safely stand up without being seen from the cove. Very slowly, inch by inch, he climbed up the side. Slowly, slowly he raised his head till he could see over the rim made by the old walls into the sunken place in the middle. A boy, smaller than himself, was lying asleep. His mouth was just open. Again Ian heard that gentle breathing noise. Ian knew that boy by sight. He had been one of those he had seen that other day, striking stone on stone to stir the deer and make them show themselves.

Ian's second thoughts came just in time to stop him from waking the trespasser with an indignant shout. If he were to wake that boy there and then and send him back to his boat with a flea in his ear, he would merely be warning the invaders. He waited, perfectly still but very angry. A stranger in the place that had always been his own and no one else's. Making himself at home too. Ian noted the empty lemonade bottle, the sucked orange, the scout-knife that had been used to cut a hole in it, the paper that had held sandwiches tucked loosely into the open pocket of the knapsack so as not to be blown away. This was no island boy either. Clever of him, whoever was behind the plan of shifting the deer, to use boys from elsewhere and to bring them by sea, so that there would be no hope of tracing them once they had done their work and gone. He saw the telescope lying close to the boy's hand. He had been using the broch for a look-out post too, just as Ian had used it ever since he could remember. Lying there, where Ian himself had so often lain, he could look out to sea. What was he watching for? Ian turned his head. Two fishing smacks. The smoke of a steamer on the horizon. He looked slowly round. What was that? A white motor yacht nosing along the coast from the north. Some rich man from Glasgow, showing his guests the beauties of the Hebrides. Ian suddenly stiffened.

What was it his father, the old laird, had said when Angus had told him that the interlopers he had chased off had landed from a small sailing yacht? 'If they're up to real mischief there'll be more of them, and they'll want something bigger than that to bring them and to take them away if they mean not to be seen by someone on the roads.' What if that motor yacht were bringing the rest of the party? That would explain why it was nosing so close along the coast. It was looking for them. That would explain what this boy was doing on Ian's private broch. He had been sent to watch for them and to signal to them where to come in. Ian grinned. Not much of a look-out, he thought, looking at the sleeping Roger. And if that motor yacht was bringing the rest of the scoundrels, why, so much the better. 'Don't chase them off,' his father had said. 'Round them up and we'll settle this deer-shifting business for good.'

He was thankful now that he had not waked Roger with an angry shout and asked him what he had to say for himself. Much better to let him sleep. Ian decided to slip quietly away to let them know at home of what was happening. But he took another look at Roger, sleeping there never dreaming that an enemy was watching him. Ian felt the pride of the successful stalker. That boy was at his mercy and did not know it. Let him sleep. Yes. But when he should wake . . . Ian grinned. He crawled silently over the rim into the hollow, and set about his work. The lemonade bottle first. Then the telescope. The knapsack. That would puzzle him. He took the sandwich paper, opened it slowly so that it should not crackle, dug in his sporran for a stump of pencil and wrote. He grinned again, took the boy's scout-knife and skewered the paper to the ground just above the sleeper's head. He listened a moment to his victim's even breathing. Then, moving carefully backwards, he slipped over the edge of the broch and was gone.

The afternoon crept on. Roger, tired out after the last two days and nights, scarcely stirred. He was waked at last by a hoodie crow which, seeing something on the top of the broch, swooped down and, not so careful as the stalking Ian, loosed a wild squawk as it flapped past only a foot or two above the sleeper.

Roger opened his eyes, stretched, yawned, sat up suddenly and remembered where he was. His hand groped for his telescope and could not find it. Puzzled, he saw it standing on its end, like a tiny lighthouse against the sky, on the edge of the hollow. Surely he had not left it there. Then, to the right of it, he saw his empty lemonade bottle with a small blue flower sticking out of it that he knew he had not picked. His knapsack had turned itself completely inside out, and was arranged like a punctured football at his feet. Gosh! He

THE SLEEPING BEAUTY

jumped to his feet and saw something else. Pinned by his own knife to the ground just above where he had been resting was the sandwich paper, with large black letters scrawled across it. Roger grinned, not too happily. It is never pleasant for a coastguard or a sentinel to find himself labelled as

'THE SLEEPING BEAUTY'

'The beasts!' he said to himself. 'The horrid beasts! They might have waked me. It must have been tea-time long ago.'

He put his knapsack right, gathered up his knife and telescope, angrily scrumpled the sandwich paper and, obeying the ancient rule, never to leave a scrap of litter, pushed it into the knapsack with the empty lemonade bottle, debated what to do with the orange skin and, seeing no rabbit hole, put it in with the sandwich paper. Then he looked down from the top of the Pict-house to Scrubbers' Bay. He saw the *Sea Bear* and, in the same moment, saw something else that made him hot to the tips of his ears. Beyond the *Sea Bear*, just on the other side of the rocky spit, a second boat was lying, a motor yacht, white, with a large deckhouse. He had no need to use the telescope to know that it was the *Pterodactyl*.

Instantly he knew what had happened. He had seen her pass out of sight to the northward. She must have steamed north until she had gone beyond the place where she had met the *Sea Bear* three days before. Then she had turned and followed the coast south again, looking into every bay until she had seen the old pilot cutter lying at anchor. They had not given her the slip after all. And who could tell how long the *Pterodactyl* had been there? Or how much the egg-collector had seen? And he, Roger, had been the look-out and had slept and never warned them that the enemy was coming back. The rest of the crew had come to look for their sentinel and, instead of waking him, had scornfully let him

sleep to wake at last with that label above his head. 'Beasts!
Beasts!' said Roger. His shame turned into anger not at
himself but at the others. For one moment he thought of
never going back at all. Then, clenching his teeth, he jumped
from the top of the Pict-house, landed heavily and set off
down the steep slopes to the cove.

CHAPTER 17

ENEMIES AFLOAT *AND* ASHORE

ROGER came down the rocks into the little bay where the *Sea Bear* had been scrubbed two days before. He looked at her lying quietly at anchor in the creek and saw that no dinghy was lying astern of her. Somebody must be ashore. He wondered who. He saw Peggy up aloft, sitting on the cross-trees, with her back towards him and guessed that she must be looking at the *Pterodactyl*. From up there she would be able to see across the lower part of the rocky promontory that divided the inlet. Some of the others were on deck, Susan, Ditty, Dorothea. He could not see Dick, Nancy, John or Captain Flint. Then he saw the dinghy, pulled up the beach at the head of the cove where the stream came down into the salt water. Somebody, he thought, must have landed to get a nearer view of the *Pterodactyl*. Oh, why had he fallen asleep and let her come back without giving them a warning? Roger did not hail his ship. He was not going to ask to be taken aboard when they had found him sleeping and left him to wake with that label at his head. He sat on his heels on the shore, hating everybody.

Aboard the *Sea Bear* nobody noticed him. Peggy, up the mast, looked down from time to time and the others looked up at her from whatever it was they were doing, but not one of them looked at the waiting Roger. He thought they were not looking on purpose to make him feel that he was in disgrace.

He was on the point of stumping away inland again by himself when he saw Dick come down to the dinghy and busy himself with the stowage of some sort of cargo. Then he saw

Captain Flint coming down the rocks on the far side of the cove and knew that he must have been looking at the enemy. Both of them were putting something into the dinghy. They had her afloat. They had pushed off from the shore. Dick was sitting in the stern and Captain Flint was rowing towards the *Sea Bear*. The dinghy was nearing the *Sea Bear* when Roger saw Dick pointing towards him. Captain Flint looked over his shoulder and changed course. In another few minutes the dinghy grounded at Roger's feet.

'Hop in,' said Captain Flint. 'You're a good look-out. Why didn't you let us know she was coming?'

'I saw her go right out of sight,' said Roger. 'It wasn't until long after that I fell asleep. I didn't do it on purpose.'

'All right,' said Captain Flint. 'Cheer up. There's no harm done. Tell you the truth, I've been to sleep myself.'

Dick, very gloomy, said nothing.

The dinghy was half full of heather. Roger did not ask what for.

Dorothea grabbed the painter which Roger threw grimly aboard as the dinghy came alongside.

'Peggy says he hasn't landed,' she said.

'He hasn't,' said Captain Flint. 'And I don't think he will tonight. Too late. Besides a chap like that thinks that everybody else is like himself. He probably thought Dick would go straight back and take the eggs. That idea will be knocked out now because we're still here, and if we'd got the eggs we'd have gone. His next idea will be that since we haven't got the eggs yet we'll be after them tomorrow, and he'll be trusting to us to show him the way.'

'We ought to sail away and then he'll come after us and leave them alone,' said Dick.

'He won't do that unless he thinks we've got the eggs in the ship with us,' said Captain Flint.

'You've got a grand lot of heather,' said Dorothea. 'I'm

sure it's going to be all right, Dick. I'm sure it is, in spite of everything.'

Dick and Captain Flint began passing up armfuls of heather. Roger climbed aboard without a word.

'I say, Roger,' said Titty, 'didn't you see him coming?'

'You know I didn't,' flared Roger. 'I think you're all beasts, putting that notice. It was a beastly thing to do.'

'What *do* you mean?' said Susan.

'What notice?' asked Titty.

'What's all this?' asked Captain Flint, as he handed up a great bundle of heather to Dorothea.

'I don't care what you say,' said Roger. 'It was a beastly thing to do.'

'But what have we done?' said Susan.

'Coming up to my Pict-house and putting that notice and going away again just because I couldn't help falling asleep. I don't believe I was asleep for very long anyway.'

'But we've never been near the Pict-house,' said Titty. 'We came straight back here from looking at the birds and we've been working ever since.'

'Well, if you didn't,' said Roger. 'I know who did. Where's Nancy?' he demanded. 'John wouldn't have done it.'

'Done what?' asked Captain Flint.

'She knows what she did,' said Roger.

'Ahoy . . . oy!'

Everybody looked round.

'There she is,' said Susan, 'and John, just coming down to the shore. Who's going to fetch them?'

'I'm going,' said Captain Flint, who was still in the dinghy. 'Out you get, Dick.'

Dick climbed aboard and looked glumly at the long net that was hanging below the boom, one end of it still plain netting, the rest of it decorated with tied-on sprigs of heather.

'We'll soon have it done,' said Dorothea.

'It won't be safe to use it,' said Dick.

Roger looked at it, wondered what it was for, did not ask and stood at the top of the ladder, waiting for Nancy.

'Jiminy!' Nancy was saying as Captain Flint brought the dinghy alongside. 'We'll just have to fend him off. It makes things a bit more difficult that's all. I say, Susan, we're starving. Just let me get my teeth into a bit of pemmican. Get out of the way, Roger. How can I come aboard with you standing there?'

Roger, red in the face, glared at Nancy. 'I think you're a perfect beast,' he said.

'Born that way,' said Nancy cheerfully. 'What have I done now?'

'You jolly well know,' said Roger.

'I don't.'

'What you did when you came to my Pict-house.'

'But I've never been to your Pict-house in my life,' said Nancy. 'I was hard at work scrubbing the day you people went off exploring.'

'Today, I mean,' said Roger.

'Don't be an idiot, Roger,' said John. 'We've never been anywhere near you. We've been right up to the hills at the end of the valley, and, I say, Titty, we saw one of your stalkers, a keeper or something. He yelled at us like anything.'

Roger's eyes opened wider. 'Gosh!' he said. 'But it couldn't be one of them. It was in English. Whoever wrote it can't have been a Gael.'

'Wrote what?'

'Get on,' said Captain Flint. 'Let me come aboard. Now then, let's hear all about it.'

'I couldn't help going to sleep,' said Roger.

'Oh, never mind that,' said Captain Flint. 'It made no difference. We couldn't have stopped her coming in.'

'We saw her when she was nosing about outside,' said Titty.

'Go on, Roger,' said Nancy. 'Who wrote what? What did he write? Where?'

'Well, if you didn't do it, it was somebody else,' said Roger. 'When I woke up, some beast had been there. My knapsack was inside out. Somebody'd put a flower in the lemonade bottle. My telescope wasn't where I'd left it. And I'd folded up the sandwich paper and put it away and somebody'd taken it and spread it out and written on it and stuck my knife into it to keep it from being blown away.'

'Where was it?' asked John.

'Just above my head,' said Roger.

'What was written on it?'

'A message?' asked Titty.

'Nothing like that,' said Roger.

'Well, what was it?' said Nancy, impatiently.

'Just something meant to be beastly.'

'But what?'

'Where is it?' asked Titty. 'It may be a secret message.'

'Code,' said Dorothea.

Roger had not thought of that. He pulled the scrumpled up paper out of his knapsack and spread it out again. Even in that grim moment, when they all knew that the *Pterodactyl* had followed them, found them and was lying just on the other side of the rocks, the sight of the three words written on the paper made everybody laugh but Roger.

'I don't think it's code,' said Captain Flint. 'Clear, to me.'

'It's serious all the same,' said Nancy. 'You didn't hear anybody or see anybody?'

'No,' said Roger.

'It must have been one of the people who stalked us,' said Titty.

'But they were Gaels,' said Roger.

'The young chieftain himself,' said Dorothea. 'He'd know English as well as Gaelic.'

'The natives are not friendly,' said Nancy. 'You should have heard the one who shouted at us.'

'What are you laughing about?' Peggy called down from the cross-trees.

'We aren't laughing,' said Nancy. 'It's going to be a lot harder than we thought. Enemies afloat *and* ashore. I say, come down. I'm going up to have a look. You come down and do your job. We've had nothing to eat since breakfast.'

'Supper in half an hour,' said Susan. 'You others, get on with the net. We may as well finish it anyhow, even if Dick can't use it.'

'Can't use it?' said Nancy, as she started up the ratlines. 'Who said he couldn't? The *Sea Bear*'s not going to be beaten by a miserable motor boat.'

'I must say, I don't like the idea of being done by that chap,' said Captain Flint.

'We aren't going to be,' said Nancy from above his head. 'You leave it to me.'

Dorothea and Titty were already hard at work, tying bits of heather on the part of the netting that had not yet been decorated. John and Captain Flint joined them. The two cooks went below.

'Come on, Roger,' said Titty.

'But what's it for?' asked Roger who, while still boiling with rage against the writer of that label, no longer thought that one of the *Sea Bear*'s crew was to blame for it. They told him and he set to work with the others, after trying for himself how good a hide it made.

'But it's going to be much more difficult now,' said Dick. 'We've got to get it there without being seen. We've got to hide from people as well as from birds.'

215

'Hiding the hide,' said Roger, and Titty knew that Roger was feeling better.

'Once you get it there nobody'll know what it is, even through glasses,' said Captain Flint.

'It's getting it there,' said Dick. 'If those birds are frightened they'll start screaming and tell him just where they are.'

'You needn't go near them till it's nearly dark.'

'It doesn't get half dark enough,' said Dick. 'And anyway I've got to get the net to the island while there's light enough to see what I'm doing.'

'You'll manage it,' said Dorothea.

Somehow, with the return of Nancy the gloom that had settled on the *Sea Bear* had lifted. Perhaps Dick alone, after his talk with the egg-collector, understood quite how awful was the danger that threatened the Great Northern Divers and their eggs. For all the others, the presence of the *Pterodactyl* meant difficulty, but difficulty that they would find a way to overcome. One after another, after Nancy came down, champing for her supper, they climbed to the crosstrees, and looked across at the big motor boat lying beyond the rocks. There she lay, the enemy, in full view, and whatever happened, they did not mean to be defeated.

At supper, down in the cabin, there was a council of war.

Nancy summed up. 'It's like this,' she said. 'There are two lots of enemies, not one. Dick's got to take his photographs without being seen by the old Dactyl. And he's got to do it without being seen by the natives. If the natives start yelling like they did at John and me, they'll frighten the birds and he won't have a chance.'

'It's worse than that,' said Dick. 'If the Gaels see me going to the island they'll start shouting, and that'll tell the egg-collector just where to look.' He paused a moment as a new thought came into his worried head. 'Look here,' he said. 'There's something else. If the natives see what I'm doing, the egg-collector's only got to wait till we've gone. Then he'll ask them. They'll take his money and show him where the nest is and we won't be able to do anything about it.'

'Great Auks for ever!' exclaimed Nancy. 'Well done, Professor. Of course that's what we'll do. We've got to use one lot of enemies against the other. Simple. We've got to find a way of making those Gaels do all their shouting in the wrong place.'

'But if they see me.'

'They mustn't,' said Nancy, 'and they shan't. Look here, Titty. About that stalking the other day. Let's hear exactly what happened.'

Titty, Roger and Dorothea, interrupting each other, told once again the story of the explorers and how they had felt they were being watched but could see nobody watching them, and how, at last, far up the valley, the stalkers had shown themselves, with their dogs, and how, with shouts in what could only be Gaelic, a foreign language anyhow, they had sent the explorers hurrying back to the safety of their ship. This time, now that John and Nancy had themselves been shouted at, the able seamen had an audience that was ready to believe. It made all the difference to the telling of the story.

'What we've got to do,' said Nancy, 'is to get them stalking again.'

'We don't want trouble with natives,' said Captain Flint. 'What sort of people are they?'

'There's a young chieftain,' said Dorothea.

'And a huge old giant with a grey beard,' said Titty.

'You saw him yourself,' said Roger. 'The dogmudgeon who wouldn't wave back when we waved to him as we sailed away.'

'And there were others,' said Dorothea. 'All savage Gaels shouting Gaelic war cries on their native hills.'

After supper, John went up to the cross-trees and reported that the *Pterodactyl*'s dinghy was still in the davits. Nobody was showing on deck. Nobody had gone ashore.

'Lying low,' said Nancy. 'All the better.'

'But what about the Gaels?' said Dick, coming on deck after doing his share in the washing up.

'They won't be out so late,' said John. 'And once we get to the loch, that shore shelves so that you can't see the ridge when you're down by the water. The only danger from that side is when you're rowing out to the island. It'll be nearly dark, and tomorrow you'll have to be there before people get up.'

With many hands at work, the net was soon ready. They spread it flat, folded it and rolled it up for easy carrying, with a rope round it to keep it from coming undone. With the heather on it, it made a big bundle, but, of course, weighed very little more than the string that had gone to its making.

'What about starting?' said Susan. 'Nobody's had much sleep except Captain Flint . . . and Roger.'

'Susan!' said Roger angrily.

'Never you mind, Roger,' said Captain Flint. 'Susan's yawning herself. She's envious of us, that's all.'

'Not yet,' said Dick. 'I ought to go as late as possible, so long as it's just light enough to see.'

'You can't go now, anyhow,' exclaimed Nancy. 'Don't all turn round at once. There's someone coming down to talk to us.'

The sun was dropping behind the hills, but high up by Roger's Pict-house two figures had shown for a moment on the skyline. They were now coming down the slopes above the cove.

'One's the dogmudgeon,' said Roger.

'I do believe the other's the young chieftain,' said Dorothea.

'It's a boy,' said Captain Flint. 'Um, I wonder if he's Roger's ingenious friend. That message didn't sound quite like a ghillie.'

'I'm going ashore,' said Roger. 'I want to talk to him.' He jumped up and was going to unfasten the dinghy's painter that was made fast astern.

'No,' said Nancy. 'Sit tight. They're coming here. Wait and see what happens.'

But the tall old dogmudgeon and the boy in his Highland dress were not at the moment interested in the *Sea Bear*. They were coming down the slopes, but moving sideways as they came. The crew of the *Sea Bear* lost sight of them, saw them again, nearer the head of the cove. They disappeared once more.

'They're going to the loch,' said Dick.

'Of course they aren't,' said Dorothea, 'or they wouldn't have come by the Pict-house. They'd have gone straight down on the other side of the Hump.'

Peggy was at the masthead now.

'Lights in the *Pterodactyl*'s cucumber frame,' she reported, and a moment later, they saw her signalling quietly with one hand.

She had caught sight of the tall Gael and the boy. Presently the others saw them.

'They must have crossed the stream,' said John.

'They're going to talk to the egg-collector,' said Dick.

'Allies already,' said Dorothea.

From the *Sea Bear*, the watchers saw the boy and the dogmudgeon climbing among the rocks and heather of Low Ridge.

'What are they waiting for?' said Titty.

The two figures were on the top of the ridge, looking down towards the anchored motor boat. They stood there a minute or two, and then turned back the way they had come.

'Funny to come all that way and not hail him in the end,' said Nancy.

'They can't be allies,' said Dorothea.

'Don't talk too loud,' said Nancy. 'You know how sound carries over water.'

The sun had gone down, leaving a golden glow above the distant hills. It was already hard to see the man and the boy against the slopes of the hill below the Pict-house, but more than once somebody saw something moving, and just for a second, as they passed the Pict-house, the two figures showed black against the sky.

'They're going back to the castle,' said Dorothea.

'Very rum,' said Captain Flint. 'But it's the other boat they came to see. They aren't interested in us.'

'They've seen us already,' said Titty.

'I wish you'd let me go ashore,' said Roger. 'If it was that boy . . .'

'He's bigger than you,' said John.

'I don't care,' said Roger. 'I want to know why he did it.'

'Perhaps he didn't,' said Susan.

'Well, who did?' said Roger.

'You ready to start?' said Captain Flint to Dick.

'Give them time to get home first,' said Nancy.

Half an hour passed. The light in the sky had faded. The shore looked dark in the dusk.

'Now,' said Nancy. 'Now's your chance. Off with you. Gaels in bed, Dactyls ditto. We'll keep watch all the time and give you a blare on the foghorn if they come ashore. They can't until they put their dinghy over. Look here. If John's going with Dick, I'll go with them and watch the *Dactyl*

220

from those rocks. I'll borrow Susan's whistle. No I won't. If the *Dactyl* launches her dinghy, I'll do an owl-call, and then the *Sea Bear* can loose a blare on the foghorn, so that Dick and John'll know it isn't safe.'

'It's all right, Dick,' said Dorothea, 'you can't do any harm by putting up your hide tonight, even if it isn't safe to use it tomorrow. No one will ever notice it if we have to leave it behind.'

'It'll be too dark if we don't go now,' said Dick, his mind made up.

John, without a word, had already brought the dinghy to the ladder, and gone down into it. Dick followed. The rolled up net was lowered in and John made ready to row, with a leg on each side of the bundle. Nancy went down with the painter.

'You ought to be in the stern,' said John, 'but never mind now.'

'Good luck,' said Dorothea.

The dinghy slipped quietly away towards the mouth of the stream.

NIGHT VISIT TO THE ISLAND

THE glow in the sky was fading as Nancy stepped ashore beside the stream, held the stem of the dinghy for a moment and then sent it afloat again, so that John and Dick could land on the other side without risking a tumble in wading across with the net.

'A very gentle owl-call when you come back,' she whispered. 'I'll be listening.'

John backwatered and then brought the dinghy in again. He and Dick landed without a sound. Carefully they pulled the dinghy up and laid out the little anchor. John swung the bundle of netting over his shoulder, holding it by the end of the rope that tied it. In the dusk, on the other side of the stream, Nancy gave them a silent wave of the hand. They lost sight of her at once as she left the stream and began to climb up among the rocks to a point from which she could look down on the enemy.

It was still light enough for them to follow without much difficulty the track they had found in the morning, leading up through heather and rocks past the waterfall and so to the foot of the loch where the folding boat lay waiting for them hidden in the reeds. It was dark enough for Dick to fall headlong over a low clump of heather, lose his spectacles and have a hard time in finding them again. He was much encouraged.

'Got them?' asked John.

'Yes,' said Dick. 'I say, I do really think it's too dark for anybody to see us from far away.'

'Of course they can't,' said John. 'And there probably isn't anybody to look.'

Dick, whenever he could safely lift his eyes from the narrow deer-track they were following, glanced up at the high ridge of the Northern Rockies that hid Dorothea's 'castle' and the cottages of the Gaels. It might have been cut in cardboard and pasted on the sky. He could see the notch in it, where he knew the road went over to the inhabited country on the other side.

'He'd have to have eyes that could see in the dark,' he said.

'There's nothing for anybody to see,' said John.

Dick remembered that an even worse danger lay behind Low Ridge on the other side of the valley, but he knew that Nancy was there and that if anyone came ashore from the *Pterodactyl*, Nancy would signal to the *Sea Bear* and the *Sea Bear*'s foghorn, blaring into the night, would warn him that it was not safe to row out to the island. It was all right. All he had to worry about was to set up the hide without frightening the birds, and to get back to the *Sea Bear* as quickly as he could.

They came to the shore of the loch, skirted round the reed-bed where the folding boat was hidden and found that the shelving bank above them shut out the Northern Rockies altogether, and gave them a skyline only a few yards from their heads.

'I thought so,' said John. 'Nothing to worry about. It's only when we go out to the island that those Gaels have a chance of seeing us. You stay here with the net while I get the folder out of the reeds.'

Dick crouched on his heels by the bundle of netting, looking out over the steely rippled waters of the loch at the dim further shore. He fingered the netting. Whatever happened he must not get into a mess in unfolding it, when the time came to drape it over the rocks and make his hide. What if the rocks were too far apart? What if they were too close together to leave room for him to lurk between them?

He heard a rustle of reeds and saw the dark shape of the folding boat moving out. John rowed her along a few yards off the shore.

'John,' said Dick quietly.

'All right. I see you.'

John brought the boat in stern first. Dick swung the netting aboard, grabbed both gunwales and scrambled in.

'It's almost as if it wanted to upset you,' he said.

'Lucky there's a bit of wind,' said John.

'Why?'

'In smooth water our ripples would run right across the lake. Anybody might notice them, even if he didn't see us. She fairly wallowed just then.'

'And it isn't only people,' said Dick. 'The ripples would tell the birds there was somebody about.'

'Won't the birds be asleep by now?'

'Listen,' said Dick.

'Ducks,' said John.

'They're up at the top end,' said Dick. 'They started talking just after we got here. But it's only talk, not fright.'

They were moving, with quick short strokes, a few yards out from the shadowy shore. Suddenly, Dick's heart all but stopped beating. There was a quick, hurried splashing in the water of a little bay, the click of stones and then the fading sound of galloping hoofs on soft peat.

'Only deer,' said John. 'Gosh! Just for a moment I thought it was somebody fishing in the dark.'

'They must have come down to drink,' said Dick, and wished his teeth would not chatter. It was cool on the water but not cold enough for that.

'We're all right so far,' said John.

A curlew whistled high overhead and Dick tried and

failed to see him swinging across the valley against the dark sky. The ducks were silent for a minute and then began talking to each other again. Staring out across the water, Dick watched the low, dark line of the island.

'Don't turn out yet,' he said. 'We ought to go a bit past it and then go out, so as to come to it from the other end without the birds seeing us.'

'Wonder what it'll be like landing.'

'I saw some reeds at the other end.'

'May be squishy,' said John. 'Better than rocks, anyway, with the folder. We'd look fools if we tore a hole in the canvas.'

Dick had not thought of that. Nothing could be worse than to tear a hole in the bottom of the boat so that they would have to stay on the island until next morning's sunlight showed them to all the world. But, if John had the danger in mind, it was all right. He thought of something else.

'We'll have to go in very gently,' he said, 'however soft it is . . . because of the birds.'

What would those Divers do? Coots, he knew from watching them on the Norfolk Broads, might leave their nests if people came near but very soon would go back. Grebes, too, never went far away. But these big, ocean-going birds, wild and shy . . . who knew what they would do? What if they deserted altogether? Almost he wished he had not come. But with the *Sea Bear* coming back on purpose, and the netting made, and the whole crew counting on him, he could not give up now. And a new fact in natural history has simply got to be proved. Even the birds would understand that if it could be explained to them. He wished it was possible to explain to them and to tell them that he meant to disturb them as little as possible.

Away to the left the dark line of the island broke the wide sheet of steely ripples. The boat had already passed it.

Nothing had happened to show that they had been noticed by the Divers. A new danger lay ahead. He did not want to go near enough to the head of the lake to change the quiet easy chattering of those ducks into the hurried flutter and splash of rising birds that would set everything within hearing on the alert.

'Now,' he whispered.

John held his right and took a gentle stroke with his left. The folding boat swung round till it was heading straight out into the loch. John steadied it, and rowing as quietly as he could, pulled for the end of the island.

'We're in full view,' he said, as the boat moved out from under the shelter of the bank, and he saw again the long line of the Rockies, black against the sky. 'But there's nobody to see.'

'We mustn't talk,' Dick whispered.

It was not human beings that mattered now. What worried Dick was the Divers. Were they both at the nest with the eggs? Or was one on the nest and the other, perhaps, keeping guard at the very end of the island where they were going to land? With every moment he was expecting to hear an angry, frightened cry of warning.

There was none, only, high overhead, a long swaying whistle, like a call out of another world.

'Curlew again,' whispered Dick.

John rowed on. Beyond him, moving against the sky, Dick saw waving reeds.

'Very near,' he whispered.

John glanced over his shoulder, stopped rowing, stooped and took off his shoes and stockings. Dick fumbled with his own.

'Keep yours on,' whispered John. 'You'll want them ashore.'

Dick waited, listening. Were both birds asleep? It seemed almost too good to be true.

John was rowing again, just paddling. Reed-tops showed on either hand. There was a thin noise of reeds against the boat. He was feeling for the bottom with an oar. He was stepping over the side. Dick, with a hand on each gunwale, knew that she was aground. The boat lurched. She was pulled suddenly forward.

'Firm enough,' whispered John. 'Come on. Step out over the bows. I'll bring the netting for you.'

'Keep it just as it is,' whispered Dick, 'or I won't be able to spread it first time.'

He was ashore. John, standing in the water among the reeds, bent over the boat, lifted the bundle of netting, waded out with only a single splash, that might have been made by a frog or a water rat, and put the netting into Dick's waiting arms. There was still not a hint that they were not alone on the island and that those two great birds were less than thirty yards away.

'Shall I come too?'

'No,' whispered Dick. 'Better only one.'

'Right.'

Dick turned . . . Had he, after all, left it too late to see what he was doing? No. It was nothing like so dark as it would have been in the south at this time of night. He could see the tufts of rank grass at his feet, and white stones, and, towards the middle of the island, big rocks, like sleeping cows, or walruses. Dick was impatient with himself at the thought. What mattered was not what they looked like but exactly how they were placed. If there was no room for him to hide within photographing distance of the nest, he might just as well have never come at all.

He moved slowly forward, putting his feet down carefully,

much bothered by his big bundle of netting. Those pale rocks ahead of him seemed to stretch clean across. He looked for a way through them and found it. He rested the bundle of netting on one of them and waited, listening. Were the Divers asleep or not? On an island like this, in the middle of a lonely bit of water, far from houses, there was nothing for them to fear, and he knew that he and John had, so far, made no noise.

He crept on. He was in the middle of the island now. Some of the rocks were already behind him, those walruses. The ones that mattered were close in front. This big one must be the rock that, when looking from the shore of the loch, he had thought would make a background to his hide. The other two must be just beyond it. He could see the tops of them, and, yes, there was a dark space between them. Crouched in there, he would be about a dozen feet from the nest on the flat grassy shore between the rocks and the water.

Only another yard. And then, at the very worst moment, Dick stubbed his toe against a stone. He did not notice the pain. That was nothing. He was wearing sandshoes and the blow of his toe against the stone had made no noise. But, by bad luck, the stone he had kicked against had been almost touching another. There had been a click of stone on stone, and that small noise had been enough and more than enough. Something was moving on the shore beyond the rocks. There was a splash. One of the Divers had flopped to the water's edge and launched itself. Dick, clenching his teeth, listened for a second splash . . . for the beating of wings on water as the bird rose . . . for the wild 'Hoo . . . Hoo . . .' that would tell everyone within hearing that the Divers were awake. He waited, listening for sounds that never came. There was no noise at all but the gentle ripple on the shore.

At last Dick moved again. Waiting was useless, now that one of the birds was gone. The other must know that he was there, and, peering into the dusk, Dick thought that he could see it, a dark lump on the shore just where he knew the nest must be. Sitting on the eggs, probably, and listening, listening, just as he was listening himself. The best he could do now was to be gone as soon as possible. But, somehow or other, he had to get that net in place.

He wished he could have used a torch. He wished there was more light in the sky. He was afraid there was too much. But if there had been less he could have done nothing. He had been right about those rocks. There was room to squeeze between the bigger rock and the two that were nearer to the nest. Between those two there was room for him to crouch. He fumbled at the knot that held the bundle of netting. He untied it. His fingers shook. He clenched his teeth so that they could not chatter, but could feel his heart beating so that he wondered the bird did not hear it. Speed. Speed. What he had to do had to be done fast. Nothing would stop the rustle of the scraps of heather on the net. He unrolled the bundle and, after a desperate moment when the netting caught on a point of rock, he spread it over the two grey lumps that were to be the walls of his hide. And still that dark lump on the shore did not stir.

The thought came into his mind that perhaps the eggs were very near hatching. He remembered a tawny owl, nesting in the roots of a tree. It had never stirred till he was within a couple of yards of it, in broad daylight, and only two days later, he had visited it again and seen the owl's two chicks, all wool except for gaping beaks. Speed. Speed. Good thing they had made the net so big. It came down to the ground on both sides of the two rocks and hung, just as he had planned, across the opening on the side nearest to the nest. He felt for a stone, found one ready to his hand, and put it on the netting to anchor it. Another, and another. He slipped round to do the same on the other side. More stones. He found them. One,

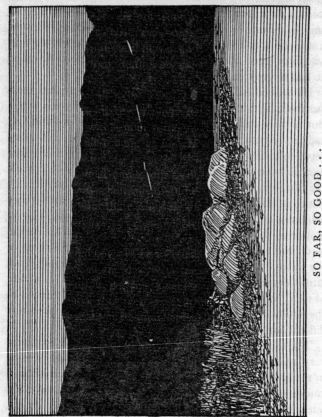

SO FAR, SO GOOD . . .

as he placed it, clicked against the rock. He thought he saw the bird move. 'Just going. Just going,' he whispered to himself.

In the dim light he had a last look over the hide. There was nothing more that he could do. Only daylight would show whether the hide would work or not. Listening for a splash that never came, he crept back through the rocks to the reedy end of the island.

There was John, standing in the water, holding the dinghy ready for him.

'Well?' whispered John.

'One bird went,' whispered Dick, 'but I don't think the other left the nest.'

'Well done, Professor,' whispered John. 'Look here. When you come to take the photographs, I've found the place for you to push the boat into the reeds. Shove her in here, well in, and she'll be hidden from both sides of the lake.'

'I ought to stop here now to save coming back again in daylight,' said Dick.

'You can't.'

'I know. I haven't got the camera here. And perhaps if I did stop it would bother them more. Let's get away quick.'

'What about the hide?'

'I think it's all right. I say. Row up the lake a bit before going for the shore. Don't let's go near their end of the island. One of them's in the water, swimming, and we'd better keep as far away as we can.'

John rowed quietly from the island until, not far ahead of them, the duck, that had been silent for some time, startled them both by sudden quacking. Then he pulled towards the shore, turned and rowed back in the shelter of the shelving bank. Dick, listening, heard no sound from the Divers. Peering towards the island in the dim light he could see nothing moving on the rippled water.

'Well, it's done anyhow,' he said, 'even if I can't take the pictures.'

'Why shouldn't you take them?'

'I can't if the egg-collector's watching. And it would be just as bad if those other people saw. They'd sell him the eggs if he offered to buy them. They'd never know how important it was.'

'Nancy's got a plan,' said John.

They came to the big reed-beds at the foot of the loch, found the place where they had hidden the boat in the morning and took her in there again, poling her through the reeds. Then Dick, like John, took off shoes and stockings and, leaving the folding boat in the reeds, they tied the painter to a stone which they dropped in the water a few feet from the shore.

'We'll find that easily,' said John. 'Just opposite this place where the bank's fallen in.'

'I've got to do it by myself tomorrow,' said Dick. 'There isn't room for two in the hide, and two of us moving about on the way there would be more likely to frighten them.'

'And to be seen,' said John. 'Yes. I'd forgotten that. Well, buck up with those shoes. Nancy'll be thinking we've sunk the folder.'

Walking back in the night, Dick with every step grew more and more cheerful. Everything that could be done had been done. Best of all, he was nearly certain that one of the birds had never left the nest. In the morning the rocks would look a bit heathery, but he did not think any bird would mind that. And John had sounded so sure that Nancy had a plan that would work that Dick himself began to think that after all he would be able to get the proof of his discovery without giving Mr Jemmerling a chance of taking the eggs. Nancy's plans always did work, even if sometimes they meant that a lot of other people had to work too. Everything was going to be all right.

It was darker than it had been, but the distance seemed shorter and soon they were coming down past waterfall and rapids to the mouth of the stream and could see the *Sea Bear* at anchor with a light glimmering in the rigging.

'Great Guillemots!' said a quiet voice from across the stream, 'you people walk like elephants. No need for an owl-call to let me know you were coming.'

'We were a lot quieter on the island,' said Dick.

'What's the Dactyl doing?' asked John.

'Gone to bed,' said Nancy. 'Their last light went out ten minutes ago. And their dinghy's still aboard. They're not trying anything till tomorrow. What about the hide?'

'It's done,' said Dick. 'And one of the birds didn't stir.'

They launched the dinghy and paddled it across for Nancy.

'Have you got a spare pair of spectacles?' said Nancy suddenly to Dick.

'I ought to have,' said Dick. 'But I went and left them behind. Why?'

'Part of our plan,' said Nancy. 'Never mind. I'll think of another way.'

'Whatever do you want them for?' said John.

There was a quiet chuckle in the dusk, but Nancy gave no other answer just then, and they were presently alongside the *Sea Bear*.

'Well?'
'What happened?'
'Have you done it?'
'No noises. We've been listening all the time but never heard anything.'

Anxious voices greeted them from the deck.

'Dactyl's never even come on deck,' said Nancy. 'He had a light in the deckhouse at first and lights in the portholes, but they've all gone out.'

'I saw them go out,' said Peggy. 'I was up at the cross-trees, but it was no use staying up there after that.'

'What about the hide?' asked Dorothea.

'I *think* it's all right,' said Dick.

'And the birds?' asked Titty.

'One went into the water,' said Dick, 'but it didn't get up and it didn't screech. I was awfully afraid it would. I'm pretty certain the other never left the nest.'

'Did you see the eggs?' asked Captain Flint.

'I couldn't have seen them without frightening the bird away. I didn't even try.'

'Netting big enough?'

'Just right.'

'So everything's ready for tomorrow? No more waiting?' said Captain Flint.

'Look here,' said Nancy. 'We haven't wasted a minute so far. Dick's got his hide and John and I have got a gorgeous plan. The Dactyl's not going to have a chance. Nor are the Gaels. Our plan's going to keep everybody off. There are lots of us. Eight, not counting you. No. Seven, because Dick'll be taking photographs. Well, seven red herrings ought to be enough.'

'Red herrings?' Almost everybody spoke at once.

'I'll explain,' said Nancy.

'Down below,' said Susan. 'There's a kettle boiling. Cocoa all round and then bed. What time have we got to get up?'

In the cabin, over steaming mugs, the red herrings worked out the plans that were to mislead Gaels and egg-collector alike and leave Dick free to take his pictures without a single enemy to see him. Only Dick and Roger said nothing at all.

Dick because he was thinking out every detail of the photographing, Roger because he had a plan of his own. He had not forgiven that stranger who had watched the sleeping sentinel.

At midnight all was peace. The *Sea Bear* swung gently to her anchor with a glimmering light above her deserted deck. The two great birds slept on their island and had forgotten the noises that had worried them. Mr Jemmerling turned in his bunk aboard the *Pterodactyl*, thinking of a huge glass case with two stuffed birds in it and the eggs that would be the crowning glory of the Jemmerling Collection. In the grey house over the top of the ridge, Ian, the young Highlander, slept without a dream. Old Angus and he, climbing home again in the dusk, had, like the crew of the *Sea Bear*, made their own plans for the morrow.

CHAPTER 19

A CLEAR COAST FOR DICK

NANCY, who had slept with the alarm clock under her pillow, had lit a Primus stove in the fo'c'sle before waking the cooks to do their duty. She had meant to wake only Susan, but Peggy had heard her too, and now John was looking in at them from the cabin.

'Skipper's still asleep,' he said.

'Don't wake him,' whispered Nancy. 'And look out for Roger.'

Roger, sleeping in the fo'c'sle, had turned in his bunk, but Susan had hung a spare sail to keep the light from his eyes and he had not moved again.

'Don't wake anybody except Dick,' said Susan, with a finger to her lips.

'No hurry for anybody else,' whispered Peggy. 'The longer Titty and Dot sleep the better.'

Everything was going well. All plans had been made the night before. Now they had to be carried out and, first of all, the Ship's Naturalist had to be hurried away to the loch and into his hide before the world was stirring. With the *Pterodactyl* in the next creek and hostile Gaels ashore, the taking of those photographs without being seen was not going to be easy. Nancy's first idea had been to send Dick off alone before it was really light, but that meant risks of other kinds. Better for him to go as soon as he could see what he was doing and as soon as it was light enough for scouts, Nancy herself and John, to signal to him from a distance if it was safe or not to take the folding boat out of the reeds and row to the island. That would be the first of the dangerous moments. The other, no less dangerous, would be later in the day when, with the photographs taken, he would have to leave the island and bring the boat back. A boat, moving on a loch, is something that can be seen for miles, but by that time it ought to be possible to have every enemy, ashore or afloat, either far away or looking in the wrong direction.

Dick had to be sent off with breakfast inside him and with food in his knapsack to eat during his wait in the hide. It would be a long wait before the sun would be right for photographing and the red herrings had decoyed all enemies to a safe distance. Oatmeal had been put to soak the night before and Susan was stirring the porridge on one Primus stove while a kettle boiled on the other, and Peggy was cutting rounds of bread to make potted meat sandwiches.

'Porridge ready?' whispered Nancy. 'I'll get Dick.'

But Dick was already awake. Bare-footed, with his shoes in his hands, he was looking from the cabin into the fo'c'sle.

'Have I overslept?' he asked anxiously.

' 'Sh!'

Nancy beckoned. 'Come along in,' she whispered. 'We don't want to wake the others yet. Sit down on that coil of rope and tuck in. The sooner we start the better.'

'I'm ready now,' said Dick.

'No you aren't,' said Susan. She gave him a bowl of porridge and a spoon. 'Pretty hot, but the milk'll cool it.'

'Here's the milk,' whispered Peggy, stirring some condensed milk into half a jug of water.

'Aren't you having breakfast too?' asked Dick.

'Afterwards,' said Nancy. 'We've got to get you off first.'

'Anything else to go in your knapsack?' said Peggy.

'No.'

'Got your camera?' asked John.

'Films?' asked Nancy.

'Let him eat,' said Susan.

'Well, he mustn't forget anything,' said Nancy. 'Once he's on his island there'll be no coming back for anything left behind.'

'I got everything ready last night,' said Dick, between mouthfuls.

'Tea,' said Peggy, putting a mug on the floor beside him.

Susan was taking the top off a boiled egg. It was a new thing for the Ship's Naturalist to be the most important member of the crew, but not one of the others could take his place and they were determined to send him off as fit as possible for the work he had to do.

As for Dick himself his mind was on the Divers. What if, in spite of his care last night, they had been frightened off by the putting up of the hide or, worse, been frightened by it when first they saw it in daylight? Birds did desert their nests sometimes and if these deserted it would be his fault for trying to photograph them. It would be as bad as if he had been an egg-collector. He swallowed his breakfast as fast as he could, refused a second egg and was ready.

They did not open the forehatch, for fear of waking Roger. The five of them tip-toed through the cabin and went up on deck. Dick ran his finger along the damp edge of the sky-light. There had been a heavy dew.

'Good,' he said. 'It's going to be a fine day. It wouldn't be any good without sunshine.'

'Plenty of things to go wrong without that,' said Nancy. 'But nothing will,' she added. 'I'd never thought about the weather. Jolly lucky it's going to be fine. He'd never wait another day, even to do the Dactyl in the eye.' They all knew she was talking of Captain Flint in a hurry to take the *Sea Bear* back to her owner.

They tip-toed gingerly on the wet, slippery deck. John

hauled in the dinghy that was lying astern. Careful not to let it bump, he brought it alongside, went down into it and sat on the middle thwart. Dick and Nancy followed.

'Don't sit on the wet seats,' Susan whispered.

Nancy grinned, but changed her mind. Susan was right. 'Much better not,' she whispered. 'You don't want to start sneezing when you're in your hide. Sit on your hands.'

Peggy was waiting to pass down Dick's knapsack. John took it and laid it behind him in the bows.

'You'd better go back to bed, you two,' whispered Nancy. 'The rest of us won't be wanted for a bit, once we've got him properly planted.'

Susan dropped the painter into the bows. John pushed off. The dinghy, moved by the tide, drifted clear. He put the oars out and rowed away to the head of the cove, to put Dick and his knapsack ashore on the northern bank of the stream.

'Off you go, Ship's Naturalist,' said Nancy. 'But don't take the boat out on the loch until we've made sure that all's clear. We're going up on Low Ridge so that we can see down on the *Dactyl* and from there we'll be able to look across the valley and see if any of the Gaels are moving. We'll stand where you can't help seeing us and we'll be able to see you. We'll signal if there's any danger from either side. If you see no signals, you can go ahead.'

'When you get to the island,' said John, 'push the boat well into the reeds where we landed last night. I showed you the place.'

'Yes,' said Dick.

'Whatever you do, don't go and forget that it isn't only birds you've got to hide from.'

'No.'

'Off you go and good luck to you.'

Dick started off. They watched him, knapsack on back,

patting his pockets to make sure nothing had been forgotten, as he hurried along at the side of the stream, climbed up by the waterfall and was gone.

They pushed off again, landed at the other side of the stream and climbed up the rocks until, looking down, they could see the big white motor boat at anchor. Her dinghy was still in its davits.

'Just waiting,' said Nancy. 'Like a snake. All ready to come chasing after us if we move. You see, as we can see him from our cross-trees, he can see our topmost from his deck.'

'Probably somebody in that cucumber frame watching all the time,' said John.

'If we sail he'll think we've got the eggs on board and Uncle Jim says he'll come after us and have another shot at buying them. When he sees we don't move, he'll be sure we haven't got the eggs and all he's got to do is to watch where we go. He thinks we'll show him the way to the birds.'

'So we shall if we're not jolly careful,' said John.

'We're not going to give him a chance,' said Nancy. 'Come on, or Dick'll be starting before we know it's safe.'

Keeping just below the skyline they moved along the narrow ridge that divided the inlets, and rose gradually towards the inland hills.

'There's the loch,' said Nancy. 'There's the place where we left the folder yesterday. Did you put it back in the same place last night?'

'Yes,' said John. 'But, I say, it's not too well hidden from this side. I can see it from here. Perhaps I couldn't if I didn't know where it was.'

'Doesn't matter anyhow,' said Nancy. 'It won't be there as soon as Dick's taken it off to the island. There he is . . . just coming to the reeds now.'

John, with the telescope, was looking at the reed-bed far

away and wondering if anybody else could have seen that black spot among the reeds that he knew was a folding boat.

'So long as he hides it properly when he's on the island,' he said.

'Telescope,' said Nancy and, taking it, carefully swept the much higher northern ridge on the other side of the valley and then focused it on the Ship's Naturalist who had moved along the shore of the loch and, using Captain Flint's binoculars, was looking across at the two scouts.

'He's seen us all right,' she said. 'Do you think it's safe for him to start? Nothing moving on that side.'

John went a few feet higher till he could just see over the top.

'Dactyl's still asleep,' he said. 'Anyhow, nobody stirring. The sooner he's at the island the better.'

'Right,' said Nancy. 'I said we wouldn't signal unless there was danger. Come on. Dick's watching us. Lie down. If we just sprawl, he'll know it means he can start.'

The two scouts threw themselves at full length on a flat rock. It was a queer way of signalling, not to signal at all, but a moment after they had lain down they lost sight of Dick.

'Good for Dick,' said Nancy. 'He's understood all right.'

'In the reeds,' said John. 'He's getting her out. There he comes.'

The little folding boat was pushing her dark nose out of the pale reeds.

'Gosh, she is easy to see,' said John.

'No eyes to look,' said Nancy. 'He's out.'

'Pretty bad at rowing her,' said John.

'She's a bit of a beast,' said Nancy. 'Never mind. He's getting her along.'

'But how,' said John.

The folding boat had left the reeds and was making a very

zigzag course of it along the shore towards the island. The surfaces of the loch, smooth in the windless, early morning, was broken by row upon row of long ripples.

'Gosh!' said John. 'Even Roger'd do better than that.'

'Nobody could do much worse,' agreed Nancy, and the two old shellbacks, one-time captains of the *Swallow* and the *Amazon*, sat up with impatience as they watched the Ship's Naturalist glance over his shoulder, pull hard with an oar, glance over his shoulder again and pull hard with the other.

'I wish I knew what time Gaels get up,' said Nancy, after another long search with the telescope. 'I can't see anybody moving.'

'Short strokes,' said John. 'Short. Not too hard. Gosh! He's spun her again!'

'She isn't like a proper boat,' said Nancy. 'He rows all right in a dinghy. But I do hope to goodness nobody spots him and comes howling down the hill to upset everything.'

'He's doing a bit better now,' said John, some minutes later.

The folding boat was coming near the island. Suddenly a row of white splashes was drawn on the water.

'That's a bird getting up,' said John. 'One of Dick's?'

'Heuch! Heuch! Heuch!' A harsh, croaking cry of fear or anger sounded across the loch.

'Golly, that's a bit of bad luck.'

John was already wriggling up to the skyline to look at the *Pterodactyl*. They had not been the only hearers of that cry. They were just in time to see the door of the deckhouse open, and the egg-collector himself, in pink pyjamas, shoot out and stand, listening, on the deck.

'He doesn't know where it was,' whispered Nancy, as the pink figure turned first one way and then the other. 'But if that bird goes and squawks again . . .'

'It's sure to,' said John.

They lay there listening, flat to the ground. The egg-collector was listening too. It was almost as if they could see his thoughts, as he moved from one side of the deck to the other and faced now towards them and now to the south. Nancy chuckled in spite of her fears and passed the telescope to John. 'He's like a pink thrush listening for worms,' she said. 'Look at the way he holds his head.'

'It was awfully loud, that bird,' said John.

'If he was down below he wouldn't know where the noise came from,' said Nancy. 'But if it does it now . . .'

At every moment they expected to hear that wild, rough squawk again, that would tell the egg-collector just where he had to look. But a miracle happened. The silence hung over the valley as if for ever, until at last it was broken by the call of a curlew. They saw the egg-collector glance up and then go quickly back into the deckhouse, shutting the door behind him.

'Sick as cats with himself,' said Nancy. 'Telling himself that curlew was all he heard and that it wasn't one of Dick's birds at all.'

'Hope that's it,' said John. 'But if he did hear it, he knows now that Dick's birds aren't far away. Hullo! Dick's got to the island.'

They watched the boat slipping into the reeds at the far end of the island. She seemed to stick.

'If he leaves her like that,' said John, 'we'll have to start signalling to tell him she's in full view.'

But, a minute later, they saw that the boat was disappearing.

'Let's have the telescope,' said John.

'Can't see her at all,' said Nancy, and handed it over.

'He's done that all right,' said John. 'Hullo. There he goes.'

They caught a few glimpses of bits of Dick as he crawled his way through the rocks.

'There's one thing,' said John. 'Nobody'd ever think that hide was anything but a lump of heather. He did that jolly well.'

'Can you see him?' asked Nancy, a minute or two later. 'I can't.'

'Neither can I,' said John.

'Good,' said Nancy. 'And that bird's never squawked again. First job's done. Ship's Naturalist's in his hide. Now for breakfast and then hard work for red herrings.'

They looked across the valley. No one was stirring on that northern ridge. They looked down to the *Pterodactyl*. No one was on deck. They took a last look at the island on the loch, a little flat island, with rocks towards its nearer end, and among the rocks what looked like a sturdy bush of heather. They hurried down to the mouth of the stream, pushed off in the dinghy and rowed back to the *Sea Bear*.

Everybody aboard the *Sea Bear* was now awake and making ready for the business of the day. Dorothea, who had waked to learn that Dick was already on his way to his island, was on deck, waiting for them. Captain Flint was sitting in the cockpit, shaving, half his face covered by a white beard of lather. As the dinghy pulled alongside, John and Nancy could hear Roger's voice, protesting about something down below.

'Hullo you,' said Captain Flint, clearing a wide red furrow in the white soap as he leaned forward to look into a shaving-glass propped against the binnacle. 'Why didn't you wake me?'

'No need,' said Nancy.

'Is Dick all right?' asked Dorothea.

'On the island and in the hide,' said John.

'Oh, good,' said Dorothea.

IN THE HIDE

'He's all right for now,' said Nancy. 'Nobody about on shore. There was just one bad moment when one of his birds let loose its howl, and the old Dactyl popped out on deck, pink pyjamas, the very pinkest, you know, strawberry ice-cream. He'd heard it all right, and was listening for it to howl again, but luckily it didn't and a curlew came over at the right moment and he bobbed in again thinking he'd made a mistake.'

'Grub!' called Peggy from below.

'Ready for it,' said Nancy. 'We haven't a minute to lose. The sooner the red herrings get going the better.'

Down in the cabin, breakfast was on the table, and Susan was wrapping up the last of eight packets of sandwiches. John and Nancy had to tell again how Dick was on the island and had safely stowed away both himself and his boat.

'Heather's grown a bit in the night,' said Nancy. 'Nothing else to show he's there, and nobody'd spot that if he didn't know exactly where to look. And now it's up to us to see that nobody even thinks of looking.'

Breakfast was quickly over. Sandwiches and lemonade bottles were dropped into knapsacks for easy carrying. Each red herring took its own knapsack, so that, in case of need, they could separate without starving. One packet of sand-wiches was left on the cabin table for Captain Flint, who was to stay aboard.

'Everything clear?' said Nancy. 'Uncle Jim at the masthead, to keep an eye on the *Pterodactyl*. He gives three long hoots on the foghorn as soon as Dick's safely back. The main body of red herrings do just what the explorers did the other day. They've got to get stalked again and take the stalkers right up the valley to the hills and keep them going as long as ever they can to give Dick time to get his photographs and bring the folder away from the island. Dick and I go and show ourselves to the *Pterodactyl*. As soon as the old

Dactyl sees Dick, he won't worry about anything else. He'll be bead sure to follow Dick, and we'll take him up the wrong valley where there are lots of lochs and he'll come chasing after us, gloating to think that Dick's showing him the way to the birds.'

'But Dick's on the island,' said Dorothea.

Nancy chuckled. 'John's Dick,' said Nancy. 'I was afraid last night he couldn't be, because of the spectacles, but we've thought of a way.'

'Roger's more Dick's size,' put in Dorothea.

'I've got something else to do,' said Roger.

'Roger can't cover as much ground as John can,' said Nancy. 'The old Dactyl may come chasing after us waving cheques and banknotes, and he mustn't get near enough to see John isn't Dick. We may have to leg it pretty hard. Off you go. I'll put you ashore and bring the dinghy back, while John's getting ready. Where's Peggy?'

'Hi!' said Peggy quietly from aloft. 'They're putting the *Dactyl*'s dinghy over.'

'Buck up and come down,' said Nancy. 'We haven't a minute to lose.'

The main body of red herrings stowed themselves in the dinghy, Susan, Peggy, Dorothea, Titty and Roger. Nancy rowed them quickly ashore at the place where the *Sea Bear* had been put on legs to be scrubbed.

'Wouldn't it be better to go up along the stream?' said Peggy.

'Galoot,' said Nancy. 'Of course not. You've got to go right up to the ridge, just like they did the other day. Titty and Dot'll be guides. They know where they went.'

'Up past my Pict-house,' said Roger.

'Nowhere near the loch anyhow,' said Nancy. 'You've got to get your Gaels stalking and keep them stalking for as long as you jolly well can.'

247

'And when they catch us?' said Peggy.

'Don't let them,' said Nancy. 'But if they do it doesn't matter so long as you've taken them far enough. You haven't been doing anything wrong. Just grin at them and be polite. Ask them how far you have to go before you can see the Atlantic. And if you can see it already, ask them what it is. Leave the talking to Susan.'

'I wish Captain Flint was coming with us,' said Susan.

'Lots better without him. You can pretend not to understand if they yell at you. Just wave cheery hands and go galloping on. He'd be bound to get into a parley. What you've got to do is to keep all your Gaels and stalkers on the move.'

Roger sat in the bows of the dinghy and said nothing. He had only one idea in his head, and that was to get even with the particular stalker who had labelled him a sleeping beauty. If Roger could meet him there would be no thought of parley or anything like it. But the others would not understand that. They hadn't fallen asleep, as anybody might, and waked up to find that some enemy had been playing round, turning knapsacks inside out and generally gloating.

The moment the red herrings were ashore and climbing up towards the Pict-house, Nancy pushed off with an oar and rowed as hard as she could back to the *Sea Bear*.

Captain Flint was waiting for her.

'*Pterodactyl*'s dinghy's away,' he said.

'Come on,' said Nancy. 'If he's ashore the sooner we show him Dick the better. Where's John? Hullo! What's all that hanging up at the cross-trees?'

'Varnish tin,' said Captain Flint. 'Hammer, marline spike, scraper and sandpaper. You don't think I'm going to perch up there with nothing to do. I'm going to take down blocks, clean and varnish, so that if those chaps on the motor boat put a telescope on me they can see I'm busy. Satisfied?'

'Good idea,' said Nancy. 'Pity you can't see the loch from

up there, but you'll be able to see the other red herrings on the far side of the valley except when the Hump's in the way.'

'If I'd known what a job it was going to be, letting Dick photograph a couple of birds, I'd have let that egg-collector have his eggs.'

'No you wouldn't,' said Nancy.

'Well, perhaps not, after I'd seen him,' said her uncle. 'Get out of the way. Where's John?'

'John!' called Nancy impatiently. 'Great Guillemots!' she exclaimed, as John came up the companion way and looked down into the dinghy with huge black rings for spectacles, done in burnt cork round his eyes with straight black lines going from the rings to his ears.

'It's the best I could do,' said John, coming down into the dinghy.

'They're not bad at a distance,' said Captain Flint, after a first astonished laugh.

Five minutes later, John and Nancy were ashore at the mouth of the stream.

'Sure I'd better not come with you?' said Captain Flint.

'And spoil everything?' said Nancy. 'No. Somebody's got to stay, to sound the foghorn and let us all know as soon as the real Dick's safely back. Three long hoots for that. And two short ones again and again, if you see any of the Dactyls coming over into our valley. I've told the others which means which.'

'What if the egg-collector's there already?'

'He'll be after us the moment he sees Dick.'

Captain Flint glanced again at John. 'I should think he'd run the other way,' he said. 'But perhaps not, if you don't let him come too near.'

'Don't wait,' said Nancy. 'Somebody ought to be up at the masthead now. Come on, John, I mean Dick. We ought to have started long ago. Look out, don't rub your eyes, or the black'll be all over your face.'

Captain Flint rowed away and Nancy and the new-made Dick set out to show themselves to the enemy.

CHAPTER 20

THE DECOYS

'RACE you to the top,' said John, forgetting for the moment that it was his chief business to be Dick.

They had worked along the stream until they were close under the place from which in the early morning they had kept watch while the real Dick rowed the folding boat to the island. They rushed up the slope so suddenly and so fast that the *Pterodactyl*'s scout had hardly time to get away. They were as startled as he was when a blue-jerseyed sailor scrambled to his feet in the heather and, without a word, bolted down the further side of the ridge towards the shore off which the big motor boat lay at anchor.

'Gosh!' said John. 'I wonder how long he's been here.'

'Not long enough to see anything,' said Nancy. 'They hadn't got their dinghy over till after we got back for breakfast.'

'Funny his bolting,' said John.

'Bad conscience,' said Nancy. 'Or terror. It was the same man who tried to get Susan and Peggy to give things away.'

'I say,' said John, remembering that he was Dick, 'you don't think he was near enough to see that my goggles are corked? I was coming uphill, head down, using my hands, and he can't have had anything like a full-face view.'

'Not he,' said Nancy. 'Take care. Don't look at the *Pterodactyl*. Pink pyjamas is out on deck looking straight at us. Binoculars too. He'll see too much if you make it too easy for him. Go on. Quick. Go on ahead as if you were in a hurry. Give me an excuse for yelling at you.'

'What for?'

'Gummock!' exclaimed Nancy. 'Hurry up. I'm looking at a nest or something. You get along quick. That sailor's stopping. And the old Dactyl's staring his eyes out. Just what we wanted. Get along. I want to yell at you and it would be silly if I yelled when you're close to me. He'd guess I was doing it on purpose. Go on. Dick's sure to have told him his name when he went aboard. Don't you see. I've got to make sure the old Dactyl knows who you are.'

John, out of the corner of his eye, saw the pink figure of Mr Jemmerling on the deck of the *Pterodactyl*. He saw the sailor looking across the water to his master as if waiting for orders. Nancy was pushing her nose into a clump of heather. John turned his back on them all and went resolutely off along the side of the ridge as if he had urgent business on hand. He had gone perhaps fifty yards when he heard Nancy hail him.

'Ahoy! Ahoy! Dick! DICK!'

He glanced round. Aboard the motor boat he could see the egg-collector, with his binoculars to his eyes. He could not see the sailor but guessed he must be somewhere on the shore of the cove. A moment later he knew that Nancy's plan had worked. The egg-collector was pointing up the valley, straight at John. Nancy yelled again.

'Ahoy! Dick! DICK CALLUM! Ahoy!'

John grinned, did not trust himself to shout back, waved a hand and waited.

Nancy came galloping after him.

'We've done it,' she said. 'I do believe we have. Those goggles are grand at a distance. One's trickling down your cheek a bit, but it doesn't matter now. It's his own fault if he doesn't know you're Dick. I've told him clear enough. He fairly jumped when I yelled your name. That sailor was just going to get into the dinghy, and the old Dactyl looked as if

252

he was going to explode with rage. The sailor saw him in time and didn't push off. The Dactyl was pointing straight up the valley. Anybody could see he was telling the sailor what to do.'

'What's he doing?'

'Coming after us.'

'What do we do? Wait for him to give a "View Halloo"?'

'Mustn't let him get too near. You've just got to go on being Dick. What would Dick be doing?'

'Looking at birds.'

'Well, look at them. That's easy. But he wouldn't be dawdling much if he was on his way to see his Divers. Come on. We'll lead that sailor a lovely dance. There are lots of lochs up this valley. We'll give him half-a-dozen to choose from and every one of them wrong. With the Dactyl thinking his sailor's close on Dick's heels there's no danger at all from him. And if Peggy and Susan lure the Gaels up into the hills there's no danger from the other side either. The Ship's Naturalist'll get his pictures and be back aboard the *Sea Bear* without anybody seeing him at all.'

'Are you sure that man's coming after us?'

'Of course he is,' said Nancy. 'Don't look round. We mustn't let him guess we know he's after us. Just keep going. When we want to make sure he's there, one of us points up into the sky ... hawk or something ... and then we can swivel round with our heads in the air and have a squint at anything we want.'

Five minutes later, Nancy stopped short.

'John! Dick, I mean. Just look at that albatross. Up there!'

John turned to see Nancy pointing up into the empty sky.

'Can't you see it?' she said. 'Pink, with green wings. And

there's another, speckled gold and purple. Go on. Keep your head cocked up to see the albatrosses and take a good squint astern.'

'Can't see the motor boat any more,' said John.

'Bother the motor boat,' said Nancy. 'It's that sailor we want to see.'

'Got him,' said John. 'He's just dodged behind a rock.'

'Where? Where?'

'There he is again.'

'Victory,' said Nancy. She too had seen the dark blue jersey of the sailor. 'And he's trying to hide from us. Grand. I knew a decoy Dick would do it. Gosh! These albatrosses give me a crick in my neck and a squint with having to look along my nose with my head in the air. But we needn't look back again for a bit. We've got him fairly hooked. We'll keep him going till he drops. Jiminy, I wish I knew if the red herrings have started the Gaels.'

'Couldn't we work up again till we can see across our valley?'

'No,' said Nancy. 'It's the one thing we mustn't do. We've got to keep him thinking that Dick's birds are not in our valley at all but in this. Come on. There's one of the lochs ahead. We'll make for that, and then go on and find another. We must take him so far that he won't have time to get back till it's over. We won't let him stop till Dick's in the *Sea Bear* and we hear Uncle Jim hooting triumph on the foghorn.'

'Still coming after us?'

'Must be. But if we keep turning round he'll know there's something fishy. No more albatrosses for a bit.' She wriggled her neck. 'We'll go on for a good long way, and then we'll both see a great auk at the same moment and swivel round like lightning to get another look at him.'

They went steadily on, aiming at the first of several small

lochs in the valley. For as long as they could, they put off seeing great auks, feeling that hard purposeful walking was the likeliest way to keep the *Pterodactyl*'s sailor hurrying in their tracks.

'Now,' said Nancy at last. 'What about it?'

'All right,' said John.

'I'll count three and then ... round like a flash and we'll spot anything moving. Are you ready?'

'Yes.'

'One ... two ... three ... Great auks!'

Round they spun and, sure enough, three or four hundred yards behind them, they caught sight of the sailor just before he dropped in the heather and disappeared.

'That settles it,' said Nancy. 'He's after us and he doesn't want us to know it. Three million cheers! Well done, the goggles! And my yelling your name must have helped. All we've got to do now is to keep him going.'

Once they knew for certain that their trick had worked and that the *Pterodactyl*'s scout was busily following the sham Dick while the real Dick was taking his photographs unseen, they began to enjoy themselves. It was, of course, a pity that they could not go up and look across the other valley to see what was happening to the red herrings, but they were going to take no risks. They knew the red herrings would be doing their best and, after all, misleading the egg-collector was the most important part of the plan, and it was silly to worry about the others while they had plenty to do themselves. They settled down to a long day of hard but joyful work. Hither and thither, to and fro, from one small loch to another, they led the unfortunate sailor. Soft marshy ground, that bore John and Nancy so long as they kept moving, let the sailor, in his heavy seaboots, sink to his knees. Once, glancing back, they saw him hurriedly emptying the water out of a boot before dragging it on again to come squelching in pursuit.

'Good thing we're not near enough to hear what he's saying,' said John with a grin.

'Oh, I don't know,' said Nancy. 'We might learn some good new words.'

The sun climbed high in the sky. Their shadows no longer ran ahead of them but dragged behind them. The day wore on to afternoon and still, like will-o'-the-wisps, John and Nancy flitted up the valley, cheered to their work by occasional glimpses of the blue jersey of the sailor far behind them. At last they began to listen hopefully for the hooting of the *Sea Bear*'s foghorn that would tell them that their work was done. They were very hot, but it was pleasant to think that the *Pterodactyl*'s sailor must be hotter still. It was long past dinner-time and they began to be hungry.

'I say,' said John. 'It's a long time since I've seen him. You don't think he's given up?'

'Dick's bound to have got his pictures by now,' said Nancy.

They stopped and looked back over a wide stretch of rocky moorland. There was not a single moving thing in sight.

'We'll have our grub,' said Nancy. 'And my tongue's hanging out for grog. If that bottle's as hot as I am, it'll burst in another minute.'

'It must be safe to stop now,' said John. 'And we ought to get a sight of him again when he comes over that rise.'

They threw themselves down on short dry heather, shrugged out of their knapsacks, opened their sandwiches and let the corks from their bottles go off like guns.

'He probably got stuck in that last bit of bog,' said Nancy, after the first few urgent mouthfuls.

'What about cleaning off these goggles?' said John. A hand that he had put up to wipe his forehead had come away with a black smudge that had reminded him that he was being Dick. 'They can't matter now.'

'They aren't quite as good as they were,' chuckled Nancy looking at him. 'But you'll only make them worse. It's no good trying to clean off burnt cork without soap. You may even need pumice stone.'

'Bother,' said John, touching his cheek with a clean finger and looking at the black finger-tip he brought away. 'I wonder if there is any pumice stone in the *Sea Bear*.'

'There'll be a file in the engine room,' said Nancy. 'We'll get the black off all right when we get back. Gosh! I wish I knew what was happening to the others.'

'There hasn't been any shouting,' said John.

'If they didn't get stalked,' said Nancy, 'they'll be pretty sick by now of being red herrings all for nothing.'

'Susan'll be glad enough,' said John. 'She didn't really much like the idea of being hunted by Gaels.'

'Uncle Jim's fault,' said Nancy. 'Rubbing it into her that we didn't want to get into trouble for trespassing. But she'll have done her best. She knew how important it was.'

'If we climbed up that ridge we'd probably see them,' said John.

'We can't,' said Nancy. 'Not with a spy at our heels.'

'He isn't at our heels now,' said John. 'But we'll be seeing him in a minute. Keep an eye on that open bit we crossed when we came up off the flats.'

They finished their sandwiches and tipped the last drops of their lemonade down their throats. They were both sitting up, looking a quarter of a mile away for a blue, plodding sailor, when Nancy suddenly grabbed at John. Somebody was watching them from not twenty yards off. Over the top of a rock they saw a battered blue sailor's cap and a startled, puzzled face, the colour of old mahogany. It was too late for John to turn over and hide the smudgy ruin of his spectacles.

TOO CLOSE A VIEW

The secret was out. The sailor, who had spoken to Dick aboard the *Pterodactyl*, knew now that this was not the real Dick and that he had had his chase for nothing. Nobody spoke. The sailor and the decoy Dick stared at each other. The sailor wiped his face with a large red handkerchief. He stared again. He stood up looking so angry that John stood up too, not knowing what was going to happen next. But the sailor just stood there staring, as if he could not take his eyes from John's zebra face. Nancy scrambled to her feet and stood beside John.

Suddenly the sailor seemed to make up his mind. He swung round and set off at a steady trot down the valley towards the distant creek.

'He's off to tell the Dactyl he's been after the wrong Dick,' said Nancy.

'Pretty good stalking on his part,' said John, 'getting right up to us like that.'

'I hope the Dactyl pays him well,' said Nancy, 'he's earned it. But I bet he doesn't. The Dactyl'll be tearing raging mad.'

'It won't take him so long to get back,' said John. 'He'll go straight instead of all over the place like we did.'

'It's all right,' said Nancy. 'We're bound to hear that foghorn any minute. Unless Uncle Jim's hooted already and we're too far away to hear it.'

'It's a pretty good foghorn,' said John. 'I wonder if we ought to have kept him here.'

'Too late,' said Nancy. 'And parleying wouldn't have worked. Nothing would have stopped him once he'd had a good look at your mug.'

'Let's get up on the ridge,' said John, 'and see what's happening in our valley.'

'Wait till the sailor's out of sight,' said Nancy.

'He hasn't turned round once,' said John.

They watched the spot of dark blue moving quickly down the valley, losing sight of it in hollows and among rocks, seeing it again as it crossed the rises in the uneven ground.

'He's going straight back,' said John again. 'Come on. From the top of that ridge we'll be able to see right across.'

They quickly poked their sandwich papers deep into the peat, sank their empty lemonade bottles in a small pool and set off, with empty knapsacks flapping on their backs.

The sailor had passed altogether out of sight and they did not catch sight of him again even when they were climbing the steep slopes of the ridge that divided the two valleys. They had their first news of something happening before they reached the top. A long shrill whistle that nobody could have mistaken for a bird's sounded from far away.

'Did you hear that?' panted Nancy, stopping short.

'Yes,' said John. 'And it's not Susan's. I know the noise hers makes.'

'That's not hers either,' said Nancy, as another whistle sounded on a slightly different note.

They fairly raced up the last fifty yards till they were able to look down into the valley beyond. Far away to the right of them they could see the little hill with the Pict-house on it and a line of blue sea. They could see just a little of one of the lochs. High above it, on the other side of the valley, smoke, drifting above the skyline, showed where the houses must be. Beginning at that end of the valley, where they knew the red herrings must have started, they searched along the opposite ridge.

'There they are,' said Nancy. 'Some of them. They've got a very long way. But who blew those whistles? I can't see any Gaels. Can you?'

'No,' said John. 'No . . . At least . . . How many of them can you see?'

'Pretty well spread out,' said Nancy. 'That's Titty and Dot down in the bottom. They've gone further than we have.'

'We've come a long way round, looking at those lochs and giving that sailor a run,' said John.

'There's Peggy's red cap ... Jolly useful for spotting purposes.'

'Not so good when she wants to hide,' said John. 'But, of course, she didn't. They'd all want to be seen to get the Gaels to come chasing after them ...'

'Red rag to a bull ... Red cap to a Gael,' said Nancy. 'There's Susan. That's four ... Another higher up ... That must be Roger. Hullo, who's that, a bit behind? That makes six.'

'But there can't be six, unless they've got Dick with them, and he knew he had to get back to the *Sea Bear* the first moment he could. But look here. There's another, right up on the skyline. Seven! I say, Nancy, you don't think Captain Flint ...?'

'He'd never leave his masthead once he'd promised to stick there ... Look! ... Look! Further up, where there's a sort of gorge going up into the hills. One ... Two ... Three ... Four ... There are a whole lot of people spread out in the heather.'

'If they are people,' said John. 'Yes, they are. I saw one stand up and then go down again out of sight. And, hullo, look at those deer.'

'Great Guillemots!' said Nancy. 'It's the Gaels. They've been stirred up all right. A regular army. Oh, well done the red herrings! There are Gaels all round them. I wonder if Peggy knows, or Susan. It looks to me as if they're walking slap into an ambush. I'm going to signal.'

'The Gaels'll see you if you do.'

'Doesn't matter,' said Nancy. 'We're miles from Dick's

loch. We've got to let them know.' She climbed up on a rock and waved a handkerchief in wide sweeps from side to side. 'You watch with the telescope and sing out the moment one of them sees us.'

'Susan's spotted you,' cried John a moment later. 'She's looking straight at us. So's Peggy.'

'Right,' said Nancy, and waved her handkerchief with two short sweeps and then a long one from side to side as wide as she could reach. Then again two short quick sweeps and a long slower one. Then again. 'Golly,' she muttered, 'my arm'll bust if they don't understand soon.'

'Peggy's waving.'

'Can't the gummock see I'm signalling?'

'Hullo! She's got it. Long ... short ... long ... short ... Answering sign. That's all right ... Now what?'

Suddenly things began to happen. John and Nancy heard two more whistles far away, and a nearer one. They saw Peggy and Susan come together, stop, look back, start to run forward and then stop again. They saw men and boys, no longer crouching, but running and leaping down the heathery slopes. They heard Susan's well-known whistle. They saw both Susan and Peggy beckoning to Dot and Titty down in the valley. More men were coming down to join the others. Below them, they saw Dot and Titty run side by side to join Susan and Peggy on the opposite slopes.

'Why on earth didn't they bolt across to us?' said Nancy.

'That's why,' said John, pointing.

'It's the dogmudgeon himself,' exclaimed Nancy, as she saw a huge giant of a man stand up, shaking his fist, close to where Titty and Dot had been.

There was no way of escape. The red herrings were surrounded. The next moment, as the enemy closed in towards them, the watchers saw Peggy signalling again, three short waves and a long one. Three short waves and a long.

'Require assistance,' said John grimly.

'I should jolly well think they do,' said Nancy.

'Come on,' said John, and with Nancy beside him went plunging down the slopes.

CHAPTER 21

THE RED HERRINGS

It was hard to say who were the leaders of the red herrings. Susan and Peggy were in charge, but naturally they depended on their guides. Titty, Roger and Dorothea had climbed this side of the valley before, had looked through the gap in the ridge and had already been stalked by the Gaels. It was Titty, Roger and Dorothea who had to show their leaders what to do if they wanted to make sure that the Gaels would come stalking them again. Roger, in a hurry to get to his Pict-house, was climbing ahead of the others. Titty and Dorothea were telling yet again, now that people were ready to believe them, exactly how they had been followed by invisible enemies crawling through the heather, and how, in the end, they had been chased down the valley by the old grey-bearded giant whom Roger had called a dogmudgeon. They told of the bagpipe music and of the grey house with the turret that lay, just out of sight, beyond the Northern Rockies.

'It can't have been really a castle, Dot,' said Susan.

'It would make a pretty good one,' said Titty.

'But how did the stalking begin?' asked Peggy.

'A dog started barking at us,' said Titty.

'There was a young chieftain watching from the tower,' said Dorothea.

'That boy who came down with the dogmudgeon last night?'

'It must have been him,' said Dorothea.

'Well,' said Peggy. 'We'll do everything you did. We needn't let sleeping dogs lie. It wouldn't be safe. They'd only wake up later and come charging over the top just when Dick's in full view.'

'We've got to be pretty careful,' said Susan. 'That first time they weren't expecting you. This time they may be too quick. If we show ourselves and don't get a good start, it'll be like poking a stick into a hornets' nest and not being able to bolt far enough.'

'Jibbooms and Bobstays!' exclaimed Peggy in the Nancy manner. 'Let's get it clear. What we've got to do is to get them tagging after us. The further we get before we stir them up, the safer it'll be for Dick. But we mustn't risk not stirring them at all. We'll get well along the ridge, and then show ourselves on their side and kick up a row till they see us.'

'And if they don't come?'

'They'll come all right,' said Peggy. 'Nancy said the dogmudgeon fairly roared at her and John.'

'Just like he did at us,' said Titty.

'So long as they don't come too fast,' said Susan. 'Captain Flint said we were to keep out of trouble with natives.'

'That's just what we're going to do,' said Peggy. 'We're going to exercise them, that's all, and keep as far out of trouble as we possibly can. What's the matter with Roger?'

Roger had reached the old Pict-house and was beckoning to them.

'Someone's been here since yesterday,' he said. 'Anyway, since I left. Look at the doorway.'

'What's wrong with it?' said Susan, who, like Peggy, was seeing it for the first time.

'There wasn't any heather in it before,' said Titty. 'Roger crawled right in.'

'There wasn't any yesterday,' said Roger. 'I went in again to look at the old biscuit box. Someone's put it there on purpose.'

The square doorway had been blocked by a big bundle of heather that had been pushed in roots first, so that from outside it looked as if it had grown there. Nobody could go into that doorway now without first taking out the heather.

'Are you sure it wasn't done while you were here?' said Susan.

'The beast might have done it while you were asleep,' said Peggy.

'He didn't,' said Roger, not liking to be reminded of the label he had found above his head. 'I looked all round before I came away.'

'The dogmudgeon and the young chieftain may have done it last night,' said Dorothea.

'Or this morning,' said Titty. 'They may have been up before we were.'

All five red herrings looked anxiously up at the ridge.

'The road goes through that notch,' said Titty, 'and Dot's castle, where they played the bagpipes, is on the other side of it, and a lot of the black houses of the Gaels, like the ones we saw in Skye.'

'We'll go well beyond the notch before looking over,' said Susan.

'I'm going to stay here,' said Roger. 'Whoever blocked up that doorway did it to keep me out. He's sure to come again to see if the heather's been moved.'

'You're going to do nothing of the sort,' said Susan.

'Rogie, you can't,' said Titty.

'There aren't enough of us anyhow,' said Peggy. 'And if one of us settles down to sleep . . .'

'There isn't going to be any sleeping,' said Roger. 'And if whoever it was thinks he can do it again . . .'

'John and Nancy have started,' said Dorothea.

Far away below them, they could see the inlet, the near cove with the *Sea Bear* at anchor, and the narrower one beyond it, running further inland, where lay the *Pterodactyl*. They could see Captain Flint in the dinghy, and knew that he must be rowing back to the *Sea Bear* after putting John and Nancy ashore.

'I can't see them,' said Titty.

'They'll have started being decoys,' said Dorothea.

'We ought to have started too,' said Susan.

'Come on,' said Peggy.

They left the hill of the Pict-house, climbed as far as the track and, after a moment's hesitation, because, remembering the first time, Dorothea was inclined to think they ought to show themselves to the Gaels, set out along the track towards the head of the valley.

From the track they had a clear view of the two lochs and the island of the birds.

'He's hidden the boat beautifully,' said Dorothea. 'Nobody'd ever guess there was anybody there.'

'It doesn't look big enough to hide even Dick,' said Titty.

'He may be taking the photographs now,' said Dorothea.

'Jolly well hope not,' said Peggy. 'If he comes out in the boat he'll be in full view before we've got the Gaels even started.'

'Don't look down that way,' said Susan. 'We know he's on the island, and we know John and Nancy are in the next valley being decoys. It's silly for us to look. We don't know that somebody isn't watching us. And if we stare down there . . . and point . . .' she added, looking at Roger, 'we'll simply give the secret away.'

'Susan's right,' said Peggy.

'I believe we ought to have gone and stirred them up first,' said Titty. 'I don't believe they'd have stalked us last time if we hadn't.'

'Not safe till we've got further along,' said Susan.

She had hardly got the words out of her mouth before they

all heard a long shrill whistle. They swung round and stared up at the top of the ridge.

'It's begun,' said Titty. 'Only last time they'd been stalking us long before we heard the first whistle.'

'Somebody must have been on the look-out,' said Dorothea. 'I say. They may have been watching us all the time.'

'Jiminy!' said Peggy. 'No time to lose. Buck up. Keep together. Easier going on the cart track. We'll spread out to puzzle them later. Go it, red herrings. They're unkennelling the pack.'

Nobody watching the little party on the hillside and seeing how, at the sound of that whistle, they set off on the run, could have thought anything but that they were up to mischief. The whistle had hardly stopped sounding before all five of the red herrings were racing along as if they had stolen goods in their knapsacks instead of harmless sandwiches.

'Go it, Susan!' cried Roger, running close behind her.

'Keep to the track,' said Susan over her shoulder, and Roger grinned as he ran. He, too, had seen the deep peat cuttings on either side of the track, and the little piles of cut peat drying for next winter's fuel.

'Stick to it, Peggy!' he called.

'You keep your breath for running,' said Peggy, not even bothering to look round.

They ran on and on, along the winding track, that dipped and climbed and twisted among the rocks and heather of the ridge. At first they thought of nothing but keeping going, sure that the Gaels were already coming after them. Then, as their trot became more and more breathless, one after another of them kept glancing up towards the skyline.

'It was like that the other day,' panted Titty. 'We knew they were there, but we couldn't see them at all.'

'I c . . . can't k . . . keep it up,' panted Dorothea.

'Easy,' said Susan. 'We've got miles to go . . . Where's Roger?'

They stopped and looked back and then at each other. There was no doubt about it. They had been five red herrings. They were now only four. Roger had vanished altogether.

'I'll have to go back for him,' said Susan.

'Susan, you simply can't,' said Peggy.

'He may have slipped and hurt himself,' said Susan.

'Not he,' said Peggy. 'He'd have shouted. He's dropped out on purpose. I ought to have guessed he was up to something. It's a pity we divided up the grub before starting.'

'Don't look back,' begged Dorothea. 'If the stalkers see us looking back, they'll think there's something to look at.'

'There's someone up on the skyline now,' whispered Titty. 'I thought it was a rock, but it moved.'

'Look here, Susan,' said Peggy. 'If Roger'd slipped or anything like that he'd have shouted. He was close behind me when we began running. We can't risk spoiling the whole plan just because Roger's being a donk and starting some silly game of his own.'

'We simply can't,' said Dorothea. 'Dick's on the island now. He's counting on us. So's Nancy, and John. If Roger gets caught it's his own fault.'

'They won't kill him even if they catch him,' said Peggy.

'We've got to count him as a baby thrown to the wolves,' said Dorothea.

'He'll enjoy it,' said Titty.

'I jolly well hope he doesn't,' said Peggy. 'A plan's a plan and people ought to stick to it.'

'There's something moving up there,' said Titty.

'It's working all right,' said Dorothea. 'Just like last time. We knew it would. Oh, Susan, you mustn't look back.'

'All right. I won't,' said Susan. 'But Roger is so awfully cheeky and after all we are on someone else's land.'

'Explorers always are,' said Titty, 'except the ones that go into the Arctic and places like that, and even bits of the Arctic belong to Eskimos and Lapps. Roger'll remember Captain Cook. He'll keep on the right side of the natives.'

'Captain Cook got on the wrong side of them,' said Dorothea.

'The inside,' said Peggy. 'I hope Roger does too. If he gets eaten he deserves it. We ought to keel-haul him when we get back. But we can't do anything now. We must keep moving. Look here, Titty, was it really like this the other day? Native noises, like that whistle, but not a native to be seen.'

'We'd got further than this before they even began making noises,' said Titty.

Shepherding the worried Susan before them, the red herrings were on the move again. It was clearly the only thing to do.

'When they started last time, we turned into geologists,' said Dorothea. 'To show we were harmless . . .'

'No need to do anything like that,' said Peggy. 'Not unless we have to think of something just to keep them from losing interest. But, I say, are you sure they're stalking us at all?'

It was hard to believe. Titty had thought she had seen a head on the skyline, but nobody else had seen it. But for the whistle that all of them had heard, there had been nothing to show Peggy and Susan that the red herrings were not getting very hot for nothing, hurrying on and on in wild moorland country without a human being in it beside themselves. Still, they could see that Titty and Dorothea were sure that the same thing was happening that had happened when they were here before. Bit by bit, they came to be sure of it themselves. Anyhow, they had gone too far to turn back now. They no longer ran, but sauntered, ready at any moment to run again.

'Don't look back,' said Peggy. 'I know what Roger's done. I believe he meant to do it all the time.'

'What?'

'Gone back to his sentry box,' said Peggy. 'You know, where he went to sleep yesterday. I believe he meant to stay there all the time.'

'He'll never have got back there without being seen.'

'He can indian very well when he wants to,' said Titty.

'John and Nancy'll be pretty furious when they hear,' said Susan.

'Cock, cock, cock . . . Go back! Go back! Go back!'

'There you are,' said Titty. 'Those were grouse, and it wasn't us who startled them. There must be somebody up there in the heather, even if we can't see them.'

'Cock, cock, cock.'

'There goes another lot,' said Dorothea, as they saw the birds whirring above the skyline.

'Go back! Go back! Go back!'

'They're saying that to the stalkers,' said Titty.

'Well, I hope the stalkers don't go back either,' said Peggy. 'I'm going to give them a wave, to make them think we've spotted them. We all will.'

And the four red herrings, looking up towards the top of the ridge, waved cheerfully at rock and heather.

There was no answer from any stalker, but they saw yet another brace of grouse get up and fly along the ridge towards the hills.

As the red herrings turned to go on, they saw a movement in the valley.

'It's the deer,' said Titty. 'We saw them last time, too.'

The red herrings had not noticed them while they lay quiet, but now saw twenty or thirty all moving together.

'I can't see one with horns,' said Dorothea.

'There's another lot coming down the slopes ... over there ...'

'They'll have been started by Nancy and John,' said Peggy. 'Gosh! I do wonder how far they've got, and if the old Dactyl's chasing after them.'

They were by now already well beyond the upper of Dick's two lochs, and could safely let themselves look across the wide valley, that stretched, with patches of green among the rock and heather, to the further ridge. That further ridge hid the valley beyond it, where they knew John and Nancy were at work, carrying out their part of the plan. Far away to the south, they could see blue hills, and, towards the head of the valley they were in, the hills rose steeply with crags and screes, almost like the mountains in their own country. But there were no farms in sight, no buildings, no people, nor any signs of people except the cart track under their feet, winding on into the hills.

'I don't wonder Dick's birds chose this place,' said Titty. 'Until we came they must have had it all to themselves.'

'What about the Gaels?' said Dorothea, and they looked again up the steep slopes of rock and heather to the skyline.

'We've been going a long time,' said Susan.

'Not half far enough,' said Peggy. 'Look here. Nobody's tired?'

'Not a bit,' said Dorothea.

'It's about time for grub,' said Susan.

'I bet Roger's scoffed his,' said Peggy.

Susan, in spite of herself, looked back.

'Susan!' said Peggy. 'You mustn't.'

'I can't see him,' said Susan.

'Good,' said Peggy. 'So long as nobody else can. Just forget the little brute. Look forward. There! There! ... Nothing there really,' she explained. 'I'm only doing a bit of pointing in case some of our stalkers may be looking at us.'

'We'd better not stop to eat,' said Dorothea.

'No need,' said Peggy.

They ate their sandwiches on the march, stopping only to drink. As Peggy said, there never was a red herring that could tip lemonade down its throat out of a bottle while prancing along on a cart track. And it was just while Peggy was making sure of the last drops of her lemonade that something that changed everything for all of them.

The three others, waiting a moment while Peggy, with her head back, held her lemonade bottle upside down over her mouth, heard a sharp click.

'What's that?' said Susan.

'Nearly outed a tooth,' said Peggy. 'Don't move. Look where I'm looking now.'

High on the hillside above them, a boy in Highland dress was watching them.

'The young chieftain,' said Dorothea.

All four of them had seen him, the same boy who at dusk had come down with Roger's dogmudgeon, had looked silently at the *Pterodactyl* and had gone silently back.

'There's something funny about this,' said Peggy. 'It was funny the way they started after us without our having to stir them up. I believe they were waiting for us, but I can't see how they knew we were coming.'

'Nobody could have known,' said Susan.

'The Gaels have second sight,' said Titty.

'They may have known about Dick too,' said Dorothea.

'No,' said Peggy. 'What Nancy was afraid of was that they'd come charging down with war cries so that the Dactyl would have heard them and known where to look. And they haven't done that. Dick's all right.'

'He's all right so far,' said Dorothea. 'And we've got them coming after us.'

'I believe they'd be stalking us whether we wanted them to or not,' said Peggy.

'That boy's signalling to someone,' said Susan.

'He's disappeared,' said Titty.

'We ought to keep moving,' said Dorothea.

It is one thing to be a red herring, purposely leading the hunt in the wrong direction. It is quite another to feel that you have no choice in the matter, and that, whether you wanted to be stalked or not, the hounds would be hot on your trail. From now on, the red herrings were thinking not only of keeping the stalkers interested but also of how to keep themselves from being caught.

They were no longer looking anxiously for signs that they were being followed. Instead, they had the feeling that every rock hid an enemy. In a queer way, the whole desolate valley seemed astir. More and more often, grouse whirred along the hillside. In the valley below them parties of hinds kept moving, throwing up their heads, waiting and then suddenly moving again.

'When do you think it'll be safe for us to turn back?' asked Susan.

'Not till we hear the *Sea Bear*'s foghorn,' said Peggy.

'We've got a lot further than we did the other day,' said Titty.

'The further the better,' said Dorothea, thinking of Dick.

'I think the stalkers have gone even further than us,' said Titty a few minutes later. 'Look at that deer.' Far ahead of them, they saw a solitary stag going down into the valley as if startled by something on the ridge.

'I've thought that for a long time,' said Peggy. 'Those grouse have been getting up further and further ahead of us.'

274

'We might not hear the foghorn as far away as this,' said Susan. 'I'm going to turn back fairly soon.'

'Not yet,' said Peggy.

'We ought to hurry on and get ahead of them again,' said Dorothea.

'No hurrying,' said Susan urgently. 'We're not doing any harm. Just going for a walk. We've got to look as if we didn't know they were after us.'

A whistle shrilled behind them. They swung round. All four of them saw a man high on a rock above the cart track.

'He may have been hidden there when we passed,' said Titty.

'We can't go back that way,' said Susan.

'We don't need to,' said Peggy. 'When it comes to going back we'll cross the valley and go back down the other side.'

'Last time,' said Dorothea, 'dogs came charging down at us out of the heather.'

'The Gaels called them back,' said Titty.

'And then that old man came shouting after us,' said Dorothea.

'We bolted like hares,' said Titty.

Susan looked across the valley. 'Dot,' she said, 'how long does Dick take to photograph a bird?'

'I don't know,' said Dorothea. 'But he said it wouldn't be any good until the sun had gone over. You see, in the morning it would be shining into the camera.'

'Anyhow, he'll have got his photographs by now. Give him another half hour to get home and then we'll work across the valley and start back.'

Susan spoke in a whisper to Peggy.

'Right,' said Peggy. 'Of course they can't go the lick we can. Look here, you two. We're going to spread out. Susan and I'll keep along the track, but you two had better begin edging down into the bottom. You won't have so far to go, if we have to bolt for it.'

'Go on, Titty. Don't wait,' said Susan.

'But we don't turn back yet,' said Dorothea.

'No. No,' said Peggy. 'We'll go on as long as we possibly can.'

Titty and Dorothea left the track and went slantwise down the hillside into the valley. Peggy and Susan strolled slowly on along the track, trying not to show in any way that they knew that an invisible army of stalkers was moving with them.

It was perhaps twenty minutes later when two loud whistles on the hillside startled them again.

'I say, Peggy,' said Susan, 'I wish I knew what we ought to do.'

They stopped and looked down into the valley. Down there, on the mosses, Dorothea and Titty had stopped too, and were looking up at them for orders. Deer were moving this way and that, for no reason that they could see.

Suddenly, with a sigh of relief, Susan caught sight of Nancy's red cap on the top of the ridge across the valley.

'There's Nancy, and John,' she said. 'Does it mean we can start back? Look, she's waving.'

'Signalling,' said Peggy. 'Gosh, and I haven't a hand-kerchief.'

'I have.'

'Quick,' said Peggy.

On the other side of the valley, they watched the flick, flick of white.

'Morse,' said Peggy. 'Bother it. I wish she'd semaphore. Whatever is she doing? All the same letter. Why doesn't she get going and say something. I've given her the answering signal. Hullo. Short ... short ... long ... short ... short. Long. One U after another.'

'Danger signal,' said Susan. 'It means, "You are standing into danger!"'

'We know we are,' said Peggy.

'Perhaps John and Nancy can see more than we can,' said Susan.

'With the stalkers all over the place, what do they want us to do?'

A whistle shrilled again on the hillside behind them, answered instantly from higher up the valley. From behind rocks, from out of the heather, Gaels were sprouting into sight. Frightened deer were streaming down from the upper slopes.

Below in the valley, Titty and Dorothea were looking this way and that.

'Why haven't they the sense to bolt across to Nancy?' said Peggy.

'They can't,' said Susan. 'Look! Look! We'd better be all together.' She blew her own whistle and beckoned.

'Gosh!' said Peggy. 'It's Roger's dogmudgeon himself.'

Titty and Dorothea had seen him too, the grey-bearded giant of a man, from whom they had fled once before, the same grim man who had watched them put to sea, the same who had come down to the water's edge last night. He was close to them. Susan was beckoning. They had heard the mate's whistle. They waited no longer, but ran to join her. The dogmudgeon turned and came after them.

'Signal again,' said Susan. 'Signal to Nancy. John'll know what to do. Quick. Tell them we want help. Three shorts and a long one. Go on. Do it again.'

CHAPTER 22

THE ROUND-UP

SQUELCHING through the soft moss of the flats, stumbling, picking themselves up and stumbling again as they struggled up the heather-covered slopes, Titty and Dorothea ran to join Susan and Peggy, who stood waiting while the Gaels closed in. The deserted valley was full of movement. Nancy's red cap, Gaels, deer ... wherever one looked something was astir.

'The dogmudgeon's coming after us,' panted Titty, looking over her shoulder, 'and John and Nancy'll be too late to do any good.'

'I can't go any faster,' gasped Dorothea.

'Stick to it,' said Titty.

By the time they came breathlessly up to the cart track on the hillside, Susan and Peggy were already prisoners. Half-a-dozen wild-looking Gaels were standing round them.

Susan was talking, rather loudly, like someone talking to the deaf.

'I'm very sorry if we were trespassing,' she was saying. 'We didn't see any notices. We haven't done any harm really, only walking. If we have done any harm it was only by mistake...' She faltered into silence and Titty and Dorothea knew that she had been talking for some time. The Gaels stared at her with grave faces but said never a word.

Peggy started the moment Susan stopped and the Gaels stared at her instead of at Susan.

'Look here,' she said. 'It's quite all right. We want to get to a place from which we can see the Atlantic. You know ... The Atlantic Ocean ... America ... Over there...'

She pointed vaguely towards the hills and all the Gaels swung round but seeing only John and Nancy hurrying across the valley they turned again to Peggy as if they were listening hard and wanted to know what she was saying.

'We're here,' said Titty.

'I wish the others would come quick,' said Susan.

'They don't understand a word of English,' said Peggy desperately.

The prisoners and their captors waited in silence, watching John and Nancy who were already climbing up out of the valley. They had passed quite close to the dogmudgeon, who had not tried to stop them but was striding steadily after them, seeming not to hurry but moving nearly as fast.

'It's all right, Susan,' said John, racing up to the cart track and slipping through the Gaels who made room for him to join the other prisoners.

'Oh, John, John, have you hurt yourself?' said Susan. 'What *have* you done to your face.'

John, who had forgotten the burnt cork, wiped his face with a hand and made it worse. The Gaels stared at him. Two of them spoke urgently to each other.

'They don't know any English,' said Peggy.

'It's all right,' said John impatiently. 'Only Dick's spectacles. What's happened?'

'Let me do the talking,' said Nancy, but even she for a moment found nothing to say to those silent Gaels who were looking now at their prisoners, and now up the ridge, as if they were waiting for somebody else.

The dogmudgeon, that old, grey-bearded giant, came striding up to them. He stood, leaning on his long staff, and glowered at the prisoners from under bushy eyebrows. He moved a little closer, to peer into John's face. There was nothing in his blue eyes to show what he was thinking. He asked a question in a language the prisoners knew must be

Gaelic. One of the other Gaels answered him, and all of them turned and looked up the hillside and back along the track.

'How far do we have to go to see the Atlantic?' asked Nancy.

The dogmudgeon frowned at her. 'You will be seeing the inside of a jail first,' he said after a pause.

'Oh good,' said Nancy. 'We were afraid none of you knew English.'

'I do not need the English to see you driving our hinds.'

'But we didn't,' said Susan. 'We weren't doing anything.'

'Look here, this is all a mistake,' said John.

'Who sent you to do it?'

'But we didn't. We were just walking,' said Susan.

The dogmudgeon turned his back on her. One of the younger Gaels spoke to another. They all turned. Titty plucked at Dorothea's elbow. A boy in a kilt came leaping down the hillside towards them.

'It's the young chieftain,' said Dorothea. 'Now we'll be all right.'

'How do you do?' said John, as the boy jumped down out of the heather on the track beside them.

'Well,' said Nancy cheerfully, 'it's been good fun while it lasted. You've caught us. One up to you. But now we've got to get back to our ship.'

The boy stared first at John, then at Nancy, but did not answer. He looked at the faces of the prisoners one after another.

'One missing,' he said in English. 'There's another boy, smaller.'

'Don't tell him,' Dorothea almost squeaked, thinking of Dick.

'It's Roger he means,' said Titty.

The boy spoke urgently and privately to the dogmudgeon.

Then he swung round and went racing homewards along the cart track.

'Hullo! Hey! You! Stop!' cried Nancy angrily.

The boy turned.

'Half a minute,' said John.

'My father will be talking with you,' said the boy, and was off again at a steady trot.

'Marrch!' said the dogmudgeon.

'What do we do?' said Susan, but there was no need to ask, for the Gaels were on the move at once and the prisoners found themselves moving with them.

'Didn't you hear?' said Nancy. 'March. That's what he said. And so we will. Simply grand. Nothing to worry about. That boy talks English. So will his father. We'll get it all cleared up later on. Dick's had lots of time to get his pictures, thanks to you. Nothing else matters.'

They spoke to each other in whispers, though the old dogmudgeon, who had shown that he knew English, was walking at the rear of the party, not close enough to the prisoners to hear what they were saying.

'How thanks to us?' said Dorothea.

'Well, look at them,' said Nancy, glancing round at the Gaels marching beside them, in front of them and behind them. 'If you hadn't brought the whole savage clan up here one of them would have been sure to spot Dick on the lake and then there'd have been a hullabaloo and in two seconds the egg-collector would have known just what he wanted'

'We haven't heard the foghorn,' said Titty.

'Neither have we, but that's only because we've come so far. Dick'll be in the *Sea Bear* by now, and Uncle Jim'll be getting sails ready and cursing because he's got to wait for us.'

'Did the egg-collector come after you?' asked Dorothea, almost running at Nancy's side.

Nancy chuckled. 'Better than that,' she said. 'John blacked first-rate goggles round his eyes, and the old Dactyl thought he was Dick and sent a sailor chasing after us, thinking he'd see Dick going to his birds. He's been safe in his motor boat all the time with no dinghy to take him ashore.'

'Where is the sailor now?' asked Dorothea, glancing across the valley.

'Caught us up at last,' said Nancy. 'And had a good view of John's face. He's gone bolting back, miles too late. Every bit of the plan has worked out like we thought it would.'

'It's only Roger I'm bothered about,' said Susan.

'Where is Roger?' said John.

'We lost him right at the beginning,' said Susan.

'I think he went back to the Pict-house,' said Titty. 'Anyhow, the Gaels haven't got him. That boy said there was one missing.'

'Probably back in the Sea Bear,' said Peggy, 'having tea with Dick and Uncle Jim.'

'I wish we were,' said Susan. 'These people are furious about something and I don't know what.'

'Jiminy,' said Nancy presently. 'If they're going to move as fast as this, it's lucky we're not in chains.'

'They're taking us straight to the castle,' said Dorothea.

'Good,' said Nancy. 'That boy looks quite decent. Rather a waste really. We might have kidnapped him if we'd known and turned him into an ally. Barbecued Billygoats! We could have kept him prisoner in the Sea Bear. Pity it's all over. But it doesn't matter. We've done what we wanted to do.'

They were walking too fast to have breath to spare for argument. Presently even Nancy stopped talking. The prisoners trudged silently back along the track that climbed slowly up the ridge on the northern side of the valley, while the Gaels leaped through the heather above and below them and the tall, grey-bearded man, Roger's dogmudgeon, strode along the track behind them, like a shepherd driving sheep.

It had seemed a very long way up the valley while the red herrings had been luring all possible enemies away so that after he had taken his photographs Dick could escape from the island unseen. The distance seemed much shorter now, with the Gaels walking as if they did not know that walking could tire anyone, and the prisoners hurrying in the midst of them, determined not to be shamed by the Gaels. Also, though the red herrings were prisoners, they walked in triumph, sure that their work was done. Cheerful grins passed from face to face, puzzling the Gaels who, for their part, were just as triumphant as their prisoners. Only Susan was troubled. John and Nancy seemed to think that two words of English talk would put things right, but Susan was not so sure. The wild-looking men and lads were walking beside them without a smile, and when she glanced back at the dour face of their leader she began to feel guilty without knowing what was the crime. Whatever it was, these people thought it was serious and, if that boy and his father thought the same, explaining was going to be difficult.

'Cheer up, Susan,' said Nancy. 'It's been a huge success.'

Susan tried to smile but could not. There was Roger to worry about as well as everything else.

Long ago they had lost sight of the young chieftain racing ahead of them to bring the news of their capture to the chief of the clan. Already they were nearing the foot of the valley and could see where the track turned through the gap in the top of the ridge. They could see Pict-house Hill and the lump on the top of it that had been a prehistoric dwelling. Below them in the valley were the two lochs with the little stream joining them. They passed the upper loch. A rise in the ground hid much of the lower loch, but they could see the island of the birds.

MAP SHOWING THEIR TRACKS

Titty suddenly stopped short and was run into by Peggy at her heels.

'Sorry,' she said. 'I thought I saw something.'

'What?'

'Something moving by the Pict-house.'

'What sort of thing?'

'Roger,' whispered Titty, glancing at Susan. 'But I can't see anything now.'

Suddenly Dorothea grabbed Nancy's elbow.

'Nancy, Nancy,' she whispered. 'Dick's in sight ... rowing ... on this side of the loch, between the island and the shore.'

Nancy's head jerked, but she did not look round. 'Don't look that way,' she hissed. 'Don't take any notice at all. They may not spot him.'

'He's in full view,' whispered Dorothea.

'Quick,' said Nancy sharply. 'We've got to keep them all looking at us. Come on, all of you. Come on, John! I'll race you to the gap!'

The prisoners broke into a weary gallop.

There was a chorus of shouts from the Gaels. In a moment some of them had closed in on the track in front of the prisoners, like sheep-dogs slowing down a runaway herd.

'It's no good,' said John. 'They've seen him already.'

The prisoners stopped. Some of the Gaels were looking down towards the loch, so that there was no point in the prisoners not looking too. There was no sign of Dick and the folding boat.

'But I saw him,' said Dorothea. 'Rowing this way. He must be close under the shore, and we can't see him now because of those rocks.

'Where's the dogmudgeon?' said Peggy.

The prisoners looked at their guards. They looked both ways along the track; they looked up the ridge and down into the valley. The tall old Gael had disappeared, and, from the direction in which the others were looking, it was clear that he had gone just where the prisoners least wished that he should go.

Susan was the first to make up her mind what to do. 'Don't stop,' she said. 'The sooner the Gaels take us to their chief the better. Till we've got things explained, we can't do anything to help Dick.'

Nancy pulled herself together.

'Susan's right,' she said. 'If we all go charging down there, with the Gaels after us, hallooing like mad, it'll undo everything we've done. We've kept the coast clear all day for Dick to take his pictures. He's been a bit long over taking them. Not our fault. But what we've got to do now is to get the valley clear again with as little hallooing as possible. Bolting's no good. Only makes them break into full cry. Come on. Sedate and proper. Pretend we've been invited wherever they're taking us.'

'But Dick,' said Dorothea. 'If he's going to be made prisoner too, hadn't we better wait for him?'

'No,' said Nancy firmly but hardly above a whisper. 'We're a crowd here, for anybody to see. The sooner the valley's empty the better. Keep on the march like a school crocodile. Pretend we haven't noticed anything. Don't look back.'

CHAPTER 23

SHIP'S NATURALIST

DICK'S was a very different day from that of the decoys and red herrings. He watched for a danger signal, saw Nancy and John lying on a rock and knew that the coast was clear. He pushed through the reeds to the hidden boat, found her thwarts wet with dew, wiped a dry place for himself to sit and poled her out, stirring the reeds and, no matter how he tried to avoid it, sending wide ripples chasing each other across the smooth water of the loch. If anyone were watching, he would see those ripples. The birds would see them too. Dick wished there were a little wind to make ripples everywhere so that his own would not be noticed. The best he could do would be to get to the island quickly and hide the boat again.

He set himself to the task of making the folding boat go straight. He decided to do as he and John had done the night before, to row close along the shore and not turn out towards the island until he could come to it from the end furthest from the nest . . . if it was a nest. Now that he was actually on his way to photograph it, he began to think that he might after all have made a mistake. No. He was sure of it. Bother these ripples. Rowing with quick short strokes, now harder with one oar, now harder with the other, he did his best with that most unruly boat.

He was half way along the shore. It would be too late to turn back now, even if he got a warning signal. There were no more friendly reed patches in which to hide until he came to the island. If now the egg-collector or one of his men should see him in the boat, the secret would be out, the egg-collector would know that this was the loch and, sooner or later, he would take the eggs and shoot the birds, in which case it would have been better if Dick had never discovered them. Oh, bother those ripples, and bother this twisting boat! And now those ducks! Three, four, five ducks splashed up off the water and flew along the shore. In the quiet of the early morning Dick heard them scattering the water as they rose, looked round and saw their flight. Would they give warning to the Divers? The worst of trying to come near wild birds was that there was no way of letting them know you were not an enemy but a friend who did not mean them any harm.

He rowed on and on. Over his right shoulder he caught a glimpse of the island. There was one of the birds, in the water, and, yes, that dark blob must be the other, on the shore. They must have seen him. Dick rowed as quietly as he could. Suddenly he heard the strong beat of wings on water. Splash! Splash! Splash! A Great Northern Diver was getting up into the air. That was bad enough. Worse was to come.

'Heuch! Heuch! Heuch!'

That angry, frightened, guttural cry could be heard for miles around.

Dick nearly caught a crab. He gripped his oars and waited. Far away, across the loch, he saw Nancy's red cap moving. He lost sight of it. He rowed on, watching desperately for a signal that would tell him that the egg-collector had heard. None came. But it might come at any moment. And the birds had already been disturbed. There was only one thing to do and that was to get into hiding as quickly as he could from birds and men alike. Dick spun the boat round and headed for the island. Quietly and fast he rowed out from the shore, came to the far end of the island and worked the boat into the reeds. He sat still, breathing fast, and looked about him. Nothing but reed tops, except over the stern of the boat.

If nobody had seen him coming across and he could work her in another yard or two, nobody would be able to see her. The Great Northern Diver, after that one dangerous cry, had not called again. Dick felt over the side with an oar and found soft bottom and shallow water, not more than a foot deep. He took off his shoes, tied the laces together and hung them round his neck. He stepped over the side, took the end of the painter and waded ashore, pulling the boat after him. He made a loop in the end of the painter and laid it round a small boulder, shifted a stone so that it lay on the rope, saw that the boat was completely hidden in the reeds and set out to crawl along the island to his hide.

His head was a whirl of question-marks. Had that raucous screech brought the egg-collector rushing up from his boat to look over into the valley? Every moment he expected to hear it repeated. Was the hide as good as it had seemed in last night's dusk? Could he reach it without being seen? Had he frightened the birds away? Would they come back?

Not Roger, nor Titty, could have kept lower to the ground than the Ship's Naturalist as he indianed his way along, trying all the time not to be visible to birds or to anybody else who might be looking. Quick. Quick. There, ahead of him, were the rocks that made the back and walls of his hide. There, as he had left it, was the heather-covered netting spread over them and hanging like a curtain across the opening between the two rocks nearest to the nest. He crawled in and waited, listening for distant shouts. He heard none. And after that first call of anger and warning, the birds had been silent. Lying like that, he could see nothing. Very slowly he pulled up first one leg and then the other. Kneeling, he looked out through the netting. There was not a bird to be seen. Both had gone. But he saw, close to the water, a flattened trodden nesting-place, a circle of broken bits of reed and a worn track leading from it to the water's edge. And there, in the middle of that round mat of broken reeds, were two greenish enormous eggs. A moment later the birds swam into view, a yard or two off shore. Very quietly, Dick took the big binoculars from their case. He could see dark blotches on the eggs, which were not really green but a sort of brownish olive. And the birds? There could be no doubt about them now or ever again. Great Northern Divers at their nest. In the British Isles, no one had ever seen that sight before. It was as if he were an astronomer looking for the first time at a new planet.

His first instinct was to take a photograph at once. But the sun was in his eyes, glinting off the water, shining straight into the camera from behind the birds. He remembered in time. It would be a waste of an exposure and he had film in his camera for only five. He had taken up the camera. Now, as he put it down again, it clinked on a stone. The birds heard it, turned and began to swim away. They were out of sight from within that narrow hide. For three dreadful minutes he thought that he had, after all, frightened them into deserting the nest. Then he saw one of them again, low in the water, only the head and neck showing. Dick watched, hardly breathing. The back of the bird showed. It was swimming as usual. Suddenly, much nearer and close in front of him, he saw the other bird swimming straight for the nest. 'It swam itself aground.' (Dick's own words, as he tried afterwards to describe what he had seen.) It swam itself aground and then, using its wings to help it, floundered across the few feet of dry land between the water and the nesting-place. 'You couldn't really call it a nest.'

It settled on the eggs, facing suspiciously towards the hide. Presently it stirred again, shuffled round, settled once more, shielding the eggs with its wings on either side. It polished its bill on its breast and then, tilting its neck slightly back and its head slightly forward, was as still as if it had been shot and stuffed and were already in Mr Jemmerling's collection. It sat there, with its back to Dick, looking out over the loch as if any danger that might threaten it would come over the water. Dick was sure that so long as he made no noise the Diver would not guess that he was there.

There was nothing to be done now but to wait, hour after hour, till the sun climbed overhead and he could point the camera through a mesh in the netting without sunlight pouring into the lens. Hour after hour. He knew he would have to wait a very long time, but the long wait, that would have been torment to any of the others, was no torment to the Ship's Naturalist. The worst of his difficulties were over. He was in his hide. The boat was hidden. Neither he nor it could be seen by enemies, no matter where they were. The birds were at peace. He had only to wait to take the photographs and by that time the others would have led the egg-collector and the Gaels away into the hills and he would be able to get ashore with the film in his camera that would prove beyond all possible doubt that the birds were nesting and what birds they were.

Cautiously, he made himself as comfortable as he could. Hour after hour went by and Dick would not have liked to miss a minute of them, crouched there within a few yards of one of the great birds he had always longed to see. He hardly noticed the passing of the time and felt, as some people feel at a circus, that it was a pity it could not last for ever.

He took out his notebook and wrote down a description of the nest and the eggs and that funny floundering four-legged walk of the bird as it came up out of the water. 'Its wings work as two of the four legs.' With Captain Flint's big binoculars he could almost count the feathers of the sitting bird, even see the slits of its nostrils. Its head had looked black at a distance, but he could see now that it had a faint shimmer of green at the back and almost a purplish shimmer on its cheeks, while the lower part of its neck looked in the sun as if it were shot with green and purple together. 'Of course, even starlings look black till you get near enough to see,' thought Dick.

Sometimes its mate swam into view far out on the loch and Dick focused the binoculars on it, watched it diving and tried to be ready for it when it came up to the surface. Several times he saw it come up with a fish. Perhaps three hours after Dick had reached the hide, he saw that the bird in the water was much nearer than it had been. It dived and came up nearer still. There was a sudden stir on the shore. Almost before Dick knew what was happening, the bird that had been sitting was flopping towards the water and launching itself with a splash. The other bird was scrambling out to take its place. Dick reached for his camera and was glad he had been too late, for the light was still behind the birds and he had been photographer long enough to know that he must have it behind the camera. The bird that had been fishing settled itself facing out over the loch and Dick was sure that it had no suspicion that it was being watched from only a few yards away. He had done a lot of bird-watching, but never such bird-watching as this and with such birds to watch.

Hour followed hour. He forgot Gaels and egg-collector and the *Pterodactyl* and the *Sea Bear* and everything else but the narrow picture before him, seen through the curtain of netting. Dick and the birds were alone. The rest of the world had melted away into nothing. Dick would not have remembered to eat his sandwiches if he had not been reminded that he was hungry by wondering what weight of fish the Diver he was watching managed to eat in a day. He did not eat all the sandwiches he had been given because when he had eaten half of them, taking them out with extreme care, a bit of sandwich dropped on the paper and that tiny noise made the bird on the nest turn its head. Dick took no more risks and was glad he had thought of borrowing a flask for fear there might be the usual pop if he had a lemonade bottle to open.

The end of his waiting caught him by surprise. He could hardly believe that he had been there so long when at last he noticed that the bird was sitting on its own shadow, and that the sunlight no longer blazed through the netting but fell from overhead. The Ship's Naturalist became all photographer. There must be no mistakes. He had film for five photographs and could not afford to waste a single one. He grew hot in the face as he remembered how often he had taken a second photograph on the same bit of film by forgetting to wind on till the next number showed in the little red window at the back of his camera. Whatever happened, he must not do that today. Then there was the question of focus. Ten to twelve feet, he thought, but wished he could measure the distance and make sure. He remembered that with a smaller aperture to the lens the focus would be deeper so that a mistake of several feet one way or the other would not matter quite so much. That meant a longer exposure. He could afford that, because the bird sat so still, but it would mean holding the camera steady for a longer time. There was nothing in his hide on which he could rest the camera. Inch by inch he changed his position until he was sitting on the ground with one knee up, close to his face. The camera would be steady enough on that knee, though it would not be too easy to see through the finder. He tried and saw a blur across the picture. Netting, of course. He had to come closer to the netting and make sure that the lens of the camera looked out through the middle of a mesh. The bird quickly turned its head. Dick froze until it turned away again. Cramp gripped the calf of his bent leg. He rubbed it silently, digging a finger into the muscle. He tried again. The bird was going to be very small in the picture. That could not be helped. The first thing he would buy when he was grown up would be a camera with a telephoto lens. Meanwhile, he must do the best he could. He set the aperture at f. 11, the speed at a twenty-fifth of a second. Sunlight. Clear sky. That ought to be enough. Everything was ready.

He took a last look through the finder. He pressed the trigger. Nothing happened. In remembering so much, he had forgotten to set the spring of the shutter. This was dreadful. He knew that his fingers were trembling. No hurry. No hurry, he told himself, forced himself to wait, set the shutter, made sure once more that the camera was in the right position and pressed the trigger.

There was a sharp click. The photograph was taken, but what was happening? The bird had heard that click. For one moment Dick thought it was going to leave the nest and give him no second chance. But no. It had turned its head sharply. Then, slowly, it did what, if he had been able, the photographer would have asked it to do. It was shifting on the nest. Full of suspicion but not yet frightened, it shifted round, while still sitting on the eggs, till it was looking straight at Dick's curtain of netting. Dick did not stir a finger. The bird's head slowly drooped. Dick, knowing that he could not be seen, reset his shutter, turned on the film for the next exposure and waited once more with the camera resting on his knee, his finger ready at the trigger.

Click.

The bird stirred again.

'Don't move! Please don't move!' Not a sound came from Dick's lips, but he felt almost as if he were shouting at the bird. And, though it lifted its head and stiffened and stared at the rocks and the netting curtain that hid the photographer, it was as if the bird had heard him and understood. Slowly its stiffness eased. Everything was as it had been. The bird was still on its nest. The photographer was still in his hide. Two photographs had been taken.

Dick waited a very long time before he dared wind on the film and re-set the shutter of the camera. With those two photographs safe, he could afford to wait, and what he dreamed of now was a photograph that should show both birds. And just now that second bird was away fishing and not even in sight. At last it swam into view a long way out.

The bird on the nest shuffled round until once more it was facing the water. 'Wants to go fishing,' thought Dick, and wondered how soon it would be the other bird's turn to sit on the nest. It was too much to hope that, now that the sun was right, he would have another chance of photographing them changing places. The bird in the water was coming nearer, but not with any great haste. Suddenly the sitting bird grew impatient. Half lifting itself on the tips of its wings, it left the eggs and flopped away into the water. Dick pressed the trigger.

Click.

If only that shutter did not make such a row. But, though Dick heard it, the bird did not, as the click came at the very moment that it splashed off the land into the water. It swam out towards its mate. Three photographs and no bad mistake so far. Hurriedly, Dick took his chance, wound on the film, reset the shutter and took the fourth photograph, this time of the eggs alone.

Only one exposure left. Again he wound on the film. Was he or was he not going to get a picture of both birds together? The light seemed very strong and, with four photographs taken already, he made up his mind to risk being a little out of focus or under-exposed, and to try to get a picture of a bird scrambling out of the water. He set the aperture at its widest and the speed at one hundredth of a second.

Something very odd was happening out there. The bird that had left the nest had not begun fishing. It was as if the two birds had something to talk about. They were slowly swimming together. 'She's telling him that it's jolly well his turn,' thought Dick. 'Or else he's telling her.' It certainly looked as if one bird were bringing the other back to the nest. With sudden horror, Dick wondered if the birds were telling each other that there was something wrong about that heathery patch that had sprouted on the rocks during the night. But the birds were coming nearer and nearer. At last one stopped, dipped its head and rested, wiping its beak on its feathers, while the other swam straight for the shore, ran itself aground and floundered up to the nest. Dick took his photograph. The bird either did not hear the click or had made up its mind that there was no need to notice it. It shifted the eggs a little with its beak, and settled on them, just as the bird out on the loch went under water for its first dive. (Afterwards, Dick was not sure which of the birds had come to the nest. It might have been the same bird come back again, or it might have been the bird that had been fishing.)

Dick wound on the film, closed the camera and put it in its case. The thing was done. In there, ready to be developed, were the first five photographs ever taken of a Great Northern Diver nesting in the British Isles. Now, for the first time for hours, Dick remembered that there were human beings about as well as birds. He pulled out his watch and could hardly believe he had been there all that time. He wished he could have stayed in the hide till dark but Captain Flint had told him to be as quick as he could, and John and Nancy and the red herrings would not be able to keep the egg-collector and everybody else away from the loch for ever. He must keep to the programme, get away without frightening the birds, take the boat back to the reeds at the foot of the lake and get his camera with the photographs in it safely back to the *Sea Bear*.

He packed camera and binoculars and flask into his knapsack but did not try to sling his knapsack on his shoulders while he was in the hide. Pulling it with him, he wriggled slowly backwards, deciding to leave the netting where it was. It would not be needed again and to move it now would scare the birds for certain. Clear of the boulders he looked anxiously up at the ridges on either side of the valley. He saw no one. Hidden from the birds, he wriggled his arms into the straps of his knapsack, and crouching low, hurried to the boat. He unfastened the painter, stepped in and, after one more glance round, pushed out from among the reeds, settled to the oars and rowed as hard as he could, quick short strokes as before, but not so carefully. What mattered now was speed. The birds were bound to see him, but the sooner he was gone the sooner they would forget that they had had a visitor.

Half way to the shore, he saw one of the birds swimming. He looked for the other on the nest but could not see it. He turned the boat to row down to the foot of the lake, and rowed, watching the island, and looking for the other bird. Presently he saw it, in the water, not far from the first. He must, after all, have made some noise when wriggling out from the rocks. He rowed on, watching, wishing the bird would go back, wishing he could let it know that now and ever after it would have the island to itself. He forgot what an unruly boat the folder was to row, and, delighted as he saw that once again there was a bird on the nest, he came to the shore most unexpectedly. There was a sudden scrunch as the keel touched bottom, followed by a surprising jerk.

Dick, startled, looked round to see a big grey-bearded man with a hand on the boat's gunwale. There was another violent jerk as the man pulled the boat ashore.

'Out of that,' said the man.

'But I've got to take the boat to . . .'

'Your wee boat will bide well enough till the laird kens what you are after.'

'But,' said Dick.

'Out of the boat and no blethering,' said the man.

Dick stepped out. He thought of nothing but the photographs in his camera. Somehow or other he had to get those photographs to the *Sea Bear*. Nobody was in sight. Dick made up his mind and bolted along the shore.

He had not gone three yards before a hairy hand was at his collar.

'That is the way you are,' said the man. 'I am not a hard man, but any more of your tricks and you will be sorry.'

And Dick found himself walking fast up the hillside from the shore with a strong grip on the collar of his coat and hard knuckles against the back of his neck.

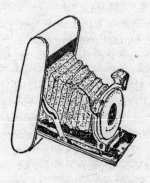

CHAPTER 24

UNWANTED RESCUER

I T was already far on in the afternoon.

The red herrings, with Gaels before and behind them, were marching along the cart track, sedate as a girls' school out for a walk, anxious only that nothing should happen to attract the attention of the egg-collector and his men. They did not think there was much danger of that because they were sure that, if the egg-collector had come ashore, Captain Flint, watching from the *Sea Bear*'s cross-trees, would at once have warned them by sounding the foghorn.

Dick, in the grip of the old dogmudgeon, was being rushed up the hillside to join them. Few prisoners can have had happier hearts. His first instinct had been to bolt for it, but though he had been captured and though the hard knuckles of the old man pressed into the back of his neck, he no longer minded that. He had caught a glimpse of the convoy of prisoners on the track high up the hillside. They had all been captured together, but they were prisoners of the Gaels, not of the egg-collector. He had seen no sign of Mr Jemmerling. He had done what he had had to do. His camera was safe in the knapsack on his back and in his camera were the photographs that would prove beyond all doubt and for ever that the Great Northern Diver had nested in the Outer Hebrides. Nancy and John would know what to say to the Gaels. They could come back in the dusk to fetch the folding boat and before morning the *Sea Bear* and her crew would be out at sea and sailing for the mainland.

Captain Flint, perched on the cross-trees of the *Sea Bear* had spent an uncomfortable day. He had given a coat of gold paint to the truck at the very top of the mast. He had given a coat of varnish to the masthead blocks. He had smartened up with aluminium paint every bit of iron work he could reach. He had smoked nearly an ounce of tobacco. He was more than tired of looking, through the pocket telescope that Dick had lent him in exchange for the big binoculars, at the *Pterodactyl* just beyond the rocks, and at the egg-collector who, much more comfortable than himself, was lounging in a deck-chair and from time to time using field-glasses to look at the masthead of the *Sea Bear*. Twice Captain Flint had gone down for a moment or two, once to get rid of his paint tins and once to get hold of his sandwiches. Each time he was no sooner back on his perch than he had seen the egg-collector returning to his comfortable chair. It was clear that just as Captain Flint was watching Mr Jemmerling, so was Mr Jemmerling keeping an eye on Captain Flint. Captain Flint had stuck to his post, though he could not help wishing that he could have exchanged the cross-trees for a deck-chair. He began to think those wretched children had forgotten all about him. Dick had probably taken his photographs long ago, and grown interested in something else. All very well. Time was going on. They ought all of them to have been back at the ship by now. Captain Flint wished Dick had never seen his birds. He wished Great Northern Divers were as common as sparrows. Most of all he wished that everything had gone as he had planned it and that the *Sea Bear* was already across the Minch, and being handed over to her owner.

Suddenly, looking up between the Hump and Pict-house Hill to the high ridge that had been named the Northern Rockies, in the hope of seeing some of his crew, he saw people moving. Twisting on his perch, he lifted the little telescope and looked again. About a dozen men and lads were walking along the hillside with at least six of the children. He could not be sure of Susan, Dorothea or Titty, but surely that was

A HAND AT HIS COLLAR

John and there could be no mistaking Nancy's and Peggy's red caps. But, instead of coming down towards the cove, they were making up towards the gap at the top of the ridge. What on earth was happening? Then he saw another man join the the rest, bringing with him a boy who might be Dick. Were they all being marched away as prisoners? Captain Flint banged his fist on the cross-trees. Never, never again, would he take children with him for a cruise. He hurt his fist but hardly felt it. He had a sudden vision of indignant mothers. He took another glance at the *Pterodactyl*. The egg-collector seemed to be asleep. Asleep or not, there was only one thing to be done. In another minute Captain Flint was down on deck and hauling in the dinghy. A minute later, he was pulling for the shore. Two minutes after that he had landed, slipped on the rocks, torn a huge rent in his trousers and was racing up the hill as fast as he could.

Aboard the *Pterodactyl*, the deck-chair was empty. Mr Jemmerling, watched no longer, was signalling. A man who had been lying in the heather with glasses to his eyes slipped down to the shore of the cove and rowed out in the dinghy to fetch his master. For some time now he had been looking carefully at the island on the loch.

'Here's Dick?'

Just where the cart track swung round towards the gap in the top of the ridge, the Gaels had stopped and looked back. The dogmudgeon with his prisoner was close behind them. In another moment, Dick, breathless, moving his head stiffly from side to side and tenderly feeling his neck, was with the others and the convoy, the dogmudgeon now at the head of it, was on the march once more.

'Did he hurt you?' asked Dorothea.

'Did you get the pictures?' whispered Nancy.

'Five,' panted Dick with a grin and a final shake of his head. 'At least two ought to be all right.'

'Did the Dactyl see you?' asked John.

'I don't think so,' said Dick. 'Anyway, I didn't see anybody. And it's all right. I saw the eggs. And one of the pictures ought to show them.'

'Why were you such an age?' said Nancy.

'Was I?' said Dick. 'I couldn't take the photographs any sooner. The sun was the wrong side. I say. Where are we going?'

'We're prisoners,' said Titty.

'I know,' said Dick, feeling the back of his neck.

'We're being taken to the castle,' said Dorothea.

'Listen!'

Once again they were hearing the noise of the bagpipes on the further side of the ridge.

'They've got all of us,' said Peggy.

'All except Roger,' said Susan.

'And Captain Flint,' said Titty.

'I say,' whispered John. 'I can see the ship. There's no one up the mast. Where is he?'

At that moment they heard him. A loud 'Hey!' came from below them. Nobody but Captain Flint shouted just like that.

'Bother!' said Nancy.

'Roger's brought him to the rescue,' said Titty.

'Who wants to be rescued?' said Nancy.

'Before we've even seen the dungeons,' said Dorothea.

'Don't stop walking,' said Nancy.

'They wouldn't let us stop if we tried to,' said Peggy.

They caught a glimpse of Captain Flint scrambling up from the shore. Then as the road dipped through the gap they could no longer look down into the valley they had left. The noise of the bagpipes was sounding close at hand. Before them were the low thatched cottages of the Gaels and the grey house with its turret that Dick, John, Nancy, Peggy and Susan were seeing for the first time.

'He'll do the talking better than we can,' said Susan.

'We could do it all right ourselves,' said Nancy.

'Here he is,' said Titty, as another 'Hey!' sounded from behind them.

Captain Flint was through the gap and running hard. The Gaels and their prisoners had reached the first of the cottages. The dogmudgeon was opening the door of a thatched building without windows, that looked as if it might be a storehouse.

'Hey!' shouted Captain Flint again.

The dogmudgeon glanced round. He said nothing, but his lips moved. It was almost as if he smiled. His had been a successful day. He had caught the children who had been driving the deer and here, falling into his hands, was one of the rogues who had sent them to do it.

Captain Flint panted up to them just in time to be hustled through the door with the rest of the prisoners. The door slammed behind them. They were in darkness. The noise of the bagpipes was suddenly fainter. On the outer side of the door a heavy bolt crashed into its sockets. They were prisoners indeed.

For a moment or two, when the bright sunlight was shut out, the prisoners were groping blind, feeling for each other and afraid to move, not knowing what there might be to trip them on the floor. Then Captain Flint got breath enough to shout once more.

'Hey!' he shouted. 'I want to talk to somebody.'

'There will be talk enough when the McGinty sees you,' came the answer from outside.

(NOTE. The name they heard was not McGinty. If the real name were to be printed here, it would tell everybody who read it exactly where the Great Northern Divers had their nest. It was necessary, therefore, to change it for another name for use in this book, and, at Dorothea's suggestion, the name McGinty was chosen, borrowed from Mrs McGinty whom Dick and Dorothea had met at Horning on the Norfolk Broads.)

'Open this door,' shouted Captain Flint.

There was no answer in English, but the prisoners could hear the Gaels talking in their own language just outside.

A little light came through holes in the thatching of the roof and, as their eyes became accustomed to it, the prisoners were seeing each other's faces, pale in the gloom where at first they had seen nothing but blackness.

'One of you go and fetch the laird at once,' said Captain Flint, in the voice of one giving an order but already not in the voice of one who knew that his order would be instantly obeyed.

There was a quiet laugh outside. The soft Gaelic talk went on but the voices sounded further away.

'They're leaving us here,' said Captain Flint. 'Well, Nancy, I hope you're satisfied.'

'We jolly well are,' said Nancy. 'The only thing that's gone wrong is your coming to rescue us when there wasn't any need. Everything's gone beautifully.'

'Has it?' said Captain Flint. 'And here we are all locked up like a lot of thieves, and heaven only knows how long they'll keep us.'

'They can't hang us,' said Nancy. 'And Dick's got his pictures.'

'But what happened?'

With that, everybody was talking at once. 'We got ourselves stalked just like last time . . .' 'It worked beautifully . . .'

'We led one of the Dactyl's men miles up the wrong valley . . .'
'We showed him loch after loch . . .' 'Do look out, John, my nose isn't as hard as your elbow . . .' 'Don't stoop . . .' 'Five photographs . . . I saw the eggs . . .' 'Ow, I've got cobwebs all over my face . . .' 'Look out, you'll be tumbling next . . .' 'Well, keep still . . .' 'Suddenly they were all round us in the heather . . .' 'We saw Peggy, signalling for help . . .' 'The young chieftain came leaping down the hill . . .'

'Yes . . . yes . . . yes . . . yes . . . But what did you do to upset these people?'

'We did nothing at all, just harmless walking,' said Nancy.

'They said we were chasing their deer,' said Susan.

Captain Flint groaned.

'Deer!' he exclaimed. 'You couldn't have done worse. Galloping about on someone else's land doesn't matter much. But chasing deer's serious.'

'But nobody chased deer,' said Nancy.

'They simply ran away,' said Titty, 'we couldn't stop them.'

'Heaven knows what we're in for,' said Captain Flint. 'I don't know what the law is in these parts. The owner may be judge, jury, jailer and everything else.'

'We'll manage him,' said Nancy. 'At least I could, if only you hadn't let yourself be caught.'

'Shut up,' said Captain Flint. 'Listen!'

Again they heard voices near by.

'Here's the laird,' said Dorothea.

'Sounds like more Gaelic,' said Captain Flint. He banged heavily on the door. 'Hey!' he shouted and then, urgently, to the other prisoners. 'What did they say his name was?'

'McGinty,' said Dorothea.

'Hey!' called Captain Flint again. 'You, outside there. Go at once and tell Mr McGinty I want to speak to him.'

Low voices spoke together outside the door, but nobody answered Captain Flint and presently the voices moved away once more.

'I don't believe they understood a word I said,' muttered Captain Flint. 'If only these chaps were Malays . . . Gaelic simply isn't fair.'

'It's all right,' said Nancy. 'Roger's dogmudgeon talks English, and so does that boy and he said his father would be talking to us. Bound to talk English too. We've only got to wait.'

'What happened to Mr Jemmerling?' Dick asked.

'Had a comfortable day,' said Captain Flint. 'Never stirred . . . sitting in a deck-chair while I was perched on the cross-trees . . . sharp edges those cross-trees have . . .'

'Was he sitting there when you came away?' asked Nancy.

'Yes,' said Captain Flint. 'He's had an easy day of it.'

'We've done him anyhow,' said Nancy. 'And now there's no hurry about anything.'

'Isn't there? We ought to be sailing tonight.'

'If we can't, we can't,' said Nancy. 'We've just got to wait.'

'I'm going to sit down,' said Peggy.

'Not on the floor,' said Susan. 'Better sit on our knapsacks.'

'We ought to be carving farewell messages on the walls,' said Titty.

'Yes,' said Dorothea. 'French Revolution. Waiting our turns and thinking of the guillotine.'

'Hang those bagpipes,' said Captain Flint.

'But they're just right,' said Dorothea. 'Better than French Revolution. Prisoners in the dungeon while the McGinty of McGinty is sitting in the hall of his castle and the piper of his clan is playing the tunes of his ancestors.'

'Well, I wish he'd shut up,' said Captain Flint. 'We ought

to be off. There's only one good thing about it all and that is that when they do let us out we'll be able to start at once. We're all here together and there'll be no hunting round for stragglers.'

'When did Roger get back to the *Sea Bear*?' asked Susan.

'Roger?' said Captain Flint peering round in the dim light of their prison. 'Why? Isn't he here?'

'No,' said Susan.

'Didn't he bring you to the rescue?' asked Titty.

'Never set eyes on him since you started,' said Captain Flint. 'Didn't they rope him in with the rest of you?'

'He wasn't with us,' said Susan. 'We don't know where he is.'

'Well, he's missed being put in a dungeon,' said Nancy. 'He'll be pretty sick about that.'

'But where is he?' said Susan. 'What'll he do when he goes back to the beach and finds nobody there? Where did you leave the dinghy?'

'Pulled well up,' said Captain Flint. 'He won't be able to get afloat and he can't come to much harm ashore. He'll just have to wait.'

'He'll be hungry,' said Susan.

'If he gets really hungry,' said Susan, 'he'll try to swim off to the ship.'

'He isn't a perfect idiot,' said Captain Flint.

'He's a bit keen on swimming this year,' said Titty.

'I ought to have gone back for him at the very beginning,' said Susan.

'Great gaping Guillemots!' exclaimed Nancy. 'Do cheer up, Susan. It doesn't matter a bit about Roger. He'll be all right. The thing that does matter is that everything's been a howling success.'

'I've got the photographs,' said Dick.

'Yes,' said Susan, 'but ...'

'Shut up, all of you,' said Captain Flint. 'Listen!'

Waiting, silent, in the dusk of their prison, they heard a very gentle tapping at the bottom of the door.

CHAPTER 25

ROGER'S DULL DAY

ROGER had waked that day with only one idea in his head: somehow or other to get even with the enemy who had gloated over the sleeping sentinel and made him look so foolish. How he was to do it he did not know but the moment he saw the heather stuffed into the entrance to the old Pict-house he took it as a challenge. His enemy had put that heather there so that he should know if anybody had used that entrance again. It was like stopping a fox's earth, to prevent the hunted fox from going to ground. Roger, the fox, instantly determined that the trick should fail. He was sure too that the enemy would come to see if the heather had been moved. It was at the Pict-house that the enemy had gloated over Roger. Very good. It was at the Pict-house that Roger would gloat over the discomfited enemy.

Getting away from the others had been easy. When the first whistle sounded and the red herrings began to run, his chance had come almost at once. He had only to lag a little, drop into one of the old peat cuttings at the side of the track and lie there while the red herrings and their pursuers moved on towards the hills. By the time he had thought it safe to put his head up and look out, the winding track had taken the red herrings out of sight. Indianing carefully, just in case some invisible Gael might be looking, Roger wormed his way back to the Pict-house and lay beside it to consider what to do next.

He had a pleasant feeling of badness, to which he was well accustomed. He knew very well what Susan and the others would be thinking of him. Anyhow, they could not be expected to understand. None of them had waked up to find

310

that someone had written a label . . . Even to himself, Roger did not repeat those loathsome words.

Carefully without touching it, he had another look at the heather that filled the mouth of what had been a passage into the Pict-house and was now the place where that enemy kept his secret store. He saw that the heather had been cleverly put in so that not a root was showing. Anybody might think it was growing there. It was as if his enemy had dared him to move the heather and put it back again so exactly as it had been that nobody could tell it had been disturbed.

Dimly, Roger began to see how he could make his enemy look foolish even if not quite as foolish as he had been made to look himself. He felt in his pocket for the string that he always carried in case it might come in useful. It was coming in useful today. He found one neat hank and a couple of loose bits. He unwound the hank and made a loop in one end of the string. Then, gently, he worked the string all round the heather just where it stuck out of the entrance. He poked the other end through the loop and pulled. The string tightened until the heather was held together like a bunch of flowers. Gingerly he lifted the great bunch of heather out of the entrance and saw that the roots, sticking out in all directions would stop him from putting it back. He joined his other two bits of string together and used them to tie up the roots in the same way. The heather, instead of falling to pieces as his enemy had planned, was a single faggot. Roger put it back in the entrance and admired it. No one looking at it from outside could tell that anything had been done to it. He had another idea, even better. He took out the faggot of heather, laid it close to the entrance, wriggled in himself and, from inside, pulled the heather back into place. Yes, the fox could lie there, hidden, in the very earth from which his enemy had meant to shut him out. All he had to do now was to wait for the enemy. The heather was itself a promise that the enemy would come, if only to see if it had been moved. Roger pushed it carefully out, and crept, blinking, into the sunshine. There was no need to wait in that dark tunnel. Far better to watch for the enemy, see him when still far away and be ready for him when he came.

He remembered the biscuit box. Dealing with the heather had put other things out of his head. He crawled back into the tunnel, felt for the box, pulled it into the light and opened it. The diary was still there, but nothing else. Roger shut the box, put it back where he had found it and crawled out once more.

He worked round to the seaward side of the Pict-house and climbed up and over into the hollow on the top of it, from which he could see out without being seen. He took his telescope out of his knapsack and looked cautiously along the hillside for the red herrings he had deserted. They had long passed out of sight beyond a shoulder of the Rockies. There were no Gaels to be seen. He looked down to the cove where, through the telescope, he saw Captain Flint busy with something, sitting on the cross-trees of the *Sea Bear*. A little further away, beyond those rocks, he could see the *Pterodactyl*. That was probably the egg-collector himself, sitting in a chair on the after deck. What about Dick? Down in the valley, beyond the Hump, the far hills were reflected in the waters of the loch. There was no wind. The island lay as if on a looking-glass. There was not a sign that Dick was there. Everything was working out just as Nancy had planned.

Roger was surprised to find that he felt a little downcast. If that enemy of his did not turn up quickly he would have to stay here all day. The others were being hunted like deer, and the more they were hunted the better they would be pleased. But it was no good thinking of running after them now. It was too late. If anybody were to see him and start shouting, as those Gaels had shouted the other day, it would mean failure for Dick and for everybody else. Roger might be forgiven for going off alone but he knew he would not be forgiven, even by himself, if he spoilt the plan of the whole ship's company. Bother! He almost wished he had stuck to the red herrings and was helping them to lead the stalkers a dance. As it was, whatever happened, he must not let himself be seen. If you are not to be seen, you must keep still, and keeping still is very dull work unless you are asleep, when it does not seem to matter.

He had never believed that time could pass so slowly. Those same hours that were going too quickly for Dick, lying in his hide with the birds before his eyes, for Roger seemed like years. Every now and then he took a wary look out from the hollow on the top of the Pict-house. Nothing seemed to change. The egg-collector and Captain Flint, one in a deck-chair and the other up at the top of a mast, solemnly kept an eye on each other throughout the endless day. Up the valley there was nothing to show what the red herrings were doing or the Gaels. No one was moving anywhere. Perhaps, thought Roger, the whole lot of them, Gaels and red herrings alike, were out of the valley altogether and climbing those blue hills. Perhaps his own particular enemy had gone with them. In the end he found it hard to believe that anybody was hidden on the island. He began to wonder whether Dick had not already taken his photographs and gone back to the *Sea Bear*. No. If he had, Captain Flint would have sounded the foghorn, to let the red herrings know their task was done. He had heard no foghorn and Captain Flint was still up at the cross-trees of the *Sea Bear*. There was nothing for it but to wait.

Roger put off eating his sandwiches as long as he could, but suddenly remembered that it would be waste if the foghorn were to sound before he had eaten them. He made a slow and comfortable meal. Then he stowed empty bottle and paper in his knapsack so as to be able, when the time came, to slip into hiding without leaving a trace. He had another careful look round, dropped back into the hollow saucer on the top of the Pict-house and lay there planning what he would do and say when at last he met his enemy face to face. One way or another, Roger would surprise him.

Suddenly he was alert. Asleep again? No. Of course he had not been asleep, not properly. But the sun had somehow made a bit of a jump to the westward. It must have been a good long time since he had last looked out and, without knowing why, Roger was certain that something was happening or going to happen. He rolled quickly over and crept up the rim. Instantly he lowered his head. A boy in Highland dress was coming at a steady lope along the old cart track from the head of the valley. It was Dorothea's 'young chieftain', the boy they had all seen with the old dogmudgeon looking at the *Pterodactyl*, the boy Captain Flint had said was likelier than any other to have written the label the mere thought of which made Roger's cheeks burn. Roger looked again. The boy was just coming to the place where the track turned up into the gap. If he was going home then Roger had waited all day for nothing. No. He had left the track and was racing towards the Pict-house, to look at the earth he had stopped and to see if his private hiding-place had been invaded again. If Roger was going to be ready for him, he had not a moment to lose.

Roger slipped down on the side furthest from the boy, crawled to the entrance, pushed his knapsack in, crawled in backwards and then, roots first, pulled the big faggot of heather after him so that, as before, it filled the opening. A little too far or not quite far enough and the boy would see that some-body had moved it.

Roger waited, listening. Close outside, a stone clicked against another. The enemy had arrived. Footsteps . . . Roger crouched in the dark inside the entrance, expecting every moment to see the heather snatched away and the enemy once more triumphant while he, Roger, had to crawl out defeated. It seemed almost too much to hope that the heather was exactly as the enemy had left it. There was silence. Perhaps the enemy had gone up on the top of the Pict-house where yesterday he had found his . . . Sleeping Beauty. Even without saying them, Roger choked over those words. Specks of light showed through the heather. Suddenly a shadow passed across them putting out one speck of light after another. They showed again. They all went out together. The enemy must be stooping just outside, looking at the heather. He must have been satisfied with what he saw, for suddenly the shadow was gone. Roger, holding his breath, heard a step or two and then no more. Victory.

Roger was on the point of dashing out to gloat and meet his enemy. He stopped. Was it victory, or was the enemy being cunning? Had he only pretended not to see that the heather had been moved? Had he guessed that Roger was inside? Was he lurking, perhaps only a yard away, on the top of the Pict-house, ready to leap on Roger from above when, thinking the coast clear, he should come confidently out? Roger waited, listening. He heard nothing. At last he made up his mind, pushed away the heather and shot out, ready for instant battle. There was no one waiting for him. He was only just in time to see that boy, running hard, disappear in the gap where the cart track led over the ridge.

It had been a triumph of a kind. That dodge with the heather had worked. The enemy had been fooled, but so long as the enemy did not know he had been fooled, the triumph had fallen rather flat. Roger climbed once more into the hollow on the top of the Pict-house.

Suddenly, far up the valley, where the track crossed a spur of the ridge, he saw people moving, a lot of people . . . the

Gaels coming back? He saw them only for a moment, as the track dipped again. They had vanished before he had time to focus his telescope.

Half an hour later he saw them again. They were very much nearer, and this time he was able to get a proper look at them, wild-looking men and boys and, walking along in the midst of them, most of the crew of the *Sea Bear*.

'Prisoners!' gasped Roger. 'They've got them all.' He counted, John, Susan, Titty, Nancy, Peggy and Dorothea. What were John and Nancy doing there? He had thought they were going to be far away in another valley altogether. Still, it was all in the plan. Nancy herself said that it would not matter if they did get captured, so long as they had drawn the Gaels well away towards the hills so that Dick could get his photographs and get back to the *Sea Bear* without being seen. But had he? While Roger was watching, he saw a sudden stir in the little crowd coming along the track. They were running. He heard a shout or two. What on earth was happening? Were the prisoners being taken over the ridge to the stronghold of the Gaels? Even that, he thought, would not matter if Dick was safe in the *Sea Bear* or lay low on the island till enemies and red herrings alike had passed through the gap and out of sight.

But what was this? A dip in the track had hid the convoy of prisoners. Now they showed again very much nearer, where the track turned up into the gap. They were stopping, looking back, waiting for something. A few minutes later he knew why. They were waiting for another prisoner. He saw the tall old man and Dick, climbing up to the track. He saw the others clustering round Dick, and the tall old man whom he had called a dogmudgeon striding ahead as the whole party were on the move again.

He must get help at once. He must signal the news to Captain Flint. He looked down at the mast of the *Sea Bear*.

For the first time, he saw no lump at the *Sea Bear*'s cross-trees. Captain Flint must have got sick of sitting up there watching the *Pterodactyl*. What was he to do? If he were to make a bolt for it, he would be in full view of the Gaels and be captured like the rest of them. Another thought struck him like a blow between the eyes. The Gaels might be coming straight to the Pict-house. They certainly would if they caught a glimpse of him. Roger rolled hurriedly over the edge of his look-out place on the seaward side, crawled round to the entrance, went backwards into the tunnel, pulled the roots of the heather in after him once more and crouched as breathless as if he had been running.

Every single one of the red herrings had been captured except himself. John and Nancy had been captured and even they had not been able to talk the Gaels into letting them go. Dick had been captured. It was lucky for everybody that he, Roger, was free. As soon as the coast was clear, he would run down to the cove, hail the *Sea Bear* and bring Captain Flint to the rescue. If he did that, even John and Nancy would have to admit that he had been pretty useful. Breathing more evenly, now that he knew what he meant to do, he crouched in the tunnel listening. He heard, faintly, the voices of the Gaels, or thought he heard them. He heard a shout, 'Hey!' the voice of Captain Flint. Then, suddenly, close by, he heard running footsteps and the panting of somebody very much out of breath. No need for him to fetch Captain Flint. He had seen them and was already hurrying to the rescue of his crew. Roger waited, smiling in the dark.

He heard no more voices or footsteps. Cautiously he pushed the heather before him and came out. Gaels and prisoners were nowhere to be seen, but he caught just a glimpse of Captain Flint disappearing into the gap. Faintly, from beyond the ridge, he heard the sound of bagpipes as he had heard them on the day the whole adventure had begun. Well, Captain Flint

was with the others now. He would make the Gaels give up
their prisoners, Dick and all. There was nothing else to worry
about. He stood beside the Pict-house, looking out over the
deserted valley, and planned to do a little gloating himself,
telling Nancy, for example, that she had had to be rescued by
Captain Flint whereas he, Roger, had remained the only one
uncaught.

Suddenly something moving caught his eye, something
yellowish, moving on the dark slopes on the further side of the
lochs. Where was that telescope? Whatever the thing was, it
was moving fast. Yellowish. Who but the egg-collector wore
mustard-coloured clothes? There was someone else. Roger
caught a sharp glint of light. It could not be . . . Yes, it was.
Looking through the telescope he saw them both clearly, the
egg-collector and another man, one of his sailors. The sailor
was carrying a gun. They were coming down into the valley,
making for the upper end of the loch of the Great Northern
Divers.

Roger's smile left his face. At the very last minute the
success of the expedition was turning into failure. The egg-
collector, while sitting quietly on deck, must have had a spy
ashore who had seen Dick leave the island. Now, with
Captain Flint no longer watching, he was taking his chance.
Chance? It was a certainty. Dick must have brought the
folding boat ashore. The egg-collector and his man had only
to cross the stream between the lochs and walk along the shore
to find the boat wherever Dick had left it. The Sea Bears
were in the hands of the Gaels. The egg-collector would steal
the eggs and shoot the birds. The whole of Nancy's plan was
crashing to disaster.

Roger thought no more of his private feud, his personal
enemy. He remembered only that he was a Sea Bear and the
only one who knew how desperate was the need for hurry. He
left the Pict-house, plunged down into the heather, raced up

ROGER AT THE PRISON DOOR

to the track and along it as fast as he could run towards the gap through which the Gaels and their prisoners had disappeared. He must let the others know at once. Captain Flint had gone to the rescue. Why was he taking so long to set them free? What on earth was he doing, parleying with the Gaels and listening to bagpipes, when every moment counted?

As he came into the gap, he expected to meet Captain Flint and the others on their way back. Not one of them was in sight, only a few of the Gaels standing beside the closed door of a thatched building, which, as he could see no windows in it, he thought must be a barn.

Roger dropped to the ground. If he ran into those Gaels he would only be captured like the others. If Captain Flint had been in sight that would not have mattered, but he was not and Roger did not know where he was. Suddenly he heard a muffled thumping, as if someone were kicking at a door. He saw the old dogmudgeon walk up to the door of the barn and listen. Then faintly, he heard Captain Flint's voice. The Gaels by the door were laughing. They were going away towards the cottages, now and then looking back towards the barn. There was another thump or two, and then silence, except for the bagpipes. Some of the Gaels had gone into their cottages. Only two were left, the tall old dogmudgeon and another, talking together just beyond the corner of the barn. Roger slipped sideways, so that the barn was between himself and them, and hurried on.

He knew now that Captain Flint was as much a prisoner as any of the others. He knew that the barn was their prison. Well, they would not let themselves be prisoners for long, when they heard the dreadful news of what was happening. There was not a moment to spare. Already the egg-collector and his man might be rowing off to the island in the *Sea Bear*'s own folding boat. Quickly. Quickly. The men behind the barn could not see him, but anybody might be looking from the cottages. He remembered those dogs that had come charging through the heather that first day. Dogs had a dreadful way of knowing you were there even if they could not see you. At any moment he might hear their loud ferocious barking. Well, he could not help that. He was close to the barn now, and no one had shouted and no dog had barked. He could hear people talking in Gaelic close by. For an awful moment he thought he had been mistaken and that the prisoners were not in the barn. They might have been taken straight to the grey house. Then he heard Nancy's voice, very loud and cheerful. He was just going to shout, but stopped himself in time. He dared not even talk loud, with the enemy so near. He threw himself on the ground and began tapping, gently at first, at the bottom of the big door.

CHAPTER 26

THE McGINTY LISTENS TO REASON

'Tap ... Tap ... Tap ... Tap ...'

'It's a signal,' said Titty.

'Hey!'

It was a very quiet 'Hey!' but urgent.

'It's Roger,' exclaimed Susan.

'Hullo!'

Everybody crowded to the closed door.

'Do be quiet,' said Nancy, 'he's saying something. Nobody can hear if ...'

'Stop talking,' said Captain Flint. 'Give the chap a chance.'

'Barbecued Billygoats!' said Nancy. 'I want to hear too.'

'Do listen!' Roger's whisper, desperate now, came under the door. 'I can't shout. They'll spot me in another minute.'

'How did you ...?'

'Listen! Listen! There's only just time. I was watching from my Pict-house and saw them. The egg-collectors must have seen Dick coming away from the island. They're in the valley now, coming across. One of them's got a gun ... Yes, a gun, I tell you. He's got a gun.'

'We've got to get out,' said Dick. 'Quick! Quick! We've got to stop him. He'll find the folding boat. He'll get the eggs. He'll kill the birds. He said he would.'

'We're done,' said Dorothea.

'We aren't,' said Nancy, 'but we will be if we aren't quick. Listen! Roger! Can you open the door?'

'I can't,' said Roger. 'I've tried.'

'Do something, Uncle Jim,' said Nancy. 'Couldn't we bust the door if we all tried together?'

'Be quiet for a minute,' said Captain Flint. 'Roger! Can you hear?'

'Yes.'

'Are any of those men about?'

'I can hear two of them talking. They don't know I'm here.'

'It's no good talking to those savages. Go straight to the house . . .'

'Where they're playing the bagpipes?'

'Get there before you get stopped. Go to the front door. Say you have an urgent message and as soon as you see anybody who talks English tell him anything you like so long as you bring him here just as quick as you can.'

'Life and death,' whispered Titty.

'It really is,' said Dorothea. 'Even now the foul murderers are stealing towards their helpless victims. And that beast'll take the eggs and Dick will wish all his life he'd never found them.' Dorothea began with a sentence in her favourite style but ended with the simple dreadful truth.

'Get into the house somehow or other,' said Captain Flint. 'If there's a butler or something and he tries to stop you, nip past him. The noise of the bagpipes will tell you where to go. Do you hear?'

There was no answer. Roger was already on his way.

'There must be somebody in the place with a head on his shoulders, if only we can get a word with him. I say, Dick, I'm most awfully sorry. That swine must have been watching me while I was watching him and when I cleared out he must have come ashore at once. My fault, but what could I do when I saw all you people being hauled off?'

'That man who came after Nancy and me must have got back and seen Dick,' said John.

'We couldn't have stopped him,' said Nancy.

Dick said nothing. He was holding his spectacles but not wiping them. He was standing there, blind, looking at the ground he could not see and thinking of the Divers betrayed to their worst enemies.

'Gosh, what's that?' exclaimed Nancy.

There was a wild Gaelic yell from behind their prison, answered by another. There was the sound of running feet.

'They've seen Roger,' said Dorothea.

'Roger's pretty nippy when he wants to be,' said John hopefully.

There was dead silence in the prison. They were all listening but the noise of the footsteps had died away. There was nothing to hear but the far-away skirl of the bagpipes.

'He had a pretty good start,' said John.

'He'll have found the front door by now,' said Dorothea. 'He'll have rung the bell ...'

'Some bells hang awfully high,' said Titty.

'He'll have jumped for it,' said Dorothea. 'The clanging bell wakes the echoes of the castle walls. If they weren't so thick we'd be hearing it.'

'Do shut up, you two,' said Nancy.

'The boat's this side of the loch,' said Dick. 'They'll have to cross the stream to get round to it. There may still be time if he's quick ...'

Suddenly in the dim light of their prison, the captives looked at each other, wondering if all had noticed that sudden break in the piping. The piper had been skirling and droning on in a wild, elaborate, endless tune. The tune had been cut off short in an unhappy wail. A minute later it had gone on again from where it had left off. 'At least,' Titty said later, 'you couldn't be sure of that, but it went on making the same kind of noise as before.'

'Roger may have startled him,' said Dorothea.

'If only he's managed to get in,' said Nancy.

'The trouble is, we don't know what sort of chap he'll find there,' said Captain Flint.

'We're going to be too late,' said Dick. Everybody turned towards him and then looked away again at once. It was too dark for them to see much, but they knew how miserable he was as he stood there with bent head, fingering his spectacles.

There was a long silence.

'He'd be back by now if he'd got hold of anybody,' said John at last.

'Here he is,' shouted Nancy.

Steps sounded outside, and Gaelic words and then a few words in English that sank their hopes once more.

'Let GO,' they heard Roger's voice. 'I'm not going to bolt.'

The heavy bolt creaked. The door opened. Roger was shot violently through it. The door slammed behind him and the bolt banged across.

'Thundering galoots we are,' groaned Nancy. 'We ought to have been waiting and gone charging out the moment they opened the door.'

Roger picked himself up.

'Are you hurt?' asked Susan.

'No,' said Roger. 'At least not much. Only a bit when I got mixed up with that bagpiper.'

'Did you see anybody?' asked Captain Flint.

'There wasn't time,' said Roger. 'I was just getting to the house when a pack of them came after me so I didn't look for any bell. I just charged through to a sort of terrace place where the man with the bagpipes was prancing. There was an old man and that boy hogging at a table in a room at the other side of the terrace. I darted across behind the piper but he turned round in his prance and I went smack into him and he came down on the top of me, and his bagpipes let out a groan and before I could get up they'd grabbed me. I tried to yell but I couldn't.' Roger wiped his mouth. 'Gaels taste pretty rum,' he said. 'Smell too. One of them had a paw all over the front of my face.'

'But what about the man at the table?' said Nancy.

'And the young chieftain?' said Dorothea.

'I don't know,' said Roger. 'They lugged me away too quick. And the man with the bagpipes hopped up and went straight on playing. I bet he got hurt all right though. He came down crash and only a bit of him was on me. My knee got scraped and I bet his did too.' Roger patted his knee, brought his hand away and licked it.

'Oh, Roger,' said Susan, 'and the iodine's all in the *Sea Bear*.'

'I'm all right,' said Roger. 'But they'll have got to the folding boat by now.'

Dick leaned against the wall. Nothing could save the birds. Oh, if only he had never told the egg-collector of his find.

'Come on,' said Nancy. 'There's only one thing we can do.'

'There's nothing we can do,' said Captain Flint.

'Yes, there is, and we'll do it. We can make such a row that they hear us in the house. We aren't gagged. We've got to make the McGinty listen to reason. Start yelling. Go on, Uncle Jim. Let yourself go. Go on. You're hailing a ship in a storm. Ahoy! AHOY!'

For a moment, Nancy yelled alone. Then the others saw her idea. One after another joined in. 'AHOY! AHOY! AHOY!'

'Never mind if you can't ahoy,' said Nancy, grabbing Dorothea by the shoulder. 'Scream. Go on. Scream as if you were being murdered. You will be if you don't. I'll murder you myself. Scream! You too, Peggy. AHOY! AHOY! Uncle JIM!'

At last even Captain Flint saw the point and sent out an 'Ahoy!' fit to be heard across the Bay of Biscay. He followed

it with another and another. Dorothea threw her head back
and screamed at the very top of her voice. Peggy did the same.
Nancy, John and Titty yelled one 'Ahoy!' after another.
Roger copied a pig being killed. Susan tried an 'Ahoy!' but
found that she too could make more noise by plain straight-
forward yelling. So did Dick. In their prison the crew of the
Sea Bear deafened each other and the row they made was
such that they heard nothing of people shouting at them from
outside. There was thundering on the door. For one second
they paused. 'Whisht, whisht!' they heard. 'We won't
whisht,' said Nancy, and the noise began again. More and
more people were shouting at them to be quiet. 'Good,'
panted Nancy between ahoys. 'If they yell too, it'll help.
Keep it up, Uncle Jim. Well done, Dot! Go it, Peggy! Never
mind about sore throats. AHOY . . . OY . . . OY . . . OY!'

There is one noise that can make itself heard over any
other noise whatsoever, and that is the noise of the bagpipes
played by a determined and indignant piper. The prisoners
were making all the noise they could and had all but deafened
each other, but through that terrific din they heard the skirl
and drone of the pipes, nearer and nearer, louder and louder,
in the ancient march now known as 'The Road to the
Isles'.

At first they hardly trusted their own ears. It was not until
the skirl of the pipes sounded close outside their prison door
that their shouting came suddenly to an end.

'It's worked,' said Nancy breathlessly.

The heavy bolt that barred the door creaked in its sockets.
The door was flung open by the old grey-bearded giant who
had captured Dick. Others of the Gaels were standing round.
Two or three women and half-a-dozen red-headed children
had come out of the cottages, no doubt, on hearing the yelling
of the prisoners. But Nancy was right. The yelling had

worked. It had brought to the prison door the man they wanted to see. A tall old man, in full Highland dress, with tartan kilt and deerskin sporran, was standing there, and they knew he could be no other than the McGinty himself. Close beside him was the boy they had seen before, Roger's enemy, Dorothea's 'young chieftain', Ian McGinty.

Roger was the first out, but, on seeing the piper, let some of the others get in front of him. 'That's the scoondrel!' exclaimed the piper. 'Running like a mad stirk!' But at a sign from the McGinty the piper was silent, scowling heavily and moving a little this way and that to keep his eyes on the one who had tripped him up, broken into the middle of a tune and, but for good luck, might very well have ruined his pipes. The young McGinty too was quick to see Roger and a slow smile crossed his face, and left it grave again.

Dick, usually slow to speak, was for once the first. 'Quick, Quick!' he said. 'We'll be only just in time. He's going for the eggs now . . .'

'Whisht!' said one of the men.

The McGinty was looking sternly over his nine prisoners. Titty said afterwards that there was a sort of twinkle in his eye, but none of the others believed that she had seen it at the time. 'He looked as grim as death', Dorothea wrote in her diary. His glance moved from one to another of the crew of the *Sea Bear* as they came blinking out of their prison into the sunshine. It rested at last on Captain Flint.

'Will you explain the reason for this appalling noise?' he asked.

'Had to make it,' said Captain Flint. 'No other way. The thing is pretty urgent.'

'We sent Roger to tell you,' put in Nancy, 'but they hauled him back.'

'That is the laddie, I tell you,' said the angry piper.

'We had to speak to you somehow,' said Nancy.

THE McGINTY AND HIS PRISONERS

'Life and death,' said Titty. 'It really is.'

'Oh, quick, quick!' said Dick.

'Whisht!' said the dogmudgeon and grabbed Dick's arm as Dick, desperate, made a sudden move.

'A noise like that does not make things better for you,' said the McGinty slowly. 'For days now you have been disturbing my deer. You have no right on the land at all. Who sent you? Who is the man for whom you have been driving the poor beasts this way and that till by now there'll not be a hind at peace this side the hills?'

'Sir,' began Captain Flint.

'If it were the children only I might suppose it was just thoughtlessness,' said the McGinty. 'But you are a grown man. You come here in two boats . . .'

'But we didn't . . .'

'That motor boat's got nothing to do with us.'

'My son and my men have seen what you were at,' said the McGinty. 'One day after another. Tell me now, what you have to say for yourself. We have little against strangers in the isles when they behave like honest folk, but the chasing of hinds out of their breeding grounds is beyond right and reason, and we'll find means to show you we'll have none of it. This is bad work you have been at, and to use children for it . . .'

'Sir,' began Captain Flint again.

'Don't waste time being polite,' exclaimed Nancy. She shot forward past Captain Flint and faced the McGinty. 'PLEASE listen!' she said.

The McGinty looked over her head at Captain Flint and seeing from Captain Flint's face that he was ready to let Nancy speak for him, looked gravely down at Nancy.

'I am listening,' he said.

'Well, please do,' said Nancy. 'There isn't time to argue. We weren't driving your deer. We were doing all we could to get out of the way. We weren't interested in deer. It was birds . . .'

'Out of season,' said the McGinty. 'Surely you're not telling me you don't know . . .'

'Oh, I know about grouse,' said Nancy. 'There are lots where we come from. Look here, Dick had better tell you. They were his birds. Birds he found. Divers. Divers nesting on your loch.'

The McGinty was interested but unbelieving. 'Yes,' he said. 'Black-throated Divers. We have them every year . . . But if you wanted to see them there was no need to drive the deer to the hills.'

'NOT Black-throated,' said Dick. 'Great Northerns. Two of them.'

'They never nest here,' said the McGinty. 'They do not nest anywhere in the British Isles.'

'But that's just it,' said Nancy. 'They do. Yours do. The first that have ever been known to. They are nesting on the island in your loch. We've seen them. Dick found them first. He wasn't dead sure, so he made a drawing and then he showed it to a man in that motor yacht . . . Look here, Dick, you'd better explain.'

'It was a mistake,' said Dick. 'I oughtn't to have shown it to him. When I went to his boat I didn't know he was an egg-collector. He tried to find out where the nest was, but I didn't tell him. But he knows now. He's going there. He wants to shoot the birds and stuff them and take the eggs to put them into his collection. You see it's the first nest ever known not in Iceland or some other place abroad . . .'

'Offered the boy five pounds,' put in Captain Flint. 'And then offered me a hundred.'

'So you . . .'

'No, no, NO,' said Nancy.

'We tried to dodge him,' said Dick.

'We *did* dodge him,' said Nancy. 'But he spotted our boat and came after us. When you thought we were chasing your deer, we were trying to make sure that he wouldn't be looking when Dick went to the island.'

'So you were after the eggs, too?'

'No,' said Dick. 'He said only the eggs would prove that the birds had nested, but I thought a photograph would do it.'

'And you got one?' The McGinty was talking in a different tone.

'Five,' said Dick.

'Some of us were being decoys to make him think the nest was somewhere else and some of us were being red herrings to keep the coast clear for Dick,' said Nancy, looking rather doubtfully at the Gaels who, whether they talked English or not, all seemed to be listening. 'But we all got grabbed by your men . . . and Dick was collared too, and Uncle Jim deserted his post . . . He was up at our masthead keeping a watch on the *Pterodactyl* . . . Everybody got grabbed except Roger and Roger saw them . . .'

'Saw whom?'

'The egg-collector and his man going straight for the loch. They've got a gun. That's why we sent Roger to fetch you. And he couldn't get to you, so I thought of howling till you came. And it worked and here you are but we're going to be too late . . .'

'We may be too late already.' Dick was desperate.

'But if the nest's on the island, your egg-collector can do nothing,' said the McGinty. 'There's no boat on the loch.'

'There's ours,' said Nancy.

'And he's seen where it is and he'll use it to get the eggs.'

The McGinty had turned away. Some time before some of the Gaels had seen a man waving his arms, running down from the top of the ridge beyond the gap. Now he was close to them, and clearly had something to say. Two large sheep-dogs, that Roger remembered very well, ran up, licked the young McGinty's hand and lay down, with their tongues out. The man, a shepherd with a crooked stick, came up to the McGinty and spoke in Gaelic. The McGinty frowned.

'This man tells me there is a boat on the loch now.'

'But we told you there was,' murmured Roger.

'Our folding boat,' said Nancy.

'Does that mean that more of your party are about?'

'No, no, NO,' said Nancy. 'That's the enemy. It's our boat but the enemy's got it.'

'We're too late,' said Dick. 'He's going to take the eggs and shoot the birds. Can't you do something to stop him?'

There was a sudden far away bang of a shot-gun in the next valley. It echoed among the hills and was followed almost instantly by another.

'He's killed them,' groaned Dick, 'and it's all my fault for having told him I'd found them.'

Those two shots changed everything. If the McGinty had been slow to be persuaded, he was now quick to act. The echo of the first shot had hardly died away before he had turned and was walking fast towards the gap in the ridge. The Gaels, who had been waiting to see what he would do with their prisoners, moved with him talking in Gaelic to each other. Whether they understood English or not, they seemed to know that their prisoners were prisoners no more. The prisoners were free. With astonishment they heard the McGinty beg Captain Flint's pardon and say something about 'murderous villains' and 'my loch!' The young McGinty, who had been spending the day in stalking the red herrings, was talking to John and Nancy. The McGinty himself began to run. The Gaels were already streaming ahead towards the gap.

The first Gael to reach the gap flung up his hand.

'He's seen them,' said the young McGinty to Nancy who was running at his side.

'View halloo,' cried Roger, who was running close behind them, happy to be leaving the piper behind who, with a care for his pipes, was not running quite so fast.

From the gap, they could see a black spot, the folding boat, moving on the loch.

The McGinty, general in command, was giving swift orders in Gaelic to his men. Most of them went racing down not towards the loch but as if they were going down to the cove and the *Sea Bear*. The shepherd, after a word with the McGinty, went off the other way with his dogs at his heels, down the heather slopes as if he were going up the valley and round the lochs from above.

'We'll make sure of him,' the McGinty was saying to Captain Flint. 'He's to land yet and get away over to his own boat. Come you with me and we'll be there before him. Eggs and birds from my loch! We'll give him no chance of getting away with either. He'll be sorry he ever put his foot ashore.' With Captain Flint beside him, he strode angrily down the hillside after his men.

The young McGinty had plans of his own. He stopped John and Nancy just as they were starting off after Captain Flint. 'They're going to wait for him coming to his boat,' he said. 'We'll do better. We'll get him as he steps out with the dead birds in his hands. You cross the burn below the loch and work round. I'll go after Roderick and his dogs and come at him from the other end. No good your coming with me. He'd spot you at once. I can get round there without him seeing a sight of me.'

'I know you can,' said Nancy with a grin.

'If only I'd known what you were doing I could have stopped him from coming ashore at all,' said the young McGinty. 'It's an awful pity you couldn't give me to know.'

'Can't be helped,' said John.

'Don't wait,' said Nancy. 'He hasn't beaten us yet.'

'He's killed the birds,' said Titty.

'Down by my broch,' said the young McGinty. 'You'll be out of sight that way. Over the burn by the stepping stones and along the loch shore.' He was off, dodging along below the track and then disappearing, showing again only for a moment at a time, lower and lower on the slopes of rock and heather.

'Come on, you others,' cried Nancy. 'Dick! DICK! Not that way. We're going to take him in the rear!'

But Dick was gone, racing headlong, hardly knowing what he was doing, straight down the rough hillside towards the loch, straight for the shore where it was nearest to the island, straight for that black spot moving on the water, the folding boat that the Sea Bears had put on the loch almost as if they had meant to make things easy for the murderers of his birds.

'Better let him go,' said Dorothea. 'If the birds are dead, he won't want to see any of us for a bit.'

CHAPTER 27

TOO LATE!

DICK, with those two gun-shots echoing in his head, could think of nothing but his birds. He thought of the great birds bleeding in the water, picked up by Mr Jemmerling and his man, their necks wrung, carefully so as not to spoil them as specimens, to be shown in a glass case, the first Great Northern Divers ever known to nest in the British Isles, with their eggs, their eggs that would never hatch, blown, dead, empty shells. If only the *Sea Bear* had never come in to that wild anchorage the birds would have been safe. If only he had never seen them . . . If only he had not wanted so badly to be sure that he was not mistaken . . . If only he had never shown his drawings to the egg-collector . . . If only . . . He ran, almost choking with misery, down into the valley, making straight for the place where he had run aground in the folding boat and been captured by that grey-bearded giant of a Gael. There was no reason in this, no plan. Simply, that place was the nearest to the island.

He could see the folding boat, with the two men in it, a long way out on the loch. Just for one moment he thought that perhaps, after all, they had failed to find the nest. But the birds were dead and had nested in vain whether the eggs were taken or not. And of course the eggs would be taken. Of course the murderer had made sure of the birds first, lest they should fly away. And only now, after killing the birds, were they rowing to the island to steal the orphaned eggs.

The men were having difficulty with the boat, the same difficulty that Dick had had himself. They were finding it hard to keep it on a course. All the same, they were close to the island before Dick came down to the shore of the loch. There was nothing he could do. Watching miserably through the binoculars he saw the boat ground. They must have seen where the bird had been sitting for they had brought the boat in only a few yards away. One man was holding her steady while the other, the egg-collector himself in his mustard-coloured clothes, stepped out with a square box of some kind that he carried by a handle or a strap. A moment later, Mr Jemmerling was stooping over the actual nest. The thing was done. The first Great Northerns ever known to nest on British soil were dead, and their eggs were to be part of the Jemmerling Collection. It was too late to do anything to help them. Dick looked desperately round and could see none of his allies. The McGinty, Captain Flint, the Gaels and the crew of the *Sea Bear* had disappeared. He was alone, watching the last act of a tragedy that he knew was all his own fault.

'Heuch! Heuch! Heuch!'

Dick stared about him. No other bird could make that yelping cry.

'Heuch! Heuch! Heuch!'

One of the birds must still be alive. Dick dropped instantly to the ground, taking what cover he could from a boulder and a tussock of rank grass. Once more, as on that first day, he was a bird-watcher, though he could not see the bird. And on that first day he had been watching birds that had no enemy. They had been quietly fishing or sitting undisturbed on their eggs. Now, everything was different. The peace of the loch had been broken by gun-shots. That cry was not the laughing 'Hoo! Hoo!' of one bird talking to another, but the harsh, guttural 'Heuch!' of a bird in fear.

Suddenly, between himself and the island, he saw a black spot moving on the water. He had the binoculars on it in a moment and saw that it was a bird's head, the head of one of his Divers. He could see the barred half-collar under the chin and the wider barred collar further down. The bird was swimming fast, showing only its head and neck. Wounded, he thought, dying and sinking as it died. But perhaps not. He remembered seeing startled grebes on the Norfolk Broads swimming just like that, with their whole bodies under water. It might be only frightened. That beast, that murderer, might have used both barrels to kill the other bird and this one might have had time to get away out of range. But what was the good of that? Widow or widower, it had lost its mate. It had lost its eggs. At that very moment Mr Jemmerling's cheeks might be puffing out as he blew first one of those great eggs and then the other and so made sure that the Great Northern Divers had nested on the island in vain. Dick turned his glasses on the island. He could see the sailor waiting in the boat and Mr Jemmerling kneeling on the ground, packing something into his box.

'Heuch! Heuch! Heuch!'

Dick stared towards the head of the loch. That cry would not have come from the bird swimming in the water.

'Heuch! Heuch! Heuch!'

A huge bird was flying fast and low over the loch. Lower and lower it flew. There was a long line of splashes, a sudden silence. Another Great Northern Diver was swimming towards the first and Dick knew that the egg-collector had missed with both barrels. Almost, Dick jumped to his feet, but he remembered in time. The two birds were swimming to meet each other. Dick found he could not see them. He put down the binoculars, tore off his spectacles, wiped them as quickly as he could, put them on again, grabbed the glasses once more and, as he lifted them, saw that others beside himself had heard those cries and seen the long, white splashing furrow ploughed by the second bird as it came down on the surface of the loch.

The man in the boat was pointing. Mr Jemmerling was

hurriedly strapping down the lid of his box. They had seen the birds. A moment later, Mr Jemmerling was in the boat and the boat was leaving the island. Dick knew that, with the eggs safely in his box, Mr Jemmerling was going to do his best to get once more within gun-shot of the birds he had robbed. This time he would not miss.

The boat was coming directly from the island towards Dick and towards the two birds which, both with only their heads and necks showing above water, were swimming side by side, this way and that.

'They're only thinking about their eggs,' Dick murmured to himself, 'waiting to get back to their nest when those beasts have gone.'

But the beasts, instead of going, were coming after the birds. At first, the sailor was pulling, with his back towards Dick, and Mr Jemmerling was sitting in the stern. Then the boat stopped and Dick saw that the sailor was turning it round. Perhaps, after all, they were going to leave the birds alone and go away. But no. The folding boat was pointed at both stem and stern and, as soon as he had turned her, the sailor began backing water, bringing the boat along stern first, and Dick saw that Mr Jemmerling was crouching in the bottom of the boat, with a gun ready, lying across his arm. The sailor was backing the boat gently towards the swimming birds and, worst of all, the birds, worried about their nest, seemed hardly to realize that they were themselves again in danger. Those two heads, showing above the surface of the water, were moving to and fro, as if driven by the boat, coming gradually nearer to the shore where Dick lay helplessly watching. It was as if they did not want to go further from the island than they could help.

Nearer the birds came and nearer yet and all the time the boat was gaining on them. Dick's hands were shaking. Again and again he lost sight of the birds while doing his best to keep the glasses trained upon them. What ought he to do? If he showed himself he might send the birds, taking him for a new enemy, swimming straight to their deaths. If he did not show himself and the birds did not fly or swim out of danger the boat would soon be near enough for Mr Jemmerling to shoot at them and it was too much to hope that he would miss a second time. Once or twice the birds went under water but each time they came up the boat was nearer. Dick found himself desperately wondering what was the range of a shot-gun. He knew nothing whatever about that kind of shooting but did know something about the length of rifle ranges. Three hundred yards, five hundred . . . The boat was already much nearer than that. It couldn't be more than a hundred yards from the birds. Less than that. Much less. Mr Jemmerling, crouched low in the boat, was stealthily moving his gun. He was going to shoot. He was going to shoot now. Dick leapt to his feet and, his throat still sore from making all that noise in prison, yelled as loud as he could and waved his arms like a windmill. Both birds dived under water, came up again far away and, with two long rows of splashes, rose into the air and flew away towards the upper loch.

'You little FOOL!' roared Mr Jemmerling.

At that moment a whistle shrilled near the foot of the loch. Dick heard it, and saw people crossing the stream beyond the reed-beds. Some had already crossed.

Mr Jemmerling and the sailor saw them too. The sailor stopped backing water and began rowing as hard as he could for the opposite shore, nearly jerking Mr Jemmerling off his balance as, holding his gun in one hand, he shook his other fist at Dick and turned to sit down once more in the stern of the boat. The hunters had become the hunted and knew that if they were not quick their retreat to the *Pterodactyl* would be cut off. Dick crammed the binoculars into their case and ran, a new hope leaping in his heart. Those were his allies working round the foot of the loch. He had seen the red caps of Nancy and Peggy. And the Gaels, wherever they were, were allies too. The birds were not dead. If only the allies could catch Mr Jemmerling and not let him escape to his boat, if only Mr Jemmerling had not blown the eggs, if only he, Dick, could take the eggs back to the nest before the birds came back after being frightened away, there was a chance, just a chance that the Great Northern Divers might yet hatch their eggs on the island they had chosen.

Dick fell, leapt up, ran and fell again, stumbling over tussocks of grass and rocks along the shore of the loch. Every time he looked over his shoulder to see how far the boat had gone, he fell over something or other if not over his own racing feet. But he saw enough to know that the boat was not making very good headway. He knew himself how hard it was to keep that boat on any steady course and that trying to move fast made it harder. He knew that the boat must be sheering this way and that and that the sailor must be having the same difficulties that he himself had had earlier in the day. He was thankful now that it was the folding boat that they had brought to the loch and not the more manageable dinghy. Now and again he heard a whistle. Now and again he caught a glimpse of people moving along the further shore. Would they be in time or would they not? And even if they were he knew it would be no good if he himself were not there too. They might stop the egg-collector, but not one of them would think of taking the eggs back to the nest. He must get there. Every minute mattered. But the eggs might be blown. The egg-collector and his man might beat the allies, get to the shore before the allies were there to meet them, get down to the creek before they could be stopped and be off to the *Pterodactyl* and away. But they might not. The eggs might not be blown.

There was a chance yet. Dick came to the foot of the lake, splashed across the stream, saw that the boat far up the lake was just coming in to the shore, set his teeth together and ran and ran and ran.

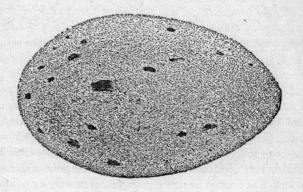

CHAPTER 28

'BUT WHAT HAS HE DONE WITH THE EGGS?'

WHEN Dick's frantic shouting broke the silence of the valley, John, Nancy and Peggy had already crossed the burn. Susan, on a stone in midstream, was giving a hand to Dorothea. Roger had slipped and was splashing up out of the shallows. Titty was close behind Dorothea. Dorothea jumped and landed beside Susan.

'That's Dick,' she said. 'Let him know we're here.'

Susan blew her whistle and blew it again, made room for Dorothea to jump to the next stone and held out a hand to Titty. Titty jumped, jumped again, wet one foot and a moment later was close on Dorothea's heels. Susan followed, thinking of Roger and Titty with their feet wet, knowing that this was no time to try to get them dry, and comforting herself with the thought that they couldn't come to much harm while they kept moving.

John and Nancy, with Peggy not far behind them, were already racing along the shore of the loch. They had heard Dick's shouting and Susan's whistle, and saw the folding boat with Mr Jemmerling and his man making straight across the loch past the foot of the island.

'Spotted us,' said John. 'Rowing like billy-o.'

'They can't go fast in the folder,' said Nancy. 'The young McGinty's right. We've a chance of catching them ourselves.'

'Two of them,' said John. 'And it's not our land.'

'It's our boat,' said Nancy.

'We can ask him what he's doing with it,' said John.

343

'We can harry him,' said Nancy. 'We can stop him landing till the rest of us come up. The young McGinty can't be far away.'

'Worth trying anyhow,' said John.

'We'll tell him he's our prisoner. If he bolts, let him. We'll go with him and see him go plump into the arms of the Gaels. They'll collar him just the way they collared us. And then we'll see the old McGinty properly in action.'

'Wish we had a rope,' panted John. 'Much better if we could manage it ourselves.'

'We're going to be too late,' said Nancy. 'But the old folder's doing its best to help.'

The folding boat was zigzagging this way and that, but it was already nearing the shore.

'I say, poor old Dick's going it,' said John. 'There he is.' Dick was already passing the reed-beds towards the foot of the loch.

'We've got to stop them,' said Nancy. 'HEY!' she shouted at the top of her voice.

The man rowing looked over his shoulder and began rowing more furiously than before.

'I say,' panted John. 'They've guessed they're cut off from the *Dactyl*. They may be going to bolt inland, and if the young McGinty isn't there to stop them . . .'

A whistle sounded towards the head of the loch. On a small promontory a kilted figure showed for a moment.

'There he is! It's the young McGinty,' said Nancy. 'Come on. We'll get them between us.'

'We can't do it,' said John. 'They'll be out of the boat and away before we get anywhere near.'

But at that moment they knew that other allies were at hand beside the young McGinty. There was a fierce, deep barking along the shore. The boat stopped. Mr Jemmerling and his man looked this way and that as if choosing a place to land. The sailor took another three or four strokes and stopped again. They could see Mr Jemmerling pointing furiously towards the shore. The sailor was rowing again. John and Nancy ran on. They could see the dogs now, splashing in the water, as well as hear them barking at the on-coming boat.

'Hold 'em! Hold 'em!' shouted John.

The boat had all but reached the shore. One of the shepherd's big dogs crouched and leapt as if to throw itself aboard. The sailor backed water. Then he pulled in again. Again they heard that deep, dangerous barking. Suddenly they saw the sailor pull in his oars, grab the gun that Mr Jemmerling had been holding and stand up in the boat . . .

As the man swung the gun towards the dogs, he staggered, made a wild effort to keep his balance . . .

'He's over,' shouted Nancy.

BANG! Splash!

The gun went off and the folding boat tipped sailor and Mr Jemmerling into the loch. It seemed to happen quite slowly. They had seen the man snatch the gun, leap to his feet to aim at the dogs and feel that the boat was slipping from under him. Then, like a felled tree, he was falling. They saw his arm fly up with the gun. They heard the bang as the gun went off. They saw the gun, loose, in the air. They saw and heard the resounding splash as man and gun came down on the water.

'He fired at the dogs!' said John.

'I hope he drowns!' said Nancy.

But the folding boat was already on the shallows. They saw the man get up, dripping. They saw that Mr Jemmerling, who had been sitting in the boat, had not fallen head first but had thrown his legs over the side. Both were standing with the water not much higher than their knees. The man was feeling under the water for the gun. They saw Mr Jemmerling give

CAPSIZE OF THE FOLDING BOAT

him an angry push. On the shore the dogs, unhurt, had been startled by the gun-shot into silence.

A whistle blew and the dogs vanished.

Mr Jemmerling and his man, leaving gun and boat behind them, waded ashore. For a moment John and Nancy lost sight of them among the rocks. Then they saw them again, floundering up through the heather towards the ridge.

'HEY!' shouted Nancy.

As she and John rushed in pursuit, they heard another shout and saw the two dogs bounding up the slope after the men.

Not far ahead of the men was a big rock with a flat, cliff-like face to it. They reached it just as the dogs were at their heels. The sailor was three or four yards in front of Mr Jemmerling. The leading dog passed Mr Jemmerling and leapt, sending the sailor headlong. Mr Jemmerling pressed his back against the face of the rock as if he were trying to push through and get inside it.

There John and Nancy found him as they came panting up from the shore.

'Good dog!' he was saying. 'Good dog!'

The dog, watching every move he made, answered with a growl.

A few yards away the sailor lay, flat to the ground, with the other dog snarling by his head, daring him to get up.

'Three cheers!' said Peggy who was the next to arrive.

'Call your dogs off,' commanded Mr Jemmerling.

'They're not our dogs,' said Nancy cheerfully.

'They're not mine either,' said another voice, 'but they'll do what I say.'

The young McGinty who, in spite of his long run round the head of the loch, was not out of breath at all, had joined them.

'Call those dogs off, boy,' commanded Mr Jemmerling.

'Watch him, Rory! Watch him, Dandy!' said the young

McGinty, and each dog gave a furious growl as if to say that he could be trusted not to lose his man.

The shepherd was coming up the slope, and both dogs looked round at their master as if to make sure they were doing right. He said a word in Gaelic. The dogs wagged their tails. Mr Jemmerling, who had been standing with his arms above his head against the rock, dropped his hands. There was a deep growl.

'If you stir he will have the throat out of you,' said the shepherd pleasantly, and Mr Jemmerling lifted his arms again and stood there not daring to move.

Susan, Titty, Roger and Dorothea arrived in a bunch.

'Oh, good,' said Titty. 'You've got him.'

'I say,' said Roger, 'who fired a gun? We heard it. Was it at you?'

'The sailor fired at the dogs,' said John.

'He didn't hit them?' said Titty in horror.

'Got a ducking instead,' said Nancy.

'What are you going to do with them?' said Susan.

The shepherd and the young McGinty were talking together. The shepherd put his fingers to his lips and whistled. There was an answering whistle from the direction of the cove. The shepherd startled them all with a long wild cry in Gaelic. Again there was an answer from far away and another from close at hand beyond the ridge.

'Just letting my father know we have them,' said the young McGinty.

'We've got them all right,' said Nancy. 'At least the dogs have. And I say, Peg, you should have seen them go kerflop out of the folder. You remember I told you it wasn't safe to stand up in it. Well, one of them did.'

'They can't get away now,' said John. 'We'd better rescue the boat.'

And then, at last, Dick struggled up to them. After running

the whole way round from the other side of the loch and getting across the stream without waiting to look for the easiest place, he was hardly able to speak.

'Have you got the eggs?' he panted, and for the first time the others noticed that Mr Jemmerling's hands were empty.

'Where are the eggs?' Dick's voice shook as he asked.

Mr Jemmerling, his back to the rock, his eyes warily watching the dog growling at his feet, closed his lips tightly. Cornered as he was, he had not yet lost hope of showing in the Jemmerling Collection the first eggs of the Great Northern Diver to be found in the British Isles.

'The birds are alive,' Dick blurted out. 'We've got to get the eggs back. Quick! Quick!'

'Where are those eggs?' asked John, but he could not help a hint of doubt coming into his voice.

Mr Jemmerling looked at him with returning courage.

'What eggs?' he asked.

'Are you sure he had them?' asked Susan.

'I saw him take them and put them in a box,' said Dick, 'before he came after the birds again.'

'He had something in his hands when the boat tipped him out,' said John.

'So he did,' said Nancy. 'I saw it.'

'Where have you put the box?' Dick asked furiously.

'What box?' said Mr Jemmerling.

Nancy turned to the young McGinty. 'Would the dogs give him a bite or two if you told them? Just a nip, to help him to remember.'

'We can't do that,' put in Susan. 'Up to now it's all his own fault.'

'I'd like to,' said the young McGinty.

'Call your dogs off at once,' said Mr Jemmerling.

'Look out,' cried Roger, 'the sailor's getting away.'

While everybody had been looking at the egg-collector

spreadeagled against the rock, his man, finding that the dog that had knocked him down had joined the other to wait, growling, ready to spring at Mr Jemmerling, had seen a chance of escape. He had crawled further away and, as Roger shouted, he had jumped to his feet and bolted.

'He's running away with the eggs!' cried Dick.

The shepherd said something in Gaelic to his dogs and in a moment, flashing over the heather, they had reached the man and rounded him up like a stray sheep. The man stood, panting, holding his hands out of the dogs' reach.

'Bring him back,' called the young McGinty.

The shepherd spoke in Gaelic again and the dogs, growling now behind him, now on one side and now on the other, brought the man back to the rock where the egg-collector had let his hands drop. Both dogs, thinking their job with the man was done, turned at once against his master, and Mr Jemmerling's hands flew up once more.

'What have you done with the eggs?' Dick asked the man.

'I've got no eggs,' said the man, and everybody could see that he had not.

'Come on,' said Nancy. 'The box must be somewhere. He must have hidden it in the heather.'

'The dogs didn't give him much time,' said John.

'He may have put it on the rock,' said Nancy. 'Great Auks and Albatrosses! It may be right in front of our eyes.'

'There's no box on the rock,' said the shepherd slowly. He was tall enough to see.

'It must be between here and the shore,' said Titty.

'The eggs are getting cold,' said Dick, 'and the birds may be back any minute.'

'It'll be where they landed,' said Nancy. 'Come on, John. You'll guard the prisoners, won't you?' She turned to the young McGinty.

'They'll no stir from this place,' said the shepherd.

'Quick! Quick!' said Dick, running down to the shore. Titty was already half way there.

'Half a minute,' called the young McGinty. 'My father's just coming.'

But nobody waited with him except Roger and the shepherd. Roger, after one moment of hesitation, decided that there were plenty of people to look for eggs and that he did not want to miss seeing what happened when the McGinty and Captain Flint met the egg-collector face to face.

Slowly, not hurrying, a group of people were coming down the ridge. There was the tall kilted figure of the McGinty. There was Captain Flint in his untidy shirt and flannel trousers. There was the old dogmudgeon. Spread out along the ridge was a line of ghillies. The McGinty's strategy had been simple. Cut the invader off from his boats and you have him. He had sent the shepherd with the dogs to see that there was no escape by land. He himself with Captain Flint and the ghillies had gone down past the Pict-house, crossed the stream at its outlet and come over by the rocks to the shore of the further cove to wait by the *Pterodactyl*'s dinghy which they found pulled up on the shore.

There, while Captain Flint had been telling the McGinty the whole story of how Dick had come to make his discovery, they had heard that third shot and the frantic barking of the dogs. Warily, in a long line, they had begun to move up the ridge towards the loch, had heard the shepherd's call and now were coming to consider what was to be done with the prisoners.

Roger looked gleefully to see how the egg-collector was taking the sight of the McGinty and his allies coming down the slope of heather at their own pace, slow, unhurried, like the march of doom.

He was astonished to see that the collector was perking up

and looking at approaching doom as if it were a rescue party. Suddenly he laughed.

'What is it?' asked the young McGinty, puzzled.

'He's more afraid of those dogs than he is of your father,' he said, and this time the young McGinty laughed too.

Roger, looking up at the ghillies, had just a moment of doubt whether he would not have done better to go with the others to look for the eggs, but as soon as he saw that the piper was not among them, he had no further worries.

'We've got him all right,' he called to Captain Flint. 'And Dick says he missed the birds. Dick saw him take the eggs, but he hasn't got them now. He's even pretending he didn't know about them.'

The egg-collector, still flattened against the rock, gave Roger an angry glance. Then, with some attempt at dignity, not very easy as his eyes kept shifting to the growling dogs, he spoke to the McGinty.

'Are you in authority here?' he asked. 'Will you kindly bring this outrage to an end at once.'

'And what outrage would that be?' asked the McGinty gravely.

'Those dogs,' said the egg-collector, 'have been deliberately incited to attack me. You will be so good as to order your man to call them off and allow me to go about my business.'

'Have you business here?' asked the McGinty, and then, suddenly, 'Was it you fired those shots on the loch?'

'I was not shooting at game,' said the egg-collector. 'My name may be familiar to you. Jemmerling. Jemmerling of the Jemmerling Collection. I am visiting the islands for scientific purposes. Allow me to present my card . . .' He made as if to take his pocket-book out of his pocket, but at the first movement there was a deep, threatening growl, and he hurriedly put his hands where they had been, flat against the rock.

'You will call off these dogs,' he said furiously, 'unless you wish to get into the most serious trouble.'

At this, as Roger reported afterwards, the McGinty always a tall man, shot up two inches taller.

The shepherd spoke quietly in Gaelic to the McGinty.

'Was it for scientific purposes that your man shot at my shepherd's dogs?'

'They were preventing me from landing.'

'From landing? Then you had a boat on my loch?'

'I found a boat here.'

'It was our folder,' put in Roger.

'I see. You stole a boat on my loch. And then?'

'I was not shooting game birds,' said the egg-collector. 'I went, for scientific purposes, to collect some eggs that would, in my collection, be of general interest.'

'How did you know they were there?'

'What does it matter?' said the egg-collector angrily. 'I knew they were there.' As he spoke his eyes wandered from the McGinty towards the shore of the loch, where John and Nancy, after rescuing the folding boat, were emptying it of water, while all the others, Susan, Peggy, Dorothea, Dick and Titty were moving slowly up from the water's edge, searching every inch of the ground, groping under every tuft of heather.

'Kindly bring this farce to an end,' said the egg-collector, 'and allow me to . . .'

'What were the birds at which you were shooting?' said the McGinty.

'Great Northern Divers,' said the egg-collector. '*Colymbus immer*. I wished to preserve them. Them and their eggs. No other collection has . . .' He broke off. His eyes were anxiously following the searchers as they worked their way through the heather. 'All the world would have come to see them, the first birds of their species known to have nested in the British

Isles. I should have had them preserved with their nest. The finest taxidermist in London . . . Your loch would be famous . . .' Again he broke off. 'My solicitors . . . the police . . . Or I will make you a fair offer. If you let me go at once, you shall . . .'

There was a yell from down by the shore. Dick, Peggy, Susan and Dorothea were scrambling through the heather to join Titty who was crouching over something. John and Nancy were running from the boat.

'She's found the box,' shouted Peggy.

'My personal property,' screamed the egg-collector.

The McGinty spoke in Gaelic to the dogmudgeon and the shepherd. The ghillies closed in round the egg-collector and his man. The dogs, knowing what was wanted of them, growled at the feet of their prisoners. The McGinty and Captain Flint left them and walked down to the shore after Roger and the young McGinty. Roger had been away first but tripped in the heather and fell headlong. He picked himself up to find that the young McGinty had passed him and to hurry after him as fast as he could.

'Titty found it,' Dorothea was saying.

Dick and Titty together were fumbling at the strap and buckle of a wooden box.

'Let me get at it,' said Nancy.

CHAPTER 29

'QUICK! QUICK!'

TITTY, like Dick, had been thinking more of the birds than of the capture of the egg-collector. Her heart, like his, had missed a beat at hearing those shots on the loch that had turned the McGinty and his Gaels into allies instead of gaolers. She had pursued the egg-collector like a young fury but without hope, for she thought that all was over, the eggs stolen and the birds dead. Then had come Dick's news that the birds had escaped and that if only they could give them back the eggs there was yet a chance that the story of the Divers might have a happy ending. The others were looking for the eggs to take them from the egg-collector. Titty, like Dick, was looking for them in the wild desperate hope that it might not yet be too late to give them back to the birds.

It was Titty who had said, 'Dick'll want the boat as well as the eggs', so that, while all the others were searching for the box, John and Nancy, after rescuing the boat, had pulled it up and were emptying the water out of it. She herself moved fast from one patch of heather to another. The egg-collector or his man must have hidden the box in the heather, not among the stones where it would easily be seen. For less than a minute the two of them had been out of sight as they ran up from the shore. They must have known that their only chance was to hide the box and come back for it later. It could not be far away. Feverishly her hands groped among the tough stems of the heather. The trouble was that she did not know exactly what she was looking for. Dick, searching a dozen yards away, had said it was a box but he did not know what kind of a box or how big. Nor did John and Nancy, though they had seen

that the egg-collector had had something in his hands. Titty
groped on and on. This was worse than hunting for Captain
Flint's cabin trunk hidden under the stones of Cormorant
Island. That, after all, had had in it only a book and a type-
writer, things that were not in a hurry. This was a matter of
life and death. Quick! Oh, quick! Life and Death! She
thought of the Divers grieving for their rifled nest. She thought
of the young Divers who might never peck through the shells
into the world outside. What was that box like? Big! It could
not be very small. And then, thrusting deep into a tuft of
heather, she doubled her fingers against something hard. There
was blood on the backs of her hands where she had scraped
them against the heather stems. There was more blood now
as her knuckles hit on a buckle.

'Dick!' she called.

Dick was beside her in a moment, the others close behind
him. He had lifted the box from under the heather and was
trying to help her to undo the strap. She heard Dorothea
saying, 'Titty found it.' She heard Dick saying, 'The buckle's
stuck.' She heard Nancy's, 'Let me get at it.'

Nancy's fingers, not trembling like Titty's and Dick's, had
unfastened the strap. Titty's head bumped on Dick's as they
bent to look in. There were the eggs, the two big oval eggs
of the Great Northern Diver, dark olive, blotched with
darker brown, each in a nest of cotton wool in a compartment
at the bottom of the box.

'Blown?' asked Dick breathlessly.

'They're still warm!' said Titty. 'I can feel them warm
even without touching them.'

'The boat!' exclaimed Dick. 'There's still a chance. Quick!
Quick! Cover up the eggs.'

The McGinty and Captain Flint were standing over them
and looking down into the box. Roger was there too, Peggy,
Susan, Dorothea, the young McGinty. Flitting through

Dick's mind came the thought that anyhow the thing was proved now. The whole crew of the *Sea Bear* and the two McGintys had with their own eyes seen the first eggs of the Great Northern Diver ever known to be laid in the British Isles. But it hardly seemed to matter. What mattered now was to get them back to the nest. He went hurrying down to the shore.

Titty heard above her head the grave deep voice of the McGinty. 'Queer that a grown man should be ready to swindle a boy for a couple of eggs.'

'It isn't just the eggs,' said Captain Flint. 'What he's after is a place in history.'

'I'll see he gets one,' said the McGinty, 'if we hear any more of him. Preserve the birds! He was for preserving them dead. And the eggs too. And taking them from my loch without so much as a "By your leave".'

'Boat's ready,' shouted John.

'I'll row,' said Nancy.

'No! No!' said Dick, thinking of Nancy pulling as in a boat race, straight for the island. That would be the last straw, even if the birds had not already been too frightened to return.

'Dick ought to do it himself,' said Dorothea.

'All right, Professor,' said Nancy. 'Your eggs.'

'I'm bringing the eggs,' said Titty.

'Yes,' said Dick. He walked straight into the water, stepped into the boat and sat down.

A moment later they were both afloat. Dick was rowing as quietly as he could. Titty was sitting in the stern nursing the egg-box. The crew of the *Sea Bear* still on shore, the McGintys, father and son, Captain Flint, the raging egg-collector and his man, watched by the dogs and ghillies, all had ceased to exist for them. Nothing mattered now but the birds. Had they flown away for ever? If they had come back would they be frightened away again by yet another human

357

visit to the island? And that visit had to be made. Would the birds, in spite of everything, come back to their nest or would they not? Everything hung on that one question. If the eggs were put back in vain, there would be only miserable failure to remember. It would be a pity that the *Sea Bear* had come into the cove instead of being scrubbed in harbour. It would be a pity Dick had ever found the birds, a pity that, after he had found them, he had not sailed away without trying to prove what birds they were.

'The island's over there,' said Titty.

'I know,' said Dick, but did not row straight for it. For a moment or two he said nothing more. Then he thought he ought to explain. 'The nest's at this end,' he said earnestly. 'So we'd better come at the island from the other.'

'But every minute counts,' Titty all but whispered.

'If we frighten them again it'll be longer before they come back.'

He rowed steadily on while Titty sat there with the egg-box, more and more afraid that they were too late and that the birds were already far away. Driven from their nest, shot at, missed, pursued again, the Great Northern Divers might have left the loch altogether and flown, despairing, on and on, northward to the Arctic. Well, if they had gone, there could be no hope of saving the eggs. They could not be kept warm for very long. Sooner or later the life that was hidden in them would fade away. How long, already, had they been taken from the nest? Things had happened very quickly. The taking of the eggs had been long after the shots, for Dick had seen it done. Then, when Dick's shout had saved the birds, the thief and his man had rowed for the shore and been caught. The search for the box had been a short one. Perhaps the eggs had been in the box not half an hour altogether. But where were the Divers? She saw that Dick kept glancing across the loch in the hope of seeing them. She too, kept looking out over the water but nowhere could she see those strange, great birds.

Suddenly Dick stopped rowing.

'There's one of them,' he whispered. 'Only its head show-ing.'

Titty stared in the direction in which he was looking, but could see nothing.

'Heuch! Heuch! Heuch!'

'That's the other one,' said Dick. 'They're coming back. We've still got a chance.'

'Hoo! Hoo! Hoo!'

This time it was not the guttural screech of alarm but a weird yelping call.

Far up the loch in the gleaming water between herself and the evening sun, Titty saw a long line of splashes as the bird came down on the water.

'I can't help it,' said Dick, more to himself than to Titty. 'I can't help it if they do see us. They're coming back. We've got to go straight to the island.'

Rowing again, as quietly as he could, he turned the boat and made straight for the end of the island furthest from the flat bit of shore where the Divers had their nest.

'Perhaps better if they do see us now,' he said presently. 'Better than if they go back to the nest before we've put the eggs there.'

'We simply must get there first,' said Titty.

At last she saw the head and neck of one of the birds, swimming as if to meet the one that had just flown down to the loch.

'We're all right,' she whispered. 'It's going the other way.'

Dick said nothing. He wanted to bring the boat in close by the reeds where he had hidden it that morning and again, in his hurry, he was finding it hard to steer. There was a gentle swish as the bows pushed into the reeds. A moment later the keel touched ground, and Dick stepped out into the water, pulled the boat up a foot or two and held out his hands for the box.

'I'd better not come,' said Titty.

'No,' said Dick. 'It's a pity even one of us has to go there. They must be watching us now.'

She handed over the box and waited.

Dick seemed hardly to have gone before he was back.

'Just where they were,' he whispered, as he pushed the boat off and stepped in. 'Lucky I'd seen how they lay . . . side by side, but not touching. That beast hadn't upset things either. He said he wanted to take the whole nest, but he didn't have time and he left it when he thought he had another chance of shooting them. He'd have had to dig up a bit of the shore. The nest looks just like it did. If only the birds come back to it before the eggs get cold.'

'That one in the water dived and came up much nearer. It's dived again. At least I can't see it.'

'We must get away,' said Dick.

They were nearly half way across to the shore, when they heard that yelping cry again.

'Hoo! Hoo! Hoo!'

One of the birds was once more in the air. It came flying overhead so that they saw its pale underneath and its great folded feet. Round it swung high above them.

'If only it tells the other one we've really gone,' said Titty.

Dick went on rowing until a long splashing furrow in the water fifty or sixty yards away showed where the bird came down.

'Are they both there?' said Titty.

Dick pulled in the oars and let the boat drift while he tugged Captain Flint's binoculars from their case.

'That one's swimming quite high,' he said. 'Its back's showing . . . Can't be so frightened . . . I can't see the other . . . Yes, I can . . . Still only head and neck . . . But they're

nearer the island . . . One's gone under . . . Up again . . . Oh,
don't let the boat rock . . . They're both swimming properly
. . . I say, one's going straight for the shore where the nest is
. . . It must have seen the eggs by now . . . It . . .' There was
a long, breathless pause . . . 'It's coming out . . . Using its
wings like flippers . . . like a seal . . . It's on the nest . . .
Here, *you* look . . . What's the matter?'

'Nothing, nothing,' said Titty impatiently, scrumpling her
handkerchief into a ball. It really was dreadful, the way her
eyes would weep when there was nothing whatever to weep
about . . . quite the contrary.

'Look,' said Dick. 'Put your elbows on your knees to keep
the glasses steady.'

Titty took the glasses and looked. For a moment the island
swung from side to side, but, as the boat steadied, she saw it,
the flat bit of shore, the rocks where heather had sprouted in
the night and yes, in front of those rocks, a yard or so from
the water's edge, a huge black and white speckled bird, with
a dark neck on which were two striped patches, the Great
Northern Diver, sitting on its nest. Its mate was swimming to
and fro in the water just beyond the island.

'Come on,' said Titty. 'Let's go and tell the others.'

'Gosh! Oh gosh!' said Dick, almost as if he were Roger,
and, blinking joyfully through his spectacles, pulled for the
shore.

FAREWELL TO THE *SEA BEAR*

Other Books by Arthur Ransome

SWALLOWS AND AMAZONS

'Watch the effect of the first hundred pages on your own children. If they want no more, send for a doctor' – *Daily Telegraph*

SWALLOWDALE

'If there is a nicer book this side of *Treasure Island* I have missed it' – *Observer*

'A perfect book for children of all ages, and better reading for the rest of us than are most novels' – *Spectator*

PETER DUCK

'One of those rare books which come from time to time to enthral grown-up people and children at once with the spell of true romance. A book to buy, to read, to give away – and to keep' – *The Times*

COOT CLUB

'There is a satisfactory realism about all that happens to the Coot Club, and the atmosphere and detail of the odd part of England where they navigate are conveyed with a charm and accuracy that only this author could bring to bear' – *Guardian*

WINTER HOLIDAY

'One could hardly have a better book about children' – *The Times*

PIGEON POST

'In its own class, and wearing several gold stars for distinction, *Pigeon Post*, by Arthur Ransome, stands head and shoulders above the average adventure book for and of children' – *The Times*

WE DIDN'T MEAN TO GO TO SEA

'This book is Ransome at the top of his form; and so needs no further recommendation from me' – *Observer*

'This is the seventh of the Arthur Ransome books about the Swallows, and I really think it is the best' – *Sunday Times*

SECRET WATER

'Once more the Swallows and Amazons have a magnificent exploring adventure, once more Mr Arthur Ransome has kept a complete record of their experiences, terrors, triumphs, and set it down with the cunning that casts a spell over new children and old' –
The Times Literary Supplement

THE BIG SIX

'The setting is once more the Norfolk Broads, about which Mr Ransome obviously knows everything that can be known. As usual every single detail of the boatman's art and craft is meticulously explored ... Mr Ransome once again equals or perhaps excels himself, and every boy who enjoys him – and every boy does – will vote this detective story super' – Rosamund Lehmann in the *New Statesman*

MISSEE LEE

'*Missee Lee*, by Arthur Ransome, seems to be his best yet. Not only are there pirates in it, but a super female pirate, Missee Lee herself, whose very surprising behaviour creates a situation far too good to be given away. This new Ransome like all the other Ransome's, is a book to buy, to read, and to read again, not once but many times' – *Observer*

THE PICTS AND THE MARTYRS

'*The Picts and the Martyrs* is quite up to the best standard of its predecessors, and to all old Ransome devotees the return to the lake of the first novels gives an added pleasure. It is impossible to finish it without wishing one did not have to leave when there are still "five more weeks of the holiday to go"' – *Glasgow Herald*

All illustrated, and published by Jonathan Cape and Puffins

THE WAR OF THE BIRDS AND THE BEASTS
and other Russian Tales

Arthur Ransome

A talking fish, a crystal palace, a saint on horseback, a sack full of devils – all of these and much more can be found in this wonderful collection of folk-tales, gathered by Arthur Ransome during his travels in Russia before the 1917 Revolution. They follow on from the hugely successful *Old Peter's Russian Tales*.

THE DOLPHIN CROSSING
Jill Paton Walsh

'"Look, son" said Crossman. "This is no kids' game. You are right about what's going on; but you haven't any idea what it is like. You would be sailing into the middle of a battlefield. They are taking men off from right under the nose of enemy guns; sitting ducks those boats will be, and no defending them possible. Let me tell you, it isn't funny being under fire. And in a boat it's worse; fire and water, either will kill you."'

This is the story of two boys, and the friendship between them during the early days of the last world war – Pat and John, both knew the risks they were running, yet took a boat to help save the stranded British army from Dunkirk. It is not a true story, but it could have been true, for there really were schoolboys who helped ferry the British army in retreat.

BLACK JACK

Leon Garfield

Young Bartholomew Dorking stood in the dark, quiet room and looked down at the coffin and the huge ruffian, lately taken down from the gallows, who lay there, seemingly carved out of stone. Suddenly he noticed that the eyes were open and staring at him with a dreadful entreaty. The villain was alive! And that was how the gentle apprentice came to find his life entangled with a murdering villain, forced to help him for fear of the dreadful crimes he would commit if he were let loose on the world.

This is a wild story, recommended for readers of eleven and over with strong nerves and a taste for melodrama.

MINNOW ON THE SAY

Philippa Pearce

The floods brought the canoe to the foot of David's garden, and the canoe brought David to Adam Codling, its proper owner. That was how David and Adam became friends, scraped and varnished the boat, and named her *Minnow*. Then they made plans for how they should use her.

Of course, they could just paddle her up and down the river, the Say, and picnic and climb the willows and fish, but Adam wanted to do more than that – he intended to use the *Minnow* to find the family treasure which his ancestor had hidden centuries before. But time was running out, and with the family in such financial trouble there was little chance that Adam would be there next summer to paddle the *Minnow* on the Say.

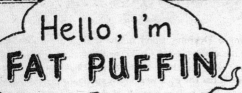

Hello, I'm
FAT PUFFIN

Would YOU like to find out more about
Puffin books and authors, enter competitions
and get a chance to buy new books?

Then join
The Puffin Club!

You will get a copy
of the Club magazine
four times a year, a
membership book
and a badge.

And there's lots more! For
further details and an appli-
cation form send a stamped,
addressed envelope to:

The Puffin Club,
P.O. Box 21,
Cranleigh,
Surrey,
GU6 8UZ

If you live in AUSTRALIA
write to: The Australian Puffin
Club, Penguin Books
Australia Ltd., P.O. Box 257,
Ringwood, Victoria 3134